LURED

A HOLLOWAY PACK NOVEL

BOOK 2

J.A. BELFIELD

LURED
A HOLLOWAY PACK NOVEL

Published by J.A. Belfield
www.jabelfield.com

Copyright © 2019 Julie Anne Belfield

Previously published as *Blue Moon* [2012 & 2017]

Cover art by Aimee Laine.

First Printing: 2012
10 9 8 7 6 5 4

ALSO BY J.A. BELFIELD

BEGINNINGS
CALLED
HEREDITARY
CAGED
UNNATURAL
ENTICED
CORNERED

THE THERAPIST

HER MANE ESCORT

LURED

For Mr B and the Mini-Me's and your understanding ways.

The music of wolves pierced the night air.

Ears twitching, I listened to the echoing calls of the rest of the pack—their announcement of readiness beneath the powerful glow of the full moon.

In eagerness, I thrust forward.

A warning growl from Sean held me in place.

My neck stretched forward; my head bobbed with my inhalations.

I took another step.

Sean's growl halted me again.

I sent him a glance, whined.

His eyes twinkled before he gave an upward jerk of his chin, and we took off.

Every one of my senses heightened as our paws pounded the earth.

Flavours, scents, culinary delights blew to me on the breeze.

I didn't rely on my enhanced vision to see. With the absence of foliage, the lunar glow left us without obstruction, lending light to the dark.

Side by side, Sean and I ran so close, our bodies' maintained constant contact, my facial hairs bristling beneath his breath every time he glanced my way.

Our ability to each understand the other's emotions, intents, needs and wants was magical—always had been.

As my paws contacted solid ground, the alluring aroma of fox invaded my path. My claws dug in, scraping up crumbling earth as I tried to stop. I spun, a patch of mud spraying my underbelly, and dove toward the scent I craved.

Sean headed to the right.

I followed.

His head lowered, feet moving faster.

I raced to keep up, reflecting his movements as he angled left and into a wide right arc.

The wind picked up, altering course, and blew the rich, meaty bouquet to my senses.

I ran faster.

My increased pace brought me to Sean's side.

The delicious freshness of the meal tugged at me like a lure.

I wanted it.

So did he.

He allowed me a second's glance before driving into the lead.

Fear oozed from our prey. A shudder wracked my body as my vision swam with bloodlust. I bounded onto Sean's back hard enough to knock him away and propelled myself from his stumbling body.

I surged forward, jaws wide, lips back, ears flattened, saliva already present.

A low scoop snatched the animal into my jaws.

My teeth clamped down. My head whipped left, right, left again.

Each jerk lessened the animal's struggles until I heard the victorious crack that resonated like thunder and vibrated through my jaw.

With each shake of my head, my teeth punctured deeper, releasing warm blood that trickled across my tongue, tantalising my taste buds, and as it pooled at the back of my throat, I let out my canine purr.

Eyes shining with his usual amusement, Sean crossed to me.

A low warning growl left my throat, but I didn't move as he rubbed along my side—his sniff of my kill didn't concern me.

After lowering to the ground, I pinned my meal between my paws and whined up at him to join me.

He heaved a sigh before settling his body down alongside mine.

His paw snuck around to draw the creature in for a taste, and my muzzle followed in search of more.

Nothing could ruin a good hunt.

1

The Porsche purred beneath my palms. Wind whipped through the gap in my window, stirring my hair into a halo. In the passenger seat beside me, my best friend, Poppy, sat shivering. "You sure you're warm enough, Pop?"

"I'm good." She pulled her coat a little higher around her wild, red curls and re-aimed the vents her way for the twentieth time.

She'd never complain, anyway, not when she understood being a werewolf notched up my regular body temperature enough that a sweater and scarf compensated for the chance at fresh air. At least she had the burgers for warmth. Brown paper bags filled with lunch pressed against her lap. I'd already eaten one while driving, but the wafts of fat-scented steam continued to entice.

Rounding the corner, I turned onto the road to the site of the pack's latest property development. Although tempted to squeal through the gates and announce my arrival in style, I figured it best if Sean continued to believe I drove like a snail when in his car, and shifted down the gears one by one.

I spun the wheel left for the turn, but braked hard at a woman standing in the middle of the gatepost.

She whirled, lids narrowed over irises of bright blue, until she settled into a look of bewilderment.

If she thought I'd missed the fleeting irritation in her expression, she was mistaken. I stuck my head out. "Can I help you?"

From beneath a full head of black waves, her cool stare trained on me, as her hands faux-flapped in front of her. "You scared me out of my wits, flying 'round the corner like that." The chill in the woman's tone matched her expression.

I scowled. "Five miles an hour is *not* flying."

"She trying to put out a fire, or something?" Poppy mumbled.

She turned from me to Poppy and quit with her hands, before circling toward the almost completed apartments.

Near the entrance, Ethan, Sean's older brother by two years, had his head in close to Connor Larsen's ginger curls, but her focus only swung as far as Connor's son.

As though aware of the attention, Josh lifted his chin, and his gaze shifted from the Porsche to the stranger. After he mumbled something to Connor and Ethan, the three men headed our way.

I glanced back in time to see a smirk cross the woman's face.

"What's she playing at?" Poppy hissed.

Shrugging, I stuck my head back out the window. "I asked you what you wanted."

She glanced back to me. "I was just admiring the apartments." At the arrival of the three men, she gave them her full attention, complete with winning smile.

"She switched that on pretty quick *for them*," Poppy murmured.

Josh smiled at the young female as he strode past her. Arms coming to rest against the Porsche's window ledge, he planted a kiss on my cheek. "You've been ages, Jem."

"Well, I'm here now."

He thumbed over his shoulder. "Who's your friend?"

"She's no friend of mine." My lip curled. "She looked like she was spying."

Josh straightened as he laughed. Obviously, he didn't get my non-joke. I'd have set him straight, but the fake, stalker-girl already had his attention, as well as Connor's and Ethan's.

"The apartments." She waved a hand to her right, lashes fluttering.

Ethan tucked his hands into his jeans pockets and rested against the gatepost. "What did you want to know?"

My eyebrow lifted as I faced Poppy.

A *'Can you believe them?'* expression showed on her face.

With a low growl of irritation, I jammed the gearstick into first. "If you want your food, come and get it," I said and drove off.

I parked near the three-storey structure and killed the engine. The second I climbed from the car, Sean Holloway came our way.

The mere sight of my mate hitched my breath and sent my stomach into somersaults.

He removed his hard hat, a rub of his hand sending his chocolate brown hair into disarray. Four days into December, and he wore only short sleeves, offering a glimpse of his muscular arms. The nearer he came, the clearer his dark eyes grew, and his widening smile flashed teeth that glowed against the golden skin of a man who spent his life outdoors.

Poppy laughed from the other side of the car. "You two look at each other as though you've been parted for decades."

Sean reached me, tangled his fingers into my hair, heaved out a deep sigh as though relieved I'd made it in one piece, and drew me in for a kiss. Eyes locked, our bodies met as though drawn by a magnetic force. Our tongues darted out, sampling the delicacy of the other, and my right foot left the ground, my body swaying with the headiness of the moment.

"Did you bring food?" he asked as his lips freed me.

"Of course."

He sent Poppy a grin over my shoulder. "Joining us for lunch, Poppy?" He made it sound like we had a table reservation at a high-class restaurant, rather than squeezing into the portable onsite cabin.

"Apparently so," she said.

11

"We didn't want to keep you waiting, so I'll drop Poppy home after we've eaten." I studied his eyes, checking to make sure he didn't mind, and received a nodded response.

At the passenger side, I ducked into the Porsche for the bags of food. A glance to the right showed the three pack members still chatting to the woman at the entrance. As her body language headed in the direction of flirting, my scowl returned.

"Lunch!" I shouted.

Connor and Ethan broke away.

"Bring mine here," Josh said without turning.

My brows shot up. "What?"

"I'm talking. I'll eat here." Still, I didn't warrant so much as a glance from him.

"I'm not your servant." I growled. "Get it yourself."

Connor passed behind me. "What's up with you?"

"Nothing," I mumbled, meeting Poppy's gaze.

Ethan smirked as he brushed against me and grabbed one of the bags. "I have a pretty good idea." He strode off, tossed two burgers to Josh, and followed Connor into the apartments where the rest of the pack worked.

With my scowl still in place, I plodded across to the inadequate hut.

Behind me, Sean's footsteps hit the gravel, keeping pace with Poppy's as she waffled on about cushions and throws and everything else we'd perused on our shopping trip.

I nudged the door open, flicked on the light—for Poppy's human vision more than my own—and dropped the fast food bag onto the desk on my way to the drinks counter in the corner.

"Sounds like you had a good day," Sean said, the rustle of paper telling me he wasted no time searching for his meal.

"We did," Poppy said.

I flicked on the kettle and spooned coffee into three mugs.

The intensity of the stranger's eyes, with her attention latched onto Josh like a damn fishing hook, roiled through my mind.

Looking at the apartments, my foot.

"Didn't we, Jem?"

I leaned back against the counter and took the burger Sean held out for me with a nod. "Got the cushions." I peeled back the greaseproof wrapper. "Picked up paint charts." I aimed the bun at my mouth and bit a chunk off. "Grabbed lunch." I sent him a burger-distorted smile around the garbled words.

The door swung open, and Josh entered, his green eyes sparkling beneath a mess of shaggy, dark blond curls, and a wide grin spread across his face.

My gaze flittered to Sean.

His expression matched his pack brother's like Josh had impressed him with his ability to chat with a young, attractive female.

Poppy and I exchanged another glance—a hoard of unspoken communication passing between us. Knowing Poppy also had a bad vibe about the stranger made me feel a little better.

Josh unwrapped his second burger and shovelled half into his mouth as he leaned against the counter beside me.

I peered up at him. "Who was she?"

He shrugged. "Just passing and stopped to look at the apartments."

"She wasn't looking at the apartments."

He nodded. "She lives with her sister and is looking for her own place. She said these look perfect. So ..." He shoved the rest of the burger in and chewed. "I gave her my card."

Gave her his card? He didn't even know her. I sought Sean's reaction—he still had a smile on his face. "She wasn't looking at the apartments," I said again.

"'Course she was," Josh said around his swallow. "What else could she have been doing?"

"Could have been ... spying," I mumbled.

Sean choked on his burger. "Spying?" He rubbed his hand across his mouth in a poor effort to hide his smile. "On what?"

Averting my gaze, I watched the shuffle of my feet at the floor.

"Jem?"

I lifted my face to the glistening in Sean's eyes, tilting my head as it sank in how ridiculous I might sound to him. "Josh." I cringed at the heat spreading through my cheeks, and my stare flickered away again.

Deep chuckles met my ears. Josh reached around and drew me to his side. "If I didn't know any better, Jem, I'd say you were jealous." His lips met my neck, and a little wolf nuzzling ensued.

"Hey." Sean tossed his empty wrapper at his pack brother, though his lips remained curved. "Knock it off."

Josh sent Sean a grin, but he released me, bumping me with his shoulder. "Don't worry, Jem. I'd never run off with someone who didn't have your approval."

My eyes sought Poppy's, found them already on me. Poppy knew as well as I did we'd have to hope he never asked approval for the dark-haired girl.

She'd already lost it.

Poppy glanced at me from her cocooned position in the passenger seat of the Porsche. "You really don't like the idea of other females invading your territory, do you?" she asked over the hum of the engine.

I shrugged.

"I know you have a strong bond with Josh, so I understand you feeling pushed out, but ... it's not only him, is it?"

"I don't know. It's just ..." I paused to consider. "None of them have shown an interest in women."

"Just because they haven't advertised their attraction doesn't mean the feelings aren't there, sweetie."

I didn't comment.

"At the end of the day, they *are* male. They all have a pulse," Poppy continued. "Of course they think about women."

Still, I remained mute as horrid images of sharing the breakfast table with six females rampaged through my mind.

"You're too used to having them all to yourself."

I shrugged again, trying to shove the mental slideshow away.

"You have to consider they may meet someone—date even. Surely, you don't think they've all lived their lives as monks?"

I couldn't tell her that, as a rule, the pack didn't date humans because past experience showed them the consequences could be catastrophic—not for themselves but for the humans. "I've never thought about it." I hadn't needed to.

"Oh, come on. Men have needs. Sooner or later, those men of yours will want to get those needs fulfilled." She probably thought the conversation helped.

She couldn't have been more mistaken.

My eyes had been opened to the possibility that I may not always be the sole female to interact with the pack.

I welcomed the idea about as much as a bout of diarrhoea.

2

Thursday, I woke to the usual heat of Sean's body along my spine.

"'Morning, Jem," he whispered against my hair.

I rolled in search of him. Wrapped in each other's arms, our hearts beat an unsteady tune, our breaths mingled. "Hey, baby."

"Sleep well?"

"Hmm-mm." My lips brushed across the overnight stubble coating his cheek.

His knee nudged between mine until he nestled within my thighs. "Shopping again today?"

"Hmm-mm." I tugged on his lower lip, my tongue sampling the delicacy of him. The tilt of my hips united me with his erection, and my gasp merged with his soft groan as he entered me with a gentle thrust. "Can't you come with me?" I whispered. "I miss you when I go alone."

His fingers caressed the soft flesh of my breast. "I thought you were going with Poppy." He traced my jaw with his teeth, hovered above my pulse, where he suckled before trailing down my neck to my shoulder.

On a shudder, I tangled my fingers into his hair. "Tomorrow." My body moved against him as my legs rose to entwine with his. A tilt of my head, and I encouraged his mouth back to my neck.

The journeying of his teeth and tongue sent shivers along my spine. "I'll speak to Dad, see what he says." His mouth worked my throbbing flesh.

As I found his throat and did some teasing of my own, his steady rhythm kicked in. His arm snaked beneath my back, holding me to him as he took control. Back arched, eyes connected with his, I gave myself to him. With every thrust, my body trembled, as did his. My fingers grasped his shoulders as though afraid to let go.

With the magic of his body, the heat within me, and his dark eyes brimming with emotion above, he took me over the edge until I cried out, spurred on by the deep growls of his desire.

Sean crumpled against me, breaths ragged. As his heart pounded my chest, our beats synchronised. Our gazes remained locked, moistness invading Sean's eyes, while a similar dampness misted my own.

"I love you, Jem," he said.

"I know. Why else would I be here?"

My natural response, one I gave often, always made him smile.

"Okay, you two!" Nathan, Sean's dad, boomed from downstairs. "Time to get up!"

I groaned.

A sparkle claimed Sean's eyes. "We'll get up when breakfast is ready."

"We're not your bloody slaves," Ethan called. "Get your own."

Sean chuckled, as we hauled our backsides out of bed and pulled open the bedroom door. On the landing, we both turned for the bathroom.

"Sean!"

We twisted toward Nathan—our Alpha—at the bottom of the stairs, where he stood with sternness in his pale blue eyes beneath a dark mop of hair his two sons had inherited.

With a lift of his eyebrows, Sean shrugged as though to say '*what now?*'

"You can shower separately," Nathan said. "We need to leave the house at some point today."

A common order from Nathan. He often split us up—although he did have a point. If we stepped into the generous shower cubicle together and lathered the soap up across one another's body, we'd get side-tracked, everyone would be waiting for us, we wouldn't care … they'd get stroppy.

Taking advantage of Sean's distraction, I spun for the door first.

Dressed in a green sweater and jeans, my blonde hair still wet against my shoulder blades, I jogged into the kitchen, as Sean lowered a plate holding four slices of toast and two poached eggs onto the table.

He inclined his head. "Sit."

I sent him a smile on the way to my usual spot, parked my rear on the oak-carved chair.

Ethan smirked from the opposite seat, humour lending a shine to dark eyes that matched Sean's. "Good evening."

I picked up my fork. "You're getting funnier, Ethan. You've been practicing again, haven't you?"

The chair to my left scraped out as Sean joined me with a plate of his own. He nudged a drink in front of me and pointed his knife at my food while shovelling a forkful of egg into his cavernous mouth. "Eat."

"Very masterful." My gaze lifted to Nathan on my right. "You must be so proud of your Neanderthals."

Nathan's focus never left his newspaper. "Eat your food, Jem."

"Wonder where they get it from." Toast and egg found their way into my mouth, rinsed down with a swig of coffee.

"If you want Sean to join you today, you'd better get a move on." Nathan's eyes remained downcast toward his paper. "If we don't leave soon, we'll fall behind, and then I won't be able to spare him."

Despite my mouthful of food, I smiled. I'd got my way, and would get to spend the day with Sean—alone.

Sean's increased speed suggested approval of his dad's decision, too. As soon as he finished, he jumped up from the table and sped to the bathroom.

While I waited, I cleared away the breakfast plates, piling them into the dishwasher. My head tilted at Sean's footsteps padding back across the landing. Lids lowering, I envisaged his naked body glistening from the water, steam rising from his flesh on contact with the cool air.

My eyes opened. I turned toward the stairs. Took a step.

"Sit down," Nathan ordered.

When I peered once more toward where my mind had travelled, Nathan cleared his throat. With a sigh, I slumped into my seat, glaring at Ethan's quiet snorts of laughter into his mug.

A few minutes later, Sean's booted feet carried him back into the kitchen. The dampness of his hair made it appear almost black. Along the back of his T-shirt, a line of moisture clung, where he'd failed to dry the rivulets either side of his spine.

I tracked his movements across the room to pick up his wallet and keys.

As he shoved them into his jeans pockets, he turned and sent me a flash of a grin, and my stomach tightened in response.

"Time to go." Nathan pushed up from his chair. "You won't need your keys, Sean. We'll all go in the pickup."

Sean's frown appeared fast and furious, booting his grin aside. "But ... Dad ..."

A thirty-two-year-old man being told what to do by his father could be considered quite sad, but it was the way of the pack—the Alpha said jump, we asked how high?

"You can drop me and Ethan off," Nathan said. "And I need you to make a list of the piping we'll need for the showroom kitchen. Then you're free to go, and you can collect us on your way home when you've finished."

"But ..." Sean stared down at his Porsche keys.

"Take it or leave it, Son. It's my only offer."

"Sure." Sean tossed the keys down before following Nathan to the door.

***

In the showroom apartment, Nathan strode across the lounge and tugged back the cardboard flaps on one of a dozen packages lined against the wall. "These what you hoped they'd be like?"

I smiled at the shiny, vermillion door I'd ordered for one of the kitchen units. "Perfect." I nodded to the other packages. "The white ones—are they as glossy?"

"Exactly the same, but white." His mood seemed to have improved since morning. "You want to check?"

"Sure do."

From the corner, he retrieved another flat-pack piece of cardboard and brought it over. Opening the flaps revealed whiteness as brilliant as fresh snow.

My lips curved as I ran a finger across the door's surface.

"This will be the lounge."

Nathan and I turned at Josh's voice.

He smiled. Beside him stood the dark-haired, young woman from the other day.

The hackles shot up along my spine. Eyebrow raised, I sent Nathan a sideways glance before I fixed a stare back on her.

"It's a good size." She smiled up at Josh—way up. From a vertical perspective, she had to be at least a foot below Josh's six-three height.

Josh walked over, kissed my cheek. "Are the doors right, Jem?"

I nodded but continued to watch the girl.

The girl followed Josh's every move. As he walked, her eyes tracked his legs, his arms. When he spoke, she studied his lips, his eyes. During his interaction with me, she never broke contact with him. She had to be either unnaturally interested in a man she didn't even know, or naturally very observant. I couldn't figure out which.

"This is Marianne." His hand came to the small of my back, nudging me forward a step as he gestured toward the invasion.

Face to face, I studied her. Pegged her to be around twenty-one. Without a doubt, pretty.

I saw why she'd taken Josh's attention—but her eyes led me to believe the deal went deeper than the surface, as they contradicted the outward youth she portrayed, making her look like a calculating, wise, old owl.

I didn't realise how long I stared, or that I hadn't spoken—even the narrowing of my eyes didn't register.

Josh leaned in close. "Please, play nice, Jem."

All sorts of ideas whizzed through my mind, like to drag her arse outside and request, not too politely, that she find another male to set her sights on—preferably not one from our pack. Instead, I took a step forward and extended my hand. "I'm Jem." My lips stretched in an attempted smile.

"Nice to meet you, Jem."

On release of her hand, I resisted the urge to wipe my palm across my jeans leg and turned to Nathan instead.

He frowned—probably at my outright rudeness—and offered his own hand. "Nice to meet you, Marianne. I'm Nate."

Nathan always introduced himself as 'Nathan' to strangers. He always reserved 'Nate' for friends and family.

I scowled. *Am I the only one impervious to her?*

Breakable, tiny fingers folded around Nathan's. "Hi, Nate."

"Come on." Josh stepped away from me, placing a guiding hand on Marianne's elbow. "I'll show you the rest of the rooms."

As soon as she was out of earshot, Nathan whispered, "What's up with you?"

"She's lying."

"About what?"

"She doesn't give a damn about these apartments. The only thing here holding her attention is Josh."

"Does that really matter? Josh seems content enough to play along."

21

"If she likes him, she could say. I'm sure the truth would work just as well." I sounded like a sulky child.

"Perhaps she's shy."

"Does she *look* shy to you, Nate?"

"I wouldn't know. I don't know much about women. Haven't had much experience with them."

"Except for Beth."

His gaze, as it met mine, filled with anguish, I presumed at the mention of his human wife—the mother of his two sons. Nathan had sent her away over ten years before, after Connor's wife had been killed in an attack by another pack. He believed it the only way to keep her safe. Neither Sean nor Ethan had seen her since.

Except for Beth," he said at last. "And you."

I smiled. "Surely, I'm too much of a pain in your arse to count?"

His chuckle told me my attempt at lightening the moment worked. "Jem, you overestimate yourself. Come on, let's round up and get home."

3

On Saturday, we spent the day at Poppy's for her son's birthday—a morning and afternoon of sandwich making, pirate games, and Sean chasing about the garden with the entire party of nine-year-olds, while Poppy followed him with her digital camera. Watching him expose such a natural way with kids turned out to be entertaining, enlightening, and almost heart-breaking, all at the same time.

Daylight showed the first sign of dimming, as Sean stopped the truck outside home and turned the key. Quiet met our ears, filled only by our breaths.

"What did you think?" I asked when he made no move to get out.

The question didn't really need asking. Anyone with eyes could have seen the fun Sean had at the party, reliving his youth, burning off energy.

He turned, his teeth flashing a smile. "It was awesome. Ben's so cool. Lily, too."

"That's because they have Poppy as their mum," I said. "And Jase as their dad."

He nodded and leaned back against the cushioned headrest. His lids lowered as though taking a moment for personal thought.

"Fancy a game of ball?" he asked, opening his eyes.

I smiled. "Do you really need to ask?"

We exited the car, and while Sean forked off to gather up the basketball, I entered the house through the conservatory.

"We're playing ball, if anyone's interested," I said before heading back out.

Sean and I had already pulled off our sweaters, our scrabbling for the ball well under way, by the time the others emerged and clothed me in their scents. Of course, they took his side, leaving me to chase after them like the puny kid who couldn't quite keep up—as usual.

Kyle bulleted toward their goal with the ball he'd stolen from me, and before I could reach him, he leaped, aimed, shot and scored.

A dive landed me on his back, my arms wound around his shoulders. "That was cheating. The game's barely started."

He chuckled. "You being a bad sport, Jem?"

Lips pursed, I slid down him until my feet met the ground. "No."

The game recommenced, and my muscles came alive with the exercise. Adrenaline surging, my heartbeat sped up, my breaths hastened—until Kyle tackled me, as I made a dash toward the action.

His hands gripped my waist, and he whirled me round to face the wrong way.

I growled. "You're going to be in trouble if you keep this up."

The next attack came from Daniel, the middle Larsen son. He dove for me, as I jumped for the ball, and we collided mid-air before the ball could reach me. His arms came around my waist, saving me from the blow, and our feet slammed the lawn on our landing.

"What's this? Pick on Jem day?" I nudged him away with my shoulder. "You're all as bad as Josh ..." Trailing off, I halted, my gaze scanning the garden.

Where the heck *was* Josh? He never missed out.

After a second check confirmed he definitely hadn't come out, I jogged across to the house and pulled open the conservatory door. "Josh!"

No answer. Even the noise of game play grew quiet as they paused.

"Josh! Come and play!" I called.

Feet shuffled from the lounge into the hallway.

I smiled ... until Connor appeared instead of Josh. "Where's Josh? Tell him to come out."

"He's not here," Connor said.

"But ... it's almost dinnertime."

Connor's green eyes shot to the side beneath his red hair. "He's not eating with us today."

Frowning, I took a step into the kitchen. "Is he ill?"

"No. He's gone out."

My frown deepened. "Where's he gone?"

Sean's scent spiralled through, before his feet hit the tiled floor of the conservatory. "What's up?"

I turned to him. "Did you know Josh was going out today?"

"No." He faced Connor. "Where's he gone?"

"On a date." Daniel spoke from behind us.

I whirled, checking his face, his eyes, but found no sign of a joke, despite his smile and light tone. "A date?"

He nodded. "With that girl he met. What's her name ...?"

"Marianne." I scowled as my good mood drained away.

"Yeah, that one."

Daniel seemed oblivious to my expression, as I glanced back toward Connor. Connor's gaze met mine for only a split second before he gave his attention to the tiled floor.

As I looked from one man to the next, my hands tightened at my sides, my jaw ached from the clenching of my teeth, and those hoods of mine overhung with the mega-furrowing of my brow.

Sean took a step forward, reached out for me, but I spun and headed inside, already digging in my pocket for my mobile.

"Jem?"

Ignoring Sean's call, I squeezed past Connor through to the hall. With my mobile held out before me, I scrolled down to Josh's name and hit the call button.

As I strode past the living room, a tilt of my head revealed Nathan. I didn't speak, just kept going.

25

At the end of the hall, I U-turned and raced up the stairs, two at a time.

The first door on the left led to my bedroom. I entered and slammed the door behind me.

The ring tone sounded four times, five, six, seven. Each ring frustrated me further, fuelling my impatience.

He's doing it on purpose.

Maybe he knew what I had to say.

Josh answered on the ninth ring. "Jem?"

"Why didn't you tell me you were going on a date? Is it because you're with *her*?"

"Jem?"

"Why didn't you tell me?"

"Um ... what's wrong?"

"Are you on a date? Yes, or no?"

"Excuse me for a minute." His muffled volume told me his words weren't aimed at me. The sound of his footsteps indicated movement before he spoke to me again. "Jem, what's wrong?"

"Why am I finding out from everyone else you're on a date?"

"What? I—"

"Why didn't *you* tell me? Is it with *her*—the faker?"

"*Jem!*" His tone arrived sharp.

"Don't *Jem* me." My warm temper burned. "You knew you were going on a date, and you didn't tell me."

"I haven't *seen* you." Irritation marred his tone, too.

"You've seen me all week. Was it because you knew I wouldn't approve?"

"What are you going on about? How can I tell you something I don't even know myself?"

"Don't give me that."

"Marianne only called last night to ask me out. I haven't seen you since then, so how could I possibly tell you? And what do you mean, *you* wouldn't approve?"

"*She* called you? She called *you*? That's because she has ulterior motives."

26

"What the hell are you talking about?"

"She's a *liar*," I said. "She's lied from the off and played you like a fiddle."

In truth, I realised I had absolutely no idea what I was talking about. I must have sounded like a bumbling idiot, but couldn't seem to help myself—I was on a roll, and it moved too fast to show any signs of slowing.

"You don't even *know* her," Josh said.

"That's exactly my point, *Josh*."

"*What*? What the hell—"

"You promised you'd make sure I liked anyone you dated. Do you remember that?"

"Jem—"

"Well, I *don't like her*!" I hung up on him.

My chest heaved.

The tremble of my hand affected the mobile I held before me, as I waited to see if Josh would call back for round two.

He didn't.

My frustration expanded, but the more time that passed, the longer I had to think. As my pulse returned to normal, my breathing followed suit, and my brain evaluated what I'd just done.

I groaned.

What right had I to tell Josh who he could or couldn't date?

No right, that's what.

Who was I to insist he seek approval for any women he liked?

No one—not even family ... not in the literal sense of the term.

I had to be the biggest let-down of a surrogate big sister ever.

"Shit!" I kicked at the divan.

I owed him an apology—big time—but couldn't bring myself to call him back.

Probably wouldn't answer, anyway.

"Shit! Shit! Shit!" A stomp of my foot accompanied each curse.

What if he was on his way home? What if my ranting had incited him to cut his date short? He could be raging mad and already coming to have it out with me.

"Oh, you idiot."

With another groan, I tossed my mobile onto the bed, rubbed my hands over my face. Only as I fisted them in my eyes did I realise the threat of tears.

What the heck's wrong with me?

Jealousy hadn't sparked the outburst. Something more than that. Would I have gotten so mad if it had been a different girl he'd taken on a date?

I very much doubted it. I just couldn't figure out why I had such a problem with her.

Clatters carried from the kitchen, as footsteps bounded up the stairs.

I tilted my head.

The bedroom door handle squeaked, and the door swung open to reveal Sean. "Come and eat, Jem."

"I'm not hungry."

"You need to eat."

"I've upset Josh," I said.

"You can apologise."

I shook my head, my mouth bearing the burden of my frown.

Sean stepped into the room and pulled me close. "He'll forgive you, Jem, once he's cooled off."

Inhaling his calming scent, I leaned into him. When he drew me to his side and herded me toward the door, I didn't protest, hadn't the energy—I'd used it all up on Josh.

In the kitchen, the others had already started eating. When Sean drew back my chair, I slumped into it and ignored the attention of the pack, peering down at my dinner as though potatoes had answers.

From his usual seat beside me, Sean reached for my fork and held it out to me. "Eat."

I took the cutlery, poked at my cottage pie. Knowing he wouldn't leave me alone unless I obeyed, I prodded up a miniscule forkful and steered it into my mouth, raising my eyebrow at him in a '*happy now?*' expression.

With a smile, he leaned over and snared a far bigger blob on his own fork and waved it beneath my nose, until I relented and ate it.

As I'd no wish to endure the embarrassment of being fed in front of the others, I forced one mouthful after another down.

Halfway through my meal, I dropped my fork and pushed up from my seat. "I should call him back."

Sean tugged at my arm, parking me back on my rear. "Leave it, Jem."

"I should .... I was horrible to him." With a groan, I leaned forward, holding my hair up to prevent it stroking mashed potato on my plate.

"Talk to him tomorrow," Sean said.

I shook my head, clambering from my seat.

Back through the hall, I rounded the newel post, jogged up the stairs, and snatched my phone off the bed. I hesitated only a second before I hit redial.

It rang for ages. Maybe he'd no intention of ever talking to me again.

My chest tightened at the thought.

His answer jolted me back. "What now, Jem?"

"Josh, I'm sorry."

"Okay." His tone chilled me.

"I had no right to speak to you that way."

"No, you didn't."

I sniffed. "I'm sorry."

His sigh travelled the connection to my ear. "I know." His voice had softened. "Can we talk about this tomorrow?"

"Sure," I mumbled.

"Bye," he said and hung up.

Josh hadn't sounded as though he'd forgiven me, or that he would.

The thought of losing the bond I shared with him tugged at me. I'd grovel if I had to—except over what I'd said about *her*. After spending hours awake thinking about it, I realised I'd meant every word—even if some of it hadn't made any sense.

Little conversation arose over breakfast. The further through my sausage and tomatoes I chomped, the quieter I grew, the more reflective I became as my mind worked its way through the apology I had to give.

I'd never forgive myself if unsuccessful.

My urge to get the apology over and done with had me sending impatient glances toward the stairs, as I waited for Sean so we could leave. Sensing eyes my way, I turned to meet Ethan's gaze over the rim of his mug.

His dark orbs shifted to the left, toward his dad.

Expecting admonishment for my antsy behaviour, I looked toward Nathan, but he stared with such intensity at ... nothing ... he didn't even seem to notice our scrutiny.

Both Ethan and I faced him for seconds.

Nathan's expression didn't change.

My attention re-met Ethan's, and I gestured with my eyebrows, hoping to portray my question, *what's up with your dad?*

Ethan gave the tiniest of shrugs.

Something was definitely up with Nathan, and I didn't think it had anything to do with Josh.

When it finally reached time to head to Connor's, we took our usual route through the forest in wolf form.

Weekly visits meant regular changes—something strongly encouraged by Nathan. He said it aided in retaining mental balance and control, and kept the twitchiness that occurred if a body's needs weren't met at bay.

Not that any of us minded.

I watched Nathan as the four of us raced forward.

Although a quieter character than the younger pack members, Nathan loved his runs as much as the rest of us. His body language, his focus, his rumbling growl, though, told me the day's exercise lacked its usual enjoyment.

I glanced sideways at Sean, caught him eyeing his dad, before my eyes retrained on Nathan.

Something bugged him, for sure.

The five mile stretch to the Larsen household didn't take long to cover. We sent a call of approach, alerting them to bring clothing out for us—a routine none had bothered with before I entered the pack.

Embarrassment over nudity didn't lie within any of them. *I* had issues over seeing Sean's family with no clothes on.

The way-too-long running sweats, which had been left on loan, told me I'd run out of gear at Connor's—again. I rolled up the legs and tugged an equally large T-shirt over my head. After a glance to ensure Sean had dressed, too, I broke out of the forest onto the Larsen lawn and found Josh on the patio.

Sean reached me and kissed my cheek. "Go on ahead. I'll wait for the others."

I nodded and strode across the grass to Josh.

His head hung low, hands in his pockets. When I neared, he lifted his lashes, giving a small smile.

I stopped in front of him. "Josh, I—"

He turned and walked away.

I stared at his retreating back, until he paused at the back doorway to the house and peered over his shoulder.

"Come on. We need to talk," he said.

I followed him in, through the kitchen, the hall. Connor's house had pretty much the same layout as

Nathan's—as though designed by the same person. As we turned for the stairs, I spotted his two brothers and dad in the living room. They each sent me a smile.

Josh ascended the stairs. My eyebrow lifted for a second, before I fell into his shadow behind him. It took Josh's long legs only a few strides along the landing to arrive at the second room on the right. He allowed me a brief glance, pushed open the door, and went inside.

Reaching the doorway, I leaned against the frame, as Josh sat on the bed.

The first time I'd entered Josh's room, it'd rendered me surprised. The many images of his mother in there held sharp contrast to the sparse adornment of family pictures in Nathan's home. Josh had been only thirteen when the outside pack had killed his mother a little over ten years before.

Josh's beckoning finger brought my attention back to him. When I didn't move, he came over and took my hand, walking me to the bed and drawing me down with him as he sat.

I lifted my bare feet, tucked my knees beneath my chin, wrapped my arms around them.

"Are you going to tell me what's wrong?" he asked.

I shrugged.

"What was yesterday all about, Jem?"

My shoulders lifted and dropped again.

He sighed. "So ... you're not going to talk to me about it?" He swung his feet up and lay back against the pillows, folding his arms behind his head. A flicker of pain visited his eyes when he looked at me.

"I told you yesterday I was sorry. You're the one who didn't sound like you accepted it." My voice came out weak. *So much for repairing the damage.*

He nodded, and we simply sat for a few minutes, gazes on each other.

"Josh, I'm sorry, okay? I was a total arse yesterday, but ... you could have said something. I can't believe you'd leave your dad to tell me ..."

"You have a problem with me dating, Jem?"

I shook my head because I didn't.

"You just have a problem with Marianne?"

Picking non-existent fluff off the duvet cover, I thought about telling him no, but nodded.

"I like her. Why can't you just be happy for me?"

I didn't answer. What could I say? That I had a bad feeling about her? How ridiculous and insubstantial would that sound?

"Are you jealous?" The frown overhanging his dulled eyes told me his words held no joviality.

I shook my head.

"I know I can't have you ..."

At his quiet mumble, I studied him closer.

"Should I just mope around because of that and never bother looking elsewhere?"

I didn't know what to say. I'd always believed Josh's feelings for me were given in a playful sense—nothing more, nothing less. The way he looked at me and the deepness of his voice had me reconsidering what I'd always thought to be harmless fun.

Specks of rain hit the window. Although I gave the quiet patter my attention, Josh's heavy stare remained on me. "When that girl first showed up ..." My lip went to curl, until I chewed at it. "... and you showed an interest in her, it made me realise ..."

"Realise what, Jem?"

I looked back at him. "That I've grown used to having you all to myself. Not just you, Josh—the entire pack. Poppy told me it was selfish. She said you all have needs." I half smiled. "I guess she's right, maybe I am being selfish. It's just ... I don't know."

Only our breathing filled the room again, until I broke the silence. "I've no right to expect you all not to date. I know that. How unjust would that be when I have Sean? But it ... would be easier to deal with if your females were ..." I swallowed down my discomfort. "Someone I didn't mind."

"Why do you have a problem with her?"

"Because I know she's lying about her interest in the apartments just to get to you."

His jaw tightened. "So, what? What's wrong with her lying because she finds me attractive? All women do it. You're all manipulative. You all make stuff up just to get a man's attention, and then, once you've got it, ask him out, or something."

I threw my hands up. "And you know this, how? From your vast experience with the opposite sex? Have you even had any experience with women, Josh?"

He glared before he reined it in, letting out a heavy sigh. "Not really."

My lips curved at his naivety.

"But I like her," he said.

The arc of my lips switched to a downturn. "I know."

"And I want to see her again. Can't you accept this is what I want?"

My poorly contained sigh escaped through my nostrils. "I can try."

"Can you please not make things difficult for me if she comes round again?"

"I'll try."

"Will you at least try to be nice to her?" His green eyes beseeched. "For me?"

I studied his lovely face, reached out to tug at his erratic hair that had grown into a curly mop. "I'll try my best ... for you."

Smiling, he took my outstretched hand. A gentle tug urged me down beside him. I brushed my lips across his cheek, nestled my face into his shoulder. As he pulled me close into his body heat, I breathed out my relief.

It didn't take long for footsteps to climb the stairs. My face remained burrowed when they entered the bedroom, and the mattress depressed behind me as a heavy weight climbed on.

"This a private party ..." Nuzzling teased the back of my neck. "... or can anyone join in?"

I tilted my head to allow Sean's lips easier access.

"I can't believe this," Josh said. "I finally entice Jem into my room—alone—and you turn up and spoil my fun."

Sean's chuckle vibrated along my spine, and I giggled. "You forget too often, Josh, that Jem is my woman." Sean's words held no warning, no malicious intent, only a regular banter.

Josh rolled toward Sean, and I found myself sandwiched between two rock hard chests.

As Sean's hand stroked across my stomach, it fluttered.

Josh slid his hand down and grasped my thigh, tugging at me until my face pressed into his chest. "Maybe we could come to an arrangement. It's unfair that you keep her all to yourself."

Sean drew me back to him. "I don't do sharing. Sorry. It's in my nature to be territorial."

The rumble of laughter brewed within their chests.

Josh wriggled closer. "How about a threesome?"

Sean laughed, shifting closer against my back. "Interesting idea."

The two of them squashed me until my nose and mouth were buried against Josh, my rear heated by Sean.

"I can't breathe." The fabric of Josh's T-shirt muffled my mumble.

"You hear something?" Sean asked.

Josh chuckled. "No."

I tried to push out my arms. Sean and Josh had them pinned. I struggled against them, my grunts turning into a low giggle. "You'll be sorry when I pass out from the fumes of smelly armpit."

"Hey, I don't smell."

As soon as Josh lifted his arm and sniffed there, my fingers located his ribcage.

He squirmed against the tickling contact, rolled over laughing.

Sean's hold lessened, and I made my escape to kneel on Josh's stomach, tickled him some more. Giving me the upper hand ... until Sean joined in the game—on Josh's team.

Two against one? I never stood a chance.

4

Monday lunchtime, donned in humungous, waist-high coveralls, and ugly, steel-capped boots Nathan insisted I wear, I tried to ignore the calls of, "Hey, Jem, nice outfit," as I headed inside the showroom apartment.

The plastered walls had been prepared the afternoon before, and awaited my magic touch. In the kitchen, after filling a tray with brilliant white emulsion, I balanced the roller against the lip and climbed the stepladder.

The ceiling didn't take long to coat, and I moved to give the lounge its first lick. I'd covered almost a quarter when Josh showed up, bearing a steaming mug of coffee.

I clattered down and danced over to Josh with a smile. Mug in hand, the steaming aroma travelled up, as I inhaled, sighed, and sipped. "Thanks, Josh. I needed this."

"So I see." His gaze travelled the walls and returned to me. "I'm impressed. You haven't got any paint on you."

"Very funny. I am capable of doing stuff without making a mess."

"Yes, but ..." He paused at his mobile ringing and pulled it from his pocket. His focus flicked from the caller display to me. "It's Marianne."

I willed my brow not to crease. "You'd better answer it, then."

He seemed unsure as he hit the connect button and put the phone to his ear. "Hey, Marianne, how are you?"

"Pretty good—even better now I'm talking to you."

My enhanced hearing caught her words without effort, and it took restraint not to stick my fingers down my throat.

Josh grinned. "Did you have a good time on Saturday?"

"Of course. We should do it again sometime."

"I'd like that."

I considered moving away so I wouldn't have to hear them any longer, but didn't.

"Listen, are you busy right now?" Marianne asked.

"I'm working."

"Oh ... it's just that I was coming past that way. I made you some tea. What with the weather being so cold, I figured you could use something to warm you up."

"You've made me tea?"

As Josh met my stare, my eyebrow lifted.

"Would it be okay to drop it into you? I won't get in your way."

Nooooo! my mind screamed. I willed my head not to shake, kept my mouth shut. My teeth clenched with the effort.

Josh combed his fingers through his hair. "That would be great."

"Would it be okay to come in to you? Or would you rather come out and meet me at the gates?"

Josh turned toward the window. "You're here already?"

"Yes."

"You may as well come on in, then. I'm just in the apartment—the one I showed you ..."

"I know," she said. "See you in a few seconds."

Josh hung up. "Marianne's here."

My head bobbed. "I heard."

"Please ..."

"I'll try."

"Jem." His eyes pleaded.

"I'll *try*," I said again.

Marianne waltzed into the room brandishing a silver—single-serving—flask. "Hey, Josh."

What sort of woman made flasks for men they barely knew?

Skinny-fit jeans accentuated her slender figure, and her matching cable-knit jumper and gloves, and her gilet enhanced the dowdiness of my coverall. Even my thrown-into-a-scrunchie hair faded into the background beside her lush, dark waves cascading in perfect twists.

She approached Josh with lips spread wide, teeth revealed, eyes sparkling. The instant she turned toward me, all warmth faded, despite the smile that remained fixed in place. "It's nice to see you again, Jem."

Josh's body tensed.

Although I wanted to tell her to take her stupid flask and disappear, I'd made a promise to Josh. "You, too." My jaw almost seized in the effort to remain polite. "I have work to do." I placed my foot on the bottom rung of the stepladder.

"Do you want this now, Josh?" she asked.

Unable to help myself, I glanced over my shoulder.

Marianne smiled as she handed it to him. "You look as though you could use warming up."

Warming up? Josh stood before her in nothing but a muscle vest and had not a goose bump in sight.

"Thanks." He took it from her and twisted the lid, and his entire face scrunched up.

The flower beds in Poppy's garden smelled more consumable than whatever the flask held.

My foot relocated to the floor, and I moved closer. "Tea?"

Marianne smiled. "Yes."

"Doesn't smell like tea to me."

"That's because it's herbal. I make it myself. It's very good for your health, Jem. Helps you stay strong."

Josh held out the flask as though diseased, and my hand lifted to smother my smirk. He glanced up, panic widening his eyes.

I barked out a laugh, but choked it back with the pretence of a cough. "I'll, um ... put that in the office, if you like. You can have it when you take your break later."

I didn't wait for him to respond, just took it from him as my strides carried me past. By the time he mumbled a *thanks*, I'd already left the room.

From the snug bucket seat of the Porsche, I cruised the country lanes toward the DIY Depot across town, with scarf circled around my neck, and Sean's rock CD blasting through the speakers. Through the open window, the icy cold wind whipped my hair about my head, and taking advantage of the lack of police cars prior to hitting town traffic, I drove way too fast, in a desperate need for coveralls that fit.

I barely met any other vehicles during my recklessness. Only a Nissan and Volvo came toward me, and a sleek, black Lexus, whose driver also didn't seem averse to breaking the speed law, stuck in my rear-view throughout.

When I reached the depot car park, I took the Porsche slow over the speed bumps and, after parking up, headed in.

On the way to the protective clothing department, a set of bathroom taps caught my eye, and I veered right. The chrome contours slid beneath my inspecting fingers. My lids lowered as I pictured them on the suite I'd ordered—white curves amid silver walls to match the taps—until a deep unease settled over me.

My shoulders stiffened as my eyes flew open. A discreet inhalation revealed nothing to set my alarm bells ringing.

To the left, my gaze met that of a middle-aged man, with thinning hair and a paunchy stomach. Beyond him, a younger guy in jeans and T-shirt, his hair gelled.

Behind my other shoulder stood a couple, both with their hands on a pushchair.

I stared hard at the woman for a few seconds, before turning my attention to the only other occupant in the bathroom aisle, a middle-aged woman with rich chestnut hair.

She held a brochure, seemed to search the shelves for something.

Still nothing—within visual or sniffing range—to cause concern.

Shrugging it off, I reached up for a set of the taps and ducked off to find the coveralls I'd come for.

Wednesday morning, donned in my ridiculous white coverall and ugly boots, I began to decorate the walls of the apartment. With each sweep of the paint roller, my body relaxed. The sounds of the others doing their manly jobs and quiet tunes from the radio added to it.

After an hour, Sean arrived. My arm continued to move, as I assured him I was okay and allowed him a kiss to ease his withdrawal. With the promise of coffee on his next visit, he headed back out.

Once again, I slipped into a trance-like state. My mind daydreamed about Sean, what I'd very much like to do to him, *with* him, about the forest and hunting—all the good thoughts that aroused my body as well as my brain.

Footsteps entered the apartment, disturbing my blissful oblivion, and neared the room I occupied.

I turned, and my gaze fell on Marianne.

"Hello, Jem."

Remembering my promise, I nodded and tried a small smile on for size—it didn't fit very well.

"Is Josh about?"

"Didn't you ring him first?"

"I tried, but he didn't answer." She smiled as her cool stare travelled over me. "I assumed he couldn't hear it."

Teeth gritted, I studied her for seconds, while my inner attitude warred against the politeness I knew I had to offer. "I'll try his number ..." ... *if it'll get rid of you.* I retrieved my mobile from the window ledge and dialled.

Josh answered straight away. "Missing me, Jem?"

"Always." I smiled. "Marianne's here."

"Where?"

"Down here ... with me."

Silence.

"She did try calling you, but she said you didn't answer."

"I didn't hear it."

I glanced at Marianne. "That's what she said."

"Tell him I brought more tea," Marianne said.

I reined in my smirk. "She's made you more tea."

He hesitated, may even have groaned, but covered it well. "Okay, tell her I'm coming."

I hung up. "He's on his way."

"Thanks." She sent me a smile sweet enough to rot teeth.

"Sure." I put my phone down, returned to the ladders and my painting.

"Did you choose this colour?" she asked.

I nodded.

"It's nice."

Maybe if I ignored her, she'd get the hint and wait outside. I'd done what she wanted. How much did she expect from me?

"I could help you out ... if you needed it. I'm good at painting."

I paused mid-roll, peered over my shoulder.

Her expression flashed to her faux friendly smile, yet I didn't miss the calculating glint she had in her eyes.

My brow lifted, as I prepared to give her a special look of my own, one learnt from Poppy, but Sean appeared in the doorway. His gaze met mine over Marianne's head as though checking my mood at her being there. As she turned toward him, I shrugged.

Sean gave her his attention before she could spot our exchange. "You here to see Josh?"

"Yes."

"Does he know you're here?" He glanced at me as he spoke. Perhaps he didn't trust me to behave civilly.

"Yes. Jem let him know." She pointed a thumb my way like she considered him incapable of figuring out who she meant. "You're Sean, right?"

"That's right."

"I'm Marianne." She extended her hand.

I scowled.

"Yes, I know." Sean smiled as he allowed her a short handshake and stepped around her. "Jem, I'm about to make drinks. You want another?"

My eyebrow arched up.

"Stupid question?"

I gave a slow nod.

With a chuckle, Sean about-turned.

As soon as he'd gone, I wished he hadn't. Marianne looked at me like she expected me to strike up friendly chatter.

When familiar footsteps travelled across tiles, a sigh of relief eased past my lips.

Josh stuck his grinning head around the doorframe. "Marianne."

She mirrored his expression. "Josh."

Gag!

"Everything okay?" Although he spoke to Marianne, Josh faced me.

"Yes, thanks."

"Jem says you made me some more tea."

"Yes, I did." She took another single-serving thermos from her shoulder bag. "I hate to think of you being cold."

Behind her back, my headshake accompanied my eye roll. I could, I guessed, understand her thinking Josh wasn't as warm as usual—his sleeved T-shirt replacing his regular vest confirmed it—but no one in their right mind would look at Josh and believe the guy to be cold.

Josh, though, broadened his smile and took the Thermos from her. "Thanks." At least he showed no eagerness to get the lid off.

My head tilted at footsteps outside, and my nostrils flared as Sean squeezed past the two of them with a mug in each hand.

"You found each other, then?" he asked.

Marianne nodded. "I was offering my services to Jem before." She turned to me. "You didn't say, Jem, if you needed any help or not."

I took my coffee from Sean and sipped, giving me time to formulate a decent excuse. "Actually, you're not covered on the insurance to work in here." My lips almost curved in smugness as I shrugged. "It's against health and safety regs."

"Oh, well ... never mind." Frostiness flashed in her eyes for a split second before she peered up at Josh. "Can I speak to you for a minute?"

As soon as Josh shepherded her into the lounge, placing his flask of swamp water on the window ledge en route, Sean leaned in close to my ear. "Well done."

I tilted my head. "For what?"

"For being polite to her when I know you can't stand the sight of her."

"What makes you think that?" I whispered it in a tone I knew would reach only Sean's ears, thanks to a special connection that gave us the ability to communicate without anyone else overhearing. I half laughed at his raised eyebrows.

"What's wrong with her, anyway?" If he'd eavesdropped at all while I'd ranted at Josh on Saturday, he'd have had an idea.

Sitting on the top step of the ladder brought me almost to Sean's eye level, and his warm breath hit my cheek. From my position, I could see Josh and Marianne, and the sharpened icicle glances she sent my way, until her attention returned to Josh and her entire demeanour shifted faster than a flickering holograph.

"Have you seen the way she looks at me?"

Sean angled his face toward her. "Hmm. Maybe you should try smiling at her."

"I have tried smiling at her."

He gave a throaty chuckle. "That's not a smile, Jem. That's baring your teeth. You'll frighten her."

44

"She's not afraid of me."

"Flask?" Josh's voice carried through to us.

"The one I brought your tea in the other day?" said Marianne. "If I take it back with me, I'll have a spare one at home."

"Oh ... um ..."

"Josh said he hasn't seen that flask since you took it from him," Sean whispered.

"That's because I threw it in the bushes."

He snorted. "What if Josh wanted it?"

"He didn't. He was just too polite to say. I helped him out."

Josh moved to the doorway and stared pointedly at me. "Jem, do you remember where I put Marianne's flask?"

I hopped down to the floor. "Sure, I'll fetch it."

"Sounds good," came Daniel's voice, as I passed back through the foyer with the retrieved flask in hand.

I turned the corner, to find him standing beside Josh, the two of them so similar in appearance—both with wide smiles.

Even Sean wore a grin.

Handle hooked over my finger, I strode across the room to Marianne. "Your flask."

"Thanks, Jem."

When her fingers folded around the cylinder, she gave a slight tug—one that may well have hurt a weaker person.

A low warning growl left my throat before I could stop it, but I reined it in lest Marianne heard.

The tilting heads of the boys told me it hadn't gone undetected by them, though—as did the disappointment flashing within Josh's eyes—and I streaked back to the kitchen.

Tuning out the conversation in the other room didn't come easy, even as I picked up my equipment and stepped to the wall.

Footsteps followed behind me. I didn't turn, but I identified Sean by his scent and the way his body met my back.

His breaths hit my ear as his arms circled my waist. "Talk to me."

What could I say? Marianne tried to hurt me? How petty would I sound? I stayed mute.

"You think I didn't hear?"

My shoulders lifted, as my head tilted at the farewells being bid in the next room.

"See you this weekend," Josh said, as Marianne's steps carried her off.

Quiet mumbles passed between Josh and Daniel before dwindling away to nothing.

"You think Josh didn't hear it?" Sean asked, bringing me back.

He received another shrugged response from me.

"You really don't like her, do you?"

I considered giving another shrug, but didn't do lies or evasiveness with Sean, so I shook my head.

"Is it because she's after Josh?"

"No. I just don't like her."

"But, why growl at her? She look at you funny? What?"

"She bloody pulled that flask off my finger like she was trying to hurt me."

"Do you think she intended to hurt you?"

Back to non-vocal responses, I jerked my shoulders up.

"And why throw her flask in the bushes? You must have known she'd want it back. How'd you know Josh didn't want it?"

I glanced to my right, at the fresh Thermos still sitting on the window ledge. "If he wants it so bad, why didn't he take that one?" Sean leaned over my shoulder, and as his cheek brushed mine, I twisted my head to see him. "You didn't smell the other one. It was disgusting. I helped him out."

46

His eyebrow lifted. "And you took no personal pleasure from throwing it in the bushes, at all?"

I held my finger and thumb close together. "A little."

His chuckle resonated within his chest, sending vibrations along my spine. As I leaned into him, he took the paint tray from me, planted it on the stepladder. Bringing his hands back round, he unzipped my suit.

It took him seconds to release my upper body from the tissue-like garment. When his fingers feathered across my stomach, down low to my hip line and back up to cup my breast, I almost groaned.

I reached up and tangled my fingers in his hair. His breath warmed his trail of kisses across my shoulder and up my neck, to my ear, where his teeth tugged on my lobe. Twisting to face him, I drew him closer, and my parted lips met his as our gazes locked.

His tongue arrived for a taste. The musky scent oozing from him and the proximity of his body offered comfort, as a ripple washed through me—one I knew he'd created.

I clutched his T-shirt and swept it over his head.

As Sean freed it from his arms and tossed it aside, my palms slid across the firm muscles of his chest. My lips and tongue took over the caress, and as my teeth scraped across his hardened nipple, Sean gave a low growl, and fisting his hands in the papery fabric of my suit, he tore the rest of it away from my body, sending the tattered shreds to the concrete.

My fingers suddenly frantic, I reached for his buttons, freed his waist of his jeans. A quick shove sent them down until stalled by his boots, my lips travelling his flesh as I bent, sliding back up again as I straightened.

His hands grabbed my hips, and I collided with the wall. Sean's body crushed mine, as his mouth did my lips, and his dominant nature arrived to take the reins.

Evidently, he had about as much patience as me.

With his tongue delving, the kiss deepened. Gazes connected, our breaths hastened, and the beat of our hearts increased.

Fingers prying beneath the fabric, Sean urged my underwear south, and with it slid out of our way, my thighs embraced his hips, and I pressed into him.

A throat cleared near the doorway.

Our heads whipped round.

Daniel stood with his head low in an obvious attempt not to look, and Sean gave a low growl. One of warning. Of *Why the hell are you here?*.

"Your dad's on his way down," Daniel mumbled.

"Stall him!" Sean's snapped command merged with a snarl.

Daniel hesitated for only a second before nodding. The door closed on us, and his footsteps crossed the outer room, fading as he left us alone.

Sean didn't wait for Daniel's retreat—he'd already nudged his boxers to join his rumpled trousers. Hands back on my hips, he lifted my body then lowered me onto him.

My gasp, as he entered my body, met with his rumbling one. My eyes closed in satisfaction before reopening to watch him.

Soft moans left us both as he thrust.

His teeth worked my throat. My nails drew blood from his shoulders, and Sean's growls attacked the quiet of the room.

With each movement, we trembled. With each growl, each moan, we shuddered.

Nearing our peaks, our sighs of desire crescendoed into cries of pleasure, each of Sean's calls shooting my body closer to climax.

I brushed my lips across his cheek to his ear. "Come with me, baby."

As our gazes relocked, he moved faster. The small space filled with low echoes of our passion as flames licked along my body.

At the moment my body convulsed in orgasm, Sean's knees collapsed beneath him, and we both landed upon the floor, me astride his lap. My fingers smoothed across his shoulders and the damage my nails had caused. The kiss I allowed him arrived slow, tender.

"You have paint in your hair, Jem." Sean's husky chuckle hit my chest.

I reached back to investigate.

"And you have paint on your back."

A small smile spread my lips.

"And your gorgeous arse is now an interesting shade of green."

At my snort, he laughed again—until Nathan's deep tone alerted us of Daniel's poor attempt to hold him off, and Sean's eyes widened.

Clambering up, I reached for clothing at the same time as Sean.

He slid his boxers and jeans over his hips, tugged his T-shirt back on.

Thanks to Sean's destruction of my painting suit, I had only knickers to cover my lower half. My spare suits lay in the other room—with Nathan.

Sean chuckled behind me, as I took a deep breath and yanked open the door. I strode straight for my suits and pulled one on.

Nathan's nose wrinkled, scrunching up when Sean stood in the doorway.

The paint across my back tightened as I moved. I must have looked a real mess—confirmed when Nathan returned to staring at me.

Connor and Daniel joined in.

Suited up, I acknowledged the knowing glance of Daniel, sent him a small smile, but avoided the understanding appraisal of the two older pack members as I hightailed it into the kitchen.

A gentle nudge against Sean's back sent him to the wrong side of the door, and I swung it shut, leaving him to deal with his dad.

"Sean?" Nathan asked in his voice of disapproval.

At least our escapade had gotten Josh off my mind.

With a stifled giggle, I went back to work.

Thursday equalled my day off, and a chance to spend some girl time with Poppy.

As I hung up on Sean's third phone call to check on my safety, Poppy turned to me, her eyebrow raised. "Withdrawal symptoms?"

My lips curved. "Of course."

She turned back to the black skinny jeans in her hand. "Things okay with you and Josh?"

"I suppose ..." I'd already told her by phone about the argument and making up with him. She also knew exactly what I thought of Marianne's creepy tea brewing. "Until she turned up again, yesterday."

"She came to the site again?"

I nodded. "She brought him more bog syrup."

Poppy's brows lifted. "She made him more tea?"

My head bobbed again. "And she wanted her other flask back."

"Ha!" Poppy snorted. "Did you fish it out the bushes, then?"

I smiled. "Yep."

"Did she suspect?"

"Probably. She'd have to be a moron to believe Josh is drinking that dishwater of hers."

Poppy dropped the jeans into her trolley. "Is it really that bad?"

"Nope. It's worse. And I'm certain the conniver tried to hurt me when she took it off me."

"She tried to hurt you?" Poppy-the-parrot asked.

I told her how she'd taken the flask from me.

"What a bitch." Poppy's defensiveness resonated in her tone.

"Yep. And I'm sure they were making plans for the weekend. Plans I'm certain Dan's involved in. Plans they stopped talking about when I stepped into the room—ones Josh has yet to mention to me. If he thinks my eavesdropping lets him off telling me himself, he's mistaken."

Poppy smiled. "I'm sure he is. He'll tell you, though, especially after Saturday."

I frowned. "Do you think I overreacted on Saturday, Pop?"

"How important is Josh to you?" she asked—the exact response as when I'd asked her by phone.

I arched my eyebrow.

"Stupid question. How important is it, to you, that he not get hurt?"

My expression didn't waver.

"How much do you dislike this girl?"

My eyebrow lowered to accommodate an impressive scowl.

"Me, neither. So, no, I don't think you're overreacting when you put it into perspective with your feelings. But you have to remember, Josh is old enough to make his own decisions. He'll figure her out soon." Poppy-the-sage rubbed my shoulder. "You just have to be there to save his fall when he does."

"I guess."

"So ..." She nudged me with her hip. "Two weeks 'til Christmas. Any idea what you're getting Sean?"

"No." My pulse picked up a notch at the thought of finding the perfect present for our first Christmas together. "What am I supposed to buy him?"

She started to walk off. "You'll think of something."

"No, I won't. I'm useless at buying presents."

51

"Don't be silly." She peered over her shoulder as she sashayed away.

"I'm not." Shaking my head, I trailed behind her. "I haven't a clue what to get him."

"Sean would be happy if you wrapped your body in tinfoil and offered yourself to him on a plate, Jem." She grabbed my trolley to pull me beside her. "Quit worrying over nothing. You'll find the right thing."

I nodded. "I will."

"Yep." She gave a small laugh as she continued along the aisle.

"No problem," I muttered.

No problem at all.

The filled-to-capacity trolley made me grateful Nathan had insisted I bring the pickup. Poppy drew alongside me with her smaller trolley, as I came to a stop beside the truck. She rambled on about Christmas, while I distracted myself by loading the numerous bags into the bed.

As I reached down for the last three bags, the uncomfortable sensation of being watched prickled the back of my neck—exactly how it had in the DIY Depot.

Scouring the car park, I sampled the air, my ears strained for those damn alarm bells.

"Jem?"

I held up a finger. Poppy simply completed loading the shopping, while I scanned left to right.

A woman, strawberry blonde, tall, hourglass figure. Mature couple, evidently still enjoying each other in their entwined method of walking. Empty red Fiesta. Empty blue Polo. Woman loading a small child into the rear of a petrol-blue people carrier. Black Lexus with a woman in the driver's seat.

My eyes followed the path of an elderly lady walking at the speed of a slug.

Something still niggled.

An empty green Golf. An old man who appeared to be struggling with his climb into his Berlingo. Teenager mounting a scooter. A handful of trolley collectors.

Something still niggled, something about that damn Lexus.

My gaze skimmed back.

Someone had been in there a moment before, but it stood empty. I thought back to the chestnut hair I'd spotted through the windshield. Something bothered me about that, too, though I couldn't put my finger on it.

"Do me a favour, Pop?"

She dropped the final bag into the truck. "Sure."

"Do the trolley return and take them past that black Lexus. See if you can get a look inside."

Although her eyes held confusion, she headed off without question, moving across the car park as if she had all the time in the world. Alongside the Lexus, she tilted her head, a discreet move as though to look over the car.

A couple of minutes later, she returned. "Just some woman bending over to reach into her handbag on the passenger floor."

My gaze remained fixed on the black vehicle. What the heck had me so antsy?

"What's going on, Jem?"

I shook it off. "Just a niggle."

5

The following morning, as I gave the showroom bathroom its first coat of paint, I thought, again, over what to do for Christmas. Thanks to Poppy's reminder that only two weeks remained, panic mode had kicked in, and the stupid subject refused to budge from my mind.

It took until the second coating of Silver Quartz before the beginnings of an idea formulated—a good one. That didn't mean it would be easy to accomplish. Nathan would take some serious buttering up. Lost in the low squelch of the roller, I formulated my plan.

Mid-morning, as the bathroom embraced its new colour, Josh visited me. When I turned to him, with his head bowed and bearing coffee and a doughnut, I suspected the time had arrived to share his weekend plans.

"Thanks." I smiled as I took them and walked through to the lounge, with Josh in tow. Planting my rear on the window ledge, I took a bite of the sugary cake, failing to catch the jam as it oozed down my chin.

Josh reached out and rescued it on his thumb, licking himself clean. "I thought I should warn you I'm going out with Marianne again on Sunday." His gaze stayed on me as he spoke.

I stopped chewing for a second. "Why Sunday?"

"That's when she invited us."

My brow arched. "Us?"

He dug his hands into his jeans pockets. "She asked if Dan wanted to double date with her sister."

My doughnut lodged in my throat, and a quick swig of coffee disguised my groan.

Marianne poaching on Josh concerned me enough, without her doubling up and dragging Daniel into the mix.

I relaxed my clenched jaw. "Does that mean you won't be there when we come for dinner? You missed our time together last weekend."

The excuse sounded lame, but Josh smiled. "No, Jem." His fingers trapped my loose hair, tugging a little. "We'll only be out in the morning. Dad said he'll get dinner ready an hour later, so we'll be back for it."

I studied him, sipped my coffee, holding my frown at bay when it attempted to creep in. "Okay."

His brows lifted. "Okay?"

I nodded.

"You're giving me permission?"

My shoulders shrugged.

"So ... if we're into asking permission of one another, where was your request on Wednesday, Jem?"

I stared at him.

"I know very well what you and Sean got up to in that bloody kitchen." He pointed behind himself as he grinned. "Dan couldn't wait to tell us when he got home. I can't believe you got away with it."

My lips twitched. "Neither could we."

"You got lucky." Josh leaned in and kissed my cheek, his breath warming my face as he pulled back. "But next time? Remember to come ask me if it's okay first." His chuckle followed him as he walked off.

"Touché," I whispered with a half-smile.

Sneaking from bed Sunday morning, without disturbing Sean, took skill, but a tiptoed trip down the stairs and into the conservatory unhindered proved my covert antics successful.

Just as I'd hoped he'd be, Nathan occupied one of the chairs. He sat so immobile, I thought he was asleep. Eyes half open in a lazy, contented way, he stared toward the garden from beneath the pitter-patter of rain on the glass roof.

As I curled into the willow chair beside his, the slight flare of his nostrils told me he'd acknowledged my presence.

"You're up early," he said.

"So are you."

"Yes, but I'm always up early. You, on the other hand, aren't."

We fell quiet for minutes. My breathing slowed, as I leaned back into my seat, and my mind filled with the hypnotic sounds of the weather. I closed my eyes, tired still, thanks to my early morning.

"Did you want to speak to me about something, Jem?"

My lids remained lowered. "What makes you think that?"

He chuckled, its deepness bouncing like a bass drum within the small enclosure. "You must want something. You're never awake at this hour. And when did you ever climb from bed without Sean to accompany you?"

He'd come to know me well. Smiling, I opened my eyes. "I need to ask you something."

He twisted in his chair and faced me.

"I need your permission for something. If you give it, then I need to ask for your help." I shrugged. "I doubt you'll even give the permission, though, let alone the help."

"Now you have me intrigued."

My shoulders hunched in an exaggerated shrug.

"Ask me, then."

"I want to do something special for Sean ... for Christmas, as it's our first together—well ... this time, anyway."

He smiled, as he did every time I made reference to my history with Sean.

"I've been racking my brain to come up with an idea that'll mean a lot to him—something he'll treasure. When I finally thought of it, I realised my biggest obstacle was you."

His eyebrow lifted. "I'm not a total ogre, you know."

My lips curved. "You're not even a bit of one."

"So, tell me. What do you want?"

I took a deep breath. "I want to make a scrapbook of photographs for Sean. I know there's none around the house, but I figured you must have some hidden away somewhere. Josh's room is full of pictures of his mother ..."

Nathan frowned. "You want the scrapbook to contain pictures of Beth?"

"Yes. Well, not just Beth. Pictures of me, too, and other people important to him. And Poppy has pictures of us from last weekend. I thought I'd get one blown up and framed." I paused for breath. "I just thought he'd like it, that's all."

His expression remained negative. "Tell me, Jem. Why do you think there aren't photos around the house?"

"I know you believe cutting the connection with Beth keeps her safer, Nate." The pack that incited him to hide her was the same one that slaughtered Connor's wife. "But you know Sean would keep it somewhere secure. I don't believe for one minute you haven't any pictures of her." I watched him as I spoke. "If Connor was trigger happy with a camera, you most likely were, too."

As he continued to study me, the lines lessened across his brow.

"I didn't want to go behind your back. I wanted to speak to you first. Like I said, I want your permission."

He leaned back in his seat. "I don't know, Jem. I'm not sure it's—"

"Please, Nate."

"Can't you just buy him clothes?"

"I don't want to bloody buy clothes for him. I've thought so hard about this. This is the only idea that feels right"—I pressed my hand to my chest—"in here. That's why it's so important to me."

"I'm just not sure it's a good idea."

"He misses her."

His pale blue eyes held intensity when he swung back to me. "He speaks of her with you?"

"A lot. He misses her like crazy. It hurts him, not seeing her. I'm sure having pictures—memories—would mean a lot to him."

He leaned forward until his elbows came to rest on his thighs, rubbed a hand over his lowered head.

After a long silence, he lifted his face to me, some kind of inner emotion warring within his eyes. "Okay. You can have the pictures."

My eyebrows shot up. "I can?"

"Yes. But you *must* keep them safe, understand?"

A sigh of relief escaped as I nodded.

By the time we headed indoors at Connor's, the rain had weighted each of our clothing.

As usual, I headed straight for Josh's room, though his and Daniel's absence felt like a tangible oddity throughout the house.

In his wardrobe, I found jogging bottoms, jeans, shirts, T-shirts, vests, shorts—every one of them too big. Josh's less broad shoulders made his stuff my best fit, though, so I nabbed a pair of jersey, drawstring shorts and a T-shirt and crossed the room to extend the loan to a pair of his boxers.

Sitting on the bed beside his table, my attention snagged on the array of framed photographs it housed. Josh's mum, Nadine, had passed on her dark blonde hair to her two youngest sons. Only her hazel eyes were recognisable in Kyle's face, his red hair having been inherited from Connor.

The pictures depicted the entire family in informal poses with goofy grins. Nadine alone, a warm smile on her face, or one with a much younger and ganglier Josh—obviously pre-puberty—with his arms around his mother's waist.

Sean entered Josh's room a lot. I wondered how hard he found it, knowing Josh had been permitted images of his mother, when Sean had nothing as a reminder of Beth. At least, I guessed, Sean had the knowledge that his mother still lived and breathed somewhere. Josh only had pictures.

The fresh T-shirt I pulled on turned out not to be as fresh as estimated and stank of Josh, as did the shorts I swapped sweatpants for. Thankfully, I liked Josh's scent. As my hips wriggled in, and I cinched the drawstring, the deep rumble of an engine rolled beneath the window—Daniel's Hi-Lux.

My body seemed to relax at their return.

I hadn't even reached the bottom step when my hackles rose. My hands tightened as I turned the corner, and my legs became leaden.

Upon entering the kitchen, I halted. All air seemed to vanish, as if it had been sucked from the room, until I could scarcely breathe.

My worst nightmare had come true.

"Hello, Jem."

I tried to rein in my scowl at Marianne's greeting, but didn't succeed. Eyes narrowed, I took everything in—pans bearing serving spoons spread across the table, sliced meat on a plate in the centre, the whole pack, bar me, surrounding it.

I turned toward my seat beside Sean.

Taken.

By Marianne.

My fists curled further, and my breaths deepened.

From Marianne in *my* seat beside *my* Sean, my attention lifted to the woman standing behind her—and I almost did a double take.

Marianne and her sister looked so alike, some kind of scientific experiment must've been involved in their creation. They had to be twins—I guessed identical. The only feature to set the two apart came in the other's hair, brushing her chin in its short bob cut.

Two of them.

Just great!

I looked back to Marianne. "You're in my seat."

"Oh." She and the clone moved in unison, as Marianne scraped back my chair. "Sorry, Jem."

I ignored the apology and sat the second she'd left.

The pack's stares weighted my movements, as I spooned vegetables onto my plate, speared beef and Yorkshire pudding with my fork, piling it alongside the veg. With my gaze averted, I poured a generous helping of gravy over it all.

Josh's stare drilled into me the heaviest, yet I couldn't bring myself to look at him.

He'd disappointed me—pure and simple.

He could have warned me. Would it have been so difficult for him to pick up the phone and let me know his plans?

Tension mounted in the warm kitchen, coiling muscles around the room.

Their invasion upon our Sunday ritual filled me with agitation too thick to be controlled. The silence deepened—other than the clink of cutlery as I stabbed with viciousness at my food—and my irritation spiralled right along with it.

Glaring at my meal, mouth full, I mumbled, "Nobody hungry?"

"No," said Josh. "We'll have ours later."

My hand paused mid-stab, yet I didn't raise my head. "So, you're not eating with us ... *again*?"

"Come on." Josh urged his chair back. "We'll go in the living room."

Tempered breaths made it difficult to swallow. I gave up on chewing, half tilted my head to watch them leave.

From beneath hooded brows, I tracked the path of the two girls, followed by Daniel.

Josh's swagger and balled fists told me just how furious I'd made him.

He clenched and unclenched his fists, jiggling something around his wrist. For reasons I didn't understand, the second my brain drank in his new adornment, a low rumble built in my chest, and cold dread settled into my stomach.

I whipped out a hand and snared his arm, gripping tighter when he yanked back. Standing, I raised his wrist. "What the hell is this, Josh?"

"None of your business."

Eyes narrowed, I glowered at him. "Where did you get this?"

"It's none of your business." He growled, snatching his arm away.

Through strength lent of temper, I dragged him back and poked the bracelet with a finger. "Is that ... *hair*?"

"Let go!" Josh's jerked retraction of his arm snapped me to the side.

A snarl bubbled in my throat, cut short by Marianne stepping back to the kitchen doorway. "Is something wrong?" she asked.

I glared at her, pointed to Josh's wrist, which he did a poor job of concealing in his pocket. "Did you make him that?"

Her eyes widened.

"Jem!" Nathan said.

"This bracelet is fucking made of hair." Why the bracelet being made of hair bothered me, I didn't know, but it did—big time. That it matched the dark colour of Marianne's only added to my concern.

"Jem, mind your language at the table," Nathan said.

Sean's fingers folded around my arm, but I shrugged him off, my focus still on Marianne. "Did you make this?"

"I ..." The tremble of her hands and moistening of her eyes did not go unnoticed. For the first time, she looked afraid of me.

"Jem?" Sean's tone arrived quiet as he took my arm again.

I snatched it away, rage twisting my features as it merged with unexplained panic. "Did you make him this fucking bracelet, Marianne? Yes, or no?"

Her hands lifted to cover her eyes. Sob-like sounds left her lips. I didn't believe for one minute the tears would be genuine.

"Nice one. Now look what you've done." Josh's arm settled protectively around Marianne's shoulders, and he led her away from me.

As they entered the living room, his words of apology to her drifted through.

I took a step forward. "Don't you dare apologise to her on my behalf!"

Josh's head poked back round. His bared teeth offered an imposing attitude usually hidden beneath his relaxed personality, and his eyes darkened as he shook his head. "Too far, Jem."

My fist impacted with the doorframe, the jolt spiking through my forearm.

"Sit down," said Nathan.

I whirled on him.

"Sit down, and eat your food."

My barely eaten meal still sat on the plate. I reached over, shoved it halfway across the table toward Connor, gravy splattering on the oak top. "Give it to your damn guests. I've lost my appetite."

Before they could retaliate, I rounded the table and flew out the back door.

As I sprinted across the lawn, my hands tore at Josh's clothing. The rending of fabric should have encouraged me to ease off, but only made me shred harder, and grey, Josh-scented scraps of cotton floated to the grass.

By the time I crashed through brush into the forest, feet pounded the ground behind me. "Jem!"

I didn't pause, or slow, but surged forward—in the beginnings of a change as well as my run.

"Jem, wait!"

Mud splattered the backs of my ankles. Sean would be upon me any second. He'd need to be quick, though. Ripples had already staked a claim to my flesh.

"Please, wait!"

The first shot of agony hit me like a cattle prod. I gasped, tilting my head at a quieter sound from Sean behind, as the sensations of my change affected him. Still, I didn't stop, but pushed faster.

"Please." His breaths arrived loud. "We need to talk about this."

I almost stumbled in my haste to get away. When his fingers brushed my hip, I snarled.

My chest heaved. My heart pounded. Tears threatened to blur my vision.

As splintering pain stabbed my limbs, my knees folded, dropping me to the ground.

Sean crashed into my side, his body bowling over mine. He rolled through mulched leaves before coming to a stop, and he spun, naked, facing me in a crouch.

Glaring at him, I pushed the change on a little further.

"Not yet." His jaw tensed. "We need to talk about this."

Breaths burst from me in short spurts. I spotted the throb at his temple, knew my lack of control held responsibility for its creation.

"Will it help, at all, if I tell you I think Danny and Josh were wrong to bring those girls here unannounced?"

I studied him—his bunched muscles and intense eyes.

"Will it help if I tell you you're not the only one to have alarm bells ringing about that damn bracelet?"

My head tilted as my brow furrowed.

"I felt something off about it, too," he said.

I stared harder, but only sincerity greeted my scrutiny.

"The second you said hair, something inside clicked. Like a—"

"Flicker." My voice arrived deep. "Like a memory you couldn't quite grasp onto."

"Yes." He nodded. "Can you explain that to me?"

Confusion re-creased my brow. Sean never asked me questions about our past—he usually had all the answers.

"You felt it, too. What made you panic so bad?"

"I don't know," I said.

Both still crouched, palms flat against the forest floor, I realised my body had calmed, the ripples had vanished. My body was no longer under attack from the agonizing reconstruction of my form.

"We should go back," he said.

I shook my head. "Not with them there."

"I meant back home."

I released a small sigh, watching him for a few beats. "So, we'll go home?"

He nodded. "We'll wait for Dad. Try to explain what bothered us."

"Do you think he'll listen?" I didn't think so. He'd looked seriously pissed at me.

"We'll make him listen." Sean smiled as he stood and stepped toward me with his hand outstretched.

I took it, allowing him to pull me to my feet and encase me in his arms. "How long do you think we have before he gets back?" My cheek pressed against his chest.

"An hour, maybe." His breaths hit my crown, their warmth contrasting against his cold flesh.

I swept my hands over his back, across the contours of his shoulder blades. When I looked up at him, he brought his mouth down for a kiss.

His heady aroma filled me with a deep inhalation.

"Run with me," I whispered.

His lips curved against mine. "Always."

Harsh pounding bounced inside my head, before I roused enough to understand the reality of the racket.

"They're back," Sean murmured against my ear.

A glance at the illuminated digital numbers of the clock showed five pm had arrived without my realisation. After our run, we'd returned home and enjoyed a private session of lovemaking in the empty house. Falling asleep had been unintentional.

More bangs echoed through as the door vibrated beneath heavy blows. "Come on, you two!" Nathan's voice boomed through the wood.

"We're awake," Sean said.

"Good!" The door swung wide, and Nathan strode across the room. His body shadowed the bed as he leaned forward, looming over us. He pointed his finger at me. "Your behaviour at Connor's was unacceptable."

"Dad, listen—"

"No!" he snapped, turning back to me. "I know you dislike Josh's new girlfriend, but when you are in their home, and Josh brings her there, you have no right to react the way you did."

The duvet slid from Sean's chest as he sat up. "Josh should never have brought those girls there in the first place."

Nathan glared at his son. "That's beside the point. The point is that Josh and Daniel brought humans home today, and once they were there, there was little we could do without making a big deal out of it and drawing attention to ourselves. But you"—he prodded his extended finger in my direction—"managed to make more out of it than that. And what the hell was the deal with the bracelet? What were you thinking, screaming at Marianne over something she gave him?"

"Actually, we've been waiting to talk to you about that," Sean said.

Hands on hips, Nathan glowered from Sean to me, back to Sean.

I hadn't moved since his intrusion. Only my face peeked out above the duvet—seemed safer that way.

Nathan brushed his hands across his hair, lowering them again with a nod. "Okay, get up. I'll wait downstairs. Then you can explain to me exactly why I've spent the best part of the afternoon dishing out apologies on your behalf."

One more parting glance to each of us, and he marched from the room. The door rattled as he slammed it closed.

6

Nathan's heavy gaze settled on me once in the kitchen. "Talk to me, Jem, and make it good."

I sent Sean a glance before giving a small nod. "Well, for reasons I can't explain to myself, let alone you, the moment I saw that bracelet on Josh's wrist, something twisted inside me."

Nathan's expression didn't waver. "Try to explain it."

I blew out a small breath. "Seeing the bracelet seemed to trigger a memory—one I can't quite piece together—and it sounded an alert that something was amiss."

Nathan turned to Sean. "Do you know what memory she's talking about?"

Sean shook his head. "No, but I think it's one we both have. It's just buried too deep. Neither of us are getting all the details, but as soon as Jem recognised the bracelet as being made from hair, something clicked inside me, too."

Nathan swung back to me. "Are you sure this isn't just because Marianne gave it to him?"

I returned his hard expression with one of my own.

"I know you don't like her."

"I don't trust her."

"Because she's after Josh?" Ethan piped in from across the table.

"This isn't about jealousy, Ethan. Before she'd even spoken to Josh, I felt there was something off about her."

"Because she's young, fit and after Josh?" Ethan asked again.

"No." My fist thumped the table. "It has nothing to do with any of that. I just don't trust her."

"Why not?" Nathan asked.

"I ..." I pinched the bridge of my nose. "I don't know, but ... man, it's an intense vibe I get off her."

"Do you understand how much you've upset Danny and Josh over this?"

I nodded. "I have a good idea."

"You've got some serious apologising to do," he said. "I will not have discord amongst my pack. Do you understand?"

My gaze dipped. "I'll apologise to Connor for behaving rudely in his home. But Josh and Dan ... they should never have brought them—"

"You *will* say sorry," Nathan said.

"What about them?" My tone bordered on sulky. "Do they have to say sorry?"

A mixture of exasperation and an underlying hint of temper moved across Nathan's features and chilled his eyes.

"When Josh and Danny are ready to apologise to me for their inconsideration, feel free to send them my way, and I'll say sorry in return."

"You're behaving like a child," Nathan snapped.

"No, Nate." My other fist hit the table with a quiet thud. "I'm behaving like the only female member of the pack, whose relationships are under threat. And not just by the presence of female humans, but female humans I don't trust." My fingernails dug into my palms as my hands clenched tighter. "I'm behaving like a female pack member who cares about the male members of this pack. One who doesn't want to see Josh get hurt. Like—"

Nathan held up his hand. "I get it." His lips gave a slight twitch.

I uncurled my hands, placing both palms atop the table as I waited to see if he'd speak.

After a long silence, he said, "Tomorrow, you and Josh will sort this out between the two of you. You will both apologise—"

"But—"

"You will *both* apologise," he repeated. "I will keep an eye on Josh's new girlfriend, and decide if she's up to

anything. And you two"—he pointed from me to Sean—
"will try to remember what disturbed you so much about
that bracelet."

Connor paused in his work, as we climbed from the
truck Monday morning.

"Where's Josh and Danny?" Nathan called the second
his boots hit dirt.

Connor pointed over his shoulder. "They're inside. You
want them?"

"Yes. Tell them I want to see them in the cabin."

Connor nodded and strode away.

"Now!" Nathan called before adding, "Please, Connor."

Connor continued walking, gave another nod.

Not really wanting to be around for the boys' ticking off,
I made my way in to get on with my painting. One leg in
my coverall, I lifted the other to feed through, when
footsteps in the outside hallway pricked my ears.

Following Connor past the open doorway to the
apartment, Daniel and Josh peered my way.

At the lack of warmth in Josh's eyes, the smile I'd been
about to give evaporated. A hollow void expanded within
my chest—my emotional defence against dealing with the
hurt.

Making up would not be easy.

Ignoring the physical symptoms caused by Josh's glare,
I stirred the Roman Stone emulsion. The globby liquid
spiralled around like a whirlpool, and I lost myself in its
squelchy tune until blobs flicked into the air and thick
paint spatters decorated the concrete floor surrounding the
tub.

My mind wandered to the day before. In bed, Sean and I
had almost induced migraines with our desperate attempts
to recall whatever had bothered us so much.

Before Sean and I re-met, each had been aware of the
other, thanks to us both experiencing dreams with the

starring roles played by ourselves. Every dream, we'd learned, represented memories of past lives together. Sean's eight years of memory-stirring dreams surpassed my couple of months' worth, but none of them had helped. Whatever had us alarmed—if something from a previous existence—refused to fully surface.

"Jem?"

My arm jerked up at the interruption, and more emulsion sloshed over the side. Wiping my hands down my trouser legs, I stood and turned to face Daniel.

"I'm sorry ... about yesterday." He shrugged. "I tried to talk him out of it, but he wouldn't listen."

I slid my hands into my pockets, pulling the coverall tight over my shoulders as I dug down. "So, you didn't want to bring them home with you, then?"

"Of course I did." He raised his hands, showing his palms. "But I knew we'd probably get into trouble."

"But he wouldn't listen?"

He hesitated, but shook his head.

"Don't you find that odd, Danny? Josh not listening to you over this?"

Daniel shrugged.

"Don't you think there's something off about her?"

His gaze returned to me. "Actually, she seemed really nice, Jem."

My eyes narrowed, but I kept my scowl at bay.

"Her sister seemed really nice, too."

I almost questioned how, if related to Marianne, she could seem nice, let alone *really* nice. "Is she like Marianne?"

"A little. In some ways." He smiled. "Her mannerisms, some of the words she used were the same. But she was a nice girl."

I gave a nod, hopefully succeeding in hiding my disagreement. "What's her name?"

The green of his irises warmed. "Amber."

"And you had a good time with Amber?" As my frown tried to sneak in, I ran a hand over my brow.

His smile suggested I hid it well. "Yeah, I did."

I drew in a deep breath. "You'll see her again?"

"We never got as far as talking about it."

Because of me? Maybe I'd scared them off. Perhaps they realised they'd bitten off more than they could chew once they saw the boys came as a package deal with the rest of us. *Man, I sound selfish.* I pushed the thoughts aside. "I'm really sorry, Danny."

He took a step forward. "Me, too."

I trampled through the spilt paint to cover the remaining ground, stretched up, and wrapped my arms around his neck.

Daniel offered a tight hug as he lifted me and pressed his face into my hair.

"We okay?" I murmured.

"We'll always be okay."

Josh, though, would be a challenge.

It took much longer for Josh to come.

To begin, I told myself his being the instigator had earned him a detainment by Nathan.

Deep down, I knew he was probably too mad at me to apologise.

Over an hour after Daniel had left me alone, Josh's familiar footsteps entered the apartment.

I put down my paint roller and turned.

Josh came to a stop at a distance and rested his hands on his hips. Head hung low, muscular shoulders high and tense, he trained his sights on his work boots. "I'm sorry." His voice came out gruff. Without awaiting a response from me, he spun and strode from the room.

I frowned. "Josh?"

He didn't stop, not even a pause—just kept moving.

I took a few steps. "Josh?"

He reached the door to the outside hallway, rounded the frame and stormed off, his pace increasing as though to put distance between us.

Disappointment swept through me—anguish, too. Beneath those, my temper brewed as I pursued. "Josh?"

His palm pressed against the glass door at the main entrance, pushed it open. After a glare over his shoulder toward me, he marched off, leaving the door to swing shut in my face.

Stunned, I watched him for seconds through the glass. Temper evaporated, as a deep ache settled inside my chest, and a tear of desperation leaked out.

Brushing it away, I shoved through the door. "Josh?" I picked up my pace, until almost at a jog to catch up with his long strides, and tugged on his arm.

He snatched it away.

I grabbed it again.

Josh growled at me.

Darting forward, I raced in front of him, blocking his path.

He went to walk around me.

I sidestepped to prevent him.

"Move," he said.

Another tear pushed out as I shook my head.

He stepped to the other side.

Again, I moved into his path and stalled his escape.

"Get out of my way."

I stood my ground.

Josh grabbed my shoulders. A breath of relief shuddered from me—until his hold tightened, and he swung me from his path. "I've got nothing else to say to you, Jem." He strode away again.

I watched his receding back, swiping a hand over my eyes when my vision blurred.

From one of the upstairs windows of the apartments, Ethan stared down, and I mentally willed him not to tell Sean.

Ahead, Josh entered the cabin and sealed himself inside, and taking a deep breath, I marched over and let myself in.

Josh stood in the coffee corner with his back to me, spooning sugar into a mug. He didn't turn as I closed the door.

"Josh?"

No response, not even a grunt.

Another tear escaped. "Josh?"

Although he ignored me, the clang of the teaspoon against the side of the mug told me enough.

"Josh? *Please* ..."

"What, exactly, do you want from me, Jem?" His voice came out deep and measured.

"I don't ..."

"Nate told me to apologise. I did it. Now, what do you want?"

"I—"

"What am I supposed to do, exactly?" His voice deepened further. Tension raised the set of his shoulders, as he made a slow turn, his jaw tight and gaze burning. "I have feelings for a woman who belongs to someone else, and it's wrong." He waved his hands in my direction. "So, I show an interest in someone else, and ..."

"Josh?"

"And it's *wrong*," he growled over me.

I lifted a palm. "Listen ..."

"I go out on dates, and it's *wrong.*"

"Please, Josh ..." Another tear fell.

"I bring my date home with me, and it is *wrong.*" His volume increased with each word, while I watched him through my abstracted vision. Josh's hands fisted as he roared, "She gives me a fucking gift, and *it's wrong!*"

My own hands contracted, but not from temper. My feet shuffled in a manic fashion on the hard floor beneath me, as the shake of my shoulders affected my entire body.

"I breathe. It's wrong. I smile. It's wrong. I try to get on with my life and meet someone new. I try to be happy, to do things that make me happy. And still, it's fucking wrong. What, exactly, do you want from me, Jem? You don't want me, but nobody else is having me, either? Is that it?"

I didn't respond—could think of nothing to offer.

"*What*?" he barked.

My eyes blinked wide as my body jerked.

"What is it, exactly, you expect from me?"

I tried to murmur a sorry. Thanks to the tremble of my lips, it came out a small incoherent mumble.

"I know." He nodded as he perched on the desktop. "I know. How about you tell me what I'm allowed to do? Because I'm obviously expected to dance to your bloody tune. So, come on. Tell me what you want."

My eyes had given up on their attempts to focus as I shook my head.

"Tell me what you want from me."

I gave another headshake, jerked and robotic.

"What? You're not going to tell me?"

I averted my eyes, aimed my fuzzy gaze at the floor.

"Nothing, then. That's exactly what I thought." He pushed to his feet, brushed past me and booted at the door three times until it bounced open.

I tracked the sound of his receding footsteps—and heard his words when he spoke.

"Hey, Marianne."

With a muffled growl of frustration, I shut the door.

7

The veneer of the desk did not make a good pillow, but hiding out came at a price and lack of luxury seemed a small cost to pay. If Sean saw how upset Josh had made me, the distress would extend further than it already had. I refused to be responsible for a rift between him and Josh, too.

The ring of my mobile disturbed my thoughts. Temptation to ignore battled strong, but if it was Sean, and I didn't answer, he'd come looking for me.

It took effort to unfold my body from its crumpled position, to tug the phone from my pocket and check the display. Not Sean. Jess, my sister.

I hit connect and placed it to my ear. "Hello, Jess."

"What's wrong?" she asked.

"You called me, remember?" My voice sounded lacklustre, even to my own ears.

"What's wrong?"

"Aren't you supposed to be at work?"

"I am at work. What's wrong, Jem?"

"Shouldn't you be working?" I asked.

"I'm a multitasker. Tell me what's wrong."

"Nothing," I mumbled.

"Liar."

My sigh arrived heavy.

"Come on, tell me. You sound about as happy as a slug beneath a pound of salt."

"I've fallen out with Josh."

"Oh. Well, it's hardly the end of the world," she said, faux chirpy.

I sniffed at the snot clinging to my nostrils.

When I gave no other response, she asked, "Okay, what did you fall out over?"

"He's got a girlfriend."

"Ah." She paused, then, "Jealousy is such an ugly beast, though, Jem."

I scowled at yet another accusation. "I'm not jealous."

"Of course you're not."

"Why would I be jealous? I've got Sean, for goodness sake."

"So, if not jealousy, what's the true problem?"

"I don't trust her. She's up to something, and Josh isn't listening to me."

"Up to something, how?" Jess's tone became serious as she entered 'problem-solving' mode.

I breathed out a small huff. "Where would you like me to start?"

"The beginning is probably best."

"Well, first she was spying on him, but pretended to be looking at the apartments ..." I took a minute to explain Poppy's and my initial encounter and impressions.

"So, Poppy doesn't like her, either?" Jess asked.

"No."

"Hmm, Poppy's usually on my wavelength in her opinions of people."

"I know."

"Is that it?"

"What do you mean?"

"You're not that fickle. What else has this girl done to annoy you?"

"Josh took her on a date without telling me." My voice rose in annoyance at the memory.

"Uh-oh."

"I know ..." The next few moments I spent recalling my reaction to Josh's first date with Marianne, and how we'd made up—leaving out the part about Josh's sort-of confession about his sort-of feelings for me.

"Is that all?"

"I wish." I ran my hand over my forehead to smooth out the creases there. "She keeps turning up here. And she

76

keeps bringing this crappy homemade herbal tea of hers. 'I can't stand the thought of you being cold, Josh'," I mimicked in a Marianne-like squawk. "Josh hasn't been cold since the day I met him."

"Herbal tea?" Jess asked. "Homemade?"

I huffed down the line at her. "That's what I said."

"Hmm."

"What does *hmm* mean?"

"I take it Josh has kept on seeing her, from how upset you sound. What else has she done?"

"Yeah, now she's dragging Dan into it, as well. She got him to double date with her sister on Sunday. And her bloody sister is like a mutant *replica* of her. So, now I have two of them to contend with, like mini-clones."

Jess snorted. "Mini-clowns?"

I rolled my eyes. "*Clones*. But that's not the only thing griping me."

"So, what is?"

"Josh and I just had an almighty fight."

"Why?"

"Because he and Danny brought the girls home with them after their date—against pack rules. And I didn't take it so well ..."

"Hmm-mm."

"Especially not when I saw some flipping bracelet on Josh's wrist—some gift from his *girlfriend*." My lip curled.

"What sort of bracelet?" Jess's all-business tone re-emerged.

"Made from hair the exact same colour as Marianne's, if you must know."

Static silence filled the line.

My head tilted. "Jess?"

No response.

"Jess?"

"Shush, I'm thinking."

My fingers drummed out a beat of impatience on the desktop as I slumped low in the swivel seat.

"The tea?" she said at last.

I straightened. "What about it?"

"What does it smell like?"

I screwed my eyes up in concentration. "I could smell woodiness in it, I guess."

"What else?" she said, her voice stern.

My face tilted to the ceiling. "Earthiness."

"Woody and earthy smells?"

"Yes, Jess, but—"

"Anything else? Liquorice? Can you smell any liquorice in there?"

"I, um ..." My mind reached into my memories, recapturing how disgusting the liquid had smelled. "Yes," I said after a few seconds. "Now you mention it, I think I may have detected a hint of liquorice in there."

"Well, shit!"

"What?"

"Well ... shit!" she said again.

"Bloody what?"

"How many flasks has Josh had?"

Sirens began their tune of disquiet in my head. "None." *I think.*

Her heavily released breath buffeted against my ear. "Keep it that way."

I frowned. "Why?"

"Just make sure he doesn't drink them."

"Jess, what's wrong with the tea?"

"I think this girl is binding him," she said.

My frown deepened. "What do you mean?"

"It sounds like Josh has bagged himself a witch."

"What the heck?" If the statement had come from anyone else, I'd have dismissed it. From Jess, however, who believed herself to be a reincarnated witch, and who I knew had creepy spell books stashed under her bed, the enlightenment didn't sound quite so lame. I had little option but to take her seriously.

"And said witch is binding him," Jess said.

"What do you ..." On the verge of repeating myself, illumination brightened my brain until it flickered into motion. "She's *binding* him?"

"That's what it sounds like to me."

"How are the tea and bracelet going to do that?"

"The drink sounds like a summoning tea, so she can command him to do her bidding. I'm not one hundred percent sure, so I'll look into it further. But the bracelet being made of hair? That sounds like the same kind of binding that was performed for you and Sean."

My mouth opened, hanging there as I absorbed her words. "How could you know anything about our binding ritual, Jess, if Sean and I can't even remember it?"

Silence, then, "Oh, um ..."

"Jess?"

"Well ... okay. Do you remember when you first told me about Nathan's history lesson?"

By history lesson, she actually meant when Nathan panicked me half to death, by announcing my importance as the first ever female werewolf in werewolf history. My still being a mere human at that point helped my acceptance of the information not one bit. Of course I remembered it.

I offered a hesitant, "Yes."

"And do you remember when you asked me to look it up and see if it was possible for two people to be bound for eternity, like Nathan claimed had happened to you and Sean?"

Another hesitant, "Yes."

"And do you remember I asked if you wanted me to look up about the pack history regarding you, but you said not to bother because I wouldn't find it, and I said I'd look anyway?"

Something told me I wouldn't like what Jess had to tell me, but I still answered, "Yes."

"Well, I looked. And you were right. I couldn't find any pack recordings about you anywhere."

I expelled the breath I held. "Like I told you."

"I know. But there *are* recordings of you and Sean, Jem."

"What?" My whispered tone came out higher than intended. My throat did its little constricting trick—it had done that a lot since Marianne's appearance.

"I found recordings of your existence," Jess continued, "of the two of you together. Well ... I presume it was you two the information referred to, anyway. I mean, there's only one recorded successful eternal binding spell, and that particular one states the binding was performed for two werewolves. So, I figure it had to be about you and Sean."

"But ..." My jaw dropped until I worked it back up. "You never mentioned this."

"That's because the only information I had then was that it had been done. I didn't know how, or for whom," she said, her tone defensive. "But ... since then, I've found more information."

"What? How? For goodness sake, where?"

"Think about it. As far as your binding went, werewolves weren't the only race involved."

I scrunched up my eyes until my temple throbbed and a wave of dizziness swept through me. "Witches," I muttered. "Holy shit, Jess."

"Correct," she said. "It took me a while to find it, but I did. If you know the right places to go, there are records— grimoires— with witch histories in them. They also contain successful or powerful spells and rituals, dark or forbidden magic. All the stuff that can only be read if you have the right connections, because it would be really bad if they fell into the wrong hands."

"Oh, God!" With a groan, I rubbed at my face.

"You and Sean are in one grimoire, along with a detailed description of the binding ritual used and the incantations spoken. It was all in there, including the admission that it was believed to have worked so powerfully because you'd already been bound and connected to him by the bite."

"Tell me." I dropped my hand to the table-top. "Tell me about the ritual."

"Are you sure?"

"I need to know. I need to understand what triggered my reaction to Josh's gift."

"Well ... if you're sure."

Get on with it, already, I wanted to yell. "I am."

"Okay. So, you and Sean exchanged wreaths that had been made from your hair—his for you, yours for him ..."

No sooner had the words left her than a switch clicked inside my brain, like an attempt to send through a surge of information. My lids lowered. Fluttering images danced about behind the shield. Jess continued to speak, but I no longer defined her words. With the striving cogs inside my mind almost loud enough to hear, the throb at my temple spread across my sinuses. I massaged the ball of my free hand into my eye socket to stem the pain.

My lids flew open. "Oh!"

"Jem?"

"I think I remember it."

"You—"

"I *remember* it," I said. "My wreath." I gestured to my neck as though I expected her to see. "I made it from my own hair, like you said. My mother insisted on it. Sean made one, too, from his hair. And we exchanged them. In the forest—we were in the forest." I closed my eyes again to draw forth the image and took a deep breath. "The moon was whole that night." My voice dropped to a murmur. "It ... it was the eve of our wedding—or, at least, I was wearing my wedding dress. I think ... I think our hands were sliced with something, I'm not sure what. And we seemed to be mingling our blood ..."

"Amazing—"

"No! Not mingling, that's not right. We ... *exchanged* blood," I corrected. "We weren't alone, and there was chanting, or something. Words—binding words. And we recited about fate and destiny, but I've already remembered those words, so ..."

"Oh, my—"

"Candles." I reopened my eyes against the vividness of the memory. "We were within a circle of candles." My breaths arrived faster. "I ... I can't recall anything else."

"Holy shit, Jem! You really *were* there. It's exactly as described in the records."

"How long have you known about this, Jess?"

A brief pause came through before she said, "Since October."

My eyebrows shot up. "And you didn't think to mention it?"

"If you recall, you asked me not to tell you anything that might freak you out."

"Yes, but—"

"You said if I found anything I thought you'd rather not know, then I should keep it to myself."

I couldn't dispute her. I had said that. "Even so."

"Look, I had every intention of telling you. At first, I wanted to be certain I'd got my facts right. Then, once I'd convinced myself it couldn't possibly be about anyone else, I was waiting ... for the right moment."

I let out a long, low groan.

"I'm sorry, but I was going to tell you. I swear."

My whole life, since I'd learned of Sean's existence, since I'd met him—everything—it all seemed a lot for one person to have to take in.

"Jem?" Jess's voice sounded tentative.

"What do I do now?" I asked.

"About what?"

The door to the cabin pushed open. As Nathan stepped inside, his gaze met mine, and he inclined his head.

I held up a finger to request a minute. "About the witch," I said into the phone.

Nathan nodded, coming farther in and shutting the door.

"Stick close to her," Jess said. "And leave me to do some digging."

"How am I supposed to stick close to someone who knows I don't like her?"

"Turn it around. Be nice."

"How the heck am I supposed to be nice to someone I can't stand the sight of?" My gaze remained locked with Nathan's.

"You will have to try if you want to help Josh."

"But—"

"Have you never heard of the expression, keep your friends close, but keep your enemies closer? It's a rule I find works very well for me. If you push her away, you'll push Josh away. If she's binding him, he will not listen to you—or anyone else, for that matter—if you have something bad to say about this witch. The only chance you have of helping Josh is if you watch him like a hawk. And you can't do that if you're barely speaking. So suck it up, befriend the witch, and play nice."

My eyes closed for a moment as I released a groan.

"In the meantime, I'll dig deep and see what I can find out about her. See what's growing on the grapevine. You said her name is Marianne?"

I lifted my lids, stared back at Nathan. "Yes."

"Surname?"

My shoulders shrugged. "I don't have it."

"What about her sister's name?"

"Amber."

"Leave it with me. I'll go dig. I'll take the biggest shovel I have. As soon as I have something, I'll call. Witches don't like parting with info on their own kind, so play it cool and be patient. Okay?"

"Okay, Jess. Thanks."

I hung up and lowered the phone to the desk as though handing over a live bomb to a professional diffuser.

"Well." Nathan flung his arms wide. "What was that all about?"

I blew out a breath. "We have a problem."

8

Nathan's hands rested on his hips as he stared down at me.

"Marianne is a witch," I said.

"According to ...?"

"Jess." I tapped my mobile. "I just spoke to her. She said the tea Marianne keeps making Josh is a summoning tea. And she said the bracelet being made of hair qualifies it for binding."

Nathan frowned.

"That's why Sean and I recognised it as being off," I continued. "Because that was one of the things we did during *our* binding ceremony."

Exactly as mine had, Nathan's mouth opened and closed. He took a step forward. "Did you recall a memory?"

"Not at first." My gaze remained on his. "Jess helped."

His eyebrows shot up. "Jess?" I gave a slow nod, and his brows lowered to accommodate the return of his frown. "She knows about you and Sean?"

My chin dipped again.

"That's impossible." He lifted his hands up, slammed them back down on his hips. "How?"

"There are records, regarding us, in witch history," I said. "Jess has read them. And I know them to be accurate because when she said something about us exchanging hair, it jogged my memory about that evening. When I told her what I remembered, she said it's the same as what's been recorded."

Nathan raised a singular eyebrow. "So, *you* remembered?"

"Yep."

"And now witches, as well as our race, are aware of your existence?"

My shoulders bunched into a shrug. "I don't know."

Nathan fell quiet for a moment, rubbing a hand across his forehead. "Just because witches have a record of your binding doesn't mean they're aware of your return."

"I don't think Marianne's interest in Josh is connected to me and Sean, if that's what you're worried about."

He stared hard at me for seconds, his mouth a grim line. "You asked Jess for suggestions before you ended the call, yes?"

"She said she's going to see what she can find out about Marianne and her sister. In the meantime, she said I have to be nice to Marianne." My scowl returned. "Jess said if I'm horrible to Marianne, I'll push Josh away." I matched his serious expression with one of my own. "He's no longer under your command, Nate. Marianne is controlling him now."

A flash of fury chilled Nathan's eyes.

"And she said make sure he doesn't drink the tea."

Nathan groaned, reaching up to brush a hand across his hair.

My pulse increased. "Nate?"

"It's too late ..."

The chair rolled back as I stood.

"He's drinking the damn thing now."

My dive for the door sent the chair crashing into the wall at my rear.

Nathan's hand covered mine, holding the door in place. "You can't just go charging over there."

I wiggled the handle, growling when Nathan held it steady. "I need to stop him."

"Did you listen to a word your sister said?" His free hand slid around my waist, and he swivelled until we faced back inside the cabin. "Play nice. Isn't that what she told you?" He took my shoulders, spinning me round to face him. "You'll go nowhere but backward, if you don't handle this with a little delicacy—especially if Jess has her suspicions correct."

It took effort to calm my heaving chest. My gaze darted around until I'd gained self-control and they settled on Nathan. "What do I do?"

"You go over there ..." Calm words spoken with a hint of the snarls he often repressed. "And you repair the damage already done."

My cheeks bulged with my huge pout.

"Jem?" Nathan urged.

I heaved out a sigh. "Sure. Whatever it takes, right?"

He patted my shoulder. "Whatever it takes."

I hit the showroom apartment just in time for lunch. Pausing in the doorway gave me a chance to scan the room's occupants, Daniel, Kyle, Connor, Ethan, Sean.

Josh and Marianne.

Sean rummaged into the brown paper bag on the floor. "You timed that well." A flick of his wrist sent a burger sailing toward me.

I caught it. "Thanks."

The air in the room lacked the tension I expected it to hold, telling me details of the argument Ethan witnessed had spread no further than Nathan.

I left the warm depths of Sean's eyes and met Ethan's questioning gaze. I smiled, giving the tiniest of nods. For Connor, Kyle and Daniel, their food held more interest than me—typical Larsen behaviour.

With his body half turned away, Josh partly obscured my line of vision to Marianne, but as though she sensed my stare, Marianne tilted to the left.

As Nathan's instructions echoed in my head, I dismissed my unwrapped burger and walked over to her, ignoring Josh when he turned and frowned.

Her eyebrow lifted. "Jem."

The pack probably thought I had plans to tear her up some. If not for my phone chat with Jess and Nathan's orders, a little shredding could well have been on the agenda.

"Hello, Marianne." I practiced a smile, impressing myself with my efforts. The mild surprise in Marianne's eyes helped it to widen, despite my lips trying to curl. "I owe you an apology." *Damn, that was hard.*

Josh's high shoulders drooped an inch, while the curious attention of the others burned from my right.

My gaze remained on Marianne's. "I was out of order yesterday. I had no right to speak to you the way I did ... and I'm sorry."

A flash of irritation sparked her eyes for a nanosecond.

I curbed my smile, as it tried to take over my lips, and held out my hand. "I'd really like it if we could start afresh." With the ball in her court, I awaited her next shot.

Her calculating eyes took me in for too long, before she smiled, reached out, and shook my offered hand—though I guessed I'd left her with little choice. "Of course. I'd like that, Jem."

The urge to squeeze harder than necessary overwhelmed me. I really wanted to. Maybe bring tears to her eyes. After a longer handshake and much more physical contact with the witch than I wanted, I let go. "Thanks. That's very generous of you."

With one last smile for emphasis, I returned to my burger and crossed the room to Sean. My expression faded the second I turned away.

Sean's head tilted as his eyes drew me in. "Jem?" His mumble arrived no louder than a sigh.

I bit down on my meat-filled bun and chewed. "She has no idea who she's messing with," I whispered.

"You going to enlighten me?" Sean asked, after the others had all dispersed for work.

I climbed the stepladder, sat at eye level with him, and told him of my memory recall.

His brow wrinkled as he listened. "If it was the eve of our wedding, I don't understand why I'm not getting it."

"I know," I said. "You dreamt about the wedding ceremony, as well as our ... love making in the barn." As a particular favourite of our dreams—for us both—talk of it provoked smiles in the two of us. "I don't get why your mind would skip the part in between."

He tugged on a loose strand of my hair. "Me neither."

"But," I said, considering again, "if you think about our wedding night dream, weren't you wearing something around your neck in the barn? I'm certain you were, now I think about it."

Sean's eyes grew distant and focused. "That's right. Some kind of ... braided necklace." His hand signalled where it would have rested against his chest. "Made from—"

"My hair," I finished.

His head continued bobbing as though the dots connected in his mind. "So, this means, what? That Marianne is—"

"Binding Josh to her," I said.

"But ..." His frown returned. "Why?"

"Jess is going to find out."

"Jess?"

I nodded. "Jess called me. She recognised what Marianne had done. It was Jess who prompted me to remember."

His eyebrows scrunched. "Jess?"

It took only a couple of minutes to run through the revelation that witches knew, as well as werewolves, about the binding ceremony that took place between Sean and me.

His frown lines deepened, when I explained how Jess had found a record of it. "And this grimoire, or whatever it is ... where did she find it?" he asked.

"I didn't think to ask. Does it matter? Surely, even if someone else reads it, they won't connect the story to us?

Witches can't recognise werewolves ... so, how would they know it's us?"

"That's not what I was getting at, Jem."

"Then, what?"

He stared into me. "This grimoire? Aren't they like ..." He seemed to search for the right words. "I'm pretty sure grimoires are a record—a witch's record—of tried and tested spells. Is that right?"

I shrugged. "Something like that."

"And they get passed down from generation to generation? Like with our histories?"

"I guess. So?"

He took my face between his palms. "That binding ritual could only have been recorded by you or your mother, Jem. At some point, the particular grimoire that holds the details of our binding belonged to *your* family."

My mouth formed a silent 'O' as the implication of his words sank in.

"So, we should find out where it is," he said. "Because, theoretically, that book belongs to you."

My distracted mind resulted in a half-hearted attempt at cooking dinner. I forgot about the sausages I'd put in the oven to brown, and we ended up eating a couple of gammon omelettes each. The entire time, Ethan nagged about how dinner never burned when he had cooking duty.

As soon as the last of the meal had been eaten, I cleared the table and turned to study the three men, left to right— Ethan, Nathan, Sean. "I don't want to tell you I told you so, but I did." The more I'd thought about it over the course of the day, the more annoyed I'd grown. If they'd all listened to me, instead of laughing at the ridiculousness of my unease about Marianne, Josh wouldn't have been in such a mess. "I told you there was something wrong with her. The first day I saw her, I told you there was something funny about her. If you'd listened to me, instead of—"

"You're right." Nathan broke into my monologue.

I lifted an eyebrow.

"You're absolutely right." He rubbed a hand over his head, roughing up his hair. "You said you had a feeling about her, and I should have taken notice. You did exactly what I've always told you to do. I've always encouraged you to let us know if something seems off, and when you did, we didn't listen. I'm sorry."

Ethan and Sean turned from Nathan to me, their brows high. Their reactions told me Nathan didn't have to admit his errors very often.

"Have you told the others about this?" I asked Nathan, meaning the Larsens.

"Connor knows. But not Dan or Kyle. Josh has been with them all day, so I didn't get the chance. And I've asked Connor not to talk about it this evening, in case Josh overhears. The last thing we need is Josh eavesdropping on his family, while they accuse his girlfriend of being a witch. If that happens, it'll push him farther away ... if your sister's right about this."

"She's right." My hands came to rest on my hips. "I know she is."

"Have you spoken to her about Josh drinking the tea yet?"

"No. I doubt there's a lot we can do about it now. Even if Jess comes up with a solution, I know nothing about the art of potion making, or spell casting." At a hopeful glance from Nathan, I added, "Despite my distant upraising."

He nodded again—he seemed to be doing a lot of agreeing.

"So, I take it the plan is still to play nice to the witch and pretend I like her?"

"I know it's going to be hard for you, Jem," Nathan said.

I scowled. "You have no idea."

His head bobbed—maybe he had no other answer.

"And we watch Josh like a hawk?"

"Yes," he rumbled.

I dipped my chin. "Of course, we wouldn't have to watch him at all, if—"

"We *know*, Jem."

"All I can say is, you'd better hope Jess finds out what they're up to. And if she finds out what they're up to, and it isn't good? You'd better hope she comes up with a fix."

I caught the wince in each of their gazes. To rely on an outsider for help went against everything they believed in—especially when that outsider arrived in the form of a female, a human, and to top it all, something resembling a witch.

9

Momentary disorientation greeted me, as I blinked in the darkness. A partial moon provided a sequinned glow to the furnishings of the bedroom and glittered with each raindrop that hit the windowpane. Beyond the glass, ever changing clouds ruled the dark sky.

The dream I'd left behind had taken me beyond sleep, and I rolled out from beneath Sean's leaden arm and climbed from the bed. Rummaging through the laundry pile, I found a sweatshirt and a pair of his thick socks and pulled them on, before a glance to the left brought the outline of his fantastic body into view. With a smile at his soft, slumber-fed breaths and the serenity of his features, I grabbed a blanket from the chair, wrapped it around myself, and headed for the bathroom—the place with the best view of the forest.

Despite being a female, despite some of my most terrifying moments having occurred in the forest, I'd never been afraid of it. Its appearance only enchanted, drew my body into the pull of its sanctuary. I opened the window to maximum capacity, climbed onto the sill, and rested with my feet dangling against the brick of the house.

The rear of the property provided more shelter than the front, but even the thickness of the socks provided inadequate protection against the cold wind, and the gale tugged at the edges of my blanket, its icy chill taunting the flesh of my exposed legs.

As I watched, the high branches of the forest battled, as the wind constantly swirled, changing direction, and the structures stretched one way before reaching toward another with the grace of a natural ballet.

"Jem?"

I tilted my head at Sean's low murmur behind me. Thanks to the encompassing whirlwind, even his scent had escaped detection.

Soft footsteps crossed the bathroom to me. His body brushed mine as he took up position beside me on the window ledge.

I turned to his naked, shuddering body and held out a corner of my blanket. "Want some?"

He shuffled in closer. Still facing the room, his arms wrapped round me as I cocooned us in the folds of fleecy fabric, his cheek coming to rest against my shoulder. "What's up, Jem?"

"A dream. I think."

His lashes tickled my skin. "What'd you dream about?"

"That night. The night of our binding."

We fell quiet for minutes. Only the onslaught of nature and the mechanics of our bodies made sound.

"Did you get anything else?" he asked after a while.

"I get the sense there were four people there. At first, earlier today, when I remembered, I thought there were just the two of us and my mother. Now, I think there may have been a fourth person, and I can't for the life of me get a clear picture of who it was. It just ... bothers me." I toyed with the strands at his crown. "The whole thing bothers me. You not remembering bothers me. I don't know ..."

It's bothering me, too," he said.

I nodded, and we returned to quiet. At least my irritation at not having all the answers began to fade. With Sean beside me, my body and mind relaxed.

"So ... you planning to stay out here all night?" When I didn't answer, he nudged me with his hip. "Aren't you cold?"

"My feet are bloody freezing."

"Come back to bed with me." Without awaiting a response, he slid me to sit across his lap, before leaning around to close the window and shut off the breath-stealing gusts.

I reached up a hand, cupped the back of his neck and brought him down to brush my lips across his. "Promise me you'll watch out for Josh."

His eyes stared into mine. "You know I will."

"Promise me, Sean, you won't let her take him from us."

"I promise."

I folded into his arms as he lifted me, and once back in bed, his body, his scent, the comforting whispers of his deep, velvety voice caressed me into a state of calm until sleep once again moved in.

The winter sun hung low in the sky Tuesday morning, but while it gleamed at me in the rear-view mirror of the Porsche, it couldn't obscure the fact that I had a black Lexus on my tail.

I'd have shrugged it off as nothing, but the deal with the witches and the black Lexus from the week before brought my niggle to the surface.

I hadn't gone with the others that morning, which only added to my worry.

The second time, when I had a bad feeling about a Lexus parked outside the supermarket, I'd left the house alone, too.

The third time resulted in a black Lexus in tow as I flew around country lanes toward Derby.

Coincidence?

I peered for about the four-hundredth time in my rear-view mirror. Whoever drove the Lexus seemed to know to keep their distance.

If I slowed, they hung back and retained the gap.

When I sped up to lose them, they did, also.

I turned right, they turned right—turned left and they followed.

Definitely not coincidence!

After about forty minutes of the Lexus clinging to my rear bumper, I scanned the road signs for a lay-by alert.

If they had any sort of intentions toward me, surely they'd take the opportunity and follow. "Only one way to find out," I murmured.

Another five minutes passed before a sign forewarned of an upcoming lay-by. I checked my speed, dropped down to sixty, down to fifty. When the turn-off came into sight, I flicked my indicator to give the Lexus fair warning and slowed even further. The black car matched my speed through every reduction.

Spinning the wheel to the left removed the Porsche from the road, and I recognised the escalating roar of a floored accelerator a split second too late.

As the black Lexus whizzed past at rocket speed, the only glimpse I caught of the driver was a flash of rich chestnut-coloured hair.

"Shit!"

I slammed the gearstick into first and wheel spun for the exit.

A flash of bottle green to my right hit my periphery, and I stomped down on the brake, the tyres struggling for traction on the gravel road, but managed to stop a fraction shy of collision.

The Jaguar's driver sent me a disapproving headshake as he swerved past.

Ignoring him, I pulled out behind and continued my chase, but winding curves made it impossible to get by.

The black car vanished from sight.

Ethan walked my way before the Porsche had even come to a standstill, when I pulled in through the site entrance.

My eyes narrowed as his head ducked in through the window, as his lips brushed across my cheek—a most unusual action for Ethan unless I'd done something worthy of praise.

"Heads up, Jem," he whispered.

Head tilted, I forced my lips to spread. "What for?"

"She's here."

My smile wavered.

"And she's not alone."

I reached up to his cheek, held him close to conceal my vanishing smile. "Did she bring her sister?"

He gave a nod, his mouth set in a firm line. "And I think Marianne brought her along to try the same with Dan as she has with Josh."

My chest constricted. "Why would you think that?"

Ethan's expression matched my emotions. "Because Marianne wasn't the only one to walk in carrying a bloody thermos. That's why."

At his words, I clambered from the car, all concerns over the black Lexus gone. "Did your dad talk to Kyle and Dan?"

"Not yet." His arms drew me into a bear hug, as he angled my face away from the apartment windows.

Did I look that panicked? "So, Danny doesn't know?"

Ethan shook his head.

My pulse increased. "Where's Nate?"

"I was just looking for him when you showed up."

"And Sean?"

"Upstairs. He's my next stop if I don't find Dad."

I glanced around Ethan's shoulder toward where the witches had to be. "Okay, go find your dad. I'll see if I can stall Danny from drinking the tea."

Ethan released me and strode off toward the cabin, and I took a deep breath and headed for the shit-covered fan.

In three seconds, I'd taken it all in.

Daniel sipped with caution at the thermos in his hand, nose twitching like crazy at the steam drifting from its content. Josh mirrored him, but with no hesitation—gulping and swallowing it down. Two witches, one as smug as a bird with a worm, the other twitchy as heck when her gaze landed on me, sat with them.

I should have known I would arrive too late, should have realised Josh would encourage his brother to drink the tea.

An unspoken curse echoed in my mind, as I lifted my lowered head, smoothed out my frown and crossed the room. "Marianne."

The witch smiled. "Hi, Jem."

I wondered if my expression looked as false as hers.

Unfortunately, Josh's lack of understanding of the opposite sex lent him no favours. He'd been right in saying women were manipulative, but he had no realisation of just how much talent existed in the gender-oriented art.

I turned my attention to Marianne's clone and extended my hand. "Amber, right? You didn't exactly catch me at my best the last time we met."

She allowed my hand a brief shake. "It's good to meet you properly, Jem."

"So," I said to Daniel, "who's on lunch duty today?"

I hadn't spoken to Josh since he'd yelled and stormed out on me, and I paid him no attention then, either. I'd caught him watching me, though, since my apology to Marianne, and spying when he thought I couldn't see. Hoping Josh would come to me when ready, I'd ignored him every time.

A small smile played on Daniel's lips. "Um ... you?"

"Nuh-uh." I shook my head with a grin. "No way. I did the lunch run three times last week. It's your turn, Dan."

He lowered his thermos, let loose his puppy eyes. "Please, Jem. If you get behind, we can all chip in when we've finished. If I get behind, Nate gets on my case like a pit bull with a damn—"

"I can hear you, you know."

Daniel whirled toward the doorway.

I smothered my smirk as I twisted toward Nathan's huge form in the opening.

He turned from Josh, chugging from his flask, to Daniel who still sipped at his. When he met my gaze, I tried to give a discreet expression of apology.

Barely moving enough for the others to detect, he nodded. As Connor came up behind him, performing the same rapid evaluation as our Alpha, Nathan stepped into the room.

Marianne smiled. "Mr Larsen?"

"Connor," he said.

"We wanted to apologise for interrupting your meal on Sunday."

"Not a problem." He remained in the doorway. "Water under the bridge, by the looks of things."

"Even still …" Marianne took a step forward. "We'd like to make it up to you."

Connor didn't speak, just raised his eyebrows, as mine knitted.

"We were hoping you'd accept an invitation for dinner with us," Marianne said.

Still, Connor remained mute. I figured he struggled with niceties for someone whose intentions toward his sons he didn't understand.

"On Sunday?" she continued.

"We usually eat with Nate and his family on Sunday's," Connor said at last.

"Well, that works out just fine." She turned to Nathan. "Because the invitation was for all of you."

Connor's mouth seemed to struggle to respond, but Nathan cut in with, "That's very generous of you, Marianne."

A hint of triumph sparked her eyes. "So, you'll come?"

"As long as you understand Jem is considered a member of my family, yes," he said.

"Oh, well …" At Marianne's sideways glance, I sent her my best smile beneath Josh's watchful gaze. She turned back to Nathan. "Of course, the invitation is extended to Jem, too."

"Excellent." I offered her a jiggle of my eyebrows. "I'd love to come."

Marianne grinned as if she'd won the lottery. "Sunday it is, then."

"I'm surprised you accepted Marianne's invitation, Nate," I said later that evening.

Lifting his focus from his newspaper, he glanced across from his armchair in the corner of the living room. "I wanted to find out where they live."

Good idea. I gave a slow nod.

"And I'd rather Josh and Dan, if that's who they're really intent on getting there, had us as escort. Better that than them spending more time alone with them. The last thing we need is Danny turning up with a bracelet to match Josh's."

"You're right. She wasn't happy, though, when you insisted I be included."

"No."

"She didn't hide it very well, either. It got to her, I think."

"Probably. But she hid it well enough for Josh to miss it."

"She could fart in the bath and laugh it off as the weather, and Josh would miss her bullshit."

Low chuckles emanated from Sean and Ethan.

Nathan's lips twitched. "Possibly," he murmured, returning to the printed news in his lap.

Tired from my lack of sleep the night before, I yawned. My arms stretched up, muscles tensing with the movement, and my back arched into a shuddering finale.

"What was keeping you awake last night?" Ethan asked.

I rubbed at my face. "Did I disturb you?"

"Nah. I just heard a noise, checked to see who it was and went back to bed."

A swing of my legs laid them across Sean's lap as I snuggled into the sofa cushions. I twisted to look at Nathan. "Did I wake you, too?"

He studied me for a few seconds before giving a small nod.

"So much for trying to be quiet," I mumbled.

Nathan folded his newspaper and set it aside. "Something on your mind, Jem?"

"No more than the rest of you."

When Nathan and Ethan continued to stare, Sean said, "She dreamt about our binding ritual."

"D'you remember more?" Ethan asked.

"Just that I think there were two people there with Sean and me that night. Not much else, really." At his raised eyebrow, I added, "I couldn't see them. I don't know who it was."

"Maybe it'll come to you." Sean's finger trailed the length of my calf down to my ankle.

"Maybe." I stretched into him, practically purring at his contact. "Or maybe it will come to you."

An hour later, the mechanical whir of the disc drawer announced Ethan's feeding of a film into the DVD player, and Sean lifted his head from the sofa back, opening his eyes. "Good idea. Action, horror ...?"

"You wake up for a film, but not to talk to me?" Ethan said over his shoulder.

Sean chuckled. "I wasn't asleep."

"It's action," Ethan said, messing with the channels.

"Cool." Sean lifted my legs and climbed to his feet. "Anyone for snacks?"

"Not for me," I mumbled.

"Crisps," called Ethan after him. "And Snickers."

As soon as Sean left the room, Nathan aimed his stare my way.

"If you're tired, Jem, wouldn't you be better off with a blanket?"

My lips formed *what* as my eyes narrowed.

With his eyes, he gestured to the stairs.

Frowning, I pushed up to look at him properly.

His head and hand tilted toward the stairs, and again after a quick glance toward Ethan.

Although I'd no idea of his motive, I swung my legs down and climbed to my feet. "I'll grab one from the bedroom." I paused in the hall. "Baby, I'm just going up for that thick blanket. You want anything?"

"No, I'll share yours."

I gave a nod he couldn't see and continued upstairs into our bedroom. The blanket from the night before sat in a crumpled heap beside the bed—the exact spot Sean had tossed it to after he'd dragged me beneath the duvet into the warmth of his arms. Remembering our love making session in the middle of the night brought a smile to my lips—until Nathan's steps sounded behind me.

When I straightened and turned, he didn't speak, just beckoned with his finger and carried on along the length of the landing.

Curiosity insisted I follow.

The second door on the right concealed Nathan's bedroom. He opened it and went in, and I followed, coming to a stop in the middle of the room.

Nathan leaned close. "Remember this number. One, nine, seven, two. Can you remember it without writing it down?"

"Sure. What's it for?"

With another beckon of his fingers, Nathan pulled open his wardrobe doors. The gentle sliding of hangers made little noise as he parted the clothes to reveal a safe.

I looked from the metal cube to him. "You've given me your safe combination?" At his nod, I asked, "Why?"

He brought his arm around my shoulders. "Because you asked me for pictures of Beth," he murmured. "And they're all in there."

A small smile formed on my lips.

"There are some in a folder," he said. "And there are some in a box. Do not take any out of the folder," he added. "The folder holds my personal favourites. Do you understand?"

I nodded, grinning. "But I can take some from the box?"

"Yes." He rubbed his hand up and down my back. "Yes, you can have some from the box."

"Thank you."

"I'm trusting you, Jem. There are a lot of personal items in that safe," he continued. "Including Beth's address ..." His eyes locked with mine. "So, I'm laying a *lot* of trust in you with this."

In other words, he trusted me not to scribble it onto a piece of paper the second I laid eyes on it and pass it onto his sons, neither of whom had the address.

I gave him a smile of reassurance. "Okay."

Despite knowing I'd have an overwhelming urge to do exactly what Nathan didn't want me to, I knew I couldn't. The message that he'd never given his safe combination out before came through loud and clear. Under no circumstances would I let him down—especially when the trust had been placed as a result of a request I'd made.

Boredom from yet another action film toppled me into the land of nod. The second my brain acknowledged the scene, with myself as the leading role, I knew I'd entered the depths of a dream.

For whatever reasons, my dreams weren't like those of others. I didn't observe from within my body, but as a ghostly spectator through my own point of view.

As my subconscious took control, I watched myself and Sean bound about, his arms around my waist, as I grasped his shoulders. Our laughter came freely, louder even than the music that spurred our actions, and I took delight in witnessing the expressive joy on our faces.

As the small crowd of onlookers clapped their encouragement, we laughed, our eyes radiating a warm glow.

Sean whirled my body around and around until my long, white dress swirled about my ankles. With each spin, I tightened my hold on him, and the fastenings of his white shirt loosened until his collar hung wide. The disarray of our attire appeared only to add to our delight as we laughed harder, and though dusk neared, the high colour of our cheeks still revealed itself in the waning light.

As the energetic dance came to its conclusion, the watchers moved forward to join our fun, and Sean retook the waist of my dream self, lifting me high into the air. On lowering me, he held me close, sliding my body down his own.

Buoyancy enveloped me as I watched the spiralling dance, intensifying until a strong sensation of floating dominated my mind. With each surge of weightlessness, I appeared to grow farther away, and the scene before me became the scene below.

A roll of my body disturbed my flow. Another almost twisted me away.

"Jem?"

I blinked, but the dimmed lighting appeared too bright to my sleep-heavy eyes, and my lids lowered again.

"Jem?" A soft shake of my body accompanied my spoken name.

I blinked again ... and again ... until Sean's face swam into focus. As my brain roused, and I spotted the wide grin spread across his lips, I realised my own face sported a smile. I couldn't help the small snort of laughter that burst out.

Sean chuckled. "I didn't mean to disturb you. You sounded as though you were having fun."

I reached up for his smiling face. As I stroked along his jaw, he leaned into my touch.

"I was going to carry you to bed." His words told me I still lay on the huge sofa. "But just as I went to, you started laughing."

Checking we had no company, I drew him down for a kiss, my lips already parted and ready as he met them.

He pulled back a fraction. "And you were twitching like crazy." Light danced in his eyes. "What were you dreaming about?"

"I think it was part of our wedding." I brushed my lips across his again. "We were dancing about like a couple of loons."

His chuckle rumbled across my chest. "It's a good one."

Instinct kicked in, and our lips met. My tongue darted out as did his. Without moving away, his hands worked beneath me and lifted me to his lap, where his strong arms wound around to carry me.

With my body clinging to his in return, we kissed our way up the stairs and into bed.

The approach of his footsteps told me when Josh finally came to me Wednesday lunchtime. They stopped in the doorway to the guest bedroom of the show apartment. I didn't turn, simply continued my up and down arm sweeps, moving the roller across the wall. Having waited that long for him to see sense, I figured a few minutes longer wouldn't kill me.

He must have suspected my awareness of his presence. I knew he watched me, the heat of his stare all but set my back alight.

Still, I didn't turn.

An unsubtle throat clearing broke my roll. With no more than a slight falter to my movements, I continued as though I hadn't heard.

"Jem?" His voice arrived low, his tenor deep—whether from his difficulty in approaching me or emotions, I didn't know. Either way, he sounded off.

My arm paused before I returned it to its downward journey.

"Jem?" His tone didn't alter, other than to reflect a hint of urgency.

The roller came to a standstill. My head tilted to the side.

"About the other day ..." Behind me, Josh drew in a deep breath, stepping closer. "Will you look at me?"

To remain facing away took all of my will power when his voice, so brimmed with passion, urged me to turn to him and cross the gap.

More footsteps brought him so near, his breaths warmed my exposed shoulder. "Jem?" He took my arm. "Please ... turn around."

I angled my head only far enough to peer at his fingers wrapped around my bicep. As their heat radiated onto my skin, I longed to respond, to lean into him. I'd missed his contact—the banter we shared. A few days weren't a long time. Without my friend, they'd seemed an eternity.

As I turned and raised my eyes to Josh's, relief seeped into his.

He released his hold of me, lifted his hands and raked fingers through his mess of hair. "Jem ... about the other day ..."

I set my tools down on the window ledge and stalked off.

He spun as I passed him. "Jem?" His confusion-filled voice echoed deeper than ever.

I'd bided my time, waited for Josh to come to me, yet apprehension about my plan resounded in the silent prayer my mind sent out. *Please let him follow. Please let him follow.*

No footsteps suggested he didn't.

I almost paused in the living room, thought about throwing as much pain as possible into my expression. It wouldn't have been faked. Josh *had* hurt me—even if he hadn't acted under his own influence at the time.

Teeth gritted against indecision, I kept walking, mental pleas continuing to murmur inside my mind. If he didn't follow, my ego would be crushed, but I had no choice. Josh needed to figure out on his own how much our friendship meant to him.

God, please let him want it enough.

As I reached the apartment door, the scuffle of boots on concrete announced his pursuit, and I blew out a breath.

"Jem?"

As I rounded the corner, pushed against the heavy panel, and swung outside into the crisp air, I wondered if Josh noticed I'd taken the same route he had, when he'd turned his back on me.

His long legs gave him the advantage, and he reached the entrance before the door had even clicked shut. "Wait!"

Six more steps, a few metres covered, and Josh arrived right behind me. He grasped both my arms, pulling my body close against his own. "Please don't do this."

In natural response, my head tilted as his murmured breaths seeped through my hair.

"I'm so sorry. I—"

"You're asking me to listen to you, when you wouldn't show me the same courtesy on Monday?"

"I was an arse." He blew out a gust, the force of it hitting my neck and sending my hair across my cheek. "I don't know what came over me. I was just so mad at you, I couldn't even think straight."

"You hurt me," I told him.

"I know." His arms wrapped around my upper body. "I'm sorry."

"I even made up with Marianne ... for you. And still you blanked me."

His head brushed my cheek as he nodded. "I've been such an idiot."

"At least my apology to you sounded like I meant it. You didn't mean it. You couldn't have sounded any less sincere on Monday."

"I mean it now, Jem. I'm—"

"How do I know this isn't just another order from Nate? How do I—"

"Are you even listening to me? Do I sound as though I don't mean it?"

I gave a small headshake. "No."

His sigh hit my skin, before he retook my shoulders and turned me to face him. His eyes searched mine, the green hue of them darkening with intensity. "Forgive me."

I studied him for a long moment and gave a slight nod of my head. "But if you ever—"

"I promise," he cut in as a smile pulled at his lips.

My own mouth curved in response. The second it did, his arms slid around me, and my feet left the floor. His embrace drew me close until only Josh's scent reached me, but a lift of my eyes showed Nathan by the apartment entrance.

I suspected he'd been there awhile, confirmed by his nod and smile. I returned the expression and buried my face into Josh, lids lowering as I inhaled the aroma I'd missed out on for days.

His arms tightened, and as his nose nuzzled deep enough to tickle, a small giggle escaped me, and I twisted my neck away, my eyes opening.

To Marianne.

I'd seen some cold glares in my time. None of them chilled like the one Marianne sent me right then, and I met it with the brightest beam I could muster while clinging even tighter to Josh.

Any decent person would have alerted him to her presence.

I had no intention of playing nice.

As my fingers brushed up to tangle in Josh's hair, as my nose pushed deeper into the crook below his ear, as my sighs announced my contentment, my gaze remained on Marianne.

For almost five minutes, she stood, her eyes icing over to Antarctic proportions, before Josh's head lifted from my throat. A flitter of surprise crossed his face on his inhale, and he turned. With a quiet chuckle, he greeted her as though his nuzzling nose hadn't caught up with the fact we had company.

"Marianne."

Her rapid switch of persona took visible effort. "Josh, hi. I brought you your tea." Her clawed fingers held out the silver thermos to him.

As Josh stepped forward to take it, his insistent arms dragged me forward for the ride

My lips twitched in pleasure at Marianne's furious expression. *Round five to me, witch.*

10

As soon as the men left for work on Thursday morning, leaving me alone for the first time all week, I pulled out my mobile and dialled Poppy's number. "I'll be a little late picking you up this morning," I told her as I climbed the stairs. 'I should be with you about eleven or so."

"That's okay, sweetie. Whenever works," she said.

I opened the door to Nathan's bedroom and headed straight across and pulled open the wardrobe doors. "And is there any chance you can bring your camera?" The hangers squeaked across the rail when I nudged them aside to reveal the safe. "I'll explain why when I get there."

"Sure," she said, her voice full of intrigue. "See you later."

I hung up, tucked my phone into my pocket, and dropped to my knees. With a deep breath, I keyed in the combination and pressed the enter button, the green light flashing my success. As I reached for the safe door, the amount of trust Nathan had laid on me popped into my head and paused my action. Shaking it off, I yanked open the safe, stuck my hand inside and folded my fingers around the box and folder lying on top.

Nathan may have said I couldn't *take* any of the folder-bound pictures, but he hadn't said I couldn't look.

I ignored the safe's other contents and carried the photographs across the room. Nathan's mattress lacked the firmness of ours as I climbed onto it and bounced beneath my crawling knees. Once settled, my eager fingers revealed the concealed.

The folder held only a small collection of photographs, maybe twenty, if that. I took out the first one and found myself face-to-face, for the first time, with the woman to whom I owed a great deal of gratitude—the woman who played a huge role in Sean's existence.

Shuffling back nearer the window, I lifted the picture into the light.

I knew Sean's and Ethan's eyes had to be from elsewhere as they didn't match Nathan's, but to see them peering out from the face of a woman I'd never met jolted me. For sure, the two brothers replicated their dad in looks, but faced with their mother, the reason Sean's features housed softer lines than the other Holloway men showed.

Beth's light brown hair, cut in a chin-length bob, suited her strong face. Her healthy complexion and deep eyes painted her as an attractive woman, in a handsome kind of way. If the picture gave any true indication as to the woman within, her stare matched her sons' for intensity.

I returned the image to the folder, took out a second. She didn't stand alone in it—both she and a young Nathan grinned at the aimed lens. His arms wrapped around her from behind showed her height to be a couple of inches taller than my five-seven.

I switched for the next picture, one with the two of them dressed for their wedding, and it stirred something inside me to see the way Nathan looked at her. I'd seen that exact expression in Sean's face whenever his sights set on me. The image radiated Nathan's adoration for his wife, making it easier to understand his drastic decision to send her away when he thought it the only way to keep her safe. I realised, for the first time, how terrified he must have been to go to such lengths.

After almost ten minutes of perusing Nathan's private shrine, I discovered two images of them sitting with a baby in Beth's lap. I paused before lifting up the next picture. It showed an unmistakable, tiny Ethan beside them, looking down at another baby as though wondering how the being had joined the family.

"Sean," I whispered, a small laugh bursting out.

With the proud parent pictures aside, I took the final three from the folder. As soon as I saw them, I recognised them as being far newer than the others. Nathan, in the one, looked no different than he had that morning, and I knew right away, it had been taken since Beth's departure. Had Nathan even bothered to show the latest editions to his sons?

Sighing at the sadness of the whole situation, I turned my attention to the box. With a lot more pictures to get through, I pondered less over each until I reached more childhood ones: Ethan alone, Sean alone, the two of them together and with their mother, the entire family—the boy's body changes at puberty easy to spot.

Humming and harring for too long, I narrowed my choices to twenty-five and, once I'd returned them to the safe in their own pile atop the others, I hit the road.

"This is a brilliant idea, Jem." Poppy slid her camera's memory card into the photo machine. "Sean will love this," she continued, as images began to appear on the small screen in front of us. "Didn't I say you'd figure out what to get him?"

Smiling, I studied my second batch of pictures of the day—ones taken at Ben's birthday party. We took a few minutes to flick through. Poppy had taken more of Sean and me together than I remembered.

"I'll get all of those." I nodded. "And one of you lot, and one of him with Ben, one with Lily."

We scanned through to find the ones I requested. When we came across the ones with Sean and Poppy, I burst out laughing. "Oh, yes. I have got to get him one of those."

"If he sees these, Jem, he may realise he's with the wrong woman and elope with me."

"Don't be ridiculous, Poppy. You'd never leave Jase."

"And Sean would never leave you."

I sighed. "Yeah, I know."

"My dream is shattering before my eyes," she said with flair.

I gave a quiet snort. "Now, which one shall I get framed?"

Poppy flipped through the images and tapped the screen. "Definitely that one. The two of you are looking so adoringly at each other."

I peered down at the picture, its likeness, minus wedding garb, to the one I'd seen of Nathan and Beth screaming out at me. "I agree."

Within minutes, I had the photographs in my hand. Our first Christmas together, my first present to him.

Rather than feeling daunted by the ever-looming date, an overwhelming sense of anticipation and excitement washed through me.

For the first time since Poppy had reminded me, I couldn't wait.

11

Trying to keep Josh from the evil clutches of Marianne, while on her home turf, concerned the crap out of me. Somehow, she'd managed to visit the rest of the week, clone in tow, and catch Josh whenever I'd nipped out. Reasons such as crystal balls had sprung to mind for her master evasion techniques, and the creepiness of it all brought with it an air of trepidation, when Nathan pulled up outside the address Marianne had given.

Connor's truck parked in front of us, as Nathan turned off the engine and peered at me over his shoulder. "Now, remember, Jem. Keep your cool. If they bait you, do not bite. You do not want to undo what you've repaired."

"I know." Vibrations in my pocket drew my attention down before the loud ring of my mobile pealed through the cab. I wriggled my fingers in to retrieve it, glanced down at the display before answering. "Hey, Jess."

"How are things going?"

"Not bad ... at the moment."

Josh appeared outside my window, one hand tapping the glass as the other beckoned at me to get out.

"One second, Jess—too many ears." I lowered the phone, waving it at Josh. "It's my sister." He nodded and grinned at me, and I tilted my head toward Sean, murmured only to him, "Carry on in. I'll see what Jess has to say and follow."

He turned to Nathan. "Dad, let's go. Jem can come in when she's finished her call."

"Don't be long," Nathan ordered over his shoulder.

The three doors opened, and the men climbed out.

As soon as they'd gone, I returned the phone to my ear. "I'm back." My gaze followed them down the path to a terraced, brick house.

"So, how are things really going?" Jess's voice brought me back.

"Not bad. Josh still adores me."

She gave a small laugh. "Well, all's right with the world, then."

"Especially as we made a bit of progress on the identity front," I said, ignoring her sarcasm. "How about you?"

"Nothing concrete yet. Just a few rumours, which have been shared by mentioning the sisters' names. What have you found out?"

The door swung open, and Marianne appeared in the frame.

"Well, as I'm now sitting outside an address with Marianne inside ..."

She took a step back, and Josh and Dan trailed inside, followed by the entire pack. A gulp lodged in my throat at their disappearance into the witches' abode.

"Don't you think that's a bit risky?" Jess asked. "You don't know—"

"We're all here," I cut in. "Marianne invited us to dinner. She said it's to make up for disturbing our meal at Connor's last week."

"Bullshit!"

"Yep. She wasn't too happy when Nate insisted I be invited, too. Somehow, I don't believe I was part of her plans."

"Ha!" Jess barked. "So, when are you all going in?"

"I've sent the others in without me so I can talk to you." My eyes narrowed at the front door of the house swinging open again. "Hang on. Somebody's come to the door." I took in the appearance of a girl with ash blonde curls tied back into a wild ponytail. "And it's somebody I don't recognise."

"What's going on?"

The blonde girl lifted her hand and wiggled her fingers—at me.

My eyebrow lifted. "She's waving at me."

"Friendly wave, unfriendly wave ... piss-take wave?"

"Well ..." I waved back in a half-hearted manner. "She's smiling."

"Wave back," Jess said. "Play along."

"I did."

The girl stooped low to the floor.

I frowned. "What the hell's she doing now?"

Her hand shook from side to side as though sowing something across the doorstep.

"What *is* she doing?" Jess asked.

"Chucking something on the ground by the looks of things."

The ponytailed girl straightened and went back into the property, the front door left wide in her wake.

"She still there?" asked Jess.

"No, she's gone back in."

"So, go take a look."

Go take a look, I mouthed as I pushed open the truck door.

Apprehension dominated the speed I walked up the path, and I hesitated halfway down. "Maybe I should just go in. If they're up to something, I don't really want my boys in there alone."

"Call me if you need anything."

"Okay." I hung up.

A few more steps took me to the front door. My chest heaved with the deep breath I drew, and lifting a foot, I went to step through—and halted.

The open doorway showed a long, narrow hallway that gave off a tunnel-like effect. I peered down its length. Although I heard the pack and female voices, I saw no one.

A tilt of my head helped locate them toward the rear of the property, and I lifted my foot again, went to step through the door.

I halted again.

Eyes narrowed, I stared into the empty space and tried again.

Same result. Although the impact didn't bring pain, I appeared to be hitting an invisible wall.

I shuffled back down the path a few steps and redialled Jess's number.

"Problem?" she answered.

"I can't get in."

"Have you tried knocking?"

"You're funny. You know that?" I said. "There's nothing to knock. The bloody door's wide open. I just can't get through."

After a few seconds of quiet, she said, "The girl you saw was, what? Sprinkling something?"

"That's what it looked like."

"Take a look. See if it's visible."

I moved back to the step and dropped into a crouch, frowning when I spotted a fine powder spread in a line across the threshold. I straightened and stepped back again. "It's a powder."

"What colour?"

"Red. Brown." I shrugged at the empty garden. "Brownie-red."

"Well, shit!"

My pulse increased. "Why do you say *well, shit,* every time I mention something these witches have done?"

"Because the sly bitches have taken advantage of you not entering with the men."

"In English, please, Jess."

"The dust you can see across the doorway is red brick dust. If you place it across your thresholds and windows—any possible entrance—it prevents anybody entering who wishes to cause you harm."

"But—"

"Do you wish to cause this Marianne harm, Jem?"

"Well ... not today, particularly," I murmured.

Jess laughed. "How much have you fantasised about hurting this girl?"

I scratched at my head. "I may have closed my eyes once, or twice, and imagined how it would feel to rip out her throat."

Her second laugh prickled my eardrum. "And therein lies your problem. You can't cross the threshold—not while you want to do her harm."

My fists clenched, helping my cause not one bit. "Damn."

"Jem?" Nathan's deep voice bounced from one wall to the other in its passage along the narrow hallway.

"I'll be there in a sec," I called back, before hissing into the phone, "What do I do? I'm going to look a right idiot if I have to admit I can't get through the door."

"There isn't—"

"Can't I just brush it off, or something?" I squatted back down by the step.

"No."

I reached out with my fingers anyway. The invisible barrier prevented me even reaching the dust. "Shit!"

"Are you coming in, Jem, or what?" called Josh.

"Coming. Won't be a minute," I sang back. "Where's bloody Sean when I need him?" I muttered.

A shadow coated the carpet from the end of the hall, and my head snapped up as I stood.

Marianne.

"Got to go," I whispered into the phone. "Witch alert." I hung up, slid it into my pocket, and watched Marianne's slow saunter toward me.

A smirk played on her lips as she reached the door. "Aren't you coming in, Jem?"

I folded my arms across my chest and stared at her.

"Everybody's waiting." Smiling wider, she took a step back, waving an arm toward the room that housed the others.

I moved forward … and hit the barrier for the fourth time. It took a whole lot of effort to suppress the growl bubbling in my throat.

At footsteps hitting the path behind me, I turned to see a small girl with brown hair bounding toward the house.

Her red lips and unusual green eyes greeted me as she skipped past. "Sorry I'm late."

"It's okay, Zoë." Marianne flattened to the wall as though to allow her through. "We haven't started yet."

My feet followed the young woman. Without incident, the newcomer entered the house. On her tail, I hopped for the doorway.

No entry.

Marianne smothered her mouth with her fingers, her eyes sparkling with malice. As her hand lowered, her smile twisted into a downturn, her entire body leaned toward me, and the humour vanished from her bright blue irises. "You think you can outwit me, Jem?"

My head lowered, but my gaze remained on her. "I don't think. I know I can."

Her body moved closer. "Well, you can't get in here now, can you?"

The raised step brought her to my level. A quick dip of my eyes revealed her almost venture to my side of the doorway—almost, but not quite.

I'd have to fix that.

My lip curled, as my gaze rose to meet hers. "You may think you can keep me away, but you can't," I growled. "Your petty games are nothing but a bore to me."

She took a tiny step forward.

I couched my smile. "You think Josh will ever be more interested in you than he is in me?"

She took another step, a sickly scent wafting from her body. "Josh isn't interested in you. Why would he want an old woman, when he can have someone young and beautiful like me?"

"Well, don't you just have tickets on yourself?" Another brief glance checked the position of her feet, before I locked eyes with her again. One more step and I'd have her.

"Jem?" Nathan boomed.

I shuffled a foot back.

"Run along, Jem." Marianne's face became a picture of ugliness as it twisted further.

Attention flitting between her eyes and her feet, my body moved back another couple of inches.

"Jem!" Nathan shouted.

Marianne matched my backward movement with a forward one of her own. "Run along, *dog* ..."

My head whipped up.

"Your *master's* calling."

My hand shot out. I grabbed her throat. A thrust of my arm to the right took her feet from the floor and sent her to smack into the bricks at the side of the door. She barely had time to grunt, before I pressed my hand hard onto her larynx, and pushed my face close with a quiet snarl. "You think I don't know what you are, witch?"

Her eyes widened, yet her lips produced nothing but gasped breaths.

"You think you can take away my family? I've got news for you, *Marianne*. You have to go through me first. You think I don't know what you've been doing to Josh? You must have realised I knew the second I flipped about the bracelet, because nobody's *that* stupid," I said. "But I suppose you must be stupid, because only a moron would keep coming back."

Her mouth opened and closed. Her eyes bulged a little, too.

"Maybe if I just snap your neck, be done with it ... then your hold on Josh will be broken."

She gave a frantic headshake, hindered by my grasp.

"Jem!"

At the call of my mate, my head tilted. When Marianne's feet flailed beneath her, I loosened my grip a little.

"It won't work," she rasped. "Killing me ... won't work."

"No?" I smiled. "Doesn't mean I wouldn't enjoy doing it."

"Jem!" Curiosity and impatience tinged Sean's tone.

"Coming, baby," I called.

"You ..." Marianne gasped

I lifted my fingers, raised an eyebrow.

"You're not even tame," she said. "You think you can huff and puff—"

A hand tightening cut her off. Her gasp squeaked out. I squeezed that one quiet, too—though her words clanged around inside my head until they had my attention.

I peered down at the doorstep. *Huff and puff?* "Bloody brilliant."

Confusion filled Marianne's wide eyes.

"That is a brilliant idea, Marianne, even for you."

Her frown almost folded her head in half with its deepness.

I laughed, snatched away my hand. She landed in a heap on the ground.

Back at the threshold, I dropped to my knees, lowered my head and blew—as hard as I could.

The strength of my breaths hit the dust, lifting it into the air and sending it floating away, to land in scattered formation. With Marianne on my side of the dust, I guessed it would no longer hold effect. I couldn't have been more right.

"Genius." I sent one final grin to the frightened witch, crossed the doorstep, and entered the house.

12

A trio of shocked female faces greeted me, as I stepped into the dining room. An encompassing smell as sickly as a honey and fruit cocktail swamped the air, while seven male werewolves sat around a huge dining table, their twitching noses following every tiny movement of the women at the far end of the room.

Controlling the twitch of my eyebrows, I headed straight for Amber and held out my hand. "Good to see you again." I smiled. Maybe I should've taken up acting classes with my improved skills.

With a grin of her own, she accepted my handshake. "Hello, Jem."

I held on for a moment too long as I inhaled. Amber definitely expelled the sickly-sweet smell. I turned my attention to a somewhat plump young woman behind Amber's shoulder.

Wide, hazel eyes shone beneath frizzy hair that, no longer tied back, fell across her face. *Brick dust girl.*

I offered my hand to her. "Hi, I'm Jem."

"Nice to meet you."

I stared hard at her flickering eyes, gripped tight onto her clammy hand, and held a smile in place at her hastened breaths.

"Oh ... sorry," she eventually said. "My name's Stephanie."

"And I'm Heather," a tall girl cut in over her shoulder, her tone more confident than Stephanie's. She wore her dark brown hair and fashion glasses with ease, too. "I've been dying to meet you. Marianne's told us so much already."

"I just bet she has." An almost silent chuckle from Sean accompanied my quiet utterance, as I stepped around the plump girl toward Heather. A second waft of the alluring perfume drifted up as I accepted the outstretched hand of the confident girl. "Jem," I said as we shook.

Although Sean's eyes found mine when I turned back to the pack, his nose wrinkled as wildly as the other men's. Whatever the witches had dabbed on themselves had the boys' attention for sure.

Not good.

"What took you so long?" Sean whispered.

Nathan's eye flicker suggested he caught the minute movement of Sean's lips, yet he didn't turn. He seemed only to have eyes for the sweet-smelling women.

"Just a minor setback," I murmured, frowning at Nathan's lack of interest. I understood the witches smelled good—they made me want to sniff at them some more, too, maybe take a little bite just to see how they tasted—but they seemed to have a much stronger effect on the men around the table.

Sean's eyebrow gave a slight lift. At my whispered, "Later," his attention zapped back to the three women carrying in plates.

I turned to Amber. "Would you mind if I used your bathroom before dinner?"

"Sure," she said. "It's directly ahead at the top of the stairs."

"Thanks." If I didn't limit my smiles, I'd have jaw ache before long.

My fingers wove into Sean's hair as I passed, mostly to remind him of my existence, and I left the room. A right turn brought me to the foot of the stairs, located between the dining room and the front room, which I presumed to be some kind of lounge. I peered toward the front door. Closed. Where had Marianne gone? I checked the other way along the hall. No sign of her. With a deep breath, I mounted the stairs.

The bathroom door stood ajar right where Amber said I'd find it. I went in, locked the door, and rang Jess.

"More problems?" she asked.

"Not really. I'm inside now. I pissed Marianne off so she stepped across the dust ... then I hurt her—a little—and blew the dust out of my way."

Jess laughed. "Sounds like you're having fun."

"Oh, yeah, a great time," I muttered. "And the party hasn't even started yet."

"Okay, so you're in. What now?"

"Well, there are more here than just Marianne and Amber—the flipping house is full of witches. And they're all wearing some type of perfume. I mean, the exact same perfume. It's weird. But even weirder than that? The men are all bloody gazing at the witches with dreamy eyes."

"Does the perfume have any distinguishable scents?" she asked.

"No specific ones I can detect any stronger than others. It just smells sweet. Why?"

"Sweet?"

"Yes ... sickly. Like sweet enough you'd consider eating them for dessert, sweet. Why?" I lowered the toilet lid and sat. "You think the perfume is doing something?"

"It sounds to me like they're pulling out all the stops," Jess said. "If I'm right ..."

"Which you usually are," I said.

"Which I usually am," she parroted. "It sounds like a bidding potion that a witch would dab herself with, to entice a man to do her bidding in a seduction sense of—"

"They're trying to seduce them?" My hand tightened on the phone.

"Yes."

"No wonder I wasn't part of their plans." I groaned, rubbing at my face. "What should I do?"

"Where are you now?" she asked.

"In the bathroom."

"And everyone else is ...?"

"Downstairs."

"So, you're upstairs?" she asked. "Alone?"

"Yes," I said with an eye roll.

"So ... go mooch. See if you can find the potion. You can bet your life it's there somewhere, like a personal supply."

"Okay." I slid back the bathroom lock, hesitating as I grasped the door handle. "But, why?"

"Because," she said, her tone exasperated, "if you can't beat them, join them."

"Ah." Pausing, I pulled open the bathroom cabinet for a quick scour. Toothbrushes and paste, shower gel, shampoo, facial wash, tweezers—nothing resembling any kind of perfume. "Not in the bathroom."

"Try the bedrooms. And remember, you need to be quiet about it."

"No, really ... you *think*?" I whispered, as I eased down the bathroom door handle.

Her giggled response tugged my lips into a grin, as I crept across the landing to the first bedroom door. I nudged it open and stepped into the room. A moment of visual scouring preceded a few inhalations. "It's not here."

"You didn't even look."

"I can't smell it. If they used it in this room, I'd pick up a hint of it, but there isn't one."

"Oh." She fell silent for a moment. "Cool way to search. You know, I'm missing a pair of really stinky socks I've been searching for, for weeks—"

"Ha, bloody ha, Jess." I tiptoed back across the landing, pushed open another door. As soon as I stepped inside, it hit me. "Bingo."

"You got it?"

"I've got the room." I moved forward. "Now, I just need to find the stuff."

"So, get looking, then."

"What do you think I'm doing?" I crossed to a dressing table beneath the window.

The entire bedroom looked like a throwback from the fifties. Lace doilies adorned every one of the aged wooden surfaces. On top of the dresser's centre doily sat a bottle.

I picked it up, and my lips curved as I pulled out the stopper. "Well, that was easy. They didn't even bother to hide it."

A tilt of the bottle sent splatters onto my T-shirt. I poured some onto the stopper, flicked some onto my stomach beneath my clothing, a few flecks onto my jeans. I shoved the stopper back in to catch some more and used it to dab scent beneath my ears and on my wrists.

"Is it the right thing?" asked Jess. "Have you found it?"

An upward flick sent a few specks to land between my modest breasts. "Yep." Another, higher, sprayed my hair.

"Okay, so dab some on ..."

"Done ..."

"In moderation," Jess finished. "It's powerful stuff, Jem. Only use a tiny amount, do you understand?"

I glanced down at the patches of oily stains across my clothing, at my wrists where I'd put more than one helping. *Hmmm.*

"Are you listening to me, Jem?"

"Sure. Don't go overboard."

"That's right." Her heaved sigh travelled the line. "And flush the rest down the loo. That way, they can't apply more to themselves to strengthen their own aroma."

Back in the bathroom, I disposed of the bottle's contents, and flushing the toilet solidified my reason for venturing upstairs.

"Done?" Jess asked.

"Yep." I frowned when I caught sight of my spotted T-shirt and jeans, but with a roll of my shoulders, I shook off my concern. "Time to hang up, Jess. I'm going into battle."

"Good luck," she said with a laugh.

***

126

Every crevice, nook and corner of the house held no scent other than the one I carried upon my body. Neither the dinner, nor any of the people occupying the house, reached my senses. And I would have been able to pick them up—if not for the potion excessively splashed about myself.

One step into the dining room told me my efforts had been worth it, though. The noses of the pack all turned to me like a Mexican wave at a rock gig. Within a second, their nostrils switched from twitching to full-out flaring, as though overcome by the need to get more.

Grinning, I lifted my sights to the five witches. From them, my attention circled the seating arrangement—Josh, at my end of the table, Sean to his left, Nathan, Ethan, Heather, and Stephanie who leaned back as though in a bid to remain concealed. At the head of the table sat Marianne, glowering down the generous length of wood in my direction; to her left, Zoë, Amber, Connor and Kyle, ending with Daniel to Josh's right.

Twelve seats. Twelve bodies.

My eyebrow lifted.

"Oh." Marianne smirked, waving a hand toward her sister. "We were supposed to bring in that extra chair for Jem."

I held her gaze. "Don't trouble yourself. It's not a problem." My lips twitched as a solution came to me. "In fact ..." I headed for Josh, lifted my leg up and over his lap. "I'm sure I'll be quite comfortable here."

Allowing Marianne the best grin I had in my acting portfolio, I lowered my bum.

As soon as it hit Josh's lap, his arms took hold and tugged my body backward. His nose burrowed into my neck, his long, slow inhalation a wind buffer against my ear.

Potent?

The vibrations of Josh's body hit my back in waves.

Understatement, much!

Marianne lowered her head and glared.

Ignoring her, I took in the delicious-looking spread of food across the table, before peering round at the men. "This looks amazing, doesn't it?" I picked up my fork. "I'm absolutely ravenous."

Marianne's bright eyes turned frosty as she smiled. "Then, please eat, Jem."

Her expression told me she'd figured out what I'd done. It also made me cautious of the food she'd invited me to sample. If the spread contained anything intended for the men, it would be in my system the second I ate it.

In for a penny, and all that, I reached out and helped myself to a couple of gammon slices. Tongs had been left for the roast potatoes. I used them to snare one, pausing when my hand came near and I saw the green specks coating its surface. "What's on the spuds?"

"Basil," said Heather with a smile.

Thanks to my aroma, I had to bring it right beneath my nose to confirm her answer. Satisfied, I dropped it onto my plate.

As though taking my cue, the others did the same—everyone except Josh, who'd yet to remove his nostrils from my flesh.

I reached down and parted his knees enough for me to fit between. "If we sit like this, Josh, you should still be able to eat around me." I slid forward an inch.

His arms tightened. "No." He drew me back to my initial position.

"*Josh!*"

I couldn't mistake the warning Sean's tone held as he leaned out of his seat toward the two of us, his eyes glinting toward Josh. Sean had never warned Josh before about the affectionate behaviour he showed me, but he shuffled forward, bringing his seat with him. His dark eyes met mine. "Sit with me, Jem."

"It's okay, baby. Let me sit with Josh through dinner, and you can have me for dessert."

Like he misconstrued my words, his eyes darkened until he looked as though he could quite happily eat me there and then.

As Josh's hand trailed a slow circle across my stomach, a gulp threatened to bung my throat.

Sean's eyes followed the movement. His jaw tightened when Josh's other hand joined in the fun.

At chairs shuffling across carpet, my head jerked up. One by one, the other men inched closer to my position. Hungered eyes locked onto me, making no attempt to disguise the extended flare of their nostrils.

I narrowed mine at them. Did they even realise what they were doing? As I studied their altered behaviour and their rapid loss of control, Jess's words bounced around in my head. *It's powerful stuff, Jem.*

Damn right about that.

Josh's arms tugged me back further, as though a sliver of air provided too much of a gap.

Sean glared at him. The first tremor visited his lips.

I couldn't see Josh, couldn't read his expression, but the unmistakable swelling that greeted my backside told me what had Sean so worked up, and my pulse fluttered like a bag in the wind.

"Sit with me," Sean murmured again.

I stood, but Josh hauled me back down. It took effort to unpeel his vice-gripping fingers and unfold his arms. I managed to get as far as standing again, before Josh shot to his feet behind me.

Sean flew from his chair to my side. His arm enfolded my waist, steering me toward him. He pressed his cheek against mine, aiming his sights at Josh, and a low growl vibrated up from his throat—one that would have been inaudible to the witches.

Josh gave a low growl in response before sinking back into his seat.

The witches remained silent, eyes wide or narrowed, brows creased—hands clenched, in Marianne's case. Their furious expressions reflected they'd never intended the pack to fight over *me*.

Sean lifted me until my legs had cleared Josh's lap and dragged me to his chair. When he sat back down, his arms took me with him. I'd barely gotten comfortable, before his nose nudged into my hair. "What have you done, Jem?"

"Later," I murmured. "Let's get this over with and get out of here.

13

Dinner could not have been more uncomfortable. Josh dropped half of his food en route to his plate. Sean smeared gravy into my hair when he failed to fully close his mouth, while burrowing and chewing at the same time. The rest of the pack clattered forks to their plates in between mouthfuls and sat gazing my way like halfwits during each round of mastication.

Maybe the mingling of my wolf scent with the potion had created the adverse effect. I didn't know. It didn't matter. I'd waded out of my depth, and it took all of five minutes to wish I'd listened to Jess before indulging in a frivolous dousing of rape juice.

When the meal came to its conclusion, and the witches refused our offer of assistance with the tidying up, I couldn't have been more relieved.

I tilted my face to Sean's at my cheek. "Can we leave now?" I whispered.

He leaned in close to his dad, mumbled the request to him.

Nathan nodded and pushed to his feet. "Thank you for the meal, ladies, but we really should be on our way."

Ethan, Connor, Kyle and Daniel stood also—like robots trained to act on command.

I straightened my knees until on my feet, Sean's body following like a conjoined twin connected to me at both hips.

Josh reached my side so fast, his chair toppled on one leg before flopping back down with a thud.

Alarm flitted across Marianne's face, but she controlled it and stood also. "Do you and Danny have to go, too, Josh?"

My gaze went from her to Josh.

Josh turned to Marianne as if she'd handed him the most difficult decision in the world. His eyes shot sideways toward me, back to Marianne, to me again, back and forth.

I took a step closer. "Aren't you going to come home and play, Josh?"

His head swivelled toward me, his face lowering until his stare met mine. The feral glint of his eyes revealed the predator I'd never witnessed outside of Josh's wolf form, and his expression sent a shiver through me. "We won't be staying today, Marianne."

My lips twitched in triumph.

"Are you sure, Josh?" Marianne asked, her tone sultry.

Without turning from Josh, I caught the subtle nearing of Marianne as she rounded the table. "Play with me?" I whispered.

Josh gazed down at me, eyes glazed over. "I need to go home." Huskiness dominated his tone.

"Dad," Sean whispered, "we need to move."

At times, enhanced hearing came in handy.

"Thanks again, ladies." Nathan headed for the door.

Ethan's, "Thanks," and, "Bye," came next. As he passed behind me, his deep inhalation reached my ears.

The other four witches climbed to their feet, as one male after another turned to leave, uttering appreciation and farewells on exit.

Josh took a step closer, seriously infringing on my personal space.

Sean's erection pressed into my back.

"Let's go," I said.

Sean remained close enough to trip me on my walk for the door. Heat at my left told me Josh mirrored Sean's proximity on my other side, and Sean's hand grasping my hip and pulling me into him suggested Josh stuck nearer than he liked.

As I'd seen the glint in Josh's eyes, met with the physical reaction of his lust, Sean's territorial protectiveness seemed reasonable.

Fresh air encompassed me when I stepped from the house. My strides carried me along the path to the gate. At the lack of heat to my left shoulder, I spun.

Back at the doorstep, Marianne's fingers clutched at Josh's arm as she stretched up to offer her cheek.

Josh's lips met her skin, his nostrils working overtime, telling me he detected Marianne's personal helping of the good stuff.

"It's a shame you won't stay," Marianne said.

I shot down the path, urged up onto my toes.

"Josh, you promised you'd play with me."

At the sound of my voice, his head tilted, and his unsure expression fixed on me. A slide of my fingers between his mouth and the witch's cheek helped to cure his uncertainty, and with a good dose of my scent-soaked wrist to lure him nearer, his eyes closed. When they reopened, he barely looked human.

"Come on." I reached for his hand, fingers still at his cheek, drawing him with little effort along the path as I made my way backward.

Sean greeted us at the gate, his hands taking my hips. "Your ride's over there, Josh."

"I'm riding with you." Josh's tone held no room for discussion.

"Let's just get out of here," I said.

Sean led us back farther until the truck door opened with a metallic sigh at my rear.

I stepped to the side, nudged Josh toward it and pushed at his rear until he'd climbed in and sat. Sean took my arm, but I shook my head. "You next."

The others had already climbed in. From the truck in front, the Larsen men craned their necks in my direction. Ethan's face pressed against the glass to my left.

Sean hopped up into the vehicle, shoving at Josh's legs with a growl. "Move up."

I turned back to face Marianne with a smile. "Well, this has been fun ... hasn't it?" I took a step closer to the garden wall. "We'll have to do it again sometime."

She gave no verbal response. Only fury coated her otherwise attractive features, and I found myself hoping I'd left no part of me in her house as visions of voodoo dolls with pins stuck in their brains sprung to mind.

Even so, unable to help myself, I mouthed *Loser* at her before turning away and climbing into the truck.

The second we left the witches' house, Nathan wound down the truck windows, but no amount of fresh air could eliminate the smell.

Ethan faced forward in his seat, long, shallow breaths seeping past his lips. Nathan's hands gripped the steering wheel so hard his knuckles turned white. Sean sat with his free hand braced against the seat in front, his jeans in danger of ripping at the seams of his crotch. To his right, Josh made no effort whatsoever to hide his ever-increasing arousal, and he constantly peered over Sean's well-placed arm until he practically hung off him like a chimp from a branch.

Nostrils twitched and flared, and I thought the insufferable journey would never end, but the gates came into sight, and I unclipped my seat belt, hand on the door catch as Nathan swung onto the driveway. Before the pickup had even come to a standstill, I swung out, hopped down, and strode for the house.

Sean and Josh reached my back before I'd barely twisted the lock open on the front door. I shoved into the hallway, tossed the key to the table, and leaped straight for the stairs.

Sean's feet hit each step as mine left it.

"Jem!" Nathan shouted.

I'd only made it halfway, but I turned to look down at him.

From amidst the rest of the pack, all of them with their gazes lifted to me, Nathan stood with his hands on his hips. "I need to speak to you."

I indicated with my head. "Come up."

"No. Not the bedroom." He stared hard, his jaw clenched. "In the living room."

A small bubble of panic formed at the six huge men I just tried to escape blocking my path. With a jerked nod, I descended—past Sean whose eyes followed me, past Ethan whose hands covered his nose as he turned away.

Two down, four to go.

Jaw tight, I lifted my arms to encompass my head and barged past the rest of them without stopping, ignoring the nose that attached itself to my shoulder.

I made it into the living room and walked to the farthest corner.

"Stay out!" Nathan boomed.

The door slammed shut. Nathan leaned against it for a few seconds, stiff arms braced. His loud inhalations came deep, shallow, deep again as though he attempted to regulate the amount of the scent he absorbed but failed.

I'd never seen Nathan so un-composed.

He pushed up and moved to the other side of the room. When he turned, sweat coated his brow. The muscles of his tensed biceps strained against the sleeves of his shirt. With glistening eyes, he stared at me. "What did you do, Jem?" His voice, scarcely more than a growl, sounded even less controlled than he looked.

The second I opened my mouth, I knew I'd be in big trouble, so I remained mute.

Nathan growled as he rubbed his hands over his hair, across his face. He moved to the sofa and started to sit but straightened. He stared down at his crotch, back up to me. "What did you *do*, Jem?" He crossed to the window, chest rumbling as he fumbled with the catch. When he eventually got it open, he shoved the glass wide and stuck out his head.

"Shall I start at the beginning?"

"I don't really care where you start, as long as I get answers."

"Okay, well ... when I was outside, talking to Jess on the phone, one of witches placed red brick dust across the door ..."

He twisted and grimaced over his shoulder. "What the hell for?"

"Because, according to Jess, if you sprinkle it at entrances, anybody who wishes to hurt you is restricted and can't enter."

Nathan's expression remained unchanged.

"Jess was right. I couldn't get in."

"But ... the door was wide open."

I stared hard at him. "Yes, I know."

He turned toward the outside, falling quiet for a moment. With a rub at his hair, he peered back. "So, they didn't want you in there with us?"

My head gave a single shake.

"But you got in."

I shrugged. "I outwitted Marianne, managed to shift the dust so I could enter."

He nodded. "Okay." Another gulp of air from outside, and he said, "So, why didn't they want you in there?"

"We both know they never wanted me there from the start. I think they had plans for you."

He turned back and fully faced the room. As soon as he did, his nose scrunched up, eyes darkening. He groaned, his clenched hand pointed at me. "You did something, didn't you? You did something to us?"

"I—"

"Why do I have an almost uncontrollable urge to have sex with my son's mate? Can you tell me that?"

"Well, I—"

"*Tell me*." The rise and fall of his chest deepened as did his voice.

I took a step back. "Maybe you should move back to the window."

"I don't want to." He let out a low snarl, tugging at his hair. "And I don't know why." As though at odds with what he wanted to do, he made his way back to the window in a two steps forward, one step back kind of fashion. At any other time, I'd have found it hilarious.

I waited until he'd reached his goal. "Listen, Nate. When I came into the dining room, it was clear the witches were up to something."

He leaned his head out farther and twisted to peer at me through the glass to his right.

"Did you even notice how you all stared at them with hungry eyes? I figured out it was how they smelled that had you all interested," I said. "So, when I went up to use the bathroom, I called Jess. She told me it was a kind of seduction potion used to make them irresistible. Her advice was for me to put some—"

"This is witch magic?" Nathan's brows bunched to meet in the middle as his eyes narrowed.

I nodded.

"This—the way we're all being toward you ... this is witch magic?"

Another nod.

"But the witches didn't have this effect on us."

"That's because I kind of put too much on." I rubbed the back of my neck. "A lot too much. I didn't think I'd get this strong a reaction."

"Didn't Jess tell you how much to use, for goodness sake?"

"Yes ... after I'd already painted myself in it."

"If you wash it off, will it go away?"

"I don't know. I guess so."

"Then, do it ... before we decide we can't contain ourselves any longer." When I didn't move fast enough, he snapped, "Shower, Jem! Now!"

***

A backward kick of my foot sent the bathroom door swinging, and I'd lifted the hem of my soiled T-shirt before it even slammed shut. Next, off came my jeans—underwear, too. I carried them all like something diseased, opened the bathroom window, and dropped them outside for later disposal.

At feet hitting the stairs, my head tilted.

The steps reached the landing.

I really hoped whoever had come up would head into one of the bedrooms.

One long stride became two. Three.

I spun.

According to Sean, there hadn't been a lock on the door in years. Four more strides, and I'd be too late.

A fourth step.

"Shit!"

Two left.

I dived for the door. As my hand grasped the inner handle, a downward tug from the other side dragged it farther.

As the door burst open, I stumbled back.

Sean barged his way in. An echoing *thunk* filled the space on the door's collision with the wall. One final step, and Sean's fingers folded around my wrist.

His arm snatched back, hauling me upright. I expected him to check me over, ensure he hadn't hurt me. Instead, his hands gripped my hips.

My body flew through the air, too fast for my mind to register, and my back smacked against the tiled wall.

A small grunt burst out, as Sean's body crushed mine. He ducked his head to my neck, attached his nose to where my increased pulse pumped the erotic scent to him in waves.

"What the hell did you do?" The nearness of my flesh to his mouth distorted his mumbled words.

"It's just a perfume. All I need to do is wash it off, and this will stop."

His eyes bordered on black as he lifted his face and emitted a low growl. "No." With his hips pinning me, he leaned his shoulders far enough back to tug off his T-shirt.

When he pressed back against my nakedness, my pulse soared. "What you're feeling right now isn't real." I took his face in my hands, lifting it to mine. "It's a *spell*, Sean."

His eyes closed. He swayed. His lids lifted as though in slow motion, and as a smile spread across his lips, my breath caught.

He could not have looked hornier. The steady drum of my heart missed a few beats. With a whispered, "*Jem,*" his mouth melded to mine.

I shouldn't have responded, knew I shouldn't, but couldn't help myself. Sean's lazy busses were excellent—his snogs awesome. Notch those up to his lust-induced, frantic, tongue-teasing kisses, and they rocketed way out into orbit. Not to mention his air of frustration with his mussed up hair, his glistening eyes, and I was his.

My lips parted. The dart of my tongue offered me a taste. I raised my legs and circled his hips, my pelvis pressing into his eagerness.

His chest pounded against my breasts. "A spell?"

I gave a frantic nod.

His lips linked back with mine.

A low groan of pleasure left me. I grasped onto his shoulders as my body arched into him, his sweat-coated flesh slick beneath my palms.

He pulled back. "What kind of spell?" His ragged voice matched the heave of his chest.

"A seduction spell," I said. "It makes men lust after you, but I put too much on. That's why I need to shower."

My back skidded along the wall as Sean shuffled us toward the corner cubicle.

His gaze stayed on me, remained locked even as he reached out a hand to grope for the tap. He managed two whole seconds before his face reburied into my collarbone.

No longer only taking a sniff, his teeth scraped across my flesh, inducing quiet gasps from my lips. As my fingers weaved into his hair, his oral visit evolved to small bites along the length of my shoulder. Each sent a surge of heat to my groin, and a tilt of my head offered him more.

The music of water on glass told me Sean had turned on the shower while I'd been too lost in the pleasure of his teeth to notice, and he deposited me inside the cubicle.

I stepped back until beneath the spray.

As I reached for the door, Sean urged past it and joined me, both of us naked, both breathless.

"This—" He pointed at no particular part, but rather at all of my body. "This is powerful."

"Yes," I said.

A step forward brought him closer. His hands pressed to the glass above my shoulders, his body pushing mine back until the cold surface greeted my rear, and his mouth revisited my shoulder.

As his teeth made bigger demands of my flesh, I closed my eyes.

Deep feral grunts filled my ears, and my arousal added to the swirling aromas.

At a sharp pain, I cried out, my eyes shot open, and the unmistakable metallic tint of my blood united with those already present.

Sean lifted his head, sought my eyes with his.

I caught the crimson coating his lips, before he slammed his lips against mine hard enough to bruise, and his fingers dug into my hips with enough force to mark.

As the release of his pheromones intermingled with the atmosphere, my own nostrils flared in greed to drink in his aroma of excitement.

With the urgent tugs of Sean's hands, my body bowed, and my throat expelled his name on a whisper.

His teeth caught hold of my lip, cut through the delicate tissue. Releasing a mewled cry, I clutched at his shoulders.

His face drew back. His wild eyes reconnected with my shoulder and the slow trickle that made its way down my arm.

Low rumbles resonated inside his chest as his face lowered. He licked over my bicep, one long fluid journey to the wound. My fingers tangled into his hair, and shudders ran through his body, matching my own.

From my shoulder, he skimmed across to my neck. His mouth suckled and nibbled on the tender spot below my ear. I tightened my hold, giving a long moan as my writhing body pushed into him.

The rumble in Sean's chest built into a growl, the vibrations throbbing through me. With a snarl that echoed in my ear, his teeth circled the flesh coating my pulse.

I stiffened, bracing for the bite.

With my neck in his jaws, he stood rigid. His chest heaved. The clench of his fingers dug into me like clamps, as guttural grunts escaped the corners of his mouth.

In an effort to remain still, I closed my eyes, tried to steady my chest. Sean and I stayed like that for seconds, until his hands, mouth, body released me.

When I opened my eyes, Sean stood beneath the wide spray. The powerful jets pummelled his head and flattened his hair across his brow. Rivulets of water cascaded down his shoulders. His flexed arms showed every muscle, as did his legs, shoulders.

As my eyes roamed every part of him—from his intense, dark stare, to his torso, over his powerful limbs, his *erection*—my stomach tightened and moisture escaped to my thighs.

I took a step forward, stretched out a hand.

He shook his head, flecks of water hitting me.

Every nerve ending tingled for his touch, and I reached again.

"Wash it off," he growled through gritted teeth.

I frowned. "Sean?"

"Please, wash it off." Each word arrived slow and measured. "I don't feel in control of myself."

"Baby—"

His eyes glistened. "I don't want to hurt you."

My mouth closed on further protest. "Pass me the soap."

"I can't." The muscles worked along his jawline. "If I move, I might ..."

"I have to come closer to reach the soap."

He closed his eyes. If at all possible, his muscles strained further as if he readied himself.

I took a step forward, manoeuvred around him until my fingers found the shower gel and bath rose. "If I'm going to get this off, we need to trade places."

I took his arm, steered him around me until the spray hit my shoulders and head. I kept my focus on him as I shampooed my hair, twice, scrubbed across every inch of flesh until my natural odour returned. The longer I washed, the less tension claimed his body.

When his eyes opened, moisture invaded them as they swept down to my shoulder. "I'm sorry."

"Sean, I—"

"I hurt you." Pain consumed his eyes as he rubbed a hand across his sodden hair. "I'm so sorry."

I shook my head, taking a step forward.

His arms came around me, and his body shuddered as his nose buried into my throat. "You smell like you again." His hands hooked beneath my rear. A lift of my body brought my gaze to meet his. "Don't ever do that again."

"No," I murmured.

As his face lowered, a tilt of my head allowed him in, and his tongue tended to the wound he'd inflicted.

My body trembled at his contact, and once his tongue had done its job, his lips took over, their sweet caress a sharp contrast to his earlier passion.

His feet shuffled until we met the tiled wall. His hands slid around to part my thighs and hook them around him.

Beneath me, his arousal beat out his willingness as he claimed my lips with his.

His actions held only gentleness, as though an attempt to eradicate his earlier lack of control. The feathering of his hands brought shivers forth, while mine found solace in the texture of his hair, in the movement of muscle beneath my palms.

"I love you, Jem."

"I know you do. Why else do you think I'm here?"

His deep chuckle hit my lips, and they curved in response.

Enveloped within the strong hold of his arms, he lifted my body and lowered me onto him. Filled by him, my gasp arrived on a sigh, and he made sweet love to me with a tenderness that produced gasps and low cries.

14

A split second of silence followed my explanation to Sean's dad and brother that night.

"You did *what*?" Ethan asked.

"I doused myself in a perfume I found in one of the bedrooms," I said for the second time. "In the hope of counteracting the effect they were having on you."

"Counteracting?" He snarled, pushing to his feet. "*Counteracting*? Do you have any idea how much I wanted to—"

"Yes," I cut in. "I picked up everyone's feelings loud and clear."

"Do you have any idea how much danger you put yourself in today?" he asked, and I flinched at his tone. "If any of us had less control, you would have been in serious trouble. As it was, Josh barely contained himself."

I remained quiet about Sean's lack of control.

"Watching Josh, with his hands all over you, when I ..." Ethan paused, his chest rising with each inhalation. "Josh was lucky I didn't tear him apart." His face lifted to the ceiling, his hands coming to rest on his hips. "And all because of some bloody perfume."

I watched his frustration in every move he made.

He turned back to me. "Why, Jem?" His palms lifted. "Why would you put yourself at risk like that?"

"Please, Ethan. Sit down, and I'll explain everything ... from the beginning."

He stared hard at me before lowering to the sofa. His elbows rested on his knees, mirroring Nathan's position, while I took a few minutes to explain about the brick dust.

"So, when I came in and saw you all had your bloody noses and wistful eyes pointed at them, I knew they'd tried to keep me out for a reason." I faced Nathan. "You foiled their plans by insisting they extend the invitation to me. I don't think they ever intended me to be there." My attention returned to Ethan. "I only used the perfume to get you all to focus on me. It probably would have been okay, if I hadn't overindulged. But that's beside the point now. It worked. That's all I wanted—for you lot to come home. Even Josh followed like a lost puppy ..." Frowning, I trailed off and, climbing to my feet, paced the carpet beneath the window. "Nate, if someone called you a dog, would it concern you at all?"

"It depends how it was said. Why?"

I halted, looked around at the three men. "Because Marianne called me a dog."

Nathan's eyebrow arched.

"But it was more than that, it was the *way* she said it."

"How?" Nathan asked.

My hands slid into my jeans pockets. "Nastily enough that I grabbed her by the throat and pinned her to the wall."

Sean chuckled. "You pinned her for insulting you?"

"It was more than an insult." At their blank expressions, I said, "Okay. Suppose I tell you the way she said it made me concerned she knows what we are?"

"Why would you think that?" Nathan asked, as all three of them sobered.

"Because she said it when you called me in, and she said, *run along, dog, your master's calling*. And then, she said something about me huffing and puffing." When the men's expressions reflected confusion over concern, I lifted my hands. "Fairy tales? Who's afraid of the big bad wolf?"

Nathan's eyes sharpened. "Do they realise who you are?"

"How can they? Our names aren't in the witch records, just the circumstances. If they've pegged me as more than Sean's girlfriend, they probably just think I'm a female werewolf—no more, no less."

"Did Jess find anything out about them, yet?"

"Nothing concrete. She's still looking."

"Do you think you could ask her to look faster?" asked Nathan. "Because we have at least five witches who live only thirty minutes away, and when they're not trying to bind or summon us, they want to seduce us for reasons I can't even fathom. Add in the very strong possibility that they know what we are—we need to find out about them ... and fast."

"I'll call her first thing."

Ethan stood from his seat. "I'm going to bed." He walked as far as the door before pausing. "I still can't believe what you did today, Jem. I have spent the entire afternoon disgusted with myself because of what I felt like ..." He shook his head and left the room.

After an hour of listening to Nathan and Sean ramble on about the witches—bouncing ideas back and forth, Nathan insisting we all should ensure Josh and Daniel were never left alone with Marianne and the clone—my mind still hadn't erased the distraught expression Ethan had sent me on his way out the door.

Waiting until Sean headed off to the kitchen to make drinks, I excused myself and went upstairs.

At Ethan's bedroom, I raised my hand to knock, but, instead, tugged down the handle and pushed open the door. No artificial lighting coated his personal space, and the closed curtains prevented any offering from the moon.

The mattress creaked beneath my weight as I sat on the end of his bed, where I studied his closed eyes and his dark outline, silhouetted against his white pillowcase, his arms tucked behind his head. "I know you're awake."

"Go away, Jem."

"Not until you hear me out." I tugged on his jeans hem, but it retracted as his knees drew up.

He rubbed at his face. "You have no idea what you did."

"I saw."

"So, you can see feelings now?"

When I didn't answer, Ethan pushed up the bed until sitting against his headboard and stared straight at me. "Shall I tell you how I felt? Help you understand?" He turned toward the window, lines tugging the skin beside his eyes. "I felt like ripping your clothes off and ... fucking *mauling* you, Jem. I don't believe I would have given a shit if it was what you wanted, or not." His voice remained deep, full of pain. "If not for my self-control, that singular part of my rationality screaming that my urges were wrong ...". He turned back to me. "You wouldn't have stood a chance. Do you understand what I'm saying to you?"

I swallowed hard. "Yes."

"And because of it, because of *you*," he continued, "I have felt nothing but contempt for myself. I believed it was me behaving that way. How could I feel like that toward my sister?" With a groan, he rubbed at his face like he could erase his emotions. "That's been going around and around inside my head all afternoon ..."

"I'm sorry."

His fisted hands pressed to his eyes. "I felt sick to my stomach."

I shuffled farther onto the bed, went to reach out, but thought better of it. "Please, give me a chance to explain." Waiting until he'd lowered his hands, I continued, "I know I shouldn't have poured that bloody stuff all over me ... *now*. But I only did it because I was afraid for my boys. My gut went cold with dread when Jess explained what she thought their intent was. I did what I had to do to get you all out of there. Please don't ask me to apologise for that, because I would do it again in a heartbeat. I'm sorry for the way it made you all feel—truly sorry—but if it wasn't me, it would have been them. I liked the choice of me better. I didn't like what I had to—"

"You looked to me like you were enjoying yourself, with Josh all snuggled into you," he said.

"Ethan, if you were me, and you'd just done what I did, would you have given those witches the slightest inkling that the behaviour of your fellow pack members was terrifying the shit out of you?"

He leaned forward, dropping his hands to his lap. "We ... we *frightened* you?"

"Yes," I admitted. "Even Sean almost lost it with me in the bathroom. So, if you think I don't understand how I affected you all today, you're mistaken."

"Are you okay?" he asked, his eyes glistening through the darkness.

"He realised what he was doing and stopped. I wouldn't have minded, except I was kind of enj—"

His hand pressed over my mouth. "Seriously, Jem—too much information."

I smiled, nudging his arm down. "So, will you accept that I'm sorry?"

"Yes," he said with a sigh, and I crawled across his covers.

"Thanks," I said, as his arms folded around me.

The spoon clinked against the cup in the corner of the cabin the next morning. I lifted my gaze toward where Connor made his tea, and caught the flash of dark hair beyond the open door.

My chair wheels gave a small squeal, as I pushed to my feet. "She's got some front, showing up here after yesterday."

"Who?" Connor peered back over his shoulder, taking a sip of his drink. "Marianne?"

I moved closer to the opening as Marianne's double trotted on her heels. "And her bloody clone."

"Who's chaperoning?" Connor came to stand at my shoulder. "You or me?"

A tilt of my head brought his face into view. "Do I get to hurt her if I go?"

"I've never seen you like this toward anyone before."

"Maybe because I've never disliked anyone the way I do Marianne. Did Nate tell you I think she knows what we are?"

"Yes, he did." His gaze narrowed as it flitted toward the two women nearing the apartments.

"You have any ideas on the why of it all, Connor?"

"No. But I'll be thinking harder on it now." He waved his mug forward an inch. "Go on. Check what they're up to. After yesterday, I doubt I'll be polite. I'm just not that good an actor."

My eyebrow lifted. "And I am?"

"Good enough for Josh and Danny. It doesn't matter about the girls. After yesterday, I reckon they know exactly the regard you hold them in, and I'm pretty sure the feeling's mutual."

"Maybe I can get Marianne on her own again, have another little chat."

Connor chuckled as he herded me to the door. "Go. They're already peering through the windows for my boys."

"Sure, okay." Pausing, I turned back. "I really am sorry, Connor, about yesterday."

"It's forgotten. Now go."

I jumped down the steps, my feet hit gravel, and I marched across to the witches, on the verge of letting themselves in. "Hey!"

They turned. Their expressions suggested they'd thought the absence of the Porsche meant no me.

"Well, well, well, you're a glutton for punishment, Marianne. Wasn't falling short of your goal yesterday enough for you?"

"I have no idea what you're talking about." She smiled—a sickly one that bordered on psychotic. "Besides, I'm not here to make pathetic small talk with you. Amber and I have come to visit Josh and Daniel."

I pointed toward the flasks they each held. "Brought them some more of your special tea, I see."

Marianne's smiled vanished. "None of your business."

"Hmm. If you say so."

"Is Josh here, or not?"

I held out my hand. "Why not just let me deliver the tea?"

"Because I know he won't get it."

"And he can't possibly survive,"—my hand snatched out for the flask—"without his daily dose of bidding potion, right?"

Marianne blinked, before she lifted her eyes and glared at me.

Concern filled Amber's expression as she tracked from her sister to me.

I smiled at them both, unscrewing the flask lid. "So, suppose the flask has an accident, loses its contents ..." My nose twitched, the second the steam escaped, and my brows tightened above my narrowing eyes. "This is a different tea."

Marianne's grin spread across her lips.

"Okay," I said, "what concoction are you trying to pollute him with now?" I looked at Amber. "Is this the same one you're hoping to get Danny to drink?"

Amber's mouth opened and closed, as her stare flitted from her sister to me again, and Marianne's dominant role stuck out like an emo at an Elkie Brooks concert.

"Whatever this game is you're playing—you know you can't win, don't you?" I said to Marianne.

Her lips curved. "I always win."

"Not this time," I said. "I won't let you."

At movement beyond the glass, my gaze lifted to see Daniel headed for us.

I reined in my groan and straightened. "Tell me what's in the tea, Marianne."

"No."

After a quick glance at the witch, my gaze fixed on Daniel and his wide smile. "I could make you tell me."

"Do it, then," she sneered.

I almost did, even took a step toward her. My right hand gripped the flask tight until the lid etched its shape into my left palm with the pressure I exerted. If not for the swinging door at their rears, I probably would have hurt them both—gladly.

"Hey." Daniel grinned as he crossed to Amber.

Amber's shoulders visibly sagged. "Hello, Daniel."

"Been here long?"

Amber sent a fleeting glance my way, and my glower dared her to say anything. "Not long," she said.

Daniel switched to the evil twin. "I take it you're looking for Josh."

"Jem was just about to call him for me." Marianne smirked at me, her eyebrow and head cocked in a 'get out of that one' gesture.

"Yes, I was." With little choice, I wriggled my mobile from my pocket and dialled.

"Missing me already, Jem?" Josh answered.

"Of course. Are you busy?"

"Why? You need me to entertain you, sweetheart?" he asked, his tone low and suggestive.

"Hands off," Sean called in the background.

I smothered my laugh. "Very tempting—very. But I doubt Marianne would be a willing audience."

The line fell quiet.

"Josh?"

"Is she listening to this?" he whispered.

"Nah—I'm not even near her."

Daniel lowered his head as a small chuckle snorted out.

"That's good. I don't want—"

"So, shall I tell her you're coming down? She brought tea, and it's a new one. She sure knows how to spoil you ..."

"Okay." He laughed. "I'll be down in a minute."

I clicked off, tucking my phone back in place. "Done."

"Thanks, Jem." Marianne beamed.

"No problem." I toed the dust-coated ground. "No problem at all."

The two witches turned their attention to Daniel, and switching off to the pukifying conversation happening among the trio, I lifted Josh's flask to my nose for a closer sniff.

The distinct flavours of wood, spice and grass with an underlying sweetness drifted into my nostrils.

After a quick check assured me nobody showed me any interest, I drew in a deep breath, lifted the flask to my lips and, despite the moronic proportions of the act, took a sip.

Every feature on my face revolted against the taste of wood, grass, possibly cayenne, honey—pretty much as the tea smelled. I peered down into its murky depths, wondered about their latest intentions, and sampled a second sip, followed by another.

By the time Josh pushed through the glass door, the flask had lost half its contents.

15

It took a whole lot of creeping to Nathan to get the day off work on Tuesday. Eyes wide, lower lip pouting, my sorry voice explained that I'd get no more opportunities to complete my Christmas shopping, if he didn't let me go before work broke up the next day.

He'd hesitated—of course he had—and brushed at his hair, while his eyes reflected his contemplation, but the vibration of his mobile had broken into his thoughts. Whatever he'd seen on the screen had creased his brow, and he'd walked away with a mumbled, "Okay then, Jem."

Desired result achieved.

Once out, I chose the department store on purpose. Not only would it save the hassle of car park switches, but it would have everything I sought—a bonus I sorely needed with Poppy's absence, thanks to her obligatory lunch with her mother-in-law.

On the third floor, rows and shelves of photo albums confronted me, though it took only a few minutes to locate the right one—warm cocoa, leather bound, manly. And around two corners of the six-foot high maze of aisles, I found the picture frames. From the unnatural blues, I padded to the wooden ones—but barely had chance to study them before a blur darted past the end of the row.

I flicked my gaze up and caught the chestnut head before it disappeared around the corner.

Not again.

Attempting not to look like an inept spy on a stealth mission, I speed-tiptoed forward, eyes narrowed. As I passed a hanging-set display, I slipped my shopping bag over one of the wire hooks and shimmied to the end of the aisle and rapid-peeked around the corner—there, back, fast.

Nothing. The woman had to have come that way, though. So, where had she gone?

Even checking the other side of the row bore no fruit. Had she even been there to begin? Maybe one niggle too many had started to affect my imagination?

I rubbed at my face as I mumbled to myself about paranoia. "Get a grip, Jem."

I spun the way I'd come, turned the corner and froze.

Up ahead, chestnut woman stood with her back to me, up on her toes and peering around the far end of the aisle.

"Looking for something?" I whispered beneath my breath. "Or looking for *me*?"

My trainer-clad feet made little noise, as I crept along the length of tiled floor behind her. No rapid movement. No casted shadows. She showed no awareness of my presence.

I came to a halt three feet from her. "Why are you stalking me?"

Her shoulders stiffened before her hand lifted—to her mouth, I assumed.

"If you wanted to follow me unawares, you should have practiced a whole lot harder before you—"

She turned, folded her across her chest, one hand reaching up to support her chin as she looked down at me—and my mouth hung open for a half second.

Because only someone related to Sean would have the exact same eyes as him. Not even the change of hair colour to that in Nathan's photographs could divert my attention from them.

I dragged my fingers through my hair. "Beth? What are you doing? Do you have any idea how much trouble I'll be in with Nate, if he finds out you're—"

"You know who I am?" Her voice came deeper than I expected, carrying husky undertones. When I nodded, she frowned. "How?"

"Photographs."

Her eyebrows lifted. "Nathan has pictures of me on show?"

"No," I said with a small headshake.

She seemed to regard me for a few seconds before she spoke again. "How long have you known I was following you?"

"Since I kept spotting your hair." I shrugged. "And do you drive a black Lexus, by any chance?"

She gave a half smile. "I guess I'm not very good at this tailing game."

"You're better than Sean."

The smile on her lips widened.

"It took me about thirty seconds to make him when he first stalked me."

"Shame on him." She gave a quiet laugh, sobering as her gaze travelled over me, head to toe, shoulder to shoulder.

When her scrutiny became uncomfortable, I asked, "I take it you know who I am?"

"You're Jem." Another smile accompanied her matter-of-fact tone.

"Then, it's a pleasure to meet you, Beth." I held out my hand, and she took it.

"You, too."

"But seriously," I said, "do you understand how much trouble I'll be in, if Nate hears about this?"

Her lips twitched. "Will you tell him?"

"He'll know." I shrugged. "Do you truly believe I won't mention this to Sean? Do you have any idea how hard it will be for him to know I've seen you, when he spends every day missing you like crazy?"

Her fingers tugged at her lower lip as her eyes moistened, and I cringed.

"That was really tactless. Sorry."

"You shouldn't apologise for being honest."

We returned to studying each other for a few seconds, before I remembered my abandoned shopping.

"Excuse me for a moment." I held my finger up, walking the ten metres to grab my stuff. When I returned to Beth, I asked, "Can I ask why you've been following me?"

She glanced away, looked back. "Nathan has told me a lot about you. About how happy you make my son. I was curious."

I could accept that. If I'd been her, and a female lived in my house, with my family, when I'd been sent away, my curiosity would have been alight, too.

"Are you busy?" she asked.

I lifted my shopping basket. "Christmas shopping."

"For Sean, by any chance?"

"Some, yes."

"Do you mind if I join you?"

At her request, my inner conflict kicked in. I really wanted to get to know the woman more. Should I, though? Knowing how much trouble it would get me into with Nathan? Should I take an opportunity Sean had been denied for years? My warring emotions battled it out as I stared up at her.

Beth reached out, placed her hand on my shoulder. "How about if you don't answer?" Her head dipped to my level. "How about if I just take it upon myself to tag along?"

"I'm not sure ..."

"I'll even save you the bother of confessing to Nathan, by calling him myself to let him know what I've done." Her convincing tone placed emphasis on the *I've*.

Against my better judgement, I shrugged. "It's a free country." I broke eye contact, kicking a toe against the pale floor. "If you happen to be in the same departments as me, or the same aisles

..." I looked up again. "It's hardly a crime, right?"

***

"So ..." I turned from the picture frame I held to Beth. "... is it just curiosity that's had you chasing me everywhere? Or is there more to it?"

She smiled. "Nathan told me you can be pretty sharp."

"He said that?"

"Yes, he did." She gave a small laugh that sounded more like a chuckle.

I remained quiet, hoping for my answer, as I stuck the broad, dark-oak frame in the trawler net with the album.

"Do you want the truth, Jem?" Her head cocked to the side. "Of course you do, now I've said that." She stared at me as though expecting a response. "Okay, the truth is I have a ... another reason for following you."

I turned to fully face her. "Go on."

"Well ... a few weeks ago, I asked Nathan if I could come home."

My muteness returned. Mostly because I didn't know what to say.

"Would you like to get a coffee, find somewhere more comfortable to talk about this?"

Though my eyes narrowed, I gave a small nod. "Sure."

The restaurant resided on the top floor, and we carried our cappuccinos to a booth tucked into a far corner. Neither of us said anything, as we emptied sugar into our mugs and stirred the liquid into a swirl of froth.

I placed my spoon aside and took a sip. "So ... you asked if you could come home?"

Beth nodded.

"What did Nate say?" I asked, lowering my mug.

"At first?" She sighed. "You'd think I'd suggested we go bungee jumping, or something equally radical."

I took another sample of my coffee.

She went to take a drink, too, but paused in the motion. "Okay, I offered you the truth, so I'll give it." She blew out a small breath. "I used you being there with them as a bartering tool. I waited ... to see how everything worked out for you—"

"How much has Nate told you about my life since being with Sean?"

"Everything." The reach of her hand to enclose my arm reflected the emotion of her voice.

"You understand I was bitten because of another pack? And that said pack kidnapped me?"

Her fingers tightened their hold. "Yes."

I stared at her. "What the heck made you think that was a good bartering tool to convince Nate?"

"Because, despite everything that's happened to you, you *are* okay, Jem." She released my arm, rubbing it before withdrawing. "That was always my aim. See for myself, to check. Even with the threat of another pack, everything worked out."

"But there was no guarantee it would."

"Yes, I know." The darkness of her eyes intensified. "But if you thought you would be in as much danger as you ended up in, would you still have stayed?"

My jaw tightened. She'd cornered me and knew it, because she already knew what my answer would be. Seconds passed before I said, "Yes."

"Why?"

"Because ..." I lifted a hand, lowered it again. "Because it meant I could be with Sean."

Her eyes softened as she smiled. "Well, maybe I'd like that opportunity. I'm so tired of hiding away, Jem. I haven't seen my sons in ten years. Ten—"

"I'm not saying you shouldn't come back, Beth."

She closed her mouth on whatever protest she'd been about to give.

"But I think it would be wrong to mislead you into thinking there's no danger. I'm in danger every day— every time I leave the house." She went to cut in, but I held my hand up to stop her. "That doesn't mean I don't agree with your coming back. Because I think it would work out all right. I think there are enough of us to try our best to make it be okay. And I know what a difference your physical presence would make to Sean's and Ethan's lives—Nate's, too, no doubt." I took a deep breath. "So, if you're expecting me to argue Nate's corner ... I won't. I do believe you should be there."

Her lips curved as she heaved a deep sigh.

"But if you tell him I said all this, he'll string me up for definite."

She breathed out a small laugh, matched by one of my own that dwindled as a thought occurred to me.

"When did you say you asked him?"

Beth shrugged. "A few weeks ago."

I nodded. "I suppose that would explain his moods lately."

"Moods?"

"Well, not moods, exactly. It's just been obvious he's had something on his mind. He's been ... stricter, I guess."

"Ah." She sighed. "When I nagged him enough to consider it, he said he had to be sure everything was as it should be first. Maybe he needed to be sure you were all taking precautions, before he brought in extra responsibility."

I nodded in agreement. "You realise Nate only behaved the way he did because he was terrified of losing you, like Connor did with Nadine, don't you?"

"Of course. I'd never seen Nathan truly afraid before that day. If not for that ..." She shrugged.

"You should know that what I have to say next is not to make you feel better, but because I believe it's the truth."

Her eyes tightened before she smiled. "Okay."

"I think you've found it difficult to accept that they allowed me to stay ... in the beginning, I mean, when I was still ... like you."

Beth's head cocked side-to-side.

"I've only ever believed it was because of who I was. If it were anybody else ... some random person, Nate would never have allowed it. Do you understand what I'm saying?"

"Yes ... and thanks." She took my arm again. "Listen, I'm a little hungry. Would you stay long enough to eat with me ... please? I'm quite enjoying your company, truth be told. That's if you're hungry."

A quiet laugh drifted past my lips. "I'm always hungry."

"You would be, wouldn't you? I'll grab us a roast." She got to her feet, already turning away. "My treat."

As I watched her grab a tray and join the short queue, I wondered if Nathan would relent, allow her home, and how that would change Sean, Nathan, Ethan—everything. I'd spent months wondering what Sean's mother would be like, what kind of woman had married into a family of werewolves and nurtured two teens through puberty when they hit their first change. Not for one minute had I expected I'd feel so comfortable in her company.

When my mobile rang in my pocket, I drew it out and checked the screen before answering. "Hey, baby," I said with a smile.

"How's your day, Jem?" Sean's deep voice asked. "Everything okay?"

How was I supposed to answer that? *Well, I'm just sitting here watching your mother pay for the meal she invited me to eat with her?* "I'm having a good day," I managed.

I would tell him. How could I not? Just not before Beth had spoken to Nathan.

"So ... where are you?"

Beth turned from the cashier with a tray in her hands. Steam spiralled from the plates and two mugs it bore.

"I'm in a restaurant, in a department store." I smiled. "I'm just about to have lunch."

"Lucky you. I'm absolutely starved, but I've got to finish this plastering before I can head out for something ..."

160

Beth slid back into her seat and placed the tray on the table, handing my food to me.

"You could have asked Dad to let me come with you."

I inhaled the rich meat and fresh vegetable scents, smiling when my stomach growled its approval. "How could you have come with me when I'm Christmas shopping?"

At my words, Beth's head shot up.

Sean chuckled. "Are you buying presents for me?"

Beth leaned forward to whisper. "Would it be too invasive if you allowed me to listen to him?"

I grinned at Sean's question. "Maybe." Switching to loudspeaker, I positioned the phone beside my plate.

Beth gave a nod of thanks.

"If I ask, will you tell me what?" Sean asked.

"No." I snorted. "It's meant to be a surprise."

His voice dropped, tone deepening. "I could make you tell me."

Beth's fingers rose to her mouth, smothering silent amusement.

"You can try as hard as you like, but I won't tell you." I picked up my cutlery, speared a chunk of carrot. "It's a surprise."

Another of Sean's chuckles travelled the line and would have tightened my stomach, if not for my company. "I'd have fun trying, though."

"I'm sure you would."

"In fact, just wait until later. I'm going to—"

I almost choked on my food. "I'm not having this conversation with you right now." I dipped my head to conceal my embarrassment from Beth. "I have you on loudspeaker so I can eat, and someone might overhear."

His next chuckle more than tightened my stomach. "Okay, okay. What time are you out until?"

"How would I know?"

He sighed—no doubt at my all-too-often response. "Okay, I have to go. I'll speak to you later. Make sure you call when you leave the store."

"What makes you think you won't ring me before then?" I asked around a roast potato.

"Jem?" he said, his tone a plea.

I rolled my eyes. "Okay, I'll call."

Two seconds later, we hung up. I sent Beth a smile before giving my meal my full attention.

Her hand folded around mine, paused it mid-lift to my mouth. Her eyes, as ours met, brimmed with emotion. "Thank you," she said.

16

"Would you mind my company for longer?" Beth asked, as we left the restaurant.

I tucked my hands into my jeans pocket. "Actually, I could use some help. I don't have a clue what to buy Nathan—or Connor. Ethan should be easy, maybe a T-shirt—something butch."

Beth chuckled.

"And I should be able to get away with pretty much the same for Josh, Dan and Kyle."

"How are they?" she asked. "Obviously, Nathan keeps me informed, but a woman's point of view may tell me something he hasn't."

"They're okay," I said. "Josh and Dan are dating ..."

Her brows lifted as she smiled.

Not particularly suicidal, I deliberately failed to mention the pack's current problems, but deciding it unfair to mislead her into believing Josh and Daniel had found someone to settle down with, I said "But their girlfriends are nowhere near good enough for them."

Beth's brows lowered, and when I didn't elaborate further, she asked, "And Connor? How does he seem to you?"

"He's doing okay."

"That's good," she said.

The trip down on the escalator interrupted our conversation, and in the men's department, I headed straight for the underwear. Rails of boxer shorts sported a whole host of colours, patterns and fabrics. I located the silk pairs, testing their texture against my fingertips. Beth stayed with me without interruption, as I studied one pair after another, until I settled for silk in the same deep blue as my eyes—a favourite shade of Sean's.

From there, we tag-teamed in our T-shirt perusal. Finding one which would not only fit, but that Ethan would wear offered a challenge all on its own.

"This one?" Beth held up her third option—black with white lettering across the front that read, 'Boys will be boys'.

I grinned. "Perfect." It went into the basket.

Metal scraped across metal as we pushed hangers of T-shirts back and forth, and I pondered over a collection depicting cartoon characters.

"How did you and Nate meet, Beth?" I asked.

She smiled. "We were both at school."

"You went to the same school?"

"Yes." She chuckled. "There were mixed schools in our day, you know."

"No, I didn't mean—"

"I know. Just teasing."

I drew out a green polo shirt I thought would suit Kyle.

"Nathan went to my school, but he was two years above me," she said. "And he was extremely fit, in more than one sense of the word."

I contained my laugh, disguising it with a hand to my mouth.

"He played on all the sports teams. That's how he caught my eye. Apparently, it's how I caught his, too." Her gaze was on me, but she didn't appear to focus on anything other than her memories.

I almost joined in her daydream—Nathan, young and chasing girls? Too funny.

"Nathan was never interested in all the popular girls in school." She paused. "They were interested in him, though. Maybe because the further through school he went, the ... bigger he grew." She turned to me at last. "He had the attention of almost everyone—he *and* Connor. But he ignored that. They both did." A smile coated her lips. "Until they saw me and Nadine one day, doing laps around the track. The football team was training in the centre, while we ran circles around them—literally." Her finger indicated the route they'd run. "It took a few laps to understand we were being observed. We were more interested in sport than makeup and mini-skirts, so we weren't really used to being watched by boys."

I smiled like a goon at Beth's recollection. "So, what happened next? Did they ask you out? I didn't realise you and Nadine were friends before you met Nate. Did you go on double dates?"

She laughed. "Yes, yes, and yes. But it wasn't Nathan who did the asking. He got Connor to do it. Even then, he wasn't used to people telling him no, and I think he was afraid of his first refusal. With Connor doing the dirty work, it would seem like he had the knockback, rather than Nate himself."

I laughed at the idea of Nathan being unsure over anything— could hardly picture it.

Beth held up the T-shirt she'd clutched throughout her tale. "Do you like this one, Jem?"

"It'll be okay for Dan." I tucked it into the net with my other buys, before nudging back to the subject. "So, how old were you?"

"When I first dated Nathan?" She smiled. "Fourteen—I thought I was pretty cool being asked out by an older boy. Everybody else suddenly decided I was worth knowing, too."

I pursed my lips. "Yeah, that can happen."

"I wasn't really interested in them, though. Once we'd been out a few times, the four of us pretty much kept to ourselves. Nathan even stayed on in sixth form, instead of heading off for college, just so we could spend more time together—mostly because his father tried his best to prevent it outside of school hours."

"What was he like?"

"Nathan's father?"

I nodded, selecting another T-shirt from a rail.

"Rob was ..." She hesitated, seemed to think about it. "There's a lot of him in Nathan. But Rob was less refined, less polite, and extremely contemptuous toward us mere"—she dropped her voice to a whisper—"*humans.*"

My eyebrows lifted. "How did Nate get away with seeing you, then?"

"He proposed as soon as I was old enough." She smiled. "And then, once I'd turned eighteen, we ran off and married behind Rob's back. After we returned, Nathan threatened to leave if his dad didn't accept me. The arguments lasted only as long as it took for me to get pregnant. The promise of his first grandchild gave Rob enough incentive to stop trying to drive me away."

"It must have been tough."

"Certainly tougher for us than Connor and Nadine. They waited until we'd paved the path before they followed. But with Nathan as Alpha's son, they both knew he'd have more chance of getting Rob to come around. And, as his only son, he did."

"When did he tell you? Did you know what he was before you married him?"

"Of course." She gave a quiet chuckle. "We were still young when I found out. Of course, I knew the first time we spoke that there was something different about him. He wore an element of danger like a permanent aftershave." Her gaze locked with mine. "I'd spent my whole life living by the book and obeying my parents. As soon as I knew Nathan was capable of being ... *bad* ... I was pretty much hooked."

I laughed. "How young were you, exactly, when he told you?"

"He didn't tell me, Jem. He *showed* me. He'd reached sixth form by that time, and his father had insisted the relationship end, so we took every opportunity we could together." She smiled again. "Nathan had a habit of convincing me to skip certain lessons. Usually maths. One Friday afternoon, he told me he'd meet me outside the gates, take me for a romantic stroll through the woods. Romantic strolls with Nathan often led to ..." She waved a hand, grunting a small laugh. "Some things you don't want to hear."

I shook my head, but smiled. "No, I don't."

"Nathan didn't tell me the real reason for the walk until we got there. He told me he was in love with me, but he couldn't go on without showing me who he really was. *I need to be certain you'll still want me, Beth*, he'd said. Like anything could change that."

My brow creased. "Weren't you afraid? Shocked?"

"Afraid? No, I've never been afraid of Nathan. He was never anything but protective. As for shocked? Yes, of course I was. But at the same time, I wasn't really that surprised." She gave another of her low chuckles. "It turned out to be yet another thing he made easier for Connor. Can you believe they talked me into telling Nadine?"

A small snort burst out. "How did she take it?"

"She laughed, said I was crazy and hadn't she told me to quit watching horror films."

Listening to Beth's running commentary of life as a teenager and the difficulties of dating a werewolf ensured the afternoon passed with ease. On familiar ground, the conversation flowed right out of her. While she talked, I shopped. I received a second call from Sean, and a third one arrived while Beth picked out a quality bottle of brandy for Nathan and a twenty-five-year-old whiskey for Connor.

Sean's final call at almost four disturbed my checkout. "Kyle and Dan have asked me to go Christmas shopping with the three of them. Do you mind?"

"Of course not," I said.

"I'll see you this evening, then."

I smiled down the line at him. "Baby, you can see all of me, if you're good."

His deep chuckle rumbled through the connection and remained with me for minutes after I hung up.

Rain had fallen during my time in the store, and my feet splashed through puddles en route to the car. Street lighting reflected in every wet surface. The Porsche glistened, exposing its bright yellow individuality amongst the surrounding vehicles of greys and blues.

Beth chaperoned, standing to the side and watching, while I piled my goods into the boot. As I slammed the lid down, a strange sadness settled in.

"I should go." I thumbed toward the car, even though I didn't feel ready to say goodbye. "I'm supposed to be on dinner duty tonight. If I'm not back in time, and Ethan gets impatient enough to do it himself ... I'll never hear the end of it."

Beth's eyes appeared as dark as the blackened sky above. "Does he treat you okay? Ethan, I mean ..."

"Yes."

"That's good. I know he can be a bit ..."

"Intolerant?"

Beth chuckled. "Yes."

"He's a pain and everything, but he treats me right."

"Good." She smiled, before it diminished and she grew serious. "Listen, Jem. I know it's a lot to ask, but would you consider exchanging numbers and keeping in touch?"

My gaze went from her to my feet, as I considered what I should do. Did I want to keep in touch? Of course I did. Should I, though? I didn't know.

"If it will make things difficult for you, I won't call. But it would be nice to have a direct line to someone who can tell me about my sons." She ducked down, as I lifted my face. "Plus, I can give you a heads up when I'm ready to tell Nathan about today."

I blew out a breath, but nodded, despite knowing the bother it would get me in. "Sure."

I recited my number, and Beth keyed it into her phone and rang mine. "Save that number, Jem."

I lifted my stare to Beth's. "I will." Reaching for my door, I stepped away. I'd barely made contact with the handle, when she took my shoulders and turned my body into an embrace that could only be described as motherly.

Her lips skimmed across my cheek. "I can't thank you enough for today. It's meant a lot to me."

My heart pounded most of the way home. The speed of the car nowhere near matched my preferred pace, and the Christmas traffic should have irked me, but I welcomed its detainment. If Beth had called Nathan straight away, he'd be furious. Beth could convince herself as much as she liked that she could talk Nathan into laying the blame onto her, but I didn't buy it.

Nathan most certainly wouldn't.

By the time I parked the Porsche on the driveway, five o'clock had come and gone.

I paused in the hallway, nostrils flared, and stilled the rustle of bags as I listened. The truck outside announced a presence, as did the patter of water coming from the bathroom.

"Jem, is that you?" Nathan asked.

"Yeah." I mounted the stairs and turned into my room, hiding my purchases in the wardrobe, before continuing on to Nathan's bedroom.

He lifted his head as I rounded the doorframe. "Good day?"

I tried to decipher if his words held hidden code. Deciding they didn't, I nodded.

He returned to his open sock drawer, stuck in a couple of pairs from the top of his dresser. "You know Sean's gone out?"

"He called and told me."

Nathan nodded, still tidying his clothes.

I went farther into the room and dropped my voice. "Is it okay to get those pictures from the safe?"

He sent a glance toward the bathroom, where the shower still played. "Be quick," he said with a nod.

It took less than a minute to open the wardrobe, key in the combination, and reach into the safe for the pictures. Guilt swept through me when I spotted those of the inanimate Beth in my hands, and I looked across at Nathan, where he'd shifted to folding boxer shorts as though he couldn't possibly wear them creased.

As much as I wanted to say something, though, no amount of words would get me out of any hole I might dig if I mentioned Beth—so I clamped my lips shut and left the room.

Once I'd secured the photographs in Sean's and my wardrobe, I hit the kitchen. Before Ethan could emerge, I tossed pork chops into the oven and chopped a pile of peppers and red onions, coating them in olive oil, and added a heap of asparagus. They went into the oven above the pork, and I headed back upstairs to assemble Sean's gifts.

Filling the album with pictures brought the blank pages to life. After removing the clear wrapping of the frame, I eased off the back to insert the one I'd had enlarged. I turned it over, held it against the wall, smiling at the forever memory of facial expressions Poppy had captured.

With the two most important tasks out of the way, I made a start on the wrapping.

Ethan straightened as I trotted into the kitchen, oven mitts on as he withdrew the chops from the oven. "Note how I finish the dinner you're supposed to be fixing again?" His eyes held sternness, but the twitch at the corner of his lips gave his amusement away as he carried the plates to the table. "Why can nobody else in this house cook? Isn't it about time—"

I drew out my chair loud enough to drown his words. With a smile in Ethan's direction, I sat to await my food, turning when Nathan joined us. "Is Sean coming back for dinner?"

"He shouldn't be too late." Nathan took his seat beside mine.

I picked up my cutlery in *feed me now* fashion, and Ethan chuckled as he placed my meal beneath my nose. Although I'd eaten a cooked dinner at lunchtime, hunger had revisited in the form of stomach rumbles before I'd even reached home.

Nathan's gaze met mine. "Did you get everything today?"

"Yeh." Talking around peppers and pork mumbled my response.

He nodded, went back to his meal.

I watched him out the corner of my eye, searching for a sign he *knew*. Paranoia traded places with guilt, as my mind convinced me that Nathan bided his time, to give me chance to confess, before he ripped me to shreds because he'd had to find out from someone else that I'd met his wife.

Beth had promised to warn me before she made the call, though. Hopefully, she'd meant it.

After dinner, I sent the two men into the living room while I cleaned up. As I closed the door on the dishwasher, I glanced toward the clock.

Seven—and still no Sean.

Unsettled by his absence, I grabbed a blanket and headed out to the conservatory. The low hum of a television disappeared beneath the beat of the weather. Beyond the glass, wind howled a gale, and leaves swirled across the lawn as though running for their lives from an unseen monster, while each gust nudged the abandoned basketball a few feet.

Snuggled into the willow sofa, my body liquefied, my muscles un-tensed, and my brain hit a state of mushiness, teetering over an abyss of unconsciousness—until a trill ring penetrated my fuzzy mind.

I blinked, my body stiffening, as I recognised the music as Nathan's ringtone. *Beth?*

17

"Hello?" Nathan answered, and I turned toward his voice, pushing up in my seat when his volume dropped to a murmur too low for me to hear.

Footsteps crossed the living room. If Nathan came my way, it had to be Beth.

I tracked his feet along the hall toward me. I stared through the French doors into the kitchen.

"Stay with them." Nathan appeared in the opposite doorway. "You know what was agreed on this." Worry rushed through me, as he rounded the table. "Yes, Sean. If they go in, you go in. You have Kyle to back you up. Give him the same order." Nathan entered the conservatory and towered over me. "Here she is." He handed me the phone.

I took it, placing it to my ear. "Sean?"

"There's a bit of a problem."

My pulse thrummed. "What kind of problem?"

"Bloody Marianne has called—said she quickly needs Josh's help with something ..."

I pushed to my feet, the blanket falling to the floor.

"Obviously, Josh offered to trot along and do whatever job she wants him for."

I rubbed at my face. "Did he tell her he was out of the house tonight?"

"I, um ... yeah." He sighed. "Yeah, he did."

"Did she know you were all going?" My fingers pushed into my hair, as I stared out across the garden.

"Josh and Danny were already going. Kyle invited himself and me along later, after Josh had told her."

My hand tightened around the phone. "How very devious of her. You know you can't let Josh, or Dan, go in there alone."

"I know. That's what Dad's just said."

"If they go in alone, something—"

"Don't worry. We're all going in. It'll be okay."

My pulse faltered. "You can't assume that. You've seen what their spells can do."

"I know."

"If they're up to something, it won't be strength you'll need, it'll be wit—"

"Yes, Jem, I know," he said.

I blew out a breath, released my hair from within my clutched fingers. "Okay. When are you going?"

"Now."

Another breath burst past my lips. My pulse refused to regulate. "Stay together. Don't drink anything they offer you. And try not to inhale—"

"No fluids, or air?" Sean's chuckle did nothing to alleviate my concern. "That should give us, what? A seven-minute window to—"

"I want you to call the second you're out of there. Do you hear?"

"Sure, Jem."

"And be careful. Watch her—"

"I know."

We said goodbye. I turned to Nathan.

As wrinkles spread across his forehead, his hand forming into a tight fist, he seemed about as happy with the situation as I did.

The click of each passing second resonated in my head. I'd tried to allow the noises of nature to provide a calming therapy, but gone was my sleepiness and my state of peace. The only sound my mind tuned into seemed to grow louder, consuming my thoughts like a ticking time bomb.

Except, the only exploding would come from me, if I didn't hear from Sean.

Over an hour had passed since his last call.

My fingers traced the outline of my mobile in my pocket. What the hell could Marianne need Josh for, for so long? Even if the job required physical strength, there were four of them.

I dived up from the willow seat, stormed into the living room, and strode past Ethan to Nathan. "What's taking them so long?"

"They'll have been there less than an hour."

"Half of that is too long." Irritated by his calmness, I raked my fingers into my hair, tugging at a cluster of strands.

Nathan's stare flicked up to the clock and back to me. "If they're not home by half-past, call him."

My lips funnelled around my blown out breath, as I turned from Nathan and paced the room.

The men's attention returned to the TV for a few minutes. On my fourth width, I cut into their line of sight and drew their focus away on my spin.

Pace. Turn. A pause to check the clock. Eight-fifteen.

"I should go over there. Check they're okay," I said.

"They can take care of themselves," Ethan said.

I blew out another breath, resumed pacing. "What if they're not okay?" Turn. My hands wrung at my waist. Pace. Why would Marianne wait until she thought Josh and Daniel would be alone? A small prick of fear formed in my chest, threatening to bubble into something larger. "Something's off about this, Nate."

Ethan's gaze followed my worn path. Nathan's did, too, until I broke away to check the time. Eight-twenty.

"Okay, call him," Nate said.

I tugged my mobile from my pocket, dialled Sean's number. The high-pitched trill echoed into my eardrum.

Each additional ring tightened my chest a little more.

Each tightening of my chest matched the deepening of the worry etched across Nathan's and Ethan's faces.

I hung up, tried Josh's number. It rang and rang. Same result. My bubble of panic expanded and brought my breaths in shallow spurts.

Nathan edged to the lip of his armchair. "Whose number was that?"

"Josh's." I scrolled down to Kyle's number. Dialled. More incessant ringing. My hand gripped the phone as though pure strength could make them respond. "Kyle isn't answering, either." The heave of my chest forced my words out on a breathless pant.

Nathan pushed to his feet. "Try Dan."

I obeyed. Same result. I hung up, retried Sean's number. The monotonous tone filled my head. "Come on. Come on." I looked to Nathan. "Why aren't they answering? Nobody's bloody answering."

"I'll try Connor," he said. "See if they've gone there."

I tried to take control of my breathing, as Nathan dialled, as more ringtone buzzed through the living room.

"Nate?" Connor answered.

"Are the boys there?" Nathan's tone carried a slight waver.

"No, why?"

I pressed a hand to my heaving chest and backed out of the room.

"They haven't come here, either ..." Nathan said.

In the hall, I grappled on the table for the Porsche keys.

"And none of them are answering their phones."

I twisted the doorknob. The door made little noise as I swung it open.

"The thing is, we think they're at ..."

I stepped outside, hopping down to the driveway. As I broke into a run, rain sprayed up, soaking the hem of my jeans.

A press of my thumb unlocked the car. I glanced over my shoulder, concerned Nathan or Ethan might have heard. At the driver's side, I tugged open the door and slid into the seat.

Keys in the ignition. A twist of my hand. The engine purred to life.

As I reversed in a wide arc from the house, Ethan raced out the front door.

"Jem!"

My gaze locked with his for a split second, before I spun down the drive and out the gates.

I had to go. Had to check. No point explaining to Nathan my reasons for going alone—that if something had happened, I couldn't run the risk of handing more of my boys over to the witches.

Nathan would never understand.

My mobile rang. I snatched it up off the dash, leaning forward to see past the manic wipers.

"Jem, come back," Nathan said as soon as I answered.

"I'm going to look for them. I'm going to get Sean."

"We'll go with you."

"You can't." My breaths panted out harder than ever. "They'll take you, as well."

"Jem, I am orde—"

I cut him off. If I couldn't hear, I wouldn't have to obey.

My foot floored the accelerator. The car skidded as I took an island at sixty. I turned into the swerve, righted the car and slammed on the accelerator again.

Only a misted view showed the way, and I tugged my sleeve over my hand to wipe at the glass, yet still couldn't see properly.

Red lights grew bigger as I shot toward a vehicle up ahead. I dropped down into third to overtake it, whipping the wheel to the right, then left as I tucked back into the lane. The car behind flashed its headlights at me. I ignored it and went faster.

I pressed my hand to my chest as my panting breaths burned through me. Sweat coated my brow and trailed a steady path to my eye—my swiping hands couldn't keep up with its production.

I picked up my mobile. Tried Sean again. No answer.

Every bone in my body, every nerve ending, every cell in my brain told me something had happened.

I'd told Sean to go there, to watch out for Josh.

Me.

My roar filled the car, and as I thumped my fist on the wheel, the impact vibrated the length of my arm.

My ridiculous speeds turned what should have been a thirty-minute drive into a little over seventeen. I turned into the road where the witches lived, screeching to a halt at the kerb. My fingers snapped at the handle. My shoulder barged the door open. I scrambled around the bonnet, vaulted the gate and raced up the length of the path.

Each boom of my fist on the door matched the thumping beat within my head.

Nobody answered.

Bang!

"Open it!"

An inhalation told me *my boys* had been there, had brushed against the doorframe.

I moved to the window, bashed my fist against it.

The curtains had been removed, the house lay in darkness. Inside stood empty.

"No!" I shifted right, kicked at the door. It rattled, but didn't budge. "No!" Another boot of my foot, and the door held fast.

"No! No! No!"

The Porsche tyres squealed on departure from the kerbside. I spun around, hit the main road, and headed for Connor's. Maybe I'd missed them on the way.

My mobile rang, and the jolt of my body lifted both hands from the steering wheel, before I snatched it up. "Nate?"

"Jem, I told you—"

"Did they come back?"

"No—"

I screamed, throwing down my mobile. As it bounced onto the passenger seat, the first tears erupted from my eyes like water from a burst pipe. I tugged my hair where it clung to the perspiration across my brow.

"Jem?" Nathan's deep voice called from my phone.

I picked it back up. "They've gone. The house ... empty ... gone." Each fractured word arrived on a hiccup.

"Jem, come—"

"Sean ..." I gasped. "Gone." Tears poured over the contours of my cheeks, pooling across my vision.

"Jem, please come—"

"Sean." My body juddered, the phone slipping from my grasp and tumbling to the floor.

I swiped at my eyes. The insistent beat within my head intensified. A rub of my fingers did nothing to ease it. Shudder after shudder affected my shoulders, each flicking the steering a little off route.

No streetlights illuminated the lanes. Rain pelted the windscreen. Even the wipers struggled to block the assault. On top of those, my concentration plummeted, my tears created a shield to the outside world, and my panicking head seemed on the verge of combustion. By the time I pulled up at Connor's, my body had almost ceased to function. How I'd driven without incident, I didn't know.

I grappled on the car floor for my mobile, hit dial as I fell from the car. Rain soaked into my shirt, my jeans. As I extricated my feet from the foot-well, kicked out of the car and forced myself upright, the connection to Sean's mobile rang out.

"Jem?" Connor's voice broke through the ringing.

Phone still pressed to my ear, I looked up. Connor stepped back from the doorway and allowed me in. The expression in his eyes said it all. He hadn't heard from the boys, either.

I lowered my mobile and disconnected. Connor's stare remained on me as he closed the door. I knew my hair had tangled, that my still wet eyes would be blotchy. My feet refused to root me to the spot, and the tremble of my lips had developed beyond my control.

Upon seeing my own desperation mirrored back in Connor's gaze, an unstoppable ripple washed over me.

"Jem?" His tone held hope, pleading.

A shake of my head whipped tears from my eyes.

His hand folded around mine holding my mobile. As he urged it back up, his voice deepened. "Try again."

I redialled. It rang ... and rang—nothing, absolutely nothing.

I rubbed at my eyes, at the sledgehammer-like pain in my head.

A tingle pricked at my fingers, my toes.

I ignored it, kept my focus on Connor, as he lifted his own phone, dialled and placed it to his ear.

He fisted his hair until erratic. The shuffle of his feet grew jerkier with each ring. Connor's call received the same outcome as mine. No answer.

He hit disconnect, dialled a second time—a voice answered.

I froze.

"Is she there?" Nathan asked.

"Yes," Connor said.

"Anything?"

Connor sent me a brief glance. "No."

At Nathan's audible sigh, I could picture the brush of his hands across his hair. "Okay, there are enough of us to take one each. Tell Jem to keep trying Sean. Connor, you take Josh, and Ethan and I will do Kyle and Danny."

Connor hung up and began his call. I continued with mine. Other than the ringtones spewed out by our mobiles, the room became silent for minutes.

A tinny voice emanated from Connor's phone.

I tilted my head.

Connor's body stiffened. He hung up—redialled. Same voice.

He turned to me. "His phone has been switched off. Has Sean's?"

I waved my mobile at him. It still rang.

His mobile vibrated in his hand, before the music blared out. Our gazes dropped to it. At a check to the caller display, he shook his head at me and answered.

"Both Dan and Kyle's phones have been switched off," Nathan said.

Connor rubbed at his face. "Josh's, too."

"Sean's?"

"No, Sean's is still ringing out."

I began a slow pace along the hall—pressing my fingers to my booming temples and rubbing at the bridge of my nose, through which numbness had masked the tingling. My shirt clung to my sweat-sodden body. The ringtone continued in my ear until ... *click.*

I whirled round to face Connor, and his stare told me he'd heard. "Sean?" I whispered.

Static silence responded.

"Baby, will you speak to me? Are you hurt? Tell me where you are."

High-pitched laughter blasted from the speaker.

A chill raced along my body, a low growl rose from my throat. "Marianne, if you—"

"Jem, Jem, Jem," she sang.

"Where the hell is Sean? What have you done with him? I want to speak to him."

Another laugh greeted me.

My limbs quivered. "Put him on. Now!" The clutch of my hand threatened to destroy my mobile.

"Sorry, but Sean can't come to the phone right now."

I stumbled into the kitchen. My hand caught in my hair, fisted around knotted lengths. "If you've done anything to him, I will—"

"You'll *what*, Jem?" Her abrupt tone held nothing but ice.

"Tell me where he is." Pain cramped through my thigh, unbalancing me into a chair and sending it crashing to the tiles. "*Tell me!*"

"Sean's mine now."

"No!"

"You brought it on yourself, Jem. I would have been content with Danny and Josh, but you just couldn't leave things alone, could you?"

Needle-like shards pierced the muscles across my shoulders. "If you hurt—"

"Ha!" she blew out. "You don't even know where we've taken him. Forget him, Jem ..."

Flesh twisted at my calves, grunting a cry from me. "No!"

"He's not coming home ..."

A distorted blur claimed my vision, as I clung to the table to remain standing. The beat of my brain thudded against the inside of my skull, and tingling spread into my shoulder blades as prickles stabbed at my spine.

"Face it, Jem," Marianne said sweetly. "You've lost him."

Breaths gasped past my lips. "You will give him back!"

"Who's the loser now?"

"*No!*"

Only the disconnect tone responded.

Beyond my liquid-coated eyes, Connor took a step forward, at the same time my knees buckled. His lips moved. A jumble of words carried out.

Agony coursed through me. My mobile clattered to the floor. I forced myself to my feet, staggering toward the exit. "I have ... to get—" I gasped, as splintering pain stabbed into my flesh. My clawed fingers worked around the door handle.

"Jem?"

With a shove, the door swung open. I glanced back at Connor with his mobile pressed to his ear.

"Get over here, Nate. Now!" Connor tugged at his shirt, hauling it over his head.

New pain doubled me over. I fell outside, landing hard on my knees, and kicked against the slabs to urge me back up. With rain whipping my tortured body, I dashed for the forest.

"Jem!" Connor's footsteps pounded the soaked lawn at my heels.

I made it only as far as the first line of trees before his hands grasped my hips. A tug of his arms lifted me from the ground, drawing my body back into his.

I punched over my shoulder, booted at his shins. "No!"

His arms tightened. "You can't do anything like this, Jem." Connor's murmured tone arrived tender, but didn't hide his desperation.

I snarled over my shoulder, wriggling like crazy, scratching at his arms. "Sean needs me!"

Spewing a deep growl, I pushed forth until my change tore through me. The further it progressed, the harder Connor fought to restrain me.

My body twisted in its contorted state. Tendons tightened. My limbs deformed. Flesh stretched as muscles distorted. Cries of anguish became screams. Pleas for release became snarls.

The arrival of my wolf form shredded my clothing, and Connor's hands lost grip, as I forced myself violently through my change.

As wolf, I whipped round to face him.

Connor had crouched, his own change already begun.

My chest vibrated against the deep rumble within. The hackles along my neck and spine fluffed up to full height, and I backed away.

He gave a long, low growl. "Wait." His tightening muscles affected the density of his voice.

I moved away farther, ignoring the appeal. As I turned away, Connor's snarl called for my attention, but I didn't have time to waste.

My face lifted to the darkened branches, my forelegs pushed up my chest. Built from the thrum within, my distress call attacked the quiet, night air, and I took off.

The torrent of rain saturated my coat, weighting my body. The burden it lent nowhere near matched the guilt that consumed every part of my soul.

I'd told Sean to go there. Made him promise he'd look after Josh. I'd heard Marianne's words. If I'd just allowed her Josh and Daniel, she'd have left Sean alone.

I should never have asked him to protect Josh.

I should have done it myself.

My muscles protested at every step as I raged through the forest. I blanked them all, as well as the nocturnal sounds of wildlife and the intoxicating aromas that would normally distract me.

Blood pumped around my body at high speed. Panic shortened my breaths. My usually enhanced vision refused to focus.

I disregarded everything—even the calls of my remaining pack members—but could not ignore the gaping hole that ripped through my chest.

You gave him to her. You sent him to her. You handed him to her on a platter.

Remorse played out in my mind to the beat of my paws. Before I'd even finished one self-accusation, another began, the words merging to take over all logical thought.

A low branch battered my face. I snarled at it, smelling blood but not caring. Nose pushed forward, I spurred myself faster. I needed to get there—where, though, I didn't know.

My tongue hung out as my body overheated. Air didn't appear to reach my lungs through my constricting throat. Had my eyes been capable of crying, I knew they'd have produced tears, just as if I could produce human sound, my screams, my sobs, would have filled the forest.

Connor pursued somewhere in the distance, and the scents of Ethan and Nathan arrived on the breeze from the north—their feet no doubt hitting dirt at a greater pace than my stupid, short legs carried me.

Three against one.

I couldn't afford to be hindered. I needed to find Sean. Despite the objection of my body and my fast-approaching exhaustion, I pushed myself harder.

Three more paces, and the ground disappeared. My body dropped. A momentary splash exploded around me.

The river. In my manic racing, I hadn't noticed it.

Freezing temperatures seeped into my throbbing limbs. My legs kicked down to no effect, as spasms attacked my muscles. As my body went down, dread settled in.

I had no idea of the depth of the river, but on four legs, I'd never reach the bed and remain afloat.

Got to change back.

How could I, though, when I could no longer sense my body?

My body floated, whirled, danced—weightless. Freezing.

Even my brain froze, attempting to shut down. Surely, the numbness had to be better than the pain that awaited me at the surface?

I should just stay here.

What was there to go back up there for? Anguish? Fear?

Sean!

I gasped as his name entered my head, water leaking into my mouth, trickling along to my throat.

The sound of a muffled howl broke through.

Of its own accord, my back arched, bowed and arched again.

Intense agony spread through my skull.

My mouth opened to cry out, but the water prevented it, and more fluid entered my body.

My feet hit the bottom, sank into the soft mud beneath. Clouds rose through the black water. In a last desperate bid to rescue Sean, I pushed up with my toes.

The action cramped my calves, my feet, and spread to my thighs, while the gentle lap of water caressed my flesh, my arms, my fingertips.

Something gripped beneath my shoulders and tugged at my languid body.

Rain pattered against my upturned face.

A voice invaded my sleepy brain. "Jem? Come on, breathe."

Ethan?

It sounded like Ethan, but my brain barely registered, as the trickle of current disappeared from around me, as a deep cold slid beneath my back, and as a heavy weight pressed down upon my chest.

A raw, choking cough burned my throat. My mind could scarcely keep up, as my body flipped over, and water evacuated my lungs. It sputtered from my mouth. I gasped in air.

"Jem?"

The fingertips that took my face radiated warmth.

"Jem, speak to me."

"Sean," I rasped out on a sob.

My body shifted, to be enveloped in heat, but numbness overpowered every one of my nerve endings. With each passing second, I slipped toward the beckoning abyss. Each lurch closer loosened my limbs further, spread cold within me, and deadened my appendages.

The rise, fall, and jostling of my body suggested mobility, but how I moved, I couldn't fathom. My arms and legs swung about, my head lolled to the side.

More distant voices arrived, murmurs, extra heat. My body continued to rock, the action instilling me with a massive desire to sleep. I forced my weary eyes to open, to see something—*anything*—and caught a glimpse of the dark hair to my left, the familiar walk.

"Sean," I whispered.

I inhaled, reached out a hand to him—but he'd gone.

Everything went black.

18

Great heat enveloped my stomach, my chest, even my toes and cheek, tempting me to stay put. *Everything must be okay*, my subconscious demanded because only Sean could fill me with such warmth and security.

I flexed my stiff fingers, blinking against the darkness. Awareness crept in at a gentle rise and fall beneath my cheek, a strong heartbeat pulsing against me.

"Sean?" I reached up to trace the outline of the face above my head, along the jaw, capturing the breaths blowing past slightly parted lips.

The body shifted beneath me a little. Hands swept over my back.

I inhaled. The second I did, everything came flooding back. As intense agony stabbed through my chest, a gasp exploded from my lips.

"Shh," Ethan whispered. A gentle rub of his hands soothed again.

"Ethan?"

"You were so cold. It was the only way to get your temperature back up. You're okay now. Everything will be okay."

"How can it be?" I bit down against the tremble of my lip. "How—when Sean isn't here?"

"You need more rest."

I pushed onto my elbows, raising my face to look at him. "How can I rest? I need to find him."

"You're exhausted." He fingered my loosened hair and trapped it behind my ear.

The gesture reminded me so much of Sean that my brow folded, as I clenched my jaw to prevent the tears.

"Shh, Jem." A gentle coax of Ethan's hand pressed my face back into his warmth, but my whirling mind would allow no reprieve.

Pain cramped at my chest before expanding, as though attempting to infiltrate my veins and spread its disease. In defence, my body began to curl. My trapped feet tugged from the heat of Ethan's legs. My hands compressed into tight fists. My knees drew up. My head tucked in.

The first sob wracked through me with the power of a convulsion.

Ethan shuffled until he sat. He tightened his arms and drew me onto his lap, circling my entire body, as my limbs denied me any request to unfold.

Violent shudders clattered my teeth.

Ethan pulled me closer. "We'll get him back. We'll get them all back. I promise you, he'll be home."

Did he even realise he made promises I could never allow him to keep?

I'd been left, stuck with three men, all of whom I couldn't take on my hunt—not when they could be kidnapped, too.

My sobs and judders lessened to clear the way for strings of thought. From those threads came elucidation. I needed help of the female variety.

"What time is it?" I whispered once my voice came back into play.

"About half-four."

I nodded, the movement wiping tears into the already soaked front of Ethan's shirt. I lifted my gaze to his, blinking to clear my vision of moisture. "I need to use the toilet."

"Sure." Ethan's strong hands offered support, as I uncurled myself from his lap.

It took a second, or two, of being vertical to gain my balance, bearings and composure. The shadowed outline of the sofas emerged out of the dimness as I teetered around them for the door. In the hallway, I turned left, tiptoed down to the kitchen. My mobile lay in the centre of the table. Someone must have gone back for it. I took a step forward, folding my fingers around the metal. As footsteps came in behind me, I concealed it in the folds of my too big T-shirt and swung past Ethan.

"I won't be long," I mumbled.

The swish of socked feet against the floor told me Ethan spun to face my receding back, but I kept going.

At the top of the stairs, I cocked an ear for any sounds of life. Breaths sounded from the two bedrooms on the right, but no movement registered. I crept across the landing, praying my passage didn't disturb Nathan or Connor.

The bathroom door stood ajar. I stepped inside and closed it at my rear. From there, I crossed to the window, opened it wide and sat on the sill.

Rain still travelled in all directions with a howling wind. One press of a button illuminated my mobile screen. I scrolled down my call history, took a deep breath and hit dial.

Once second passed. Two. "Hello?" The drowsy, yet alert, voice answered at the speed of someone who slept with their phone beside their pillow, as though awaiting that dreaded call in the dead of night.

"It's Jem." Emotion distorted my whisper.

The brush of fabric announced a shift of position. "Is something wrong?"

"It's Sean." My mind struggled to verbalise it. "He's missing." Moving my lips to produce the words took effort. "Please, come. I need you."

Her breathing altered, footsteps padded across carpet. "Sit tight, honey. I'm on my way."

Minutes passed. As my body shook with cold upon the exposed window ledge, beneath a partial moon, my mind could only deal with my near future and how much Nathan would tear me to shreds when he discovered what I'd done.

When the shivers of my body threatened to topple me to the outside slab below, I pulled the window closed and left the bathroom.

Ethan blocked the stairs, his huge bulk silhouetted against what little light arrived through the hall windows. Maybe he'd come to check I hadn't leapt from the window and raced off vigilante-style.

The thought had crossed my mind. Common sense told me I should wait to speak to Jess before making plans, though.

I trotted along the landing, peering down at him from the top step.

"Jem?" he whispered. "Are you okay?"

What did he want me to say? Of course I'm bloody not?

His expression stoppered my response. The rigid set of his jaw and taut fists lent him manic appeal. He heaved a deep breath. His shoulders sagged with his exhalation. Ethan loved Sean as much as any older brother could. I'd never seen him look so defeated.

I plodded to the step before him, cupped his face in my palms. As I pulled him toward me, his arms slipped around my waist, his face buried into my shoulder, and dampness expanded across my T-shirt beneath his eyes. My hands slid around to hold him tight. "Don't worry. I'm going to find them and bring them all home. I promise."

If Ethan realised I'd given the same reassurances as he had, he didn't say. For minutes he stood before he lifted his head. His glistening eyes met mine in the darkness. "You're freezing again."

I took his hand, drawing him with me as I descended.

A brilliant glow swept through the frosted glass of the front door, bathing us in light, and we both halted. My breath caught in my throat as I spun to warn Ethan, but he already had his hand on the doorknob.

A single flick of his wrist freed the door of its restriction. It collided with the table, as Ethan lunged outside.

The black Lexus rolled to a stop on the driveway. The handbrake clicked on.

"Ethan, wait. I need to explain—"

He leaped down the steps. Shoulders braced, he strode toward the vehicle.

The bedroom doors flew open above me.

I spun toward the sound, pulse racing.

Connor first, Nathan second, appeared at the top of the stairs. They tugged on shirts as they thundered down, one after the other.

"Who is it?" Nathan asked through fabric.

They couldn't have been sleeping, as I'd assumed. My big plans to get Beth in and explain everything to her before dropping it to the men about my phone call evaporated before my eyes. I'd well and truly dumped myself in the manure.

Connor's face poked through the neck of his shirt. "Are they back? Is it the boys?"

My mouth opened and closed. I turned from the two men to look outside.

Ethan yanked on the car door, warnings about trespassing already rumbling from his lips. He swung the door wide, reached inside for the driver, and stumbled back a step as his hands lifted to rest at his nape. "Mum?" The word came out almost on a gasp.

Fury dissipated from Ethan in an instant. His shoulders slumped as he helped Beth from the car with a tenderness he often tried to conceal.

She stood before him. Her fingers reached up to his face. The slightest encouragement of her hand drew him into her arms, and his body shook while Beth provided the kind of comfort only a mother could.

"Beth?" Connor said. Deep lines cut through his forehead, as confusion consumed his eyes.

"Beth?" Nathan's uncertainty lasted only a second, before he turned to me. In that singular glance, I found incredulity and anger, but above all else, a deep sense of betrayal.

I rubbed at my head, taking a step toward him. "Nathan, let me—"

"What have you done?" He stormed out to his wife.

Connor stared hard at me. "Are you responsible for this, Jem?"

My shoulders lifted, as did my arms. "She—"

"You called Beth?" he asked.

Unable to conjure a better response, I nodded.

Connor's stare held mine as he shook his head, and I cringed beneath the weight of his disappointment.

As Nathan reached Beth, she lifted one of her arms, and he slid in to join the family embrace. The three seemed to stay like that for a lifetime, as I stood waiting for the blow I had coming.

When the three of them straightened, the two Holloway men didn't turn on me right away. Under Beth's direction, they unloaded her luggage from the boot. Judging by the number of bags, I guessed she planned on staying a while.

Ethan hauled holdalls over his shoulder. As Nathan secured the car, Beth walked across to Connor and me.

Her arms wrapped around Connor's shoulders. She pressed her lips to his cheek. "I missed you, Connor."

He returned the gestures, his bear hug lifting her feet from the floor. "Me, too, Beth. It's good to see you."

"I'm so sorry about your boys," she said.

Connor nodded, setting her back on her feet. "I know."

Beth turned to me, hauling me into her stronghold. When she pulled back, her hands rubbed the length of my arms. "You are frozen."

Our familiarity with one another didn't go unnoticed by the three frowning men, as puzzlement and dawning crept into their expressions.

I tried to smile, but couldn't manage it.

"Come with me." Her arm worked its way around my back. "I'm running you a bath."

She herded me onto the first step, as Ethan and Nathan entered the hall. I tried to twist, to take in their expressions, to explain, but Beth's hold tightened, nudging me higher.

"Jem?" Nathan said.

I turned my head, to look back over my shoulder, until Beth's lips at my ear prevented the action.

"Just keep walking," she whispered.

Deep, booming thuds against the bathroom door accompanied Nathan's shout of, "Jem!"

"Nathan, you'll have to wait," Beth snapped.

The banging ceased, but the lack of retreating steps told me Nathan hadn't moved away.

Beth nudged me toward the oversized tub, tugged at the hem of my scant clothing. I hadn't the energy to protest. When she stood at my back and told me to lift my arms, I complied.

She leaned over and stuck in her hand to swish the bubbles. "Okay, get in."

The water scalded my frozen body, but I blanked it. I drew my knees up and hugged them with my arms, disappearing inside the high-sided bath and the wisps of bubbles crackling against my chin.

"Stay in there. Don't get out until you're warm." Beth strode for the door. As she opened it, Nathan's body filled the gap. Beth blocked him, bumping against him with her hip until outside the room, and closed the door at her rear.

"I want to speak to her," Nathan said.

"Why?" Beth asked, as I titled my head to listen. "To rant at her? To tell her she had no right to contact me? Can you not see how she's feeling, Nathan? The girl's distraught."

"She didn't have a right to contact you."

"So, are you saying you wouldn't have let me know our son is missing?" Beth said.

"Of course I would." Nathan's response brimmed with passion.

"Then, what's the difference? I'd still have been here today, anyway."

"But, I trusted her, Beth. I gave her access to all your details, and—"

"What are you talking about?" Beth cut in. "I approached Jem, not the other way 'round. Jem hasn't betrayed your trust—*I* did."

Silence arrived and stayed for seconds.

"I was curious," Beth said finally. "I wanted to see what she was like, see for myself how safe her life was. So, I've been following her—"

"You've been *what*?" Nathan's deep voice growled out of him.

"Following Jem—for weeks."

Silence resettled in. I thought they'd left and I'd missed their footsteps, until thuds banged against the door.

"Jem! Get out here!"

"Leave her alone, Nathan. There was nothing for her to tell you. She didn't even know before yesterday, when she spotted me at the store—and she might not have known then, if you hadn't shown her photographs."

"She should have told me."

"I asked her not to," Beth said. "I wanted to tell you myself what I'd done. She only did what I requested."

"But—"

"And I think she's had a little too much on her mind since, don't you?"

"But ... why? Why call you? She must have known I would—"

"She's terrified. And she most probably feels alone right now."

"She's not alone." Nathan sounded offended. "She's got us."

Beth huffed. "You're not female, Nathan. You are not on the same wavelength as her. I'm the only person who can possibly understand what she's going through right now. She needed me. So she called me. Simple as that. Don't you dare blame her for this, because I will stand by her."

I smiled at Beth's tenacity.

"Okay," Nathan murmured.

"Now, what about you?" Beth's tone turned tender. "How are you coping?"

"Honestly?" The door handle to his room gave its familiar squeak before their padding footsteps followed. "I feel out of my depth, Beth."

As the closing of the bedroom door muffled their voices, I let out a deep sigh and lowered my lids. I sank low into the water, raised my face only high enough to allow air to enter or escape. The heat of the water soaked into my skin. Gentle ripples soothed every part of me.

Even if my mind wouldn't accept it, my body required a few minutes of replenishment.

No sounds reached my deafened ears, only the thick whoosh that came with being underwater. From the jumble of words that filled my head, I tried to formulate a plan.

Images and ideas flickered behind my lids. Where could the boys be? Were they okay? How could the witches have overpowered them? What had they done? Sean had gone in there alert. Kyle, too, no doubt. Were the witches more powerful than I gave them credit for? Each thought bounced aside to allow the next to move in—a circulation of mental mumblings.

A dark form blocked the light. My eyes flickered open to a huge towel levitating at the bath side, and I pushed up until my head and shoulders emerged. As I climbed to my feet, the towel circled me, revealing Ethan. He leaned in and pulled out the plug, taking my elbow to assist my climb out. My soles had barely flattened against the floor, when he gathered me into his arms.

"I owe you, Jem." His murmur hit my hair.

I tilted my face to him.

He pressed his lips to my cheek. "Because of you, Mum's home. Ten years, I've waited to see her again. Thank you."

Somewhat warmer in jeans and T-shirt, I checked the time. Almost six. I decided to give Jess an early wakeup call.

She answered after about six rings, sounding half asleep. "Flipping heck. Do you know what time it is?"

"Sorry, but this can't wait. I need your help."

"What's up?" She must have heard something in my voice, switching to alert in an instant. "Did the witches do something else?"

"They took Sean." My jaw tightened.

"They took .... They what? What do you mean they took Sean? Wh ... what happened? How?"

"They—Marianne asked Josh over last night. Said she needed his help with something." I almost spat in anger at the recollection. "He had Dan with him, like she expected, but Kyle and Sean were with them, too. None of them came home."

"D'you think she already intended to take Josh and Dan?" Jess's all-business tone set in.

I nodded, but remembered she couldn't see. "Yes."

"Are you absolutely certain that's where they are?"

"Yes, because we rang all their phones, and Sean's was the only one answered ..."

"What did he say? Did he know where—"

"It wasn't answered by him."

A moment of quiet followed, before she murmured an, "Oh," and returned to silence.

"I thought they were only after Daniel and Josh," she said after a beat. "Why not wait? Do it another time, if they weren't alone?"

"To get back at me." I growled. "She took Sean on purpose."

"Shit! Did she tell you that?"

"Amongst other things."

"Bitch."

"I need your help, Jess. I don't know what to do. I feel like I should be out there looking for them, but, damn, I have no idea where to start."

"I thought you had an address for them? Go snatch 'em back."

"They're not there." I tugged at the wet strands of hair hanging in clumped tails across my shoulders. "By the time I'd figured out something was off and flew over there, they'd ..." My breath caught. "I was too late."

"If they moved out that soon after taking them, they must have already had a new place arranged." She paused, only her breaths travelling the line. "Unless where they've gone to *is* their usual place of residence, and the house they invited you to was temporary."

I frowned deeper. "Like a prop?"

"Yes," she muttered. "Something like that."

"Have you found anything out about them, at all, Jess?"

"I was given a name to contact. I have a meet with him on Boxing Day—"

"That's three days away! I can't wait that—"

"Given the circumstances, I may be able to get him to meet with me sooner."

"Do you think he will?" A rub of my hand scruffed up my hair. "I'm going out of my mind here."

"I'll call him, see what I can do."

"What were you meeting him about, anyway?"

"I was told he used to practice in your area, so he may know if there's a coven, maybe know some of its members—their leader, even."

I blew out a sigh. "It's a start. But I need some advice for if I'm out and about. Is there a witch repellent ... something I can do? Some way of defending the house, even, if I can get the guys to stay here?" I groaned, running my hand across my face. "I can't take the risk of her getting any more of the pack. I've already got too much—"

"Calm down, Jem. Give me a minute to think."

Jess's feet padded around through the phone line, slides and scuffs sounding as though she moved stuff about, and the flittering of pages as though she leafed through one of her books.

The longer I waited, the messier my hair became.

"Why don't you give me some time to look into this for you, and I'll call you ba—"

"I don't *have* time."

"Whatever I advise you to do, I doubt you'll have everything you need on hand. When I call you back, I'll have a list of ingredients for you and, hopefully, a local address where you'll be able to obtain them. Depending on the source, you may need more than a polite request to get through the door, so you need to give me at least an hour. Okay?"

"Can't you just—"

"Even if I can get you through the door, I'm pretty certain it won't be open before nine. Either way, you'll have to be patient."

I groaned. "How can I be? I need to be looking for Sean now. I—"

"Please, Jem, patience. We'll sort this out, I promise you. But I can't give you what you need at the drop of a hat."

"One hour. Please, no longer."

"I'll try my best."

As soon as I hung up, my gaze skimmed around the bedroom. No conversation meant no distraction, and the space became nothing more than a cold, empty shell. With Sean's absence, all warmth seemed to have been sucked from the room. I jumped to my feet, flitted left and right as though a frantic enough search could locate a hint of the room's usual atmosphere. On finding none, my body shivered, and I hurried from the room, but even with the barrier, as I closed the door behind me, the chill stroked across my back like icy tentacles.

I doubted I'd ever be warm again—unless I found Sean.

My vicious headshake lashed hair against my cheek. I couldn't think like that.

Until I found Sean. I had to believe I'd find him. If not for that, I'd lose the ability to keep going. Without Sean, my life would be pointless.

As another finger of iciness trailed a pattern across my back, I shot down the stairs.

A quick peek revealed no one in the living room. I continued past, pushed open the kitchen door. Heat bled through the first sign of a crack to encircle me in its comfort.

Connor had switched from his usual position at the foot of the table to sit near the others. My focus fell on Beth in my seat—or maybe I'd spent the past four, or five, months in her place.

I took Sean's empty chair beside her, and my attention swept over the three men before landing on Nathan. I waited to see if he had anything else to say about my phone call to Beth.

He stared hard at me, until my jaw tightened.

Beth's scraping chair created a welcomed distraction. "I'm going to fix you some breakfast, Jem."

"I'm not hungry," I said as she moved across the kitchen. I lifted my hand from my lap, placing my mobile on the table in front of me.

"You have to eat."

Elbows positioned either side of my phone, I supported my head as my glaring eyes willed it to hurry up and ring. "Please, Beth. I'm not hungry."

She didn't speak, just cracked eggs into a bowl, whisking them up.

My face tilted to her, until I met Nathan's gaze again, and I returned to my phone vigil.

"Did you call Jess?" Nathan asked.

My nod took my hands along with it.

"Did she have any suggestions?"

"I'm waiting for her to get back to me. As soon as I know how to protect the rest of you in my absence, I'm going to get them back."

The men's silence spoke louder than any words. I lifted my head. They all stared at me. So did Beth—but whereas Beth's smirk appeared impressed by my idea, the three men looked offended, with their incredulous expressions and clenched fists.

Getting them to obey, I suspected, would not be easy.

19

A plate of scrambled eggs received only a cursory glance before I reset my sights on my phone.

Beth's hand came to rest on my shoulder. "If you don't eat it now, it will get cold."

"I already told you I'm not hungry."

With a small sigh, she sat and positioned my phone in the centre of the table, before sliding the plate of food beneath my nose and a mug of coffee by my elbow. "Watching it will not make it ring any sooner, Jem. You may as well eat your food while you're waiting."

"I'm not hungry."

With a finger beneath my chin, she drew my gaze round to her dark one. "If you won't eat for hunger, then eat for Sean. How do you think he'd feel, if he knew you weren't taking care of yourself? And if you're planning on getting him back? How do you expect to do that with no strength?" She raised her eyebrows, lifted my fork, and waved it beneath my nose.

I stared at her for seconds and blew out a breath, taking the fork. Despite its light texture, the yellow fluff struggled along my oesophagus and *thunked* into my stomach like a brick. I put the fork down and nudged the plate away.

Beth shoved it back, worked my cutlery back into my tightened hand. "So stubborn. This lot must be rubbing off on you."

"Eat the food," Nathan said.

With a suppressed growl bubbling deep in my chest, I stabbed at the food and shovelled it in, one mouthful after another until my plate sat empty. The fork hit the table with a clatter, as I pushed my plate aside and returned my phone to its original position.

About halfway through sipping my coffee, impatience and irritation kicked in. The scrape of my chair jolted everyone's heads up as I stood, and their gazes followed me to the other side of the room, where I peered from the kitchen window.

As I recalled my last hunt in the forest with Sean, a sharp pain stabbed into my chest. I gritted my teeth against it and began to pace.

"When did Jess say she'd call back?" Ethan asked.

"She said at least an hour." With each meet of the wall, each spin, my focus locked onto my mobile. "What time did I come down?" I asked after a few more minutes.

Connor shrugged. "Ten-to-seven-ish."

The clock read seven thirty. I ran my hands through my matted hair, suppressing a groan. In a need to do something, I walked to the end kitchen unit and opened the drawer. A pad sat on top of the contents, but finding a pen took some shuffling. When I had them both, I placed them on the table beside my phone.

"Where's the Porsche?" I turned to Connor. "Still at your house?"

He nodded. "We all came back through the forest. Did you want me to fetch it?"

"No." My rapid headshake matched the speed of my answer. "I want you to stay here. Under no circumstances can you go back to yours until this is over, Connor. The witches will have keys to your house now, so you can't go back. If you need anything, I'll get it. If you—"

"You can't seriously expect us all to hide away while you go off on some wild, solo search mission," Ethan said.

I stared hard at him. "That's exactly what you're going to do."

Connor pushed to his feet. "Now, hang on a minute—"

"No, Connor. It's nothing but male pride that created this bloody mess in the first place—male pride and vanity."

His entire face darkened along with his green eyes. "If you think, for one minute, I will sit here and allow a ... a ..."

"What?" I snapped. "A female? You don't think I'm up for the job because I'm not male, is that it? You can't stand the thought of handing the reins over to me because of some gender issues you've got going on?"

"That's not what I meant, and you know it."

"No?" My hands unclenched to point at him. "So, explain, then."

He rubbed up his hair. "I'm ... I'm just not used to sitting around and doing nothing."

"Do you *want* your sons back?"

Nathan leaped to his feet. "Now, that's overstepping—"

"No, Nate." I spun on him. "If you'd all listened to me, they would be home right now. Josh wouldn't be bloody bewitched. Danny would not have followed, and Kyle and Sean would not have been dragged into something that isn't even their argument."

Nathan's hands flew up, slapped back down against his hips. "Oh, so, we're going back through the *I told you so*'s, are we?"

I glared at him. My chest rose and fell beneath the weight of my heightened temper, and the clench of my hands dug my nails into the palms. I let out a long, slow breath. "I don't want to fight with you." I rubbed across my face as I realised I'd picked a fight with the wrong people. "It's just ... I managed to outwit her before ... I know I can do it again. I have to."

"You don't have to do it alone." Nathan's voice calmed a little, too.

"Yes, I do. I can't take the risk of losing more of you." My jaw clenched as emotion threatened to take control. I opened the French doors, stepped out into the conservatory. Even there, my facial muscles and hands refused to relax. "I should have bloody finished her when I had the chance." A warm hand came to rest on my

203

shoulder, and I turned to Ethan. "I had her. I bloody had her, and I let her go. Now, I seriously wish I hadn't. I've never wished anything more than I do that."

Ethan rubbed my arm. "You couldn't have known she had something like this planned."

"I *should* have known, should have realised she was leading up to something, that she had bigger plans. I knew she wanted Josh. I couldn't figure out why—still can't figure that out—but I knew." I ran my hands over my head for the umpteenth time. "How could I have been so naïve? Because they don't have our physical strength? If I believed, for one second, she planned to, or had the ability to take all four of them, there's no way I'd have told Sean to go in." I met Connor's eyes. "I'm sorry, but I wouldn't."

He nodded.

At the shrill ring of my mobile, our heads all whipped round as though magnetised by its beckon.

"Answer it," Nathan said.

I strode around the table, snatched up the phone. "Talk to me, Jess."

"Okay. First, I called my contact, and he agreed to meet with me tomorrow morning—"

"Tomorrow isn't soon enough. You need to meet with him today."

"Tomorrow will have to be soon enough. In the meantime, I'm sending you on a shopping trip."

"For?"

"Ingredients you'll need, if you want to protect your home, and if you want to protect the rest of the pack."

I sank into Sean's seat, picked up the pen. "Tell me."

She sounded as though she ruffled through sheets of paper. "Okay, write these down: iron beads, burdock roots—"

I tapped my pen against the pad. "How many beads?"

"As many as they have. You'll probably buy them out of their stock."

I scribbled in my unintelligible way when taking notes. "Got it."

"You'll need red thread—strong red thread. It is vitally important that it's red. Get a good few yards of it to be on the safe side."

I wrote that on my list, mumbling the words beneath my breath.

"You're also going to ask them for some centaury."

I frowned as I swept the pen across the page. "What's that?"

"It's an herb."

"Never heard of it."

Jess sighed. "It's the legendary herb of centaurs, Jem—used for protection. They may not have any. If they haven't, don't worry too much. I have some here, and I'll be with you in a few days, so I'll bring it with me."

My pen stopped moving. "You'll be .... You're coming ... here?"

"Of course. You need my help. This is simply to keep you all safe until I get there."

I blew out the biggest sigh. "Thanks."

"You're welcome," she said. "Now, write down mandrake root. You need to ask if they have some already soaked and made to order, because it's supposed to sit in water for three days. It's the affected water you're after."

"What's it for?" I asked as I scribbled.

"Sprinkled over your thresholds, it will prevent anyone with malevolent intent entering. It's more reliable than the brick dust, which you proved can be broken."

"Okay." I scrawled as I mumbled, "Mandrake root, soaked in water for three days."

"Right. You also need alcohol." More pages rustled her end. "Any kind will do."

"Sure, okay."

"And dragon's blood—"

I paused again. "There's no such thing as dragons."

"I seem to recall you spending years telling me there were no such things as werewolves, too."

A small snort broke through as I shook my head. "Yes, but—"

"Anyway, it isn't really blood from a dragon. It's the resin of the Indonesian Dracaena Draco tree. It's only called dragon's blood because of its red colour."

"Okay."

"And finally, you'll need gum Arabica," she said.

"Gum Arabica," I repeated as I wrote. "I presume, wherever I go, they'll know what all these things are."

"Of course."

"So, do you have an address for this shopping trip?"

"Yep. It's a shop called Sacred. About an hour's drive for you. This is what you need to know in order to get in ..."

I listened to her directions, copied them out and ensured I had them correct. With the request to call her back later for further instruction, I hung up and gave Beth, and the silent and watchful men, my attention. "I have to go out. While I'm gone, you all need to stay in the house."

All three men faced me, and, maybe without even realising, Connor shifted his position until he'd blocked the rear exit from the house.

"You're not running off and doing this alone, Jem." Nathan's voice came out low. "It's ridiculous."

"Actually,"—I folded the paper I'd written on and tucked it into my pocket—"what's ridiculous is you three being too chauvinistic to admit I'm right."

A flit of my eyes to the wall showed the time as seven fifty-five. Traffic would be heavy if I didn't leave, and I wanted to get to the shop for opening. I took a step around the back of Beth's chair.

Nathan shifted toward me. "You're not going alone."

"Yes, I am." As I moved again, Nathan stepped closer. "You planning to physically restrain me from going?"

"No."

As I went to walk out, though, Nathan grasped my arm, giving a gentle tug back. I looked down at his huge fingers circled around my bicep, before lifting my stare to his.

"I forbid you to leave this house alone," he said.

My glare matched the defiant tilt of my chin. "Is that an order?"

"Yes." He nodded. "As your Alpha, yes."

"And if I disobey?"

"You will not disobey me while you are a member of my pack."

My eyes narrowed, jaw tightening as I tipped up my head to study him, but he held my gaze steady, tension filling the atmosphere to bursting point. After minutes of the stare-down, I broke through the static silence. "Then, you'll have to kick me out."

Nathan tried to hide his blink, but failed. Ethan's movement to round the table reached the corner of my eye.

Beth's fingers brushed my free arm. "Jem?"

I shrugged her off. "Let go of me, Nate. I'm leaving."

"And I've just told you you're not." His hold tightened. "Not while you're under my command."

I lowered my gaze as I gathered my thoughts. Beth's fingers touched my arm again. I ignored her, raising my attention back up to meet Nathan's. "Then, consider me out of your pack." I tugged my arm free—only achievable because Nathan's lessened grip arrived with the widening of his eyes—and continued for the front door.

"Do not walk out that door!" Nathan shouted.

Footsteps hit the tiles behind me. I didn't turn. My hand snagged my scarf from the banister. I secured it around my neck as I flung the door open—and I strode one, two, three paces away before an image, idea, memory flashed inside my head and brought me to a halt.

I about-turned and re-entered the house. Beth's eyes followed me, as I stalked past her in the hallway. Nathan's fury had brightened his eyes to a brilliant blue that softened slightly as I marched back into the kitchen.

I snatched the pen off the table, turning to him. "I don't know how long I'll be gone." I lifted his shirt by the hem. "If I'm now banned, you may not see me for a while. But something tells me"—I drew an upside down triangle on the firm flesh of his stomach—"that this symbol will keep you safe."

Nathan's gaze tracked me across the room.

Ethan looked as though he might protest, as I stood before him, but he surprised me by doing the honours and revealing his bare skin himself.

Nathan's mouth opened, staying that way for seconds. I needed to move faster, take advantage of his momentary muteness.

"I have absolutely no idea why I believe this will keep you safe." The image I drew on Ethan matched Nathan's. "But it just popped into my head, and as things that pop into my head usually hold some deeper meaning than I initially realise, I'm willing to follow my instincts and go with it."

As I sidestepped to Connor, his hands smoothed over his shirt, coming to settle against his stomach.

"It's the least you can do. If I can't be here, I need to feel I've left you all with some form of protection." I grasped at his shirt, gave a small tug. "Please, Connor."

He relented, allowing me to finish.

I spun and tossed the pen to Beth. "Make sure you mark yourself, too, okay?"

She gave a slow nod, as I passed the men and ducked into the hall.

I paused at the open front door, twisted to peer back over my shoulder. "As soon as I've found them, I'll bring them home. I promise you, they'll be back."

"Jem, don't—" Nathan started.

The slam of the door cut off his words.

20

My heart beat like a bass drum, as I covered the driveway, my ears twitching for pursuit or another order from Nathan to stay.

I knew they couldn't understand my reasoning for leaving. How could I expect them to? Growing up in a male-dominant race of creatures had imbibed it into them that they were the warriors, the fighters, the protectors. They believed themselves superior. I couldn't hold their prejudices against them. They were who they were. I just had to hope they'd heed my concerns about remaining protected.

I took a right turn out the gates and hit the road with no clue where to go. I'd never heard of the address Jess had given me. At least I had my phone, could call for directions, or connect to the Internet to look it up.

My feet moved me forward on what I suspected would be a long trek. In my haste to leave, I hadn't thought to take a vehicle—but then, what right did I have to make the assumption I could? I'd just relinquished my place in the pack, hadn't I?

I ploughed on, peering ahead. The stretch of road went on longer than ever. In my head, I calculated the distance to the nearest village. From there, I could take the bus, use my mobile to locate the shop on the journey, find it on foot and get what I needed, but then what?

What the hell did I do once I've been there? Where on earth would I go?

On walking out, hadn't I made myself homeless?

Plodding on, I stepped into the road as the pavement came to an end. The traffic had already begun to build—nine-to-fivers with their day stretched out ahead of them. My normal day would have been ahead of me, if Marianne hadn't—

I couldn't force the thought out. The deep cavity within my chest expanded a little wider and a tear trickled across my cheek. I couldn't help but wonder how Sean would have received my behaviour that morning. Wouldn't he have had the exact same attitude as the rest of them? Would he not have considered it a ridiculous notion for me to assume the responsibility of rescue?

I knew he would. He had the same genes.

It took effort to drag my feet onward, my heart weighed so heavy. Cars whizzed past with no consideration for the lone pedestrian. Maybe they couldn't see me. The gloomy sky above refused to cast any generous amount of light, especially at that hour. Dressing in dark denim and petrol blue couldn't have helped, either. Only the light tone of my bare arms reflected any light.

In my urgent need to leave, I hadn't paused to consider the outside temperature. While my neck, with the scarf I'd grabbed on the way out, may have been good and cosy, the rest of me lay exposed to the cold. My arms hugged about my chest—against the incessant pain within, as much as against the chill—while I tried to ignore my predicament, my heartache, my worries.

Just as I thought it couldn't get any worse, the first flakes of snow drifted down from the clouds.

With teeth chattering like haunted dentures, I fixated on the numbness that crept into my limbs.

The snow moistened the road in no time. Car tyres swished past, headlights on full to illuminate their route. Traffic grew relentless. One car after another flashed by. A couple of horns blasted out at my invasion upon their space.

One car approached my rear, the engine creeping up with a quiet purr rather than an angry growl. It quieted even more, telling me the car slowed further, and its horn blared out.

I ignored it, but the car drew up beside me, unhurried enough to match my pace. Although obscured by the yarns of my scarf, my hearing picked up the mechanical workings of the window opening.

"Jem?" Inside the black Lexus, Beth leaned across the passenger seat, one eye on me, one on the road. "Get in the car."

I continued to walk, as impatient motorists raced past.

"Come on, Jem. Don't be so stubborn. You're freezing. How much longer do you think you'll last, dressed like that in this weather?"

"What are you doing here?" I said through numb lips.

"I'm coming with you," she said. "Now get in."

I ceased walking and turned to her, and the Lexus rolled to a stop. "Are you planning on taking me back?"

Beth shook her head. "Not unless that's what you want."

I studied her for a few seconds. "How do I know you mean it?"

Her hand fumbled down inside of her door, and she jangled a set of keys at me. "These are to my apartment. They're yours if you want them. You can stay there as long as you like."

Could I trust her? My gut said yes.

Beth placed the keys on the dashboard and leaned across to push open the passenger door. "Please, Jem. Get in."

Heat from the car's interior mingled with the outside air, drifting over me as enticement, and blowing out a deep breath, I climbed in. Blasts of warmth assaulted my face as I closed the door. Beth angled every vent in my direction until heat hit me from all sides.

I tugged on my belt, as she pulled off from the roadside. "So ... you aren't going to try to convince me to come back with you?" My teeth bashed together between each word.

"Of course I am." She smiled. "But I've seen enough of you to know how obstinate you can be. So, I wanted to make sure you had somewhere to go, in case I failed. That way, I can tell Nathan you're somewhere safe."

"And somewhere he's familiar with," I said.

"That, too."

I nodded, grateful for her honesty. My circulation pumped warmed blood through my veins as we fell quiet for a few moments. "You think I was wrong to walk out?" I asked, though it didn't sound like a question.

She didn't speak at first, as though considering her answer, and kept her eyes on the road. After a few seconds, she glanced at me. "I think Nathan is afraid to allow you to do this alone. He's afraid *for* you, Jem. But I don't believe there's any chance of you two reaching a compromise."

"Because he won't back down."

Beth shrugged. "Neither will you."

"That's because I'm right. I can't worry about them. I have too much to concentrate on. Sean needs my full attention. He needs me—"

"But Nathan doesn't understand why you'd feel the need to go this alone."

"What Nathan doesn't grasp is the concept of allowing me control of the situation. It's okay, Beth, I understand. He can't help the way he is, and I know that. Just as I can't help that I need to get Sean back ... by myself—my way."

She reached over and patted my hand where it sat in my lap. On contact, she folded her fingers around it, lifting it toward the vent. "You need to get warmer. Your hands are like ice."

I raised my other hand, too, holding them both in the stream of air. As I relaxed into my seat, my lids drooped, mind and body showing the first sign of tiring.

"Do we know where we're going?" Beth asked.

My eyes flittered open, on the edge of dozing off. I shook myself out of it, fumbling in my pocket for my mobile and the sheet of paper. It took a few minutes to figure out how to connect to the Internet on my phone. Once I had, it took half that to locate the position of the address. "Far side of town," I said. "Coppet Walk.

According to this, it's just off Bridge Street—probably an alley, or something, in between the main shops."

"Bridge Street? There's a car park there, I think."

"Dunno," I mumbled. My total skills at vehicular navigation bordered on zero.

"We'll find it. Don't worry." She gave my arm a reassuring squeeze. "Now, why don't you close your eyes again for a few minutes? I'll wake you when we get there."

I twisted my head to look at her, my brow creased.

"I promise I'll wake you. Trust me."

I did, so I nodded. With the quiet rumble of engine background noise and the minute rocking motion, I sank under.

The third alleyway we came across held the sign I'd been hoping for. "This is it. Coppet Walk."

I ducked down the six-foot wide gap with Beth at my heels. Thankfully, the fleece sweater she'd insisted on buying from the first store we passed helped maintain my body heat. The temperatures hadn't risen with daylight—may even have plummeted—and the snowflakes had increased in size and density. To an extent, the walk offered shelter with its high stone walls on either side.

Farther along, the alley opened up into a courtyard that housed a quaint gathering of small and unusual businesses—a fancy-dress store, a tiny jewellery shop that boasted all items being handmade on the premises, a candle factory with elaborately carved wax in the window, a vintage clothing shop, and Sacred.

I turned to Beth. "Maybe you should go look round one of the other shops for a while."

"You don't want me to come with you?"

"It would be better if I went in alone, as I'm not familiar to them."

"Okay." She thumbed to the right. "I'll go check out the candles."

I waited until she'd entered before I stepped toward Sacred. A bell above the door clanged on entry.

Within, shadows added atmosphere to the tiny space. Rather than making it seem dark and dingy, the interior had a mystical atmosphere that I warmed to in an instant.

A tall man stood behind the counter to the left, his fingers working hard to thread jade beads onto what looked like hemp string. He paused and sent me a small nod and smile, which I returned.

On the surface, the place could have been any other new-age type shop. The air smelled thick with the many flavours of incense. Even within their cardboard sleeves, the perfume permeated the room. Holders lay beside them in various designs and sizes, as well as burners and scented oils. Dreamcatchers hung from hooks or nails from the ceiling as well as the walls, all different in colour and size.

My head turned as two young women tapped at bamboo chimes. A natural, melodious tune echoed out to the carpet-lined walls. They laughed as though amused at their invasion upon the tranquillity of the shop, without understanding they'd merely enhanced it with the music they'd produced. Ignoring their ignorance, I continued to scan.

The two women moved across to the counter, arms laden with items. I waited with the pretence of studying the amethyst collection, tilting my head to listen in to their polite conversation. They babbled on about spending their day with boyfriends or family, about the weather and Christmas plans. A sharp pang pierced my chest, yet I continued to eavesdrop. Once the jangle of the bell declared their departure, I crossed to the counter.

The man tracked my passage, his hands flat upon the countertop. His lips spread into a courteous smile as I reached him. "May I help you?" He had a quiet voice for a tall man, but it didn't come as a surprise. For some reason, it seemed to befit his surroundings as though they moulded together into a complete package.

I forced a return smile onto my face. "I need directions to the Pagan's Pantry. I was told I might find them here."

His eyes narrowed for a split second. "May I ask who gave you this information?" His voice dropped even lower than the first time he'd spoken.

I held his gaze. "It came highly recommended to me by Marcus Fletcher."

Instant recognition entered his eyes, and his body relaxed. "If you wouldn't mind waiting for just a moment?"

"Of course not."

I went back to checking out the shop, reined in my little dance of triumph at getting past the first hurdle.

From behind came the patter and swish of a beaded curtain, followed by a call for someone named Olivia. The beads clinked again. "She'll be with you soon."

"Thanks," I said over my shoulder.

I waited less than five minutes for a woman to join us. Her height held sharp contrast to the man's as she barely reached my shoulders.

She walked over to me, arms folded. "Your list?" No greeting, no introduction, straight to business.

"I wrote it down, but it's a bit illegible."

She waved her left hand. "If you tell me, I'll remember." I gave an impressed nod and pulled the crumpled paper out. "Okay. Iron beads—as many as you have. Burdock root. A few yards of strong red thread ..."

She ticked off a finger, her lips moving with each recited item.

"Centaury—"

"Ah, that's out of stock."

"No worries," I said. "Do you have three-day-old soaked mandrake root solution?"

215

"Of course." She nodded. "I've made a few batches up this week."

"Cool. I also need some dragon's blood and—"

"Gum Arabica," she finished. When I nodded, she asked, "Will you be requiring a quill for that, or do you already possess one?"

I almost told her I'd no idea before I recalled I had to sound as though I knew my stuff. "No, I don't have one."

She nodded, ticked off another finger. "What about parchment?"

"Need that, too." If the gnome of a woman believed I needed some to use with my other ingredients, I bet she'd be right.

She gave another nod. "If you'll kindly wait up here, I'll go and collect your order."

"Sure—thanks."

She glided away and disappeared behind the hanging beads. I caught the man's stare, met it with one of my own. He didn't turn away. Shrugging in indifference, I went back to perusing the shop.

As I fingered the dangling feathers of a turquoise dreamcatcher, the vibration of my mobile tickled the top of my thigh. I drew it out, checked the caller display. *Nathan*. A deep sigh left me. I didn't want to ignore him, but I knew why he'd called and couldn't deal with that kind of conversation in front of a stranger. With a mental apology, I switched the phone off.

The woman reappeared, a box in her arms. She inclined her head toward the counter.

I strolled over, studying the box contents. "You take card payment for these?" I took out Nathan's company card, which had been in my jeans pocket all week.

"Of course." She offered her first smile.

As though on cue, the man produced a pin machine. I handed him the plastic to insert, waited as it went through, and keyed the number in before retrieving the card.

The woman's hand closed over the top of mine as I went to lift the box. When I raised my gaze to hers, she appeared to stare right into me—like a crazy soul searcher judging by her intensity. She stayed like that for twenty some seconds before she released me and took a step back.

I collected the box and went to walk away.

"You should consider the symbol of the vulva if you truly want protection," she said behind me.

I twisted, peering back at her over my shoulder.

"The triangle," she said.

"I already have."

Her hands clasped beneath her bosom. "It isn't merely your males that require protection."

I turned back to fully face her.

"Especially so close to ovulation." She smiled. "You should protect yourself."

My pulse soared. How the hell could she know any of that? How could she know about the triangles?

Or that my ovulation neared, for that matter? I hadn't menstruated once since being bitten.

"You will." She nodded with a serene smile, as though she'd read my thoughts.

Mumbling my thanks, I backed away. At the door, I fumbled at my rear for the handle. As soon as I'd created a wide enough gap, I escaped the penetrating gazes of the odd couple.

Striding toward Beth's apartment building, I took in the blond brick structure before us. Decent security supported the main entrance, courtesy of 'Holloway and Larsen Construction', where Beth tapped in a code before using her key to get us inside.

We took the stairwell situated to the rear of the main lobby. On the third and top floor, we pushed through the fire door onto the landing. According to Beth, each floor looked the same with stone-coloured walls, spotless taupe laminate tiles and four pristine, white front doors.

Beth led me to the second on the left, D3, unlocking and pushing it open to reveal warm, neutral colour schemes and orderly rooms. I wondered how long it'd stay tidy under my control.

"Obviously, this is the lounge." Beth waved her hand around as I followed her in. She pointed ahead. "Through that door is the kitchen—the best room in here. And bedrooms and bathroom." She indicated the last three doors situated within the far wall.

I nodded, as I stood holding my box of delights.

"Come on." Beth crossed the room and opened the kitchen door. "I'll make us a drink."

The oak kitchen looked like a miniature replica of the one at home. I placed my box on the table-for-two and leaned back against the counter, while she filled the kettle.

"What time are you going back?" I asked.

She placed the kettle on its stand and turned to me. "I'm not."

"No, really ..." My brow lifted. "What time are you going back, Beth?"

"You can't honestly expect me to leave you alone."

"That's exactly what you're going to do. If you stay here, after just returning home, Nate will be even madder with me than he already is."

She smiled. "Of course he won't."

"And Ethan? What will he think if I snatch his mother away, when he's only just got you back?"

"A few days—"

I shook my head. "I won't do it to him. I walked out. This is my problem."

"Why do you insist on bloody dealing with everything yourself?"

"It's the only way." I folded my arms. "I'm going to call Jess, find out what I need to do next. That will keep me occupied until she updates me on her meeting in the morning. If I still haven't got any leads, Jess will be here in a couple of days, and I'll take it from there."

"And if I refuse to go?"

I picked up my box. "In that case, I'm out of here." I left the room, got halfway across the lounge.

"Okay, okay," she said. "I'll leave, if that's what you really want."

I peered back.

"But, only on the understanding that you don't go out hunting for them alone. If you get a lead, I want your word you'll call me."

"Why? So you can drag everyone else along with you?"

"If you promise to call if you need support, I'll promise to come alone."

I faced her head-on, studied her eyes. She appeared genuine—and hurt, as though I'd offended her by not letting her stay. "Okay," I said after a minute. "I'll call if I know anything."

She breathed out a sigh and nodded.

As I went back to deposit my gear on the kitchen table again, Beth resumed making the drinks, pouring steaming water into the mugs.

"Is there somewhere round here I can get alcohol?" I asked.

"Do you think that's a good idea?" She placed the mugs on the table, urging me into one of the chairs.

"I don't want to drink it." I picked up my coffee and took a sip. "It's on my list. I need it for ... whatever it is I need it for."

Beth disappeared from the room. Glass clinked from the lounge, before she returned, brandishing a bottle of vodka. Eyebrow lifted, she presented it to me like an award.

I smiled as I took it and placed it beside the other items. "That should work."

Beth took the opposite chair, as I gave my coffee another taste. "If you get cold, the switch for the heating is in that cupboard." She pointed behind her head. "There's some nightwear and bits left behind in the bedroom drawers. If you want to use any, you're more than welcome to. And there are some clothes in the wardrobe ... although I'm not sure how well they'll fit ..."

Wouldn't be that *big on me*. No doubt due to the treadmill in the corner of the lounge, Beth had maintained a pretty good body shape for a woman in her fifties.

"There's a little food in the fridge. Make sure you eat ..."

I gave a half-hearted nod. My nose hovered above the warm steam of my drink.

"Do you have any money?"

My lids dropped.

"Jem?"

I jerked up, trying to refocus on her words.

"You're shattered, aren't you?"

My shoulders heaved out a shrug.

"You should get some rest. I could stay a while—"

"I don't have time to rest. I'll sleep later. After the jobs are done."

Concern filled her eyes. "You're going to crash if you're not careful."

I swiped a hand across my face. "I'm fine."

Beth sighed, giving a slight headshake. "Do you have any money? I can leave you—"

"I have a credit card."

Her hand slipped inside her bag. "I'm going to leave you some cash. That way you can at least get a takeaway."

"No, Beth, I ..."

She opened the kitchen drawer, took notes and coins from her purse, before dropping them in and closing it. "Just in case."

"Thanks."

Beth hovered over me until I'd eaten a bacon sandwich. Only then did she allow me to nudge her out the door with the bottle of mandrake water and instructions.

Within the welcomed silence, I tugged off my trainers and padded into the kitchen, where I placed each item from the box onto the table. A large, white paper bag held a whole load of iron beads, the woman had given me more red thread than I'd asked for, and I discovered gum Arabica came as a ground substance in a storage tub.

As I studied them, I tugged out my phone and called Jess.

"Hello," she answered.

"I've got the stuff."

"Any problems?"

"None. But the woman was weird with a capital *W*." I picked up a bead, rubbed my thumb over it. "So, what do I do now?"

"Mandrake water. Sprinkling that should be your priority."

"I've sent it with Beth."

Silence met me for a second. "Beth?"

"Sean's mum."

More silence, followed by, "I thought she was—"

"She was ... until I called her." I put the bead down as I sat. "It's a long story. The shortened version is that Beth came home because of me. I've walked out because the men are refusing to stay safe while I do what I have to do. And I'm now staying at

Beth's recently vacated apartment which she gave me the keys to."

"Well ... shit!"

"Yeah." I scrubbed at my cheek. "That pretty much sums up how I feel. But there's no time for moping. What do I need to do?"

"Grab a pen and paper and take notes."

In Beth's cupboards, I found what I needed in the form of a pestle and mortar, a jug, a sieve and a sewing kit.

With them all set out beside my ingredients, I prepared to protect the pack.

It took a while to grind down the dragon's blood resin. Once done, I put it into the jug and poured over a healthy dose of Russia's finest, adding in Jess's recommended dose of the gum Arabica. As that needed time to infuse, I turned my hand to a little jewellery making.

Burdock roots resembled fat sticks in their bought form. Sliced, they became nuggets. A stab of a skewer created a central hole and landed them the new title of beads. I pushed the red thread through an iron bead, tied a knot, and threaded it through a burdock root bead before tying another knot. I continued on. Iron, knot, burdock root, knot, iron, repeat. Working through constant stabs to my fingers, I produced a necklace big enough to circle Ethan's wolf-sized neck.

By the time I checked on the ink solution, the hour neared four. No wonder strain had visited my tired eyes. As I crossed the kitchen to flick on the light, pain coursed through my lower abdomen. I gasped, my hands clamped over it. From the initial pain came a dull ache which intensified as though spreading deep within.

I returned to my chair, doubled over at the waist, arms cradling the affected area while my brain ran through possible causes. Stress? Could the bacon have been off? When did I last have a bowel movement?

The sensation seemed alien enough for me to dismiss as I concentrated harder on the twinges inside my stomach. When the slow trickle into my underwear began, I could no longer mistake its source. The words of the goblin-like woman bounced in my head. How the hell could she have known it would happen?

Hands still clutched at my middle, I headed for the bathroom.

A little clothing removal confirmed it. I'd begun menstruating.

"Shit!" Didn't I have enough to worry about?

I had no sanitary protection, no clean underwear—nothing.

I tugged at my hair. "Shit!"

I'd have to borrow something of Beth's. Borrowing a nightgown didn't fall into the same realm as using her knickers, but with little other choice, I sucked it up.

After cleaning myself and redressing, I grabbed some of Beth's change and headed to the store.

It neared six p.m. by the time the apartments came back into sight with my arms laden with pizza and necessary supplies. Eager to dry my soaked-through feet, I picked up my pace. I'd barely taken a few steps when my phone vibrated in my pocket. I snatched it out to see Ethan's name, cut it off and hit the power button before I key-coded my way inside.

Via the stairwell, I ascended with shopping bags in one hand, pizza box balancing atop the other. At the third floor landing, I backed in through the fire door, leaving it to bang shut as I spun away and took a few steps.

I halted the second I spotted Ethan parked on the floor beside the apartment door. "What are you doing here?"

His face held nothing but relief as he climbed to his feet. "I thought you'd run off somewhere when you weren't here." He strode the few metres to me and took my shopping. "You okay?"

"Yes." I squeezed past to the door and unlocked it. As Ethan followed me inside, I took my bags back from him. "Why are you here?"

"I couldn't stand the thought of you sitting alone. Not after last night."

"I'm fine." I used the same response I'd given Beth.

I headed for the kitchen, took out the paper bag from the chemist and my new underwear, and turned to find Ethan in the doorway.

Nose twitching, he snared my arm as I went to walk past. "Why do you smell different?" His eyes darkened, as he inhaled deeper.

I shoved out the room. "Excuse me."

"Jem?" His footsteps followed me to the bathroom, stopping only when I closed the door in his face.

Brilliant.

Another complication I could do without. Hadn't I read somewhere that wolves had issues with menstrual blood? Maybe it only referred to real wolves. I knew the shine in Ethan's eyes hadn't been imagined, though.

Beneath the spray, I scrubbed with toiletries Beth had left behind. Once I'd dried off, I saw to my female needs, redressed, and edged open the door a touch.

"You supposed to smell this strong?" Ethan asked, suggesting he'd figured it out.

I peered away into the bathroom before turning back to him. "If this is going to be a problem for you, maybe you should leave."

He took a step away. "I'm not leaving."

When I ventured out and headed for the kitchen, Ethan followed. Ignoring him, I flicked on the kettle. "Are you staying for a drink?"

"I'm staying, permanent." He folded his arms across his chest, leaned into the doorframe. "I owe it to Sean to make sure you're safe. He's not here to do it himself, so somebody's got to."

Pausing as I reached for mugs, I opened my mouth to protest.

"What the hell do you think Sean would say, if I left you out here without even checking on you?" he continued over me. "He'd kick my arse, if I left you here alone. I know he would. And that's not something he's normally capable of, so he'd have to be mad to accomplish it. You can't be left alone, Jem. That's all there is to it. I don't care if you're unhappy about it. It's what Sean would want."

I stared at him. I would say he'd used Sean to get me to agree, but Ethan only said what he thought. If he said he'd done it for Sean, he had. I resumed the drink making. "Does Nate know you're here?"

"He will, by now. Mum will have told him."

I breathed a heavy sigh. "He'll be madder than ever with me."

"He'll get over it."

I handed him his coffee and leaned against the counter to sample some of my own. "You hungry?" I asked after minutes of quiet.

He shook his head.

"You should eat. You look pale."

"So should you." His head inclined toward the table and the ingredients I'd left strewn across it. "What's all this?"

"The bits I went shopping for this morning. Sit down." My lips twitched. "I made you something."

He cocked an eyebrow as he took one of the chairs at the table.

Standing behind him, I strung the necklace I'd made around his neck and secured it with a reef knot at his nape.

Ethan tugged at his new adornment, peered down at the beads with flared nostrils. "You made me a necklace out of a plant?"

"Humour me." I planted a kiss on his crown then sat opposite him. "I've still got to make some for the others. You any good at threading?"

He chuckled. "You going to make me thread beads?"

"You may as well be useful, if I have to put up with you."

"Okay." He gave a single nod. "Show me what to do."

I set him to work on a necklace for his dad, telling him to knot the thread after every added bead. When I reminded him for the fifth time, he told me to shut up and insisted his intelligence didn't match how dumb he looked.

Zipping it, I checked on the ink solution. After giving it a stir, I poured it through the sieve into a second jug, taking it to the table with me as I went across to sit.

Ethan's gaze lifted a touch. "What's that?"

"Ink I made."

He nodded and continued his task, and I slid a sheet of parchment from the protective sleeve and picked up my quill. Five letters across, five down, Jess had said, until the words formed a square.

"Okay," I murmured and began to write.

Ethan paused in his handy work. His eyes followed the scratch of the quill, to its dip in the ink and back again. Once I'd finished, I studied it.

SATOR
AREPO
TENET
OPERA
ROTAS

The words formed a complete boundary.

"What's that for?" Ethan asked.

"It has to be on display, and Jess said it will prevent evil entities from entering a room." I looked from the Sator Square to him. "So, I'm doing lots ... for all the rooms. Just in case they come back for more of you." My hand fisted around the feathered pen. "I'm not going to let that happen."

We retained eye contact for seconds before Ethan broke it and returned to his beads.

"You can take these for me tomorrow." I slid out a second sheet of parchment. "They need to be somewhere visible."

"You can bring them yourself."

I ignored him, writing again.

"This vodka yours?" His finger pinged against the bottle.

"No, it's your mum's." A sweep of my hand formed an inked 'A'. "Just used it to make my ink."

He scraped back his chair and got to his feet. "You want some?" He started opening cupboards.

"Sure, you can pour me one. Just make it small. I haven't drunk in a long time."

"The joys of a high metabolism, Jem." He turned with a smile, two tumblers in his hands. "Unless overindulgence is truly your goal, we're mostly only capable of getting tipsy."

"Hmm-mm," I uttered, as he poured the drinks.

The clear liquid swirled in the glass, as I took a sip, followed by another, and we both went back to focussing.

Ethan's beading seemed to be taking forever. He'd been at it for almost an hour and had only made one a quarter of the size of his own. Maybe his large hands and thick fingers hindered him. I didn't say anything, though. He seemed to need something to centre on as much as I did.

I picked up my refilled glass, drank some more.

"I was just thinking we could take a drive out to Marianne's house." He didn't meet my gaze as he spoke, "Maybe take a look."

I studied his lowered head, taking a huge gulp of my drink and relishing the burn it paved through my chest.

"We don't even have to get out of the truck. We could just check it out, look for any clues about where they might have moved to." He shrugged. "Might get lucky and find one of them has returned."

He still didn't look up, but he'd tempted me, and he knew it.

It took about thirty seconds to agree.

21

Forty minutes of non-talk later, Ethan pulled up to the kerb beside the terraced property. We stared out the window, necks craned as though something useful would materialise if we searched hard enough.

The engine quieted. "Come on."

I spun to face Ethan. "You said you'd stay in the truck."

"It's okay." He gave a small smile. "You've got my back. I trust you to protect me." His fingers tapped against his beads. "Besides, I have my necklace and my new non-permanent tat, too." He opened his door and slid out.

With a sigh and a rough face rub, I did the same.

Ethan locked the doors before joining me. His arm slid around my back and drew me close. Like a couple out for an evening stroll, he guided me down the road, away from the property.

At the end of the row of houses, Ethan steered us to the left, and we coursed toward the rear of the strip before we headed around the back.

Six-foot high walls defended the entire length of rear yards, with wooden gates set in to mark each individual one. He tried the witches' gate. Locked.

"You first." He took me by my waist and hoisted me onto his shoulder, before I could respond. As his head twisted toward my body, he drew in a deep inhalation.

I pushed his face away and hauled myself over the wall. My feet hit the ground on the other side. Ethan landed beside me a split second later. Side by side, our nostrils flared. From the house before us, to the properties either side, I made a thorough check to ensure nobody observed.

Satisfied, I moved forward at the same time as him, but waited while he looked through the window. He grabbed the door handle, gave a sharp yank and a shoulder shove. The wood splintered.

We didn't pause to check if the electricity worked as we entered. Our enhanced vision took in every single detail as we moved. Kitchen first. A check of the cupboards revealed naught. Dining room, where we'd eaten with them. The lounge. Nothing.

Although we suspected we'd find the same upstairs, we checked, anyway.

The place stood completely empty. Not even a scrap of paper, or button.

We returned to the truck, and my eyes misted. Beside me, Ethan rubbed at his head. I couldn't believe we'd done it to ourselves. I'd known it could accomplish nothing, yet I'd been unable to turn down the chance. Would it always be that way? Catch a glimmer of hope, only to have it obliterated by the truth that I couldn't find him?

"We have to get back," Ethan said.

I almost suggested we get back out, change forms and do a little hunting on four limbs, except if the boys' scents extended farther than the path, Ethan would have already picked up on them. Plus, Nathan would have our hides for risking exposure in a built-up area. Instead, I wiped a hand beneath my snotty nose.

"I'm sorry, Jem. This was a stupid idea."

"No." I sighed against the tremor in my voice. "No, it wasn't."

"Yeah, it was." He started the engine.

The drive home brought no more noise than the earlier one, other than Ethan's hands brushing constantly over his hair, and the small snuffles I failed to contain.

Back in the apartment, I headed straight for the bathroom to freshen up, afterward pulling on a nightshirt of Beth's. When I returned to the kitchen, I figured out the heating system and activated it.

Ethan came through from the lounge and joined me, sans boots and jeans, a bottle in hand. Without asking, he half-filled my empty glass.

The warm, amber liquid scorched as it passed over my throat, and retaking our seats, we resumed our work. Once I'd finished with my written squares, I helped Ethan out and started on a necklace for Connor. I had no idea how long we stayed there, but halfway through my third shot of what Ethan identified as brandy, my eyes refused to focus, or my fingers to work.

"Need to quit," I mumbled.

Without waiting to see if he agreed, I picked up my glass and tottered into the lounge. A teeter left, a saved wobble right, and my body attempted to sit before I'd even reached the sofa. I made it, though—just.

At a murmur from Ethan, I called out a, "Whah?"

He stepped to the doorway, indicated the phone held to his ear and ducked back out of view.

Through my struggle to concentrate, I attempted to listen in. It took seconds to deduce Nathan held the other end of the conversation, as Ethan told him about my bleeding.

"No, Dad," he mumbled. "I can't bring her back tonight. I've had too much alcohol to drive."

He didn't appear drunk to me.

"Yes, I'll try and get her to come back in the morning." His volume rose and fell. "Yes, I'm going to stay with her." He paused. "Please, don't worry."

Quiet followed before Ethan reappeared. He flopped down beside me with the half-empty bottle of brandy.

"He's mad," I murmured.

"No."

My hand refused to hold my glass steady, as Ethan leaned across and topped me up. That should have told me not to have any more, but my brain had shut down to rationality, my limbs had hit the stage of severe incoordination, and a refreshing lightness had taken over my entire soul.

I lifted my replenished glass and sipped some more. "Maybe you should go home."

"Can't." He filled his own glass before planting the bottle by his feet. "I promised Sean."

My head flipped to the side, and I stared at him through half open eyes.

He leaned over and kissed my nose—a tender gesture for such a burly man. "He made me swear, Jem, when he first found you."

My eyelids fluttered as I studied his face.

"He made me swear to protect you, to help him keep you safe. I could see how much you meant to him, so I vowed to do whatever it takes. Sitting here with you, now, is no hardship, if it keeps that promise to my brother."

I snorted out a small laugh. "But it would be a hardship, if you didn't have to?"

He shook his head, smiling. "I adore you. You know that."

Lips curving into a weird slant, I made an inaccurate swat for his arm as I attempted to stand. By the time I'd struggled upright and faced him, though, my mood had altered, my expression twisting to reflect it. "I miss him, Ethan." My voice arrived in a quiet squeak, as I pointed to my chest. "In here."

The floodgates, no longer strong enough to restrain my sorrow, splintered open. Heartache-induced sobs possessed my body. Even when Ethan stood and pulled me into his arms, my shakes showed no signs of slowing. He stroked my hair. His hand swept across my back, but sobbing at that level of commitment took it out of me, until my legs lacked the strength to support the burden of my grief and I sank to the carpet.

My fingers on his arm dragged Ethan with me. "Shh," he whispered. "We'll find him."

Hiccups erupted with each bump of my body.

"We'll get him back." His thumbs brushed beneath my eyes, clearing the pools that spilled over. "We'll get them all back."

As I attempted to regulate my breathing, my shudders showed their first signs of subsiding, yet my tears continued to spill.

Ethan planted his lips against my forehead as he scooped me up, his strength apparent in the ease with which he did it. With his arms holding me tight in his lap, exhaustion won the battle of wills.

The agonizing pounding of my head spread across my temples. The grey daylight of winter filtered through the bedroom window. A quick pat of the half-empty bed confirmed Ethan had already woken, and I pushed into a sitting position, every single muscle in my body beseeching me to stop. Even inhaling hurt like hell, though the strength of his essence in the room, combined with that of coffee, told me he hadn't been up long.

With a groan, I forced myself onto my feet and commanded my quivering legs to follow the rich wafts into the kitchen.

Ethan's gaze lifted to the doorway, when I reached it, his eyes widening. "You look like hell."

"Thanks." I mumbled. "You don't."

He gave a small smile. "You really haven't drunk in a while, have you?"

I shook my head, pressing a hand to it when the motion sparked pain behind my eyes.

"Sit down." He pointed to the empty chair, pushing to his feet. "I'll grab you a coffee."

I obeyed, as he took the couple strides to the kettle, pressing fingers to my temples at the way too loud clink of the teaspoon against ceramic. When he returned, the plonk down of the mug and the squeal of chair feet had me groaning.

After a rough face rub and a sip of my drink that almost unearthed the non-existent contents of my stomach, I picked up my beading and attempted to thread the cord through the hole, refusing to accept it when coordination refused to be my friend.

Of course, Ethan's stare laser-burned right through my brain. "When was the last time you ate?"

"I dunno." I dropped the beadwork and rested my forehead upon my folded arms atop the table. "Yesterday. Your mum made me eat before she left."

"That was lunchtime, Jem. You need to eat."

"Can't," I mumbled. "Need to quit talking 'bout food. Not helping."

The quiet tick of the clock provided a background beat to Ethan's deep breaths. Tyres splashing outside on the road indicated rain had fallen. "Let me take you home," he said after a while.

"Can't," I said. "I walked out—"

"Bullshit. You can't truly believe you're no longer welcome there."

It took great effort to lift my head. "You're safer, if I don't involve you. This is my fault. I'm going to sort it out."

He leaned forward over the table. "How exactly is this your fault?"

"Because none of it would have happened, if I hadn't turned this into something personal between Marianne and me."

"More bullshit!" His fist thumped down on the table-top, and I winced. "You know as well as I do, she'd still have taken Dan and Josh. The only difference is we've now got four brothers to get back, instead of two. "Yes,"—he nodded when I opened my mouth to speak—"the fact she has Sean makes all the difference in the world to *you*, Jem. But ultimately? Things have more or less turned out exactly as she'd intended. Come home," he said, his voice gentler. "We can help. With the things you want to make, if nothing else."

I ran my hand through my matted hair, wiping at my face.

"Please ... I want you to come home. Dad wants you to come home. Mum and Connor are worried sick about you." He leaned farther forward until only a few inches from my face. "I know that's where Sean would want you to be, because it's the safest place for you."

"Nate's mad at me," I said. "He was fuming when I walked out."

"If you walk back in there with me, today, yesterday will be forgotten. He'll just be glad to have you back."

A few moments passed before I said, "Will you do as I ask, if I return?"

"I can only speak for myself. But if it's what I have to do, in order for you to agree, then yes, I'll hand over the reins ...". His head dipped side to side. "Unless I think you're in any kind of danger I can't ignore."

My mind ran through arguments against returning, but Ethan had never lied to me. He'd also made a point I hadn't considered. If I did fall into danger, who else would I choose in Sean's absence to fight in my corner?

"Okay, I'll come. But I won't hesitate to leave again, if you tussle with me over anything."

He breathed out a sigh as he stood, messing my hair with his hand as he bent down and kissed my cheek. "Get dressed. Let's go."

Inside the house was quiet, enough so, I presumed everyone was in bed, until I spotted feet overhanging the end of the sofa through the living room door, and ducking round the panelled wood revealed Connor.

He blinked, and when he beckoned me closer, I padded over to him. Fingers folding around my wrist, he tugged me down on top of him, his bear hug a much warmer welcome than I'd expected.

My cheek squidged into his shoulder as I returned the embrace. "Sorry about my dodgy smell," I murmured at his audible inhalation.

"I can deal," he said. "It's good to see you."

Connor's chest rose and fell against me. His body warmed like an electric blanket. Exhausted still, I stayed there, listening to Ethan's footsteps shuffle around the house.

Outside, the rain gave up, allowing a little winter sunlight to peek through. Signs of life drifted down from upstairs, and Nathan and Beth descended, passing through to the kitchen.

Low conversation carried through, between father and son. Ethan's reassurance that he'd brought me back in one piece, and Nathan's praise of *good job* for getting me to agree—the last sounds I bothered to tune into before I plummeted into sleep.

I'd no idea how many *Z*'s I snatched before the trill of my mobile vibrated against my hip, and I tumbled backward off the sofa in my haste to retrieve it, slammed it against my ear. "Jess?"

"How you doing?"

"Never mind about me. Did you meet with your man today?"

"Yes."

I ran my fingers through beyond-tangled hair. "And?"

"Sounds to me like you're dealing with the biggest bunch of world-dominating wannabes ever."

I got to my feet. "He knew them, then?"

"Yes, he did."

Connor's eyebrows lifted, as he followed my departure from the room.

"What did you find out?" I headed for the kitchen, took a seat at the table. "Did he know where to find them? Are they part of a coven?"

Connor came in behind me and took the seat beside Ethan.

"It's not really something to talk about over the phone, Jem. I'd rather wait and discuss it when I get there. But no, in answer to one of your questions, he couldn't tell me where to find them, because they'd gone underground before he left."

My eyes narrowed. "You really expect me to wait until you get here to talk about this?"

"Yes. I'd prefer to do it face to face."

"So get here already!" I snapped.

She blew out a breath. "Not fair, Jem. You want me to walk out on work? What do you suggest I do with the kids?"

"But ..." I waved my hand as if she could see. "*Two days*. I can't wait that long. I need to do something now."

"Okay, listen to me." Her big-sister tone kicked in. "One—I'm coming earlier. I'll be with you tomorrow."

I winced as I experienced momentary guilt at my demands. "But ... it's Christmas—the kids—"

"They're going to Ray's in the afternoon for a few days." She meant to their father's—Jess's ex. "Secondly, I don't believe we have to worry about everything just yet."

I glared round at my companions as though they held the blame for her attitude. "What are you talking about? The witches have had the boys for over thirty-six hours. Why the hell wouldn't they already be doing whatever they've got planned?"

"Because I don't think they'll do anything until the thirty-first."

The others all stared hard at me. I knew they could hear the conversation. Even Beth leaned in close. I hit loudspeaker to save her the effort, placing the mobile down on the table. "That's New Year's Eve. What's so special about then? And more to the point, why would you come to such a conclusion? Did that man tell you this?"

"Slow down," she said. "No, he didn't tell me. What he knew was just hearsay. The reason I think they'll wait until then is because it's too much of a coincidence to ignore that they've abducted your men so close to the date of the blue moon. If I had something planned and wanted absolute certainty for its success, that's when I'd do it."

My brow creased. "The blue moon?"

"Yes. This is the year of the blue moon, scheduled to appear on the thirty-first, which is next Friday."

My fingers massaged my forehead. "What the hell is a blue moon?"

She sighed. "I thought you remembered your binding ritual?"

"Not all of it." I shrugged. "Just bits."

"Well, your binding ritual was performed on the night of a blue moon because it's believed to heighten magical abilities, and to hold a natural power that can be drawn from, or called upon."

The headache that had dulled with sleep kicked back in. "So, on the thirty-first, the moon will be blue?"

"Of course not." Her tone suggested she considered me a complete moron. "The blue moon is when a full moon is present for the second time in one month. It's rare, compared to the monthly cycle of a normal full moon, and only happens once every two-point-something years."

I brushed a hair away from my face. "So ... what are they doing that they need to enhance?"

A slight hesitation arrived. "Again, it's just hearsay. We'll talk about it when I get there."

"If you know something, I want to hear it now."
Only her breathing travelled the line, and my pulse picked up a notch. "How bad is it—what they're planning?"

She heaved a deep sigh. "I'll tell you tomorrow."

My hand fisted. "No. Now."

"It won't make any difference whether I tell you now, or when I get there. Tomorrow is soon enough."

My fist thumped the table. "I want to know now."

"Well, I'm not bloody telling you over the phone," she snapped. "I've asked you to wait. Now I'm telling you to. You can demand as much as you like, but I will not budge." She paused, maybe to see if I'd retaliate further. "There is something I want to check with you before I come, though, something I want to double-check here—to clarify what I've been told."

"What?" I sounded like a rebuked brat.

"The tea. Not the first one, the second one—you said it was different. Were you certain?"

"Yes, it smelled completely different. It tasted different from how I'd expected the first one to, as well."

"Whoa, back up," Jess said. "You drank the tea?"

My gaze lifted to the others. It dawned on me I hadn't told anybody about my tea sampling. "To begin, it was just a taste out of curiosity, but ..." I met Connor's eye. "I only did it so Josh couldn't drink as much." As he gave a small nod, I looked back down at the phone. "Why, Jess? What was up with that tea?"

"Give me the flavours again. I'll double-check on what I already think, and I'll talk to you about it tomorrow. But, if it's what I believe, it's nothing *you* have to worry about, okay?"

"Sure," I mumbled.

"Now ... the tea?"

"Honey seemed to be the strongest element, but it also had hints of grass and wood, and some spice. If I had to name it, I'd go for cayenne."

Scratching arrived through the phone's speaker as she scribbled them down. "Got it. I'll see you tomorrow, okay?"

"Sure," I said. "But promise you'll call, if you think there's anything I need to know sooner."

"Of course I will."

"What the hell won't she tell me?" I murmured as she hung up.

22

Waiting sucked—especially when I didn't know what I waited for. Once I'd finished making Connor's necklace, and one for Beth, I had nothing left to occupy me. Even pinning up the Sator Squares had done little to alleviate the ever increasing panic over what Jess could know.

Because deep down, I knew it had to be bad.

The clock read four pm, as I paced the kitchen. I mentally calculated the drive to Jess's house, wondering if she'd be angry if I showed up demanding answers on Christmas Eve. How would her kids react to their aunt turning up in no mood for festivities?

I marched through to the others in the living room. "Nate, I need the truck keys."

He cocked his head. "Where are you going?"

"Tomorrow is too long," I said. "I'm going to Jess's to get some answers."

Nathan narrowed his eyes.

"Do you really want to wait until tomorrow night?" I lifted my hands, brought them to rest on my hips. "I can't."

"If that's the soonest she can get here, we don't have much choice."

"We're only waiting because she won't tell me something unless it's in person, and because she can't get here until tomorrow." I moved nearer to him. "There's nothing to stop me from going to her. Then she'll have no choice but to tell me. I can be there by six. The sooner I know what I'm dealing with, the sooner I can plan."

Although Nathan kept quiet about my singular person plan, the glint in his eye told me it hadn't gone unnoticed.

Ethan pushed to his feet. "You can't go alone."

I sent him a scowl, looked back to Nathan. "So, can I borrow your keys?"

"We'll take my truck," Ethan said.

As Nathan turned from me to Ethan, and tension claimed the shoulders of the two men, I realised I had no chance of leaving without a fight—so I went with using Ethan's eagerness to my advantage and nodded his way. "Okay."

Nathan climbed to his feet. "How long to your sister's?"

"One and half hours—two at the most."

"And you'll call as soon as you get there?"

"If that's what you want."

I got the impression he didn't trust me to return. Maybe he thought I planned to find the witches' whereabouts, ditch Ethan, and race off to save the world—which, in actual fact, wasn't a bad idea.

I held Nate's stare, and he eventually nodded.

"Do not let her out of your sight, Ethan." His eyes never left mine. "If she looks like she's going to bolt, drag her back here—kicking and screaming, if you have to. I want you back here tonight. No later than first light. Do you understand?"

Ethan nodded. "Okay. Go."

We made it through Shrewsbury traffic, and at ten-to-six, I knocked on Jess's front door, jigging on the spot while I waited for her to answer. As I sent a backward glance toward Ethan in the truck, where I'd made him wait, the kids shouted to their mum, inside the house, that someone had knocked.

"Coming," Jess said, footsteps descending the stairs.

Following a rattle of keys worthy of a caretaker, Jess emerged around the swinging door. I stared up at my sister, her appearance a contrast to my own—brown hair and small, hazel eyes to my blond and big blues. Even our noses and mouths didn't match, yet strangers always pegged us as sisters, somehow.

She sighed before smiling, giving a slight headshake. "Why aren't I surprised to see you here?"

"Sorry."

As she peered down from the step, her gaze travelling over my face and my body, a frown crossed her features. "You look bloody awful, Jem."

My shoulders lifted in a shrug.

Jess held her arms open. "Come here."

I didn't need to hear the invitation twice. As I stepped up to her, she wrapped her arms around my back, holding me close. We stayed there for seconds before she took me by the shoulders and drew away.

"You're really not holding up very well, are you?"

I went to shrug again, but stopped myself and shook my head.

"You'd better come in."

"I'm not alone."

She scanned the darkness over my shoulder, and the narrowing of her eyes told me when she'd found the hulk in the truck. "Who's with you?"

"Ethan. He's gone all overprotective."

Her head tilted toward where he waited. "Does he know how to behave?"

Jess had never met Sean, or any of his family. In fact, I'd not seen her since being bitten, thanks to a long distance relationship we'd always had going on. I cocked my left eyebrow. "Of course he does, Jess. We're not monsters, you know."

Her lips twitched. "You'd better come in, then."

I twisted and waved at Ethan to join us and turned back to Jess, her attention pinned on the truck as though waiting for the freak show to arrive.

The dropping of her jaw told me the exact moment Ethan came into view. "Holy shit! He's fucking huge."

I almost laughed at Jess's reaction. After spending months with the pack, their sizes had become irrelevant to me.

Ethan joined us, resting his hand on my shoulder. Even positioned a step lower, he towered over my shorter-than-me sister.

Jess's mouth opened and closed as if she had something to say but thought better of it. Instead, she moved back and waved her arm in invitation to enter.

We headed straight for the kitchen. The array of flavours permeating the room identified curry as the contents of a pot atop the stove. Spiced steam brought heat to the room, enhancing that already offered by the radiators, and sweat popped out across my upper lip. As I grabbed the hem of my sweater to tug it over my head, Ethan mirrored me and removed his own.

From head to toe, Jess let her gaze travel over him, lip caught between her teeth.

I'd seen her look at men that way before. Maybe she'd change her mind once he opened his mouth.

She brought her attention back to me. "You want to know?"

"Not want. *Need*," I said.

"Mind waiting until I've fed the kids? I can pack them upstairs then, give us some privacy."

A sideways glance brought Ethan's small nod into view. "Sure."

"You're welcome to join us," Jess said. "I haven't got enough naans for the two of you, but you can share the rice and curry."

"I'm not hungry."

"Me, either," Ethan mumbled.

Jess folded her arms. "When was the last time you ate, Jem? You look like shit."

I shrugged.

"She hasn't eaten since early yesterday," Ethan said.

I sent him a glare.

"And you?" Jess turned on him. "Have you eaten today?"

"I had lunch," he said.

242

"That was six hours ago," I snapped.

"You're in no position to lecture me, Jem. I've eaten a damn sight more than you over the last couple of days."

"Okay, quit!" Jess held up her hand. "Sit down. Both of you."

Glowers passed between Ethan and me, as we took seats at opposite sides of the table. Jess withdrew plates from the cupboard, a serving spoon from a drawer. We stayed silent as she dished up the meal and carried ours over to us.

"Thanks," we said in unison.

Jess crossed back for the others. "Gus! Jake! Dinner!"

Feet pounded the stairs, and laughter preceded their barged entrance. "Auntie Jem!" Jake said. "Are you here for Christmas? Is this your new boyfriend?"

"That's a fine welcome," I said to him. "Are you too big to kiss your aunt now?"

He smiled and offered his cheek.

As I kissed him, I drew him in for a hug, peering round at Gus—always shyer than his older brother. I crooked my finger at him. He took a step forward, and a poke of my fingers to his ribcage produced a giggle. "Now, that's more like it," I said with a smile.

Jake climbed from my hold, turning to Ethan. "Are you her new boyfriend? Are you staying, too?"

Ethan chuckled. "No, her boyfriend's my brother."

"And I don't think I'll still be here in the morning," I said.

Jake's face screwed up a little, but Ethan still held his attention—Gus's, too, as he observed from beneath his brother's arm. "What's your name?"

"Ethan."

"You're big, Ethan."

Ethan smiled down at him. "I get told that a lot."

***

With the kids lured upstairs by a bowl of popcorn and a DVD, I turned on Jess. "Okay, what's going on? What wouldn't you tell me over the phone?"

She took the chair between Ethan and me, but twisted toward me. "The man I met with this morning? He used to be in the same coven as this Marianne." She took a deep breath. "As soon as I told him she was a twin and her sister's name was Amber, he had no doubts who I was talking about. Apparently, there were a few of them in the coven who wanted to ... try something different."

I frowned. "Something different? What does that mean?"

"The few witches had concerns about the ... purity of the magic they produced. They were convinced the dilution in the witches' bloodline was to blame—"

"Dilution?"

She nodded. "There aren't that many male witches left. For years now, witches have been breeding with 'normal' humans." She did quotation marks with her fingers. "Some witches worry the dilution in the blood, because there're very few purebloods left, is affecting their powers. Most simply accept it." She shrugged. "What can be done about it, anyway? It's just how things are. But some friend of Marianne's—Stephanie, I think he said her name was— has spent the last year, or so, coming up with ideas on how to boost the abilities of their offspring—"

I blinked. "Sorry—who?"

"I'm sure he said her name was Stephanie."

I glanced at Ethan, back to Jess. "That can't be right. I've met this Stephanie. She was shy and timid and—"

"He seemed to *know* she was the instigator, Jem."

"But, she—"

"She played you." Jess held my eye.

I blew out a breath, as my frustration threatened to kick in, and turned back to Ethan. He raised his palms as if to say 'How the hell do you expect me to know anything involving women?'. "Okay," I said to Jess, "what else?"

244

"My contact heard, before he left, that a handful of witches—Marianne and Amber included—decided to follow this Stephanie in her ideas. Apparently, the coven leader found out they were practising outside the accepted boundaries, but when questioned, they talked their way out of it. When they got out of control, and the coven stepped in to put their foot down, the group left. Nobody knows where they went. Rumours have it that one of them inherited a property somewhere, but nobody knows for sure."

"But ... what has this got to do with Josh and Danny?"

She peered off toward the blackness beyond the window. "The witches wanted to find another supernatural race. They looked at all kinds. Sorcerers. Vampires. Half-demons. And ..."

"And werewolves," Ethan finished for her.

My pulsed picked up when she nodded. "What for?"

She turned back to us. "Some witches consider themselves superior to everyone else. These witches were convinced, if they could find another supernatural race they deemed worthy, they could produce a master race. A stronger race, with physical powers, as well as mental—"

"*What?*" Ethan and I gasped out our response together, sending each other a glare, before I stared back at Jess. "They've taken the boys for breeding—that's what you're saying, isn't it?"

Jess nodded.

"Are you sure?" I had to check. "How can you be so certain?"

"I wasn't ... until I made the connection with their latest homebrew. I thought, at first, it sounded like the flavours to boost fertility ..."

Bile lodged in my throat. I couldn't breathe properly.

"That might explain the menstruating," Ethan said.

"You've come on?" Jess asked.

I nodded. "Last night."

Her brows lifted. "And you drank the tea, when?"

My brow creased. "Monday."

"All this is doing is solidifying my theory," she muttered.

"Okay, back up." I glanced between Ethan and Jess. "If this is truly their goal, how the hell do they plan on getting the boys to ... impregnate them? And what if it doesn't work?"

"Everything has been building up to this—the binding and summoning to get them to comply when the time's right, the fertility tea to ensure they're capable. And by waiting for the night of the blue moon, the magic of the binding, the fertility potions, the mating ritual itself—they'll all be enhanced. Powerful. They can't possibly fail."

My teeth ground within my tightened jaw, as the bubble of panic began expanding within my chest. "Are you telling me Sean has been taken by a bunch of power hungry bitches who plan to trick the boys into thinking they want sex with them just so they can get pregnant with their fucking babies?"

"Pretty much. Yes."

"Over my dead body!"

I flew to my feet with fisted hands, and Jess scrambled away. Her unbalanced chair toppled with a crash as she backed into the corner.

My glower followed her, my chest heaved. Even when Ethan stepped between us, my eyes refused to focus elsewhere.

He took my fists, but I snatched them away, sidestepping to get to Jess, to demand she tell me she'd made a mistake. To shake some bloody sense into her ridiculous shoulders, despite the conviction never once leaving her eyes.

Ethan's hands grabbed my face. A small jerk brought my attention onto him. "You need to calm down."

"How can I?" I gasped out the breath I'd held. "It's nothing short of fucking rape."

"We'll find them before then," Jess said.

"How?" My bottom lip quivered. "We have no idea where they are."

"I'll help you." Jess came around Ethan's shoulder. As his hands released me, hers took their place. "Trust me. I know what I'm doing. I promise you, we'll find them."

"Promise is a major word, Jess."

"Yes, I know."

23

The others were still up when Ethan and I returned home around midnight. When we told them of the witches' power trip, Connor and Nathan had exploded.

By two a.m., after the others had dispersed into the living room, I paced the kitchen—just as I had at one. Neither my body nor my mind would relax.

How could they, knowing what the witches were going to do to Sean—*my* Sean?

My hands curled into fists, uncurled, curled again.

How bloody dare they? What right did they have to take the boys to feed their over-inflated egos?

It was all well and good for Jess to say we had a week to find them. I couldn't wait a week. I'd go crazy—as if I hadn't already since speaking with Jess.

Ethan's bulk filled the doorway to the unlit kitchen.

I didn't even falter in my pacing, had pumped myself up too much to stop. My feet hopped with each stride, my fists jerking up and down at my waist.

"You should go to bed," Ethan said.

I ignored him. I couldn't go to bed. Not in our room. Not without Sean.

"How much longer do you think you can keep this up before you drop?" he asked.

On my pivot, I aimed hooded eyes his way, paced again.

"You're exhausting me, and I'm only watching you."

I gave a low growl. "So, go away, then." My steps picked up speed. A manic pattern affected my movements.

His footsteps approached my rear, and I spun, shooting away from him, low threats mumbling past my lips— mostly what Marianne and Stephanie had coming to them. In fact, they all had it coming—every last one of them. I wheeled to retrace.

Ethan blocked my path. He reached for my arms.

I lifted my fists, shoved past him and kept going.

"Jem, stop," he said.

I turned, took a stride.

He stopped me again.

My lips vibrated with a snarl. "Move."

"No." He grasped my shoulders.

I struggled against him, tried to break away, but he held me fast. Even twisting my arms and angling my body away from him didn't free me from his grasp.

He brought his lips down to my ear. "You should go to bed."

"No." I yanked against him.

"You need to rest."

"No!"

"Do you want to be sedated, Jem? Because if you keep this up, that's what Dad's going to do to you."

Whipping round, I sought Ethan's eyes.

"You need to rest. Please go to bed."

"I can't," I whispered. "I can't go in there. It feels wrong."

His dark eyes seemed intense, but he nodded and took my hand. "Come on." As he went to walk away, I tugged back. His tightened grip dragged me along as he glanced over his shoulder.

With little choice, I followed.

We passed the living room, turning for the stairs. "We're going to bed," he called through the open door.

He didn't stop at Sean's and my door, as I expected him to, but continued on to his own. Ethan pushed the door wide and nudged me inside. "Sleep in here. Just until he's home."

I crossed the carpet to the generous window and drank in the whitened treetops of the forest. Across the lawn, tufts of green protruded through the remaining snow. Ethan's room had an amazing view—just the sight of it sapped some of the tension from my shoulders.

I sent Ethan a small smile, helping myself to a blanket discarded across his chair. Wrapped within it, I climbed onto the window ledge and hugged my knees, watching the branches wave their greeting in the night breeze.

"Okay, now?" he asked.

I tore myself away long enough to nod at him, and catching him backing out of the doorway, I shot from my position. "Where are you going? Don't leave ... me."

His brows lifted, but he stepped back in. After ridding himself of his jeans, he climbed beneath the duvet, where he propped his back against the headboard and slid the cover to his waist. Lips twitching, he leaned across and patted the mattress beside him. "You'll sleep better lying down."

I sent the forest a last look of yearning and padded across to the bed. Matching Ethan, I fussed until my pillows would support me against the headboard, leaning back to half sit beside him.

"So ... what have you got Sean for Christmas?" Ethan asked.

His question threw me for a moment, before I answered, "Photographs, mostly."

"Photographs?" The bed dipped a little as he shifted onto his side.

"Yes." I rested my cheek against my hand. "I had some developed that Poppy took of us at Ben's birthday. And I talked your dad into letting me have some of your mum. Only, I didn't know, at that time, she'd asked to come home. I've put them in an album for him."

He smiled. "He'll like that."

"But now he's got the real thing to look at. I doubt your mum will leave now she's back, do you?"

"I hope not."

"What do you think he'll say when he finds out she's here?" It seemed to help—talking as though Sean would definitely be back.

"He'll be ecstatic, Jem. You know how he feels about her. The gifts you've chosen tell me that."

"Do you think he'll be disappointed with me for calling her?"

Ethan's shoulders shrugged against his pillow. "I'm not. Why should Sean?"

"Because I saw the look on Connor's face when he saw Beth. He wasn't—"

"It's harder for them, Jem. You have to remember that Nadine's never returning. No doubt, Connor's lot will find it hard to adjust to Mum being here because theirs can't be."

"I didn't really stop to consider everyone's feelings when I called her. I just did what seemed right."

"It'll be okay. Don't worry. By the time Mum's finished mothering everyone, they'll be glad she's here."

"I hope so."

"Trust me." He smiled. "Now, do you think you can sleep without me having to imbibe you with alcohol?"

"I'll try." I slid my hand out, linked my fingers with his, finding the contact comforting. "Thanks, Ethan."

He shuffled down the bed a little. "What for?"

"For being here." I closed my eyes.

As I pleaded with my brain to shut down, I allowed myself the pleasure of imagining the pack racing through the forest, with the fresh scent of fear enticing us in the hunt. Behind my lids, a creature darted ahead. Catching the movement, I adjusted my route to follow, pushed forth to catch up. My head hovered above, and my jaws opened wide—until an odd lightness overcame my body and the fox expanded his lead.

With an intensity beyond my command, my body floated upward, higher.

On a mid-air twist, I caught sight of myself below, Ethan beside me with his moist eyes wide and staring into the dimness of his room.

251

I tried to raise my hand, to show him my position, but nothing happened. My entire body appeared to hold no substance.

"Weird. What's going on?" I muttered.

Ethan didn't even react to the sound of my voice.

Hovering there, I detected a tug to my body, almost as though summoned, and of its own volition, my form moved across the bedroom, right for the wall.

Realising I wouldn't stop in time, I raised my hands to protect my face, and my eyes closed against impact.

When I reopened them, the wall had gone. I'd reached outside.

How, I didn't know.

A glance behind showed the house had become distant, and I drifted away as though carried upon the strength of the wind. Had I gone through the brickwork?

"Not possible," I whispered.

I entered the forest with ease. A harsh breeze caressed the high branches surrounding me, below me, inside me— yet no chill from the air encompassed me, as it should have. It seemed odd to hold awareness of the nocturnal sounds within my woody retreat, but not to actually be there—to experience them, yet not, all at the same time.

Deep calm claimed my mind, though I didn't know my destination. Once again, my subconscious had proved its dominance. It didn't surprise me; it had done it before— just never like that.

My speed increased again, until I soared up through the highest of branches before swooping back down. As I spun, swirled and whirled, I let out a giggle.

I slowed as I entered a garden. The second I recognised it as Connor's, I sensed I had a purpose for being there, and I willed myself closer.

As had happened at home, the solidity of the walls absorbed me, and I sifted through them, blinking at the simplicity with which I arrived on the other side.

It took mere seconds to catch the voices upstairs and understand I had company.

My body levitated upward in the direction of the sounds, higher, through the ceiling until I found myself in Kyle's empty bedroom.

Head tilted, I located the direction of the intruders' voices.

"Why, again, are we here?"

Amber?

"Because Marianne has been watching the other house, and not once has it been empty. This is her only chance of getting something of Jem's."

Heather arrived with Amber on the landing at the same time as I did. I darted right, into Connor's room, and pressed back against the wall. It took mental effort not to fall straight through.

Tracing their footsteps to Josh's room, I came out of my hiding place to float nearer.

"Anything?"

My hands clenched at Marianne's high tone.

"Nothing. You?"

"No," Marianne said. "Not one strand of hair. That's all I need to hurt the bitch."

"I don't think there's even any brushes in the house," Heather said. "I haven't seen any at all."

"What about clothing? Did you check the laundry basket?"

"Yep. There's only men's clothing in there."

They fell quiet for a few seconds, and I inched closer.

"But she wears the guys stuff, doesn't she?" Marianne said. "I'm sure what she wore that day we came here didn't belong to her. It was far too big. Go check the laundry again."

Footsteps came my way. I tried to step back but couldn't before Amber emerged. Though I braced for discovery as she turned the corner, her flesh swept right through me.

Amber disappeared downstairs without even a hint of acknowledgement on her face.

Adjusting my position, I brought Heather and Marianne into my line of sight.

"What if we can't find anything?" Heather asked.

"I *want* something of hers!"

My lips drew back, and a low growl formed within my chest.

"Isn't it enough that you'll soon be walking around with her boyfriend's baby inside you?"

My growl built into a rippling snarl as my insubstantial fists curled my nails into my palms.

"No, Heather. By the time I've finished with them, Sean won't even know who she is anymore. I'll be pregnant with the child that should have been hers. And I plan to ensure the stupid dog is totally incapacitated while I gleefully rub it in her face. She'll regret ever messing ..."

I lunged, teeth bared, fingers clawed, lips vibrating against the roar raging from inside me ... and flew straight through her.

Once airborne, I couldn't stop, passing the witches, the brickwork and before I knew it, I'd left the house.

I whirled, went to throw myself back in there, but like a powerful force had snuck through from behind and latched onto my navel, I lurched backward.

My body doubled with the strength of the attack. My arms and legs flung forward with the propulsion.

The reverse action through the forest offered me nothing but a rapid blur. Nausea swept through me. Dizziness invaded my brain. Minus the soaring and swooping, the trees dashed past, my vision struggling to keep up.

I sped backward over the garden, past the haze of bricks and cement. As I jolted into my supine form on the bed, I jerked upright with a gasp.

Ethan jumped up beside me. "Jem?"

I flicked his hands off as he reached for my shoulders, and bounded from the bed.

"Shit!"

Vision unfocused, I missed the door, rebounding from the wall beside it. Grunting, I landed with a heady thud on the carpet. Ethan made a dash to block my exit.

"Jem, what's going on? What's wrong?"

I clambered up and ran at him, trying to throw him from my path. "Move! You're wasting time." As he made a grab for me, I twisted away. "She's there. Marianne's there."

"What are you talking about? Where?"

"At Connor's." Another rhino worthy collision failed to shift him. "Marianne's at Connor's. Now!"

"No." He held his palms out in front of him. "It was just a dream."

I shook my head so hard, my hair whipped my face.

"Yes." He nodded. "A dream."

It hadn't been—I knew it hadn't.

Footsteps neared the door from the landing, and panic kicked in as I realised I'd never get past them all.

"What's going on?" Nathan called.

If Nathan came in, he'd stop me for sure. I had to get out. Had to check.

As Ethan tugged down on the door handle, I backed away.

Nathan pushed through. "What's going on?"

I took more steps back until my rear hit the window ledge. Behind Nathan, Beth approached. As another set of footsteps announced the arrival of Connor, I eased up onto the sill, worked open the window.

"Jem dreamed Marianne was at Connor's," Ethan said.

My feet shuffled back until my heels met with nothingness.

"Is this true, Jem?" As soon as Nathan looked my way, his eyes widened, his hands lifted. "Jem, *no!*"

I dropped.

24

My soles thumped onto the paving. Pain splintered through my shins.

I gasped, stumbling backward, as footsteps scrambled across the bedroom above me. A kick of my feet forced me upright, and I took off.

"Jem!"

At Ethan's shout, I ran faster. Snow sprayed up, flecked my ankles, its crisp iciness numbing my soles.

"Jem, wait!"

A thud hit the ground at my rear. I didn't have to look to know it would be Ethan. Just as I knew changing would be my only chance if I wanted to outrun him.

I grabbed at the hem of my T-shirt, yanked it over my head. The fabric sailed to the ground as I ducked beneath the arches.

"*Jem!*" The power behind Nathan's roar faltered my step.

I skidded and spun round.

He hung from the window, finger pointed at me. "Don't you dar—"

I slammed my hands over my ears, turned my back on Ethan closing the gap, and bolted.

As I broke through into the forest, I tore at my underwear and brought forth my change.

My feet pummelled solid dirt.

Jolts tore through my already unhappy shins with each step.

I harvested the ripples, the tingling. Invited the deformation.

The solid *whump, whump, whump* of my heart pumping the blood through my arteries matched the pattern of Ethan's feet growing closer.

Spurred on by the thought of grabbing Marianne, I kept going.

Ethan's steps vibrated the earth beneath me. The tips of his fingers brushed my elbow.

I snatched away, ducking aside.

Another reach of his hand, another dart of my body, and a stab of agony tore through me.

My shoulder dipped beneath the weight of the affliction.

Ethan crashed into my rear.

I landed hard. My chin smacked soil. My arms flailed.

The brunt of Ethan's body forced a grunt from me. As I rolled to my back, I aimed a punch for his jaw.

He barely flinched.

I brought up my legs, already altering in structure, and kicked at his stomach, his groin, his knees.

"Jem, stop!"

A snarl ripped from me.

"Stop!"

"She's there, Ethan! Let me go!"

He held my face, staring into my eyes. As if he somehow recognised my sincerity, he nodded and shoved my shoulders into the ground. "Stay here." He leaped to his feet and took off.

He'd picked up speed and disappeared before my outrage kicked in.

How could he dismiss my plea to stay safe?

As I ploughed through more of my change, agony consumed me. In my desperation to catch him, I gave no consideration to myself, in the speed with which I forced it to come—grunts, cries, growls and snarls blowing from my throat.

I pushed through as wolf and raced away.

An inhalation detected Ethan's scent. Panting, I begged my legs to work harder, and tracked his path.

Over halfway through the forest, I had him in my sights. He could run fast for a big man—especially as he only had two feet to my four.

He whirled round like he'd heard me, hands up. "Do not—"

My paws skidded against the ground. I veered off to the left.

He pounced, smacking into my side. His arms circled my chest before his shoulder sandwiched me against the ground.

I snarled. A snap of my jaws aimed to get hold of his pinning arms, as a shimmy of my body wriggled me back.

His hold tightened. "Jem, stop!"

I couldn't. Marianne could have been getting away. I kicked up with my legs, catching his thigh.

With a growled gasp, he clambered farther over me, smothering me under more of his weight. His eyes stared down into mine. "Don't make me do this to you."

Past the point of listening, I snapped for his shoulder.

He whipped his head away, deep resignation filling his eyes. Sorrow took his features for a brief instant before a loud roar ripped from him, and mouth wide, he swung his head down until his teeth locked onto my throat.

Even his human jaws held incredible strength. I wriggled but couldn't move. My inhalations arrived in short rapid spurts.

Each intake sucked Ethan's scent deep into my olfactory, so I knew when he began changing, as his wolf put in an appearance. If he completed his transition, I wouldn't stand a chance.

I whimpered in my defeated state, trapped beneath his altering shape—until images of Marianne brought a new surge of determination, and my body bucked, legs kicked, and the clash of my teeth missed his ears by only a hairsbreadth.

A low growl vibrated in my throat, but as Ethan's jaws tightened and cut off my actions and vocals, I ceased to fight. The heave of my chest met and left his—the only part of me that continued to move.

He released my gullet and stared down into my eyes. Sending me a snort, he stepped off.

Flicking over onto my paws, I advertised my wounded pride in the form of a growl. My feet kicked into the dirt for traction, my legs braced for a leap. I sprang, but got no more than a metre, before teeth clamped my hind leg and hauled me backward.

My yelp seemed to falter his attack, and he loosened his hold. His breaths travelled the length of my hind leg, hitting my rear.

I froze.

His muzzle made contact, pushing into me.

I spun to face him, sent him a snarled warning.

He didn't back off. His eyes glistened and nostrils flared as he studied me.

At a second warning, he ruffled the thick fur of my collar and licked my face.

With one final huffed snort, he raced off in the direction of Connor's house, leaving me to follow.

We changed back when we reached Connor's, and Ethan jogged into the lead before creeping along the garden close to the wall.

I tugged on his arm. "Let me go in front."

He pointed at his necklace and his still-sported triangle on his stomach. "Who do you think is better protected here?"

With no decent argument, I gave in, and we arrived at the back door in a crouch.

Ethan raised his head high enough to peer through the glass panel. "Empty," he whispered.

"Try the handle."

As he pushed upright, he waved me out of the way and positioned himself at the side of the door. He pressed down on the handle, frowning when the door nudged open. Nose pointed toward the created gap, he inhaled. When he withdrew, he beckoned to me. "If they're not here now, they definitely have been," he whispered.

"Are we going in?"

He nodded.

With Ethan in front, I tiptoed through the house, senses of hearing and smell on alert. Unable to see past him, I lifted his arm and, gripping his waist, watched from beneath there.

We reached the bottom of the stairs. Ethan inclined his head as though listening above, before we ducked into the living room. Still in our two-man train, I searched the shadows, scanning every corner of the room.

A noise from the staircase took our attention. Ethan's deep inhalations arrived loud, battling with my own. He spun at the same time as me, but, closer than him, I reached the door first and swung it wide.

I halted. Ethan rammed into my back.

Heather froze, too, as her foot hit the bottom step.

The other two witches descended, their eyes widening as they followed.

The whole episode appeared to take seconds, yet as I evaluated the situation and went to respond, so did they.

Three arms swept out from the women in a wide arc.

"Jem, look out!" Ethan's hands grabbed my hips.

He shoved me sideways—out of the path of fluids streaming from the witches' hands in our direction.

Unable to do anything else, I lifted my arms, closed my eyes mid-flight, and hit the deck beneath a shower of liquid.

I opened my eyes. Darkness filled every inch of the hallway. It took a few moments to understand I was in Connor's house and not at home.

At a curse to my right, I turned.

Ethan's naked body crouched beside me, his head bowed, hands fisted into his eye sockets.

"Ethan? Are you all right?"

"My eyes." He gave a low groan. "They aimed it straight for my bloody eyes."

"Um ... who did what?"

"They went out the front. I can't see a bloody thing. What the hell did they throw at us?"

"Who?"

"The witches."

"What are you going on about? There's nobody here besides us." I peered around, listening for sounds of other life. "Where is everybody?"

"Look out the door, Jem." He rubbed at his eyes some more. "See if they've already gone."

My brow lifted. "Who?"

"For God's sake, Jem. The bloody witches."

"Ooo-kay." My mouth carefully formed the word, and, humouring him, I reached for the front door. "Funny." My lips pursed. "It's open." I gave a shrug, pulled it inward and stuck my head outside. The driveway stood empty. "See? Like I said, no one's here. Where are the others, Ethan?"

"What the hell is wrong with you?"

I scowled over my shoulder. "There's no need for arsiness. I was only doing what you asked."

"Get me to the bathroom. I need to rinse my eyes. They're stinging like crazy."

Sighing, I turned to take his elbow. "Come on, then. This way." Taking a step up, I dragged Ethan behind me. When he tripped on the bottom one, I snorted out a laugh. "Mind the step."

"That's the whole point of you leading me, Jem," he said. "You're supposed to guide me."

"Tetcheee," I sang.

"Maybe you should just stay quiet, if you haven't got anything sensible to say."

I clicked my tongue, pulling a face I knew he couldn't see. "Last step," I said before continuing down the

261

landing. In the bathroom, I tugged Ethan over until he stood in front of the sink and turned on the taps.

Bending low over the bowl, Ethan cupped his hands, drawing up water and splashing it over his eyes.

Watching him, hearing on alert for the others, I swiped at dampness tickling along my inner thigh. When I wiped at it for the third time, I brought my fingers to my face, found them covered in red. I sniffed them. "Did I cut myself? I'm bleeding."

Ethan straightened, gazing at me from bloodshot eyes. "Jem, you didn't cut yourself. You're menstruating."

"I'm ... what?" Eyes wide, I glanced down at myself. "Shit!"

Ethan's hands brushed over his hair and a slow breath pushed past his lips. "What did they do to you?"

I looked back at him. "Who?"

The lines deepened across his brow.

"What time is it?" I asked.

Frustration pumped from him as he shrugged. "How would I know? Must be about five, I guess."

"So, where is everybody?" Something seemed really off, but I couldn't put my finger on it. "Where's Sean? Shouldn't he be here?"

Ethan took my face and stared hard into me.

"Your eyes look really sore," I said.

"They are. Find some clothes, Jem. I'm taking you home."

His tone of voice, and the way he studied me, instilled me with unease. "Aren't we running? We usually run home on Sundays."

"No, we'll take the Porsche."

I snorted a laugh at him. "Does Sean know you're taking his car?"

He nodded, but his eyes appeared distant. "He said it's okay."

I smiled. "Is he already there? They'll all be moaning if they're waiting for us to eat."

262

"Sure, Jem," he murmured. "Get dressed."

Padded up and clothed, I opened Josh's bedroom door to find a dressed Ethan leaning against the doorframe.

"Ready?" he asked.

"Yep."

"Good. Let's go." As he took my arm, he angled his body in front of mine, leading me down the stairs. He halted at the bottom. "Wait here."

"Sure, Ug."

He shook his head, as he trailed off down the hall to the kitchen. When he returned, he held the Porsche keys. Ethan stepped to the front door, stuck his head out before he drew his body back in and faced me. "Stay behind me this time."

I scowled. "Why?"

"Please." He sighed. "Just do it, okay?"

He didn't seem his usual self. His vigilant scour of the driveway on our walk to the Porsche bothered me, too.

He pulled open the passenger door and shoved me inside.

"Hey," I said, pushing him off.

He shut the door and relocked it, before jogging to the driver's side. His door opened, and Ethan slid in, one swift movement of his hand bringing the engine to a purr.

The second we hit the road, he drove like a lunatic. His body seemed to hum with anxiety.

I peered at him out the corner of my eye. "What's up with you today?"

He shot me a glance, setting his sights back on the road. Shoulders tight and hunched, he didn't even sit back in his chair—not an easy feat for so big a man in a relatively small space. "Nothing's wrong," he mumbled. "Everything's just fine."

"You don't sound fine."

"I'm peachy. Quit worrying."

The span of headlights illuminated the grey road surface before us. The forest blurred to my left as we whizzed past.

"I'm starving." I ran my hands across my stomach. "Did your dad say what we're having today?"

Ethan gave what sounded close to a groan, rubbing at his hair until thick strands stuck up in disarray.

I stared at him. "It's not a difficult question. What's for dinner?"

His sigh arrived loud. "I don't know."

I returned to watching the muted scenery. Grittiness invaded my eyes as I strained to see more. "I hate these dark evenings, don't you? Unless it's the full moon. Then I don't mind so much. But I miss not being able to sit out in the garden until late, and having barbecues. It's just been too cold this last week to sit out. Even the conservatory is getting cold. Your dad should get a radiator fitted out there ..."

Ethan made no comment to my pointless mumblings. Facing forward, shoulders bunched, his hands gripped the wheel as though his life depended on it. He only shifted position to rub at his hair, or eyes. By the time he pulled up on the driveway at home, he looked a wreck with his wild mop.

I climbed from the car. "Fancy a ball game?"

Staring over the roof of the car, he heaved out yet another sigh and shook his head.

The front door opened. We both turned, as Nathan approached with harried strides.

"I know, I know ..." I lifted my palms. "We're late. But ... I ... um ... why are we late, Ethan?"

Nathan halted. He turned from me to Ethan.

My gaze flicked beyond him, toward Connor emerging, his pace almost as fast as Nathan's.

When a chestnut-haired woman appeared on the top step, I stepped closer to Nathan and whispered, "Who's the female?"

Nathan stared at me like he thought I'd lost the plot, before glancing over his shoulder. He swung back to me. "Beth," he muttered, looking from me to Ethan.

My eyebrows shot up. "Beth?" My head tilted to the side and I took her measure, trying to figure out when she'd shown back up and why the heck nobody had told me.

"Something happened to her," Ethan said.

"Is she staying?" I asked Nathan. "Did you invite her for dinner?"

Nathan's focus remained on Ethan. "Were they there?"

I followed his gaze to catch Ethan's nod. "They attacked us with some kind of liquid," he said. "She's been like this since."

"Just ignore him," I whispered to Nathan. "He's been acting weird since he hurt his eyes."

I strolled around Nathan and his look of confusion, past Connor's of bewilderment, and up the steps to Sean's mother. "Seeing as the men are too rude to introduce me, I'll do it myself." I held out my hand. "It's nice to meet you, Beth. I'm Jem."

She frowned. I thought for a moment she'd ignore my greeting, until a hesitant hand folded around my outstretched fingers. "It's ... nice to meet you, too, Jem."

I smiled and nodded. "So, what time's dinner ready, then?" I called as I entered the house.

For the sixth time in thirty minutes, I tried ringing Sean's phone. "Voicemail—*again*."

After all the lectures I'd endured from him, about my mobile being switched on so he could call if he got the urge, Sean had the nerve to turn his off.

"Where did he say he was going, Nate?"

Nathan sighed, his expression indecipherable. "Maybe his battery's flat."

My eyebrow lifted. He knew as well as I did we always ensured our batteries didn't run low.

Connor walked over. "Here, Jem, drink this." He placed a steaming mug of milky hot chocolate beneath my nose.

"Thanks." I peered up at him. "Did Josh and the others go with Sean? Maybe you could call them to find out where they are?"

His broad finger nudged the drink closer to me. "We'll try as soon as you've drank that."

I turned toward where Ethan sat beside me, twiddling a pen between his fingers. "Did Sean tell you where he was going?" I asked.

"No." He paused in his pen acrobatics and leaned toward me.

"Don't get that on me." The thought of scribbling down phone numbers on the back of my hand made me shudder. "You know I hate pen marks."

His eyes lifted to mine. "What?" He smirked. "Like this?" His pen-wielding hand shot forward and marked the flesh of my shoulder.

I jerked away, grabbing his wrist as he attempted to bring it closer. "Stop it. I don't want bloody pen on me."

He switched hands and drew another line across my exposed skin.

Temper bubbling, I shoved at his hand. "Stop!"

Another rapid move from him scraped me. I raised and twisted my shoulder to find a third line connecting the first two into an ugly triangle. I darted my hand out, yanking the pen from his fingers. "What is wrong with you? I told you I don't like it." A flick of my wrist flung the pen into the corner of the kitchen, and I stood and stomped from the room.

In the bathroom, I flicked the tap on full, grabbed the soap and scrubbed at the pen marks. "Bloody marring my skin." I rubbed my hand up and down, over and over the same spot. "Probably gave me ink poisoning, or something."

My flesh turned red before all traces had been eradicated. I double-checked in the mirror, gave a nod of satisfaction and trudged back downstairs.

The three men and Nathan's wife hadn't moved. I sent Ethan a glare as I snatched up my drink and marched back out.

In the living room, the sofa cushions sank beneath my weight, and I curled up with my legs tucked beneath my rear.

Sipping at the chocolaty sweetness, I fussed over Sean's absence in my head. He'd never gone out before without telling me, never been unreachable. The fact that nobody else seemed to know where he'd gone—or the other three—only made matters worse.

I downed the rest of my drink, headed back to the kitchen. "You don't think something's happened to them, do you?" I swilled out the dregs that dwindled in the bottom of the cup. "This isn't like Sean. We're never this late eating on a Sunday."

"He could have gone shopping," Ethan said.

He received my best scowl, but my eyes grew weighted with the effort. I rubbed at them. "Well, I can't wait any longer." I ran my hands across my face. "I'm bloody starving. Does anybody want some toast?"

They all shook their heads, mumbling a unified, "No."

"Suit yourselves."

I popped four slices of bread into the toaster. While I waited for it to brown, my fingers drummed out my hungry impatience on the countertop. I paused to give another rub at my eyes. An massive yawn built in the back of my throat, bursting out until my mouth gaped like a cavern, and my body juddered in its aftermath.

"Tired, Jem?" asked Connor.

I turned to him, tilting my head when I found him right beside me. My eyes rapid-blinked, yet my vision refused to focus on his face. Another ground-shuddering yawn erupted. I went to lean back against the cupboard but

267

almost fell. Thinking it to be nearer, I turned to glance behind, losing my view of the room as everything blurred.

My body dipped to the side, incoordination stumbling me forward. "I don't feel too good."

"Sorry," Connor said as strong hands grasped my waist. "We had no choice."

25

A loud snore penetrated my thoughts with startling proportions. My eyes opened to slits in search of the source. As my breaths rippled across my lips like deep growls, I realised it had been me.

Even the jumpstart from deep slumber couldn't prepare my eyes to fully open. I closed them again. The light pierced like pins, anyway. Or, that could have been the drumbeat happening inside my head. Whichever held the blame, I couldn't have been any groggier if I'd been on a drink-binging hen weekend—as if I'd overdosed on sleep at the same time as not having had enough.

Voices carried to me from somewhere in the house. Drifting amidst a state of semi-consciousness, I attempted to listen in.

"I don't know what it was," came Ethan's voice. "I just know I got a much bigger hit of it than Jem, but wasn't affected like her. I can only presume it had something to do with these beads, and the thing she drew on me, but I don't know."

"Thing? What thing?"

My brain perked up as it recognised the second voice. It sounded like ... *No, it can't be, Jess.*

"Some triangle she insisted on drawing on us," Ethan said.

"Show me."

Hmmm. It did sound like Jess.

"The vulva," the Jess-alike said. "I didn't tell her to do that—which is pretty annoying because it should have been the first thing I thought of. Who told her to do this?"

"She said it just popped into her head."

"I guess there must be more witch in her than she realises ..."

Witch?

"But if she has this, she shouldn't have been affected by the attack."

Attack?

"She hadn't. She hadn't got anything," Ethan said. "She's been so obsessed with protecting us, she didn't stop to consider she may need protecting herself."

"Silly girl. Has she got one on her now?"

"Yeah. But I had to wait until she was sedated to do it. I tried to draw one on her with pen, but she freaked and washed it off—"

The Jess-alike snorted. "That's because people writing on themselves drives her insane."

Ethan chuckled. "Well, she can wash all she likes now. I used permanent marker."

The conversation had turned weird on a grand scale. Why would Ethan and Jess be chatting about stuff that made no sense? Or, speaking as though familiar when they'd never met? I swiped at my face, considered if I could still be asleep, stuck within the oddest of dreams.

"Good thinking, smart guy," she said. "So, explain to me how she's been."

"Like she hasn't a clue what's happened this week. And she has her days and times all mixed up."

"Did you get a good sniff at the stuff? How did it smell?"

"Pungent," Ethan said. "But with a definite hint of black pepper—maybe sulphur. I think it was the pepper that stung my eyes."

"Well, shit!" The Jess clone gave a small laugh. "These witches are pretty smart."

Witches? At the second mention of the reference, my mind sharpened a little.

"So, you know what it—"

"Confusion oil. That's why she doesn't know what time or day it is. Why she doesn't remember some stuff. They've mixed her head up."

What? Who?

"Can you fix her?" Ethan asked.

"Of course I can."

The power of intrigue overtook my sleep-infested head. Swinging myself up, I blinked like crazy to keep my eyes open, the living room swimming into focus. I climbed to unsteady legs, swaying once, before I got my act together and headed out there.

"I have my kit ..."

I followed the voices to the kitchen.

"... I'll make her an infusion sac she can bathe ..."

The voice trailed off, as I stepped into the room.

At the far side of the table, Jess's shoulder brushed against Ethan's, and her body leaned toward Nathan and Connor.

"Jem." She smiled. "I thought you were never going to wake up."

My gaze flitted from the men to Nathan's wife, back to Ethan and Jess. "I, um ... what are you doing here, Jess?" I scratched my head when it came out ruder than intended.

"I thought I'd visit."

"You should have called."

Her chin lifted a little as she kept her gaze on mine. "I didn't think you'd mind."

"I ... don't. I ... it's good to see you." I turned to Nathan. "Is Sean back?"

His head shook. "Not yet."

From the corner of my eye, I caught a shrug pass between Ethan and my sister. They looked far too cosy for people who'd only just met. My eyes narrowed as I studied them closer. "Do you two know each other?"

Jess sent Ethan a sideways glance before smiling at me. "Not yet."

I breathed out a laugh at the cock of her eyebrow, the sultry tone of her voice. Jess had flirted with many a man. She'd always been too good at it, and her steady gaze and the flick of her lashes told me she found Sean's brother more than attractive.

Hmmm, I thought. *This could be an interesting visit.*

"I don't want to take a bath right now," I said, as Jess tugged me up the stairs.

"Please, Jem. I made you a special scent." She sashayed backward across the landing, her hand wrapped around mine with the strength of a surgical clamp. Reaching the door, she waltzed me into the bathroom.

The water already gushed from the tap, a not altogether unpleasant steam rising to the ceiling, and I couldn't help but smile. Jess had always been enthusiastic about knowing if people liked the gifts she made for them.

"Okay, okay." I gave a sigh—an attempt to hide my amusement. "I'll take the bath, if you'll stop nagging, but I'm taking it alone. I don't need an audience."

"I don't want to watch you. What do you take me for?" She snorted. "I'm just going to give your back a little rinse over, help drive off some of that tension you have working into knots. Then I'll leave you to it."

"Can I, at least, have some privacy to undress?"

"It's not like I haven't seen it before. Just strip off, for goodness sake."

I stared at her. Her enthusiasm peaked a little high— even for Jess.

She laughed and turned away. "Okay, I won't watch. Now, undress already."

"Take a bath, Jem. Let me wash you, Jem." My grumbles murmured past my lips, my head wobbling with each one. "Get undressed, Jem ..." I tugged off Josh's clothing and tossed it to the floor.

A dip of my hand confirmed the water was hot enough, and I turned off the tap and climbed in. The liquid soothed as it flowed over my flesh, the flavours comforting like an old memory stirred of times gone past. I slid low beneath the water—only my mouth and nose exposed.

"Are you in?" Jess asked.

I peered toward her distorted voice. "Yes."

"Good. Let's start with your hair."

"Hang on a minute." I sat up, sloshing water against the rim. "I thought you were just going to clean my back."

She aimed a thick glob of unfamiliar shampoo onto her hand. "Humour me."

Before I could protest further, she slapped the cool liquid onto my head and began to massage in shampoo redolent of basil, frankincense and rose petals, all rolled into one.

I allowed my lids to droop, as Jess's fingertips worked wonders, scratching small circles into my scalp and easing the headache I hadn't managed to shift since waking.

"So, Ethan?" she asked, and my lips curved. "Is he single?"

I breathed out a small laugh. "Yes."

"Interesting. Why is that, do you think? A hot guy with the body of Adonis—it's got to make you wonder."

I almost groaned out my pleasure, as her fingers worked deeper. "It's probably because he's stuck in the dark ages with his attitude."

"A caveman?"

"Pretty much." Another small groan crept out.

"Okay, rinse."

I ducked beneath the surface. Jess reached in, smoothing the soap from my hair. When she tapped my shoulder, I pushed back up, blowing water from my face.

"Well ..." She smiled, wiggling her eyebrows. "He can drag me off to his cave anytime."

I snorted out a laugh. "You're incorrigible, Jess. You get the female equivalent of a hard-on every time you see a hunky guy. God help you when the others get ... here ..." My brow creased, yet I couldn't figure out why.

Jess peered at me. "I can't wait. Now, sit forward, while I wash your back."

My body rocked, as she swept the sponge either side of my spine, across my shoulder blades. The bathroom filled with more of my groans and Jess's laughed reactions.

Once she'd finished, she stood and dried her hands. "You should have a soak. I'll come get you when you've been in here long enough. Okay?" She stared down at me with her 'don't bloody argue with me' face, and I nodded.

Alone, I re-submerged myself into the water. A huge intake of breath allowed me to remain there for minutes, fingers and toes pointing in my floated state of total relaxation.

Within seconds, images began springing into my mind.

Me, on a frantic race through the forest—I knew, without having to be told, I searched for Sean.

Ploughing through the snow.

Being picked up by Beth.

Beth? How had she come to be there?

You called her, Jem.

Words formed arguments. Faces—none of them happy. My self-banishment from the pack. Staying at a strange apartment.

They all flitted within my brain.

Fighting with Ethan. Getting *drunk* with Ethan.

The thoughts initially made no sense, until they rearranged themselves into some semblance of order that unfolded into a bigger scene.

Everything that'd happened over the past week flooded back to me—right up until the last act before my memory became a blur.

I recalled seeing the witches at Connor's in a dream. Racing over there. Ethan's pursuit. I knew the witches had still been there despite my fears we may have missed them.

Then what?

My lids twitched, eyes flicking from side to side behind their shields.

I leapt from the water with a gasp, clambered over the rim of the tub. Feet slipping, I grabbed at a towel with one hand, as the other hauled the door open. "Ethan!" I wrapped my body as I raced the length of the landing. "Ethan!"

He reached the bottom step, as I teetered on the top. A V formed in the centre of his forehead when his face tilted up. "Jem?"

"Did we get them?" I asked.

He rubbed at his hair.

I blew out a breath and waved my hand in impatience. "The witches? Did we get them? Did we get there in time?"

His entire frame slouched. "Get dressed, Jem. Then I'll explain."

"Okay, I'm calm now," I said, feeding them an absolute crock.

When Ethan updated me on how close we'd been to the witches, and their outsmarting of us, one of the dining chairs had been sent skidding across tiles until a collision with the fridge brought it to an ear-clattering standstill, and a small crater had been created in the wood of the door to the hallway by my fist.

Connor still rubbed at his jaw, where my elbow had connected when he restrained me until Beth took over.

Beth held me tight, her hands rubbing at my shoulders, an attempt to relax muscles that refused to concede. "It's not your fault," she told me.

I didn't believe her.

"The witches had obviously come prepared for such an eventuality."

Yep. I gave her that one.

My wild, gesticulating arms and uncontrollable shakes dimmed to tremors, and Beth pulled back. Her eyes showed nothing but consternation, whereas mine struggled to hold still. My feet had trouble with the concept of staying in one spot, too.

"Jem, look at me," she said.

I did—for about a second, before my eyes darted away again. I'd never been so furious, never experienced such wrath, never wanted to hurt anybody as much as I wanted to those witches. I didn't get that way, not over people.

I could barely deal with such fierce emotions.

"Look at me." Her husky tones took on sternness, and I forced my gaze round to her, willing it to remain steady.

I'd already fathomed Connor had slipped something in my drink that morning, just as I knew they wouldn't hesitate to do it again. No way would I provoke that.

Once I'd held her stare for seconds, she gave a small smile.

"You knew they were there, didn't you?" Nathan asked.

Not quite ready for civilised speech, I nodded.

"How?"

"I dreamed it." It must have sounded ridiculous to them. It seemed farfetched to me.

"How?" Nathan repeated. "What exactly did you dream?"

I sent Ethan a brief glance, as Beth's fingers rubbed across my shoulder, and looked back to Nathan. "I dreamed I went to Connor's, and they were there."

"You just drove over there, and when you found them in the house, you woke up convinced it had been real?"

I shook my head. "I didn't drive over there."

"You ran?" Connor asked. "Did you change?"

I gave another headshake.

Everyone stared at me until Jess broke into the quiet. "My guess?"

They all turned to her.

"She flew." Jess faced me. "How long have you been astral projecting?"

All heads shot back toward me.

I squinted one eye. Hadn't Sean said something about it once, when we first met and I'd mentioned to him about the way I dreamed? I lifted my hands. "I don't know what that is."

"It's ..." Nathan turned from me to Jess. "Isn't it like an outer body thing? Like you're a shadow, or presence experiencing ... stuff ... without having to use your body to get there?"

Jess smiled, probably at Nathan's disjointed description. "Something like that. But, because you're not restricted by limitations put upon us by our bodies, you can do things you'd normally consider impossible." She stared at me. "Like flying."

"Like drifting through solid surfaces?" I asked. "I didn't use any doors in my dream. Just imagined myself on the other side, pictured where I wanted to be, and managed to get there."

All attention returned to me, their stares intensifying.

"I should have guessed, really," Jess said.

My curled hands untightened a little. "Guessed what?"

"That you could do it." Jess shrugged. "What, with your dream history."

"Because I'm weird," I mumbled.

"Not weird." She smiled. "Just ... different."

My lips twitched. After years of being called weird, odd, 'not like other people', her 'different' made a refreshing change.

"Anyway," Jess said, "what did you see the witches doing in your dream?"

I thought back. "They were looking for something—of mine. Marianne wanted it really bad. A strand of hair, or something. They even checked the laundry basket." I looked to Nathan. "And in not so many words, they confirmed Jess's beliefs. She's right about their plans for the boys."

"What exactly did they say, Jem?" he asked.

My fingers tightened around Beth's, and she squeezed my upper arm. "I don't want to repeat it. You'll just have to accept my word."

The room fell quiet for minutes, before Nathan nodded.

"If they were looking for something of yours, I'd guess it's with the intention of hurting you," Jess said. "In which case, you're lucky Ethan marked you with the triangle."

I stared from her to Ethan. "You drew on me?"

He gave a slow nod. "When you were asleep."

"You know I hate pen marks." I tugged my T-shirt up to reveal my flesh beneath. "I didn't see anything when I bathed ... otherwise I'd have washed the bloody thing off."

"You're lucky he did it," Jess said again. "If he hadn't, and this Marianne left with something of yours, you'd possibly be in quite a lot of pain right now. Was there anything of yours there?"

I shook my head while still searching for the branding. "It's irrelevant. She figured out I don't always wear my own stuff there— knew to check the men's clothing."

"They've managed to pick up a lot about you in a short space of time. She must have watched you like a hawk."

I still couldn't find the triangle. "Where did you put it, Ethan?"

"You won't get it off—it's in permanent marker. And you don't need to worry. I put it somewhere it can't bother you." He chuckled. "Unless you have a habit of checking out your own rear in the mirror."

I glared at him. "You drew on my arse?"

His shoulders jigged with his continued chuckle.

"Okay, back on track," Jess said. "Based on what I now know, I think we may have a way to find them."

The huge crater where my heart normally resided decreased in size alongside the surge of hope at her words.

"I'll rephrase." Jess glanced around at each of us, until she settled back on me. "Jem will be able to find them."

My shoulders sagged at the deflating news. "How? Ethan and I tried to look, but we got nowhere. We haven't even got a clue where to start—"

"I'm not talking about physically searching," she said. "I'm talking about mental searching."

My eyebrow rose, as I realised her insanity outweighed what I'd given her credit for. "Mental searching?"

She nodded. "I looked up spells for how to find things. It seemed the most practical under the circumstances. In theory, it's used for missing objects, and I've never personally attempted it. But, with Jem's mental strength and her connection to those she wants to find, I think she could try it on people ... and maybe even pull it off."

"What will it entail?" Nathan's tone suggested he took her seriously.

"Well, as it's a dream locator spell, Jem will have to sleep for it to work. And," she added, peering round at the three men, "not a drug or alcohol induced sleep. It has to be natural."

"But I might not sleep for hours now," I said.

"When you're ready will do," she said. "You can always busy yourselves in between—"

"In between?"

"There's no guarantee you'll succeed on your first attempt. So, you can go out, do a visual search in between to help tire you for the mental searches."

"What will you do to me to help me sleep search?" I'd already had enough witch magic for one year.

"Nothing drastic." She smiled. "I'll just make up a small parcel of heliotrope blossoms and bay laurel leaves, and you'll have to make sure you don't fall asleep without it tucked beneath your pillow. All you then have to do is try your hardest to recall any occurrences in your dreams, or anything unusual—anything that stands out. You must remember."

"You really think this will work?" Ethan didn't look as sceptical as I expected. Maybe he'd seen enough over the past weeks to develop his belief in the powers of magic.

"I think it's your best shot," Jess said, "because nobody but that group of witches knows where they are. If you can't find them by usual means, I think you have no choice but to look using alternative ways. You're fortunate

Jem is so susceptible to psychic connection, because she may be the best hope you have."

26

Jess surprised me with the contents of her large, wheeled suitcase, as I watched her make up my dream aid. Filled with an assortment of herbs, stones, resins, plants, amongst unexplainable items, its size outshone her clothes holdall by miles. I'd no idea before then just how much Jess studied the art of witchcraft, had always imagined it to be more of a hobby.

"Done," she said, waving the small bundle.

To wear me out, we headed off to hunt for the boys. When I suggested splitting into three groups of two to cover more ground, Connor's and Nathan's responses suggested they both considered me something of a loose cannon—which meant Ethan got to leave in his truck, with Jess and Beth as his eyes, while I ended up squashed between a couple of bears.

We all had our mobiles, with strict instructions to stay in touch at all times. Mine had only been switched on for twenty minutes, when it buzzed and Poppy's name glowed from the screen.

I almost didn't answer it—could barely deal with the issues right in front of me, let alone Poppy's probing mind—but I did, and it took Poppy all of two minutes to kick aside her greeting of 'Merry Christmas' and deduce all was not right.

Ignoring Nathan's headshake, I took a deep breath and explained that Sean had gone missing, along with some of his pack brothers, that Marianne had conducted it, that Jess had come to help, but left out all the extraneous information she didn't need to know, or would worry her more than she already did.

Obviously, she did worry. She offered to drop everything and race over, until I convinced her that home with her family was where Sean would want her to be on Christmas day, and she'd eventually conceded.

Though, after Poppy hung up, my hand remained by my ear for a few beats, as I hung onto the normalcy the outset of the call offered to my unstable day.

As one day merged into the next, my patience wore thin. We hunted by road, we hunted on foot, and I hunted in my sleep. Every avenue had been a dead end, a cul-de-sac of hope—or hopelessness. Each time we hunted on foot or by car, we returned home despondent—not just me but all of us. Each time I hunted within my mind, I dozed off determined to succeed but awoke with an aura of pessimism—each time more than the last.

As a precaution, Nathan had locked every window in the house—apparently to prevent me leaping up out of slumber and taking off again—as well as ensuring the doors were secured, and he held the keys himself whenever we holed in for the night.

By three days after Poppy's call, we'd searched as big an area as anybody could. We only returned to the house each day to eat, or for me to try and dream. Each time, after collapsing in a fit of exhaustion, I'd concentrated hard on Sean, Josh, Daniel and Kyle. Within sleep, my mind searched for the last item to consume my thoughts before my brain switched off to the living world. To simplify, Jess insisted I only concentrate on one of them at a time—which made the whole exercise take a lot longer than I anticipated.

Each passing day increased my desperation. I woke on Tuesday afternoon, after a catnap rich with memories of Sean, with frantic frustration in every cell in my body.

Feet plodding, I carried my disheartened soul into the kitchen.

"Anything?" asked Jess.

I shook my head, my mouth down-curved too far in misery to speak.

She studied me. "Jem, what's wrong?"

The others all turned to me, too.

"Jem? What is it?"

My bottom lip quivered, as I looked round at them all. "What if I'm having trouble connecting to any of them because ..." I couldn't finish the sentence.

Jess seemed to understand my implication. "You know that's not true."

"But, what if—"

"If that were true—"

"It could be. We can't keep denying it as a possibility—"

"Will you listen to me for one second," Jess snapped.

I shut up, but my mouth still refused to alter the line of its curve.

"One." Jess lifted her index finger. "You have been connecting, because you said you were certain you felt a pull last night ..."

I had—a distant connection when I'd focused on each of them. Just as I'd thought 'this is it', it broke—like a door slamming in my face. "But, then I lost it."

"That doesn't mean they're all on the other side of the veil ..."

I flinched.

"It probably means there's a barrier of some sort blocking you—most probably a magical barrier. You can break through if you concentrate and hold onto it, I'm sure you can." I opened my mouth, but she held up another finger. "Two, there is no way on this earth that Sean could be dead, and you not know it."

The words 'Sean' and 'dead' uttered in the same sentence worked at the raw wound in my chest cavity like a pair of forceps, stretching it beyond capacity.

"Use your head," she said in a softer tone. "'These two hearts beat as one. One cannot exist without the other.' They're the words of your binding. If Sean were dead? You'd be dying already."

What could I say to that?

Inside, I already felt dead.

I knocked before entering—though why, when at the door to my room, I didn't know.

Jess sat on 'our' bed, her suitcase open and items sprawled across the duvet in front of her. She smiled as her eyes connected with mine. "Can't sleep?"

I shook my head, nudging a velvet drawstring bag aside to make room to sit.

"You should try camomile tea. It'd relax you."

I poked at the bag I'd moved, creating small clacking noises. Loosening the neck revealed a handful of stones, and I dug in and pulled out a rugged amethyst. "I've always liked these."

"Me, too," she said.

The icy air of the room seemed to have vanished since my last venture in there almost a week before. Perhaps Jess's claim to the space made the difference.

"What are we going to do, Jess, if we don't find them?"

"I've actually just been trying to figure out if there's a way to protect the men from a distance. Of course, it would be a lot simpler if we had a photograph of this Marianne, but ..."

"What would that achieve?"

"If we had a picture of her, I could show you how to do a binding ritual."

I shook my head. "There's been enough binding. That's what started—"

"Not that kind of binding." She rested her hand against my knee. "It's a binding ritual to prevent her doing harm. Any impure intent in her plans, and she won't succeed.

Then there's the double plus." She smiled. "If you do the ritual, it'd protect you at the same time. Anything malicious she throws your way would only be reflected back at her."

"What does that mean?"

She smiled. "Whatever she tries to afflict you with will rebound and hit her instead."

I gave a small laugh.

"But, without a picture ..." Jess shrugged.

My shoulders sagged again like somebody had stuck a pin in to deflate them.

"It's going to be difficult, anyway, to figure out what to do for the best." She gave another shrug. "We have no idea of the exact magic they've used. It's always hard to counteract a spell without all the details."

"Are you saying, even if we find them, we may not be able to break the spells put on them?"

Lips compressed, she nodded. "It's a possibility."

My fingers fiddled around in the purse, clinking the small crystals against each other. The different textures rolled off my skin—rough, smooth, polished.

"I don't suppose there's a chance of Josh having had a picture of her?"

I lifted my gaze to hers. Did I think Marianne could have given a photo of herself to Josh? Her vanity would certainly make her believe he'd want one. She may even have done something to it, to strengthen her connection to him.

Without a word, I climbed off the bed and headed for Connor's temporary sleeping spot in the lilac bedroom opposite.

I found him sitting on the edge of the bed, elbows on knees, head in hands. He looked up at my cough and made a failed attempt to smile. "Hey."

"Hey." I settled beside him. "Jess had an idea that could protect the boys, if we don't get to them in time ..."

He twisted to face me.

"But it can't work without a picture of Marianne."

He averted his eyes.

"Do you know if she gave Josh a picture of herself, Connor?"

He rubbed at his tired-looking head as he nodded. "Yes, she did."

My jaw tightened despite the little ray of sunshine the admittance brought. "Where is it?"

His gaze avoided mine again. "He thought you'd be upset if you saw it, so he kept it beneath his mattress."

I gave a small smile and padded back to tell Jess we'd struck gold, before I knocked at Nathan's door.

Feet shuffled across carpet from beyond the wood, and Nathan opened the door.

"Nate, can I have the truck keys?"

His brow furrowed. "Do you have a lead, Jem?"

I shook my head. "No, but Jess believes she knows a way to protect the boys, and I need to fetch a picture of Marianne from Connor's. He said Josh has one, and Jess can't do anything without it."

Ethan's door opened behind me. "You're not going."

"But ..." I turned, lifting my hands. "I have to."

He stepped out onto the landing. "I'll go."

I shook my head. "You can't go alone. What if they've returned? Or, you get there and they take you? They could. Look how easily they attacked the two of us last time. You can't—"

"I could go with him," Jess said.

I stared down the landing toward where she'd come out and joined Connor.

"Tomorrow will be soon enough," Nathan said before I could speak. "It'll be morning in a few hours, and Ethan and Jess can go, with Connor as backup. In the meantime, Jem, you should be sleeping."

***

Thankfully, hunting with the entire pack and falling asleep as a group had accustomed me to sleeping observed. Under the watchful eye of Connor, I brought forth not images of Sean, or any of the other boys, but of exactly what I'd like to do to Marianne when I caught up with her.

I didn't acknowledge the switch off of my brain until my conscious thoughts of her made way for unconscious ones. As the familiar setting of home faded out, an unfamiliar one took its place. A large house—indicated as such by the flight of stairs leading up and another leading down.

On the far end of the landing from me stood Marianne.

My eyes narrowed, as she turned a key in a lock, one from an entire bunch which clanked with the movement. She tugged the handle, seemed satisfied when the door remained shut, spun and walked away.

Teeth bared, I emitted the low growl I had brewing.

She took the stairs that led down.

I pursued, but almost lost my levitated balance when images flashed inside my mind and obscured the clarity with which I saw my prey.

A black and white rectangle flickered on and off like a strobe light running on empty. I tried to focus on the plaque, on the black lettering it held.

The image vanished, exposing Marianne at the bottom of the stairs taking a right turn.

I copied her route and U-turned away from what I presumed to be the front door. Like an invisible sleuth, I shadowed her around a house I didn't recognise.

Travelling the length of the hallway, we passed two doors on the left, toward a third door set in the rear wall while I floated behind Marianne.

She opened the door. Bright illumination bled around the gap. Voices carried through from the other side. Marianne disappeared, closing the barrier behind her.

I shut my eyes against the oddity of travelling through solid surfaces and sifted to the other side—into a kitchen.

The room sported no modernisation, as one might've expected from a group of young girls. Only old, varnished surfaces faced me on three sides, and from a huge floor-to-ceiling pantry in one corner. The white fridge stood out as conspicuously as a mod at a rockers party.

"How are they?" As Stephanie entered through an open door from outside, my lip curled.

Marianne gave a small laugh. "Dead to the world."

"I can't understand the problem with the other one," Stephanie said.

"Me neither. We treated him exactly the same as the others, gave him the same dosage. There's no way he should have woken."

Little!

I flinched at the mind invasion, blinking to remain focused on the two women. I couldn't be disrupted, not when certain the witches were about to say something of importance.

"I dread to think what could have happened if Zoë hadn't spotted his altered position."

Marianne nodded. "We were lucky. Just a few minutes later getting him downstairs, and ..." She frowned. "You saw how he was when he woke. I'm starting to think we should leave the others under to perform the ceremony."

Stephanie's lips pursed at Marianne's suggestion. "I'm not decided yet. I must admit, I thought they'd be more domesticated than—"

Hampton!

In my mind, another word blasted out their conversation. I brushed at my dream head as though swatting a fly, tuning back into the witches' conversation.

". . .you fed him yet?"

"I'll do it now." Marianne crossed the kitchen and reached into a cupboard for a bowl. It hit the counter with a metallic bang, when she dropped it down before stepping across to the pantry.

As she returned to the bowl with a tin, I willed myself to move closer. I needed to pay attention. Every detail could be important, even if I couldn't recall why.

Little!

I kept Marianne in my sights as she opened the tin and tipped the contents into a bowl. A smirk visited her lips when she shook the last dregs from the bottom of the can.

I read the label. Meatballs in tomato sauce. *Disgusting.* My nose wrinkled as if I could smell the artificial spice and flavours of the meal.

In anticipation of her next move, I drifted to the microwave, glaring as I waited for her to come to me. My fists tightened the longer I looked at her. A low rumbling within my chest held the potential to become an impressive snarl.

My non-existent eyebrows shot up, when Marianne bypassed the microwave and approached a heavyset oak door.

As soon as she produced her jailer's keys, I suspected she didn't plan on feeding a pet. Bowl in one hand and keys in the other, a kick of her foot opened the door. The thickness of the wood showed on its inward swing. Beyond, a set of stone stairs headed down below the house.

Hampton!

I blinked the word away to watch Marianne tug on a string hanging from the ceiling. With a quiet click, an overhead bulb submerged her in light.

I went to move forward, but halted as low, resonated groans and gasps bounced up to us. I'd heard those sounds before—a lot. I didn't need to go closer to know they were the sounds of pain created by a change.

Marianne hit the halfway step, continued down.

Although incapable of finding scents, I inhaled.

"God, that's repulsive." Despite her words, Marianne's tone held only amusement.

My eyes widened when I hit the underground room. A silent gasp left my lips. If not seeing it with my own eyes, I'd never have believed it.

The cellar held even bigger dimensions than the one at home, but half of the space had been sectioned off—with thick bars, spaced four inches apart, stretched from one wall to the other, from floor to ceiling.

They've bloody made a cage.

Pots and pots of green, spiky leaves and unusual lemon flowers lined the front and back of the bars. Their presence seemed incongruous compared to the stark walls and concrete floor, the miniscule window that permitted a view of nothing but darkness, and the gasps that flew freely from the huddled heap almost cowering behind the metal rods.

"Here you go, dog!" Marianne put the bowl of cold meatballs on the floor, kicked it toward the cage. "Dinner." Splatters of sauce marked the vessel's path.

The form lifted his chocolate brown head. Dark eyes, full of odium, glowered at Marianne.

Sean!

Pain seared my chest as I took in his pulsating muscles, the shaggy coat that hadn't quite retracted into his pores. My stomach knotted at the weight he'd lost.

"Go ... to ... hell, Marianne," he mumbled through gritted teeth.

She stood watching him, a smile playing on her lips.

Sean's face distorted. His shoulders braced. A fresh gasp broke free as the contortion spread lower.

"*No!*" I flew forward, reaching for him.

His head whipped up. His glazed stare searched the room. For a single second, our gazes connected as though he'd heard me.

"Jem?" His brow creased despite the attacking contortion.

"*Sean.*" His name breathed from me on a sob, even as an invisible force tugged on my soul.

"Stay away." The words arrived as a desperate plea, before control slipped from him, and barely supported by limbs already weak, his body plunged into deformation.

Yanked from my subconscious, the final sight I took back with me was the terror in his eyes—the last sounds, the wild growls and snarls of his suffering.

The violence of my awakening hurled my body from the sofa and landed me on all fours. My chest heaved as tension bunched my muscles into rigid balls. Long, low growls vacated my vocal chords, and tingling buzzed through me like a high voltage battery.

Connor rolled off the other sofa, crouched before me. "Jem?"

My spurts of breath came too fast.

"Nathan!" he boomed toward the stairs, his hands taking my face as he turned back, his eyes drawing me in.

I fixed on his kind and worried expression, saw from the corner of my eye when Nathan darted into the room, closely followed by the others.

Nathan dropped to his knees beside Connor. "What happened?"

"It was her dream, I think," Connor said. "She was snarling before she'd even surfaced."

"Jem?"

My gaze flitted to Nathan, back to Connor.

"Look at me." Connor shifted aside to allow him to move in, and Nathan took my face as Connor had. "Breathe. Long, deep breaths ..."

His words brought awareness of my near hyperventilation. I listened to his coaxing, let his quiet murmurs guide my breaths to a safer speed. As my heart rate slowed, I realised moisture coated my cheeks from tears I couldn't recall shedding.

"What did you see?" Nathan asked.

"Sean." My voice sounded like a whimper. "They're hurting him, Nate."

His stare intensified. "Did you see him?"

291

I nodded, lifting a shaking hand to wipe the liquid before it could mar my vision further. "They've done something to him. He ... he can't control his changes. He looks ... his body ... it's wrong. Something's wrong with the changes."

"This is good," Jess said to my right.

I whirled on her, teeth exposed. "How the hell can this be good? What is *wrong* with you?"

Her palms came up. "No, no, I don't mean what you saw is good. I meant you've obviously broken through whatever barrier was blocking your connection. That's good—your progress is good." Her hands remained raised until I settled back onto my knees. "So ... how did you do it? Did you do something different this time?"

I looked from her to Nathan. "I wasn't concentrating on the boys. Before I fell asleep, it was Marianne I was thinking about."

"So, it was Marianne you connected with?" he asked.

"Initially." I nodded. "She was upstairs in a house."

"Where?"

"I ... don't know." I groaned in frustration at my lack of information, rubbing at my face, still damp from tears. "I only saw the inside of the house. Marianne was locking a door upstairs, and then she went down—to the kitchen."

Ethan moved from the doorway to sit on my vacated sofa. "You saw all of this, Jem?"

I nodded at him. "Stephanie was in the kitchen." I looked back to Nathan. "I think they've put the boys to sleep."

"What kind of sleep?" Jess asked.

I brushed my hands over my head as I recalled their conversation. "When Stephanie asked Marianne how the boys were, Marianne told her they were dead to the world."

Jess gave a slow nod as though I'd confirmed something for her. "They've put them in a death sleep."

I stared at her, as did Nathan beside me.

Her eyebrow lifted. "Like sleeping beauty?"

My brow creased. "That's a fairy tale, Jess."

"Yes, but like all good myths, there's also some truth to those stories, too." She waved her hand. "Forget it. What else did they say?"

"They spoke about one of them—Sean—about how they couldn't understand why he'd woken. They said they only just got him downstairs in time."

"Downstairs?" Nathan asked.

"In the cellar. Caged. Like a bloody animal." Sprayed spit punctuated each syllable.

"What else did you see?" Jess tapped her fingers against her chin.

I shrugged.

"You said he couldn't control himself—his changes?" she said.

Jaw tight, I nodded.

"So, did you see anything else in the cellar? Any ..." She waved a hand. "Any plants, for instance?"

My head tilted at the reminder of the flowers that had seemed so out of place in the chamber. "Yes."

"Describe them." She knelt down to my level. "What did they look like?"

I blinked for a second. "Green, spiky leaves, yellow flowers."

"Wolfsbane," said Jess and Nathan together.

I turned to Nathan. "What's that?"

"It's ... poisonous to werewolves."

"And," Jess added, "according to folklore, when confronted by a werewolf, all a witch has to do is expose them to wolfsbane, and the wolf will convert back to human form."

"He wasn't just changing to human. He looked like he was changing out of one form and straight back into another before he had the chance to recover. His change didn't even fully complete before he started again."

293

Jess shrugged. "I'd imagine if it can make them return to their human body from wolf, it could also have the opposite effect if they're human."

"How much was there?" Nathan asked.

"The cellar was full of it. They'd put it right across the front of the bars he was behind, and inside the cage, as well."

Eyes widening, Nathan looked to Jess. "He can't have been down there that long. We couldn't cope with that for more than—" His words cut off as he caught my horrified expression, but my pulse had already quickened.

"I can try again. Try and connect to Sean this time—"

"If they've somehow been blocking you, I'm not sure it will work," Jess said.

"What if the only reason I've not been able to get through is because they've been unconscious? Sean's awake, so—"

"I don't think—"

"He *felt* me there, Jess," I said.

"That's not possible." Her eyes held sadness. "Not if it was Marianne you were focused on."

"He knew I was there." My hand fisted against my knee. "When I called out, he made eye contact with me ..."

"Yes, but that doesn't mean—"

"He spoke my name. And ..." I glanced at Nathan. "He told me to stay away."

Silence captured the room, until Jess broke into it. "Just how strong is this connection you have with Sean?"

"Beyond boundaries," Nathan said. "A one-off—like nothing else ever archived."

"That's quite the understatement, Dad," Ethan muttered.

27

For the next few hours, returning to sleep became my obsession. Each time I tried to switch off, turmoil stole entrance and filled my head with images of the torture inflicted upon my mate. Thanks to that, my hands refused to unclench, my jaw to slacken, and my eyes to remain still behind lids I forced shut.

By lunchtime, I gave up and took up a new bout of pacing. After my hour spent ignoring Nathan's suggestions to calm down and rest, and snubbing Beth's urges to eat, Connor returned from his house with Jess and Ethan in tow.

Jess waved the acquired picture beneath my nose. One glance of the inanimate image of the witch made my teeth grind.

"Come on," Jess said. "You need to do this binding."

Upstairs in our bedroom, Jess rummaged around in the depths of her case and emerged with an armful of items.

As she laid them out between us on the bed, I took in each one: a small, round mirror, black glove, a reel of what looked like garden twine, black pepper, and a plastic measuring spoon.

"Ready?" Jess asked.

I blew out a breath, flexed my fingers a little. "How do you know this will even work?"

"Did the other things I told you to do work?"

I shrugged.

"Was Ethan's protection effective when you came across the witches?"

I nodded.

"So, you know I'm not spinning you yarns here to make you feel better?"

I gave another small nod.

"Good. Let's start." She pointed to the bed between us. "You're going to measure three teaspoons of pepper into the glove."

Tipping powder into a glove that looked as though it belonged on the hand of a drag queen seemed a bit silly, but I kept my mouth shut and obeyed.

Once I'd done it, she said, "Now, take the picture of Marianne and place it face down on the mirror ..."

We both turned at a knock on the door.

Ethan stepped inside. "Mind if I come in?"

I shook my head, focusing back on my spell, as he moved across and perched on the window ledge. My lip did a little more curling when I picked up the photograph.

"Face down," Jess said as if I'd forgotten already. I did as instructed, and she told me to position the glove on top of the photograph and mirror and passed me the twine. "Now, Jem, you need to secure the items together at the same time as repeating these words ..."

I absorbed the verse before murmuring the incantation I prayed would work. "I bind you, Marianne, from doing harm." I looped the string around the bundle. "Everything you say to me, and everything you do, bounces off me three times and sticks itself to you."

"Again," Jess whispered.

"Everything you say to me, and everything you do, bounces off me three times and sticks itself to you."

Jess urged me to say it again, folding her last finger to indicate it as the final one. By the time I'd finished, the twine almost covered the items.

Jess tugged one of my pillowcases off, tossing my exposed pillow back down. "Put the package inside." She passed it to me, and I did as requested. "Now, which exit is used the most?"

I glanced at Ethan. "The back door," we both said.

Jess pointed to my bundle. "If you hide that somewhere close to the back door, the ritual is complete."

When I trudged downstairs and into the kitchen, the three mature heads lifted. As Nathan's mouth opened, I waved the folded pillowcase, tugged open the drawer nearest the back door, and manoeuvred it beneath everything else in there.

"Done." I slid the drawer shut and ran my fingers through my tangled mass of hair. It hadn't been brushed since Beth had insisted on providing a little grooming on Monday, right after I'd taken my last shower. "Okay ... time to sleep."

No need to travel. No need to search. I simply imagined myself beside my mate and arrived there. The second I did, Sean's eyes sought me out, pinpointed my spectre position and connected, as we always did.

Desperation descended as I watched him. He looked even gaunter than on my previous visit. Each of his changes appeared to end farther from completion. The sounds of distress that grunted past his lips had become constant.

I slept for longer to prolong my time with him. In the hope of easing his pain, I threw effort into attempts to control his changes on his behalf. After numerous failures, I could only guess the physical distance between us was too great.

Unable to do more, I stood guard over him. At least that way I'd know of further witch visits, their ill-treatment of him, and keep an eye on his deterioration.

I spent most of my sleep time pacing his bars. He glanced up every so often, as though he'd caught the hint of me still there. Each time he did, he gave the same warning. 'Stay away'.

What did he expect me to do? Leave? He must have realised I'd come for him as soon as I had his location.

When I eventually woke, the room lay in darkness. My eyes flicked side to side as I thought back through for important details of my dream. If there had been any signs of their whereabouts, I'd missed them. Maybe I'd been too attached to Sean to concentrate on anything else. I only knew, when I hauled my weary head in search of the others, I had nothing new to report.

The spoon hit the side of the empty bowl with a high-pitched ding. I hadn't even wanted the bloody stew, but Beth's force-feeding had gotten a little out of hand, and I'd given in just to keep my lips intact.

"Happy now?" I didn't await her answer before scraping back my chair and trudging upstairs.

Jess rested against my headboard, pillows wadded around her, as I entered our room. Between scanning some kind of spell-looking book, she sent me a rapid glance.

I padded across the carpet with little noise, but my climb onto the bed and the sprawled flop of my body jostling her earned me another glance.

"Sorry," I mumbled.

When she lifted her book again, I stared at the ceiling above.

Jess seemed as much in the mood for talking as I did. Quiet descended for minutes, before she lowered her book a little. "Jem, what are you going to do with the witches once you find them?" Her tentative tone told me she'd been waiting to ask. "Do you have some sort of plan in mind?"

Fixated on a stain on the ceiling, I nodded.

She waited a beat. "Well, what is it?"

"I go in. I find the boys, locate the witches." My voice sounded robotic. "Get the boys out, hopefully undetected. Then I deal with the ones who dared take my Sean from me."

"That's a lot of *I*'s. How do you expect to achieve all of this alone?"

I twisted my head toward her. "I won't be alone."

She heaved out a sigh. "I thought for a minute you had no intention of taking Ethan." I opened my mouth to speak, but she continued, "You know he plans to go with you, anyway, right? He's been tailing you around the house." Her brows lifted. "Don't tell me you haven't noticed."

I frowned up at her.

"So ... if not Ethan ... who?"

"*You're* coming with me."

Her eyes widened. "Me?"

"I need you. If what you said about this wolfsbane plant is true, you're the only one who can shift it for me. I'll look for the boys, and you can clear the way to Sean, so I can come down and take him out of there. Then you can protect the boys, while I deal with the witches. That done"—I shrugged my shoulders against the duvet—"we bring the boys home, you can try and break their spells, and I'll grab Ethan for clean-up duty."

"Clean-up duty?"

"Yes, Jess. That kind of mess can't be left lying around for somebody to stumble on by mistake. We have to clean up after ourselves."

"You don't plan to let any of them live, do you?"

Studying her, I wondered if I was asking too much. "If you were me, and you had a soul mate you'd been bound to for eternity—one you'd spent three lifetimes with—and it felt like a part of you died whenever he wasn't within reach, and some stupid little witches took him, with the intention of raping him just to create some bloody half-breed ..." I took a steadying breath. "What would you do, Jess?"

"When you put it like that ..." She shrugged. "If it were me, and they'd taken my soul mate ... I'd rip out their fucking throats."

I kept my gaze on her, hoping she meant her words and they hadn't been spoken under duress in an attempt to show false bravado.

Her stare never wavered. "To choose to be with a person for that length of time—I mean, to willingly do that? You must have been hopelessly in love with each other. I've never met anyone who made me want to be with them for one lifetime, let alone numerous ones." She gave a small smile. "You've been blessed, Jem. That kind of commitment is worth fighting for."

As I accepted her sincerity, I relaxed back against the softness beneath my head and relocated the ceiling stain. "Nathan wouldn't allow them to live, anyway. They know too much. They're obviously insane—no way he'd sanction them walking away. I'm going to be in enough trouble for racing off to deal with it alone. I'll be in even more trouble if I don't tie off loose ends and finish the job properly."

The tiny patter of rain hit the glass of the window in a delicate timpani of nature's beat. I tuned into it, closing my eyes to enjoy the calming sounds for moments before I disturbed the peace. "If it's going to be too much for you, Jess—if you don't think you can handle it—you should say. I won't be angry with you. I'll understand."

I gave her time to answer. When she didn't, I opened my eyes.

Her scrutiny held the compassion naturally instilled into an older sibling. Very slowly, she nodded her head. "I'm in. Now, go sleep." She shoved at my legs, nudging me to the edge of the mattress. "Find him so we can bring him home."

28

I fell asleep on the sofa, as I had each time since Christmas Day, and visited Sean, who looked less healthy and more distressed than ever. When my mind told me I would soon wake up, with nothing less than sheer determination, I willed my body to leave via a different route.

On my first attempt, I sprung back into the cellar as though enclosed in an impenetrable bubble that I'd stretched out of shape. With teeth gritted, and a 'float' up to the wall on my third try, I found myself outside in the grounds.

My mind swirled at the speed of my rapid scour of the large property. I absorbed the non-standard height of the perimeter wall. Only after I travelled fields and hit a country lane did my mental curses start flying.

The second I saw the road sign, I knew I'd seen it before, had already heard the name of the village. My distraught condition had simply prevented the information from sinking in, and I hadn't accepted it for what it was.

Little Hampton.

A quiet gasp breathed past my lips as I opened my eyes to the shadowed sofa cushions. I had it, knew where they were. At last, I could take action. I just had to figure out how without alerting the others.

I peered across at Ethan on the other sofa.

One knee drawn up, resting against the back padding, the other draped over the edge, his chest rose and fell with each of his breaths.

Best chance I'll get.

My bare feet made no noise against the living room carpet or the kitchen tiles, but I cringed at the sound of the drawer as I slid it open. I reached in for the pad and pen, leaned on the countertop to write 'GOT IT!'.

As I snuck back out, I paused at the living room door. The continued rhythm of Ethan's breathing told me I hadn't disturbed him. Tiptoeing up the outside edge of each stair, I avoided the creaks I knew resided in some and ducked into our bedroom.

Jess's face had squidged against the pillow, stretching skin taut across her cheekbone. Waking her would lead to definite questions, which would lead to Nathan being suspicious the second he found us whispering in the dark, so I took a deep breath, willed myself patient, and lent my trust over to my sister to find us a way out of there.

Don't let me down, Jess.

After curling the scrap of paper into a straw-sized tube and sliding it into the folds of her curved fingers, I headed back down to lie on the sofa and pretend nothing had happened.

The sideways, covert glance Jess sent me on entering the kitchen told me she'd gotten my message, and hiding my sigh of relief took some serious suppression.

If the men noticed our exchange, it didn't show in their faces. Their bodies, however, held knotted tension— probably a mixed result of the lunar commitment their bodies would be convinced they were owed, and the eve of the blue moon being too close for comfort.

I'd have shared their agitation if I didn't have plans of my own.

Mine soon kicked in, though, when afternoon arrived and Jess had made no noise about getting us out.

As I paced my well-worn path across the kitchen, an unnatural quiet spread throughout the house. I listened for the conversation in the living room where Jess had not long taken refreshments through to the men. Only the swish of my socked feet met my ears.

I halted, tilting my head. Creeping shuffles brushed across the living room carpet. As I leaned around the kitchen door frame, Jess appeared in the hall.

A smile spread her lips. "It's time." When I stared at her, she whispered, "Are we doing this or not?"

I crossed to her, peering around her into the living room. All three men lay spread-eagled in various poses, mouths agape, soft breaths whooshing in and out of their rising and falling chests.

Jess grinned. "They'll wake in a few hours."

"You *drugged* them?"

"Seemed like the best solution." She shrugged. "Not only can we leave without them standing in our way, but I've also got the house keys"—she held them up with a smile—"expertly retrieved from Nathan's pocket. I take it the Toyota key on here is for his truck?"

My lips curved. "Genius. Where's Beth?"

"She's having a lie down, but I took her spiked drink up to her, so she'll be under by now."

My ears twitched for any sign of movement upstairs. When I found none, I said, "Let's go."

Using the 'lifted' keys, I unlocked the front door, peering over my shoulder at Jess. "Grab some duvets. The only way we'll fit all the boys in is if we load them into the truck bed. They'll need padding to protect them—especially if they're all as naked as Sean."

"Gotcha." She nodded.

As she headed upstairs, I stepped outside and made my way round to the garage, where I checked the shelves for anything that could help in a little breaking and entering. Spying a pair of bolt croppers, I smiled. "You'll do nicely, thank you very much." I unhooked them and reached up for a crow bar on the top level. "You, too." If for no other purpose, it could come in handy for embedding in someone's skull.

I headed back out to the truck to find two duvets piled in the bed. Lack of Jess told me she'd gone back in for more.

I unlocked the doors, placed my tools in the foot-well, and folded the quilts onto the back seat.

"Please tell me you didn't plan on leaving me behind, Jem."

My body jerked. Blowing out a breath, I turned to Beth. "Why aren't you asleep?"

"Because it takes a woman to recognise the deviousness and sly glances of fellow women. And because I'm not as gullible as the men." Beth folded her arms. "I didn't drink my coffee."

Jess appeared through the front door with another duvet, stumbling as she came to us.

"She didn't drink the coffee," I told her.

Her mouth opened in an 'Ah'.

"I'm coming with you," Beth said.

"No," I said.

"Yes, I am."

"I'm sorry, Beth, but I can't take you along." When she opened her mouth, I held up my finger. "One—it will be too dangerous, and I won't have time to watch your back, as well as everything—"

"I can take care of myself. I have exactly the same protection as you." She tugged at the necklace around her neck. "More so, with this."

"Two—" I continued as though she hadn't spoken, "Nate will slaughter *me* for going. If he wakes and finds I've taken you along, he'll ensure I go through endless days of torture *before* the slaughtering takes place."

Beth gave a deep chuckle. "You can't truly believe you have more hope of talking your way out of trouble without me as your backup. You must realise I may be your only chance of Nathan going easy on you when this is over."

Damn. I blew out a heavy breath. Why the hell did she have to make so much sense?

***

"So," Beth said over my shoulder, as I engaged first gear and pulled off, "I take it you know where they are."

I caught her reflection in the rear-view mirror. "Little Hampton."

"How far away is it?" Jess asked.

I braked at the gates. "I've no bloody idea."

"Tell me you know where it is," she said.

I shook my head, blowing out a breath of frustration. "I've never heard of it before."

Jess gave a small snort. "Don't you think it would be a good idea to figure out where to go *before* we head off, Jem?"

I shrugged. "I wanted to get away first. Then figure it out."

"I have my mobile," Beth said. "You drive, I'll look it up."

I pulled away again, steering right out of the gates, and stayed within the speed limit while I awaited instruction from Beth.

We'd travelled just over a mile when she tapped the back of my chair. "We're going the wrong way."

"You found it?" Jess asked her.

"If I've got the right place, it could take us a while to get there."

I sought her eyes in the mirror. "How long?"

"If these directions are correct, it's about three hours away."

I held her gaze for a moment, had no idea what she saw in mine—probably panic. We'd already hit the wrong side of three o'clock. With the early winter arrival of evening, the moon would have begun its ascent before we reached them.

I checked my wing mirrors and swung the truck into a three-point turn. As soon as we faced the right way, I hit the accelerator and pushed the pickup to maximum speed.

"Put your seat belts on," I called over the roar of the engine.

29

The sky had progressed through most of its stages of darkening and, with no rain all day, its inky blue veneer remained clear, revealing stars that sparkled like diamonds.

"Only about twenty minutes now," Beth said from the back.

I nodded, praying the Little Hampton she led us to would turn out to be the correct one.

A forlorn air filled the cab on the final stretch of the journey. No one spoke or paid attention to each other within our shadowed enclosure. We only had eyes for what lay around us.

The longer we drove, the lighter the traffic became, the more rural the landscape. I guessed not many people headed to the countryside for New Year's Eve.

I'd always believed when the clock struck midnight the rest of the year had already been mapped out based on the attitude you carried forth. What if I began the New Year without Sean? I could hardly bear to contemplate it.

A glance at the dashboard clock showed another fifteen minutes had passed, right before I spotted the black and white rectangular road sign with its bold lettering: Little Hampton.

"Okay, this is it." I drew the truck to the side of the road. "What now?"

They both turned to me as if they'd expected me to have a cast iron plan set in place—nothing quite like a bit of disappointment to spoil an already sombre mood.

"Where do we go from here?" I asked. "I mean, do we follow the road and see how far it runs before we're no longer in Little Hampton, or .... What if there are loads of side roads that need checking. Do we do those as we go?

Or, do the main road first and head back to follow those afterward?"

Jess and Beth turned from me to each other.

"Main road first?" Jess said, and Beth nodded.

The main road extended, winding and curving, for about seven miles until another sign alerted us of our approach to a new village. I swung the pickup to face back the way we'd come, and we searched for the first side road. We'd located and counted them all on our initial run through— five to the left, which had switched to our right, and four on the other side.

A check along the first to the left revealed nothing. The second on the left gave the same result. The next one led off from the right and turned out to be much longer than the other two. Although we'd come across a couple of properties during our village perusal, none of them had the crazy-high wall I could still vividly picture from my dream.

Weaving along the third road, a tingle teased at my limbs. I put it down to my mounting anxiety as the evening looked more and more like a dead end. Mentally pushing it aside, I pleaded with myself not to bring on an emotional change right then and peered harder through the windscreen.

Five minutes passed. The tingling grew stronger, demanding my attention. I rubbed at my arms, hoping to brush it away, but to no effect.

If Jess or Beth noticed my discomfort, they didn't say.

I eased up on the accelerator, lifting a hand to my brow. A wipe of the taut skin there coated my fingers in perspiration.

What the—

My entire body snapped into spasm.

A loud gasp squirted phlegm from my mouth. As my knees contracted, my elbows drew into my sides.

Jess grabbed the steering wheel.

Head flying back, my body arched against the seat.

The buck of my body flipped my head forward, until my chin smacked the steering wheel, and a small grunt pushed through my gasps.

Beth gripped my shoulder. "Jem, what's wrong?"

Agony shot through me, and a strange mewling cry filled the cabin. It took me moments to realise that sound came from me.

I tried to turn my head, but it refused to obey. I caught Jess's eyes—wide and staring—and knew the first twist of deformation tugged at my flesh.

I couldn't stay in the truck. Whether I wanted to, or not, I would soon be wolf, and I needed to get out. Giving a low groan, I fumbled with my seat belt, but my flexed fingers couldn't release the catch.

Beth reached over and unclasped me. Within seconds, she appeared at my window, hauled open the driver's door, and dragged me from my seat.

I doubled over on contact with the roadside, gasping as fire licked through each and every muscle.

It couldn't be an emotional change—not even an uncontrolled one. The intensity of the agony peaked at levels I'd never usually hit.

"Clothes," I squeaked, before a cry escaped me.

Beth tugged at my sweatshirt, bringing forth further gasps as she hauled my arms at an angle they didn't want to go. Her hands grabbed for my vest, and she sent it sailing.

With my top half free, my palms hit the ground, fingers clawing through damp, uncut grass and into the soft soil beneath.

Beth dropped to her knees before me. I tried to focus on her, but I could barely think straight, let alone see.

Fingers tugged at the waistband of my jeans. The denim chafed at my tender skin as they were yanked over my hips and legs—a moment before excruciation attacked.

My spine tightened, expanded, then tightened again. The muscles either side contorted to accommodate the altered

308

physique. My back bowed against the pressure, higher than could ever be considered natural. Head hanging low, I watched the pale hairs force out from my pores.

The splitting of my skull blinded me, followed by facial adjustments that always seemed to hurt more than anything else, and I threw my head up as a roaring growl rumbled up through my chest, ripping past lips already vibrating.

As the end neared, I almost allowed myself a small sigh of relief—until a higher control dragged me backward, and my body heaved into reversal.

Body afflicted, mind tormented, needling pain stabbed beneath my flesh. Through the transformation from wolf to human, it all became clear.

I lowered my face to bring Beth into my sights, willing my vocal chords to hurry back into play while attempting to take over and gain control of my bodily alterations.

"Sean," I gasped.

She came closer. Her fingers brushed over the sweat drowning my face.

"He's here." Although guttural, my voice sounded more human.

"Jem?" Beth glanced around, left and right, like she'd spot him any second.

"Not my change," I whispered. "Sean's. I can feel him. We must be close."

"Holy shit!" said Jess.

Attention on Beth as the reversal neared its end, I attempted to push it faster toward completion so I wouldn't become trapped within, as I knew happened to Sean—but as with the initial change, it began to go back the other way before I'd even finished. "Oh, God!" A low cry squeezed past my clenched teeth. "Not again."

Beth's fingers gripped either side of my face, held my head steady to look at her, as the change dominated once again. "Jem, you need to block it."

"Can't." My arms shook with the effort to hold me up as the second change tore at me. I couldn't fight something so powerful, didn't have the strength. The air filled with my cries, as I blocked as much of the pain as possible.

"Disconnect from him, Jem." Beth's tone held urgency.

My cries evolved into snarls as my body swayed upon trembling limbs.

"Disconnect!"

Stabbing sensations pierced each of my vertebrae as they locked, unlocked, and locked yet again. Teeth bared, lips drawn back, feral grunts growled their way out.

"Come on! You can do this."

I tried to focus on Beth's words, but disconnecting from Sean did not come naturally to me—especially not when only thoughts of how long he'd endured the torture filled my head.

"*Concentrate!*"

Her harsh words snapped me back enough to listen to her—to get a grip on my situation.

"Good." She nodded. "Keep going, Jem."

The whole incident couldn't have taken as long as it appeared to, but when consumed by agony of such depth, even ten minutes could seem interminable.

Through Beth's words and guidance, the sound of her husky voice, and the warmth of her contact, I switched off mentally to everything but that in front of me.

My body calmed, muscles relaxed. Bone structure realigned and hairs shortened. With breaths spurting out in short pants, my arms gave way, and I collapsed to the ground.

A small eternity passed before I went from sucking in cold, damp earth to drinking in much needed air. Legs still weak, I pushed to my feet, swaying in my upright condition.

Beth tucked a sweat-streaked strand of hair behind my ear.

"You should take a few more minutes, Jem."

I shook my head, bent to grab my vest.

"You're not ready. The pain's barely subsided. You're not even steady."

"Which is why I need to move now." I tugged my top over my head, shoving my arms through. "I can't leave Sean to go through that any longer. There's no way anyone can survive that countless times and remain sane. No way." I bent for my jeans, dragged them over my feet, and wiggled my hips to accommodate the snug denim.

Her hands snared my face again, holding me still. "Take a moment, Jem."

Knowing she'd never relent, I closed my eyes, took deep breaths.

Every scent on the air sucked into my nostrils. That of the countryside always seemed so much less tainted by unwelcomed smells. If not for the exhaust fumes excreted by the idling engine of the pickup, it would have been the perfect combination of flavours to lap up.

A tilt of my head followed a trail of fresh fox. On a lift of my chin, my nose bobbed and caught a stronger whiff, to the left, to the right, until smothered by the unmistakable acridity of smoke.

My eyes flew open to the overwhelming existence of the full moon.

Fixated upon the draw of its power, a small tremor worked along my spine, tickled into my coccyx. As the breeze blew over me, though, bringing a reminder that the smoke needed investigating, I followed the path the wind had arrived on.

"What is it?" Beth asked.

"Burning," I muttered. "Something's burning."

A high leap to the left landed me with a metallic thud on the proud bonnet of the pickup. I stood tall on my toes, scoured the land past the high hedgerows bordering the road on both sides.

"Where's it coming from?" Jess asked—her first words since I'd regained control of my body.

My lids lowered again as I leaned forward, sampling the air. Once more, the breeze carried the smoke. I turned toward it, reopened my eyes. An expanse of field lay beyond the barrier. With the moon's assistance, I scanned across nude pasture, taking in another high hedge a few hundred yards to the left. My sight followed it, sweeping back to the right, and my heart hammered against my chest when I spotted the high wall from my dream—about two miles in the distance.

"Gotcha."

Beth moved closer. "Jem?"

"Get back in the truck." I looked down at her before checking out the far hedgerow and calculating the direct distance to the property. "Both of you get back in. Drive along this road until you see a turning on the right—"

"But—"

"Take the turning, follow the road—"

"Jem?"

"At the end, you'll find a property." My focus remained glued to my destination. "Shut off the lights and engine before you reach it. Get out and walk on foot, if you have to."

"Where—"

"Do not allow them to see you coming." I dragged my attention away to peer down at them. "I'll meet you there."

Stepping back brought my heels to the far edge of the bonnet. I took the two steps across the metal at a run, and pushing off with the ball of my left foot propelled me over the hedge.

Landing on all fours, my knees bent to absorb the power of motion. After a split second of recuperation, I took off, my feet bashing against the soggy ground.

Unified calls of, "Jem, wait," echoed out a couple of times, before the slamming of doors, crunching gears, and a growl of the engine replaced them.

The thought of being reunited with Sean increased my pace. My breaths blew, as my heart thumped. My arms pumped as my thighs and calves burned. Spurred on by sheer determination, exhausted, hungry beyond belief, weakened by the connection to Sean's changes—it all seemed irrelevant. All I cared about was Sean and getting to him. After days of believing I'd never find him, never touch him again, smell his scent, the thought of him kept me moving without falter.

The wall neared. I didn't slow.

The higher it loomed, the faster I went.

A deep rumble from the pickup travelled somewhere to my left. I didn't wait, didn't hesitate, merely raged toward the wall that had to be at least twelve feet in height.

Within physical range, I flung myself upward. My knees bent, shoulders bunched, arms surged in reach. Fingers locating the wall's rim, I gripped, swinging my legs to the right until high enough to hook my foot up and over. Without even having to think about it, I straddled the perimeter in seconds.

Pressed flat to the obstacle between my thighs, cheek resting against the scratchy surface, I took time to catch my breath and scanned the inner garden with nostrils flared and ears twitching.

My vantage point offered a clear view of the house. Its grandness matched the impression from my initial visit to the interior. I checked out the windows, trying to get a feel for the layout, and guessed it to be living quarters on the ground floor, four bedrooms and bathroom on the first floor, replicated on the top.

Footsteps approached. My ears tuned into them. Locating the disturbance on the outside of the property and recognising Beth's and Jess's scent with an inhalation, I relaxed. From somewhere toward two o'clock, near the wrought iron gates at the front of the boundary wall, their whispered mumbles carried to me.

My focus circled back from their position to a driveway that opened out near the front of the house. Generous-sized gardens surrounded three sides, all hedged, planted and interspersed with willows and coniferous trees.

Peering back over my right shoulder, I spied the source of the smoke I'd detected, where the scent of charred wood spiralled through the air from outdoor wood burners.

The very sight of them hastened my breath and pulse, even though I found no indication of the witches' objective—no sign of them, no guests of honour, no ritualistic tools.

"Psst."

I spun toward the hissing on the other side of the wall, peered down into the shadows at Jess.

"What the hell are you doing?" she whispered.

"What does it look like? I'm casing the joint."

She let out a small snort. "We're not here to rob them."

I thought about that for a moment, about my intention to foil their plans, take their prizes, end their lives. "Actually, I'll be robbing them of plenty."

Her head tilted back. "How the hell did you get up there?"

"How do you think? I jumped."

Her eyes widened. "Bloody hell!"

"Where's Beth?"

"Checking the other way, in case you were over there."

I jerked my head at her. "Go find her and bring her round to here."

I followed the path of her moving footsteps, as she took off at a slow jog. The farther Jess went, the less audible her movements became. I almost lost track of her, as she turned the corner of the rear wall, and as I peered behind to her approximate position, my attention snagged on a rear gate, close to the centre.

One human entrance. Thank goodness I'd brought the bolt croppers.

When a door opened at the rear of the house, my head whipped back round. It didn't take long for Zoë to appear, carrying what looked like a pile of picnic blankets. Remaining as still as possible, I watched her, unsurprised when she halted amongst the scattering of heaters and began laying the blankets on the grass.

Pathetic. All their grand scale plans to harmonise beneath the stars and draw on the strength offered by the blue moon, and the best ritual beds they'd come up with were bloody picnic blankets. My lip curled at the insult.

I swung my left leg up backward and over to join my right. Fingers gripping the top of the wall, I lowered myself down. Thankfully, my feet were still bare from my roadside change and aided in my silent descent as I released my tightened fingers and dropped, hitting the ground in a crouch.

No voices, no surprised words or approaching feet suggested I'd been spotted. I lifted my head to relocate the young witch.

With her back to me, she busied herself with setting out the 'altars'. The idea of sneaking up and whispering *boo* in her ear appealed, but as I placed myself above such petty games, I crept up until close enough to wrap one hand around her waist and the other across her mouth.

Her feet left the ground, as I spun and raced back to the spot where I expected my allies to join me.

The young witch offered no struggle. I put that down to fear. When I reached the wall, I twisted Zoë round to face me. Her eyes widened, as my hand squeezed her throat to constriction, and I slammed her back against the bricks.

"Jem?" Beth whispered.

"You're there?"

"Yes. Jess, too. Where did you run off to? We were worried."

My lips curved. "I got us a present."

315

"What is it?"

"Move aside a little, and I'll pass it to you." I had to couch my amusement at the witch's sudden flail of her arms. "But be ready to act when it lands, okay?"

"Okay," Beth hissed.

I glanced at Zoë's terrified expression, allowed her a lift of my eyebrows. "Ready for this?"

The leg kick and muffled squeak she gave pretty much answered to the contrary.

I smiled. "Good."

Keeping my hold tight, I took a few paces back and bounced on the balls of my feet before flying toward the wall. I drove my body upward, the arm that held the witch shoving up at an even greater speed. Near the top of the wall, I pushed even harder, loosening my grip at the last second.

Zoë's body disappeared over the other side, and my fingers hooked the ledge just in time to prevent me falling back down.

All those basketball games had paid off. I'd just never played it with a head as my missile before, and certainly never with a body attached.

I hoisted myself up and stared into the shadowed darkness. My comrades had not reacted as quickly as I'd hoped. Wide-eyed, mouths gaping, they gawped from the young girl to me.

You want a job done properly ... I stepped off the wall and aimed for my body to land with my feet on either side of the shaken witch.

Her eyes widened. Her mouth opened.

I landed in time to cut off her scream.

30

Jess's gaze moved from me to the witch to the top of the wall. "Please tell me you don't plan to get me and Beth in there that way."

"No." I snorted up at her from my crouch. "Where's the truck?"

She pointed toward the front of the property. "That way."

"How long on foot?"

She shrugged. "There and back, five minutes, maybe."

"Okay. You collect the tools, then you can meet us back here."

Jess hesitated, almost as though she understood my reason for choosing to send her back. After a moment, she nodded and strode off.

Hand still against Zoë's throat, I pushed to my feet and hauled the witch up with me, pinning her against the wall. "Okay, I'm going to ask a couple questions. And you're going to answer them. Understand?"

Although she couldn't move her head, and my hand prevented speech, her eyes signalled her compliance.

"Good. First question, where are the boys?" I released her just enough for her to speak.

"It wasn't me. I didn't—"

I cut her off. "Where ... are ... the boys?" I said slower, before lessening my hold again.

"In the bedrooms on the first floor."

"Is Sean still in the cellar?"

A small nod gave me the answer.

"Whose idea was it to surround him with wolfsbane?"

Her eyes widened, before she said, "Steph and Marianne's."

I'd suspected as much.

"How many of you are there?" Beth asked from beside me.

"Four others. Jem's already met them all."

"Anything else?" I asked Beth. "Any other questions?" When she shook her head, I turned back to Zoë. "Okay, we're done with you."

She breathed out a sigh. "I can go?"

"No."

Confusion filled her eyes, replaced by fear a second later. "But ... but—"

Ignoring Zoë's whimpers and grunts of protest, I did what I had to do to protect myself and preserve the pack. Her body sagged a beat later, and as I released her, she slumped to the ground in a heap.

As Jess rounded the corner, I shoved the body into the shadows with my foot, hoping she wouldn't see it, but her glued gaze to the floor told me my discretion should have come sooner.

"Did you get everything?" I asked before she could ponder.

She nodded, eyes flicking between me and the shadows. "Croppers, crowbar, bats." She dragged her focus fully to me. "What now?"

"I'm going to open the rear gate and let you two in." My hands came to rest at my hips. "Then we infiltrate."

"Who goes where once we're inside?"

"We find the keys, unlock the cellar. Then, Jess, you go down and clear the way to Sean, while I head upstairs to find the others."

"What about me?" Beth asked. "Do I help Jess?"

I shook my head. "Sean doesn't know you're back. If you go into the cellar before he's fully recovered, he'll think it's a trick, or spell, or something."

"Not if I talk to him."

"I've seen how he is, Beth. Irrational doesn't cover it, and he'll never believe you. If he thinks you're one of them and attacks?" I shrugged. "You won't stand a chance. You're coming with me."

"She's right," Jess said. "Wait—what about me? Won't he attack me?"

"Hopefully not. Because he doesn't know you by sight, he might not think it's a ruse. If he questions it, tell him to follow his senses. Here ..." I stepped over to her, rubbed my bare arms and shoulders across hers. "If he doesn't believe after smelling that, you're not going to convince him."

Her brows lifted. "And if that happens?"

"Leave the cage locked and come get me. Now ... are we ready?"

"We're ready," they said together.

It took less than a minute to scale the wall, snap through the metal loop of the padlock used to secure the gate, and let Jess and Beth in. Another minute, and we'd snuck up on the house. After checking through the window and finding the kitchen empty, we entered.

"Find the keys," I said, listening and inhaling. "Big bunch, huge ring."

"Fridge." As Jess moved across and snatched them up, Sean's gasps filtered through the cellar door.

I spun round and pointed. "Open it."

She crossed the room, fiddled with the keys, and inserted one in the lock.

"Wait." Beth turned from Jess to me. "That's not a good idea with you still in here, Jem. Not with the wolfsbane."

I knew she spoke sense, yet couldn't remove myself from the proximity of my mate. He was there—right there—and he needed me. How could I walk away?

Eyes narrowed, my head tilted as though I could somehow peer through the almost non-existent sliver at the bottom of the door and catch a glimpse—until footsteps disturbed me along with a blur to my left.

Heather skidded to a halt. "What the ..."

I spun toward her, and in one stride, two, three, my arm shot straight out, and the ball of my hand collided with her nose.

Bone broke. I shoved in and up. Cartilage splintered.

Her eyes rolled, body dropped.

The only movement from her arrived in the slow stream of blood trickling from her nostrils.

I lifted my gaze to Beth's smile.

Beside her, Jess looked dazed. "She's ... dead."

"Two down, three to go. Now the odds are even." I held out my hand for the keys. "Any problems, just clear out the wolfsbane and back off to wait for me. Okay?"

As Jess turned for the cellar door, I headed for the house stairs, with Beth on my heels and Heather's ankle in my hand. We pushed open the doors we passed, dragged Heather's body behind the first one, and reached the end of the hall unspotted.

I peered up the stairs. *Stealth or speed?* If they hadn't pegged us already, we'd have more chance of keeping it that way if we stayed quiet.

Backs pressed to the wall, we ascended. Once the landing hit my scope, I paused, scanned, inhaled and listened, but picked up nothing. I went higher, hesitated to study the five wooden doors set around the space, and twisted the handle of the first one.

With a quiet click, it opened. Before I'd even poked my head in, an inhalation told me it lay empty, but I double-checked, confirming what I already figured it to be— Sean's vacated room. His scent lingered on the air and fabrics. I took a greedy gulp before I shook my head clear and withdrew.

The next door had been locked. I fumbled with the keys until it opened. When the door swung wide, I knew we'd found one of the boys, and my heart fluttered at what my gaze landed on.

From my angle, Daniel appeared dead. I crossed the room in four strides, lowered beside the single bed. My nose pressed to his throat and brushed around until I'd located the thready drum at his pulse point. When I checked his face, a tiny flutter of expelled air left his nose and bristled my skin. "He's alive."

"How are you going to get him out of here, Jem?" Beth asked. "Back through the house?"

I pushed up and crossed to the window. The ancient and outdated frames bore no locks. On top of that, they were huge—a good five feet high, at least. I unlatched the handle.

"How?" Beth asked again behind me.

"I'll carry him."

"And jump?"

I nodded and urged the window higher, cringing against the quiet grate of scraping wood.

"If you jump, with Daniel's weight on top of your own, you'll injure yourself, Jem."

I peered outside to visually measure the drop, drew back inside and turned to her. "Help me move him."

She didn't argue further, and with her assistance, I laid Daniel's body on the carpeted floor. At my indication, she helped me haul the mattress across to the window.

I shoved it through the opening, and it landed with a thud. I expected alarms to peal but none arrived, and I went back for Daniel, lifted him with a grunt over my shoulders. As I climbed onto the ledge, I wondered at the sanity of my plan—but only for an instant—and jumped.

The shock of landing jolted through my shins. A gasped cry burst from me. Even with the aid of the mattress, it hurt like hell.

Shoulders hunched, I leaned forward onto my knees and rolled Daniel over my head onto the padding. On straightening, a kick of each leg tested them for damage. Apart from a splintered scream of resistance at the altered stance, I seemed unharmed. I stuck my thumb up at Beth.

Dragging Daniel's deadweight across the lawn, through the gate and beyond the wall left me panting. Once I'd hidden him around the corner, I jogged back, took a running leap and re-joined Beth in his recently vacated cell.

Gaze aimed toward the ceiling and the third floor above, I whispered, "Any disturbance?" The other witches had to be up there for us not to have encountered them.

Beth shook her head.

I didn't know whether to be elated that we'd gotten so far with so little, or concerned over what the witches were up to out of my sight. Either way, we had to get moving. "Let's go."

The next room housed Kyle.

After he'd been serviced with the same checks as Daniel, I slung him over my shoulders—harder the second time—and manoeuvred him out to the open window, where I hoisted us both onto the ledge.

On impact with the mattress, my muscles bunched. Pain stabbed into my bones like I'd developed the worst case of shin splints in the history of mankind.

After I'd reunited Kyle and his brother, I met back up with Beth in the house. "Just Josh."

She nodded.

"I'm sending you out." Her eyes narrowed, but I ignored it. "Go for the truck. Bring it round to the rear of the house—if you can do so without drawing attention. No headlights."

Her eyebrow lifted. "And you?"

"I'll bring Josh out." As her mouth opened, I continued over her, "This is already taking longer than I want it to. I need to get to Sean, and I can't do that until I know the others are safely on their way home."

I failed to mention the whole reason I'd come in search of the others before tending to Sean was because I feared I wouldn't give a damn about them once I had him in my sights. The urge to drag his arse to safety would be too strong for me to pause and consider I had other responsibilities.

She didn't argue or question. Perhaps she understood. With a small nod, she stepped with me onto the landing and jogged her way down the stairs while I headed for the final bedroom.

As I reached for the door handle, footsteps creaked across the landing above.

I froze.

The mover paused.

"Amber, did you check if everything's ready?"

My chest vibrated at the sound of Stephanie's voice. Temptation flooded in to just rage up the stairs, punch her, maybe have another go at merging cartilage with brain matter, possibly even scout around for a pencil to stab one of them with—in the eye worked well, I believed.

"Just going now," Amber's voice called.

When footsteps swished across the upper floor toward the top stair, I backed away.

Divide and conquer made for a much better battle plan than diving into the midst feet first. I'd heard that once when watching a naff history programme in a bored stupor. Maybe I hadn't been as stupefied as I'd thought.

My hand reached out to draw Kyle's door closed as I passed, and I snuck into Daniel's room. Leaving it ajar, I hid behind the exit, waiting for her to take the prominent bait of the unsecured barrier.

No carpet coated the stairs to muffle her footsteps, and their increase in volume made them easy to trace.

I heard when she hopped off the bottom step onto the landing. The quiet hum that vibrated from her told of her excitement for the upcoming event.

When a low grunt punctuated the tune, I knew she'd spotted the open door.

My mind's eye conjured the whir of her brain while she attempted to come up with an explanation, especially as the door led to Daniel's room. Daniel had been her catch, hadn't he? I wondered if her head spun back the way she'd come, if she considered calling back up to the other two to ask if they'd opened it.

I almost shook my head at my line of thought. She wouldn't do that. To suggest they'd left the door open when she found it ajar would be to hint at some ineptitude on their behalf. I didn't believe for one second Amber would question the competence of the two witches. I'd seen the way she studied her twin, the way she'd look for guidance or reassurance. Less dominant in every way, it came as no surprise when her pause ended and she stepped toward where I waited in the shadows.

I readied myself, took control of the adrenaline surging through me and steadied my breathing. My nostrils flared on a quiet inhalation as I allowed my senses to follow her position.

The scrape of fingertips hit the door—a gentle push, only an inch or so, as though testing for surprises.

She'd have to come in farther for those.

The door nudged another couple of inches.

I flexed my toes until I stood on the tips. My heels pressed against the skirting, my back flat against the wall.

The door opened farther, faster. I could almost taste her confusion over the empty bed. She'd most likely spotted the open window. She probably wondered if Daniel had woken from his deep sleep, possibly suspected he'd opened it and leapt to his escape. That would have been my trail of thought in her shoes. She'd need to check, wouldn't want to believe she'd lost him. Maybe she could find him in the garden and redeem herself.

I knew I'd called it right, when she scurried across to the window. As soon as she passed me, I stepped out behind her, waiting for her to sense me, or turn.

She leaned out through the opening, ducked back in. Her fingers lifted to her lips as she trod backward, breaths short and shallow, before she spun.

I gave a slight wave of my hand.

"Hey."

She froze.

I sent her a smile—a decent one. Although I'd aimed to scare and terrorise, my facial features couldn't be bothered to disguise how much I'd begun to enjoy myself.

She stared, confusion and fear in her eyes—but then she went and spoiled it all by lowering her fingers and shifting her eyes toward the upper stairway.

As her mouth opened, I darted out, grabbed a handful of scalp and slammed her face down onto my upcoming kneecap.

It hurt—me—a little more than expected. I looked down at the throbbing for a second, my lips forming a silent *ouch*, and I dragged her head back up. The fact I supported her entire body weight told me I'd knocked her out cold, but I needed reassurance she wouldn't get back up once I left her.

A smile tugged at my lips as an idea formed.

Keeping my grip on her hair, my other hand grasped the back of her trousers, and I flung her as hard as I could through the gap of the window.

She speared through, performing a dive of Olympic standards, and landed on her head with a heavy crack.

I considered it information to be stored away for future use. If traditional methods of neck breaking didn't work, tossing bodies from second storey windows made a good backup plan. At least she hadn't landed on the mattress. That would have meant more work.

With a sigh of satisfaction, I went in search of Josh.

31

My waning strength couldn't hold up forever. By the time I'd slathered Josh with kisses, dragged his limp form through the gate and spotted the truck peeking round the corner, relief flooded me. I reached it, just as Beth attempted to lift Daniel onto the pickup's bed.

"You were a while." Although incredibly fit for a woman, Beth did not possess superhuman powers, and her voice panted through her hauling. "I was getting worried, Jem."

"Ran into a witch," I said.

Her eyebrows lifted. "Problems?"

"All taken care of. I want you to get the boys home, while I go back in for Sean."

She stopped manhandling Daniel and looked at me. When he slipped from her grasp, I dived forward to catch him, shoving him back up to her.

"Don't panic." I slid the body over the duvets. "I just don't think this is the right place for Sean to learn you've returned. He'll be disorientated enough without extra issues to deal with. I'll send Jess back with you ..."

"But, then—"

"... and I'll ring Ethan before you leave and ask him to come and help. I'm exhausted, Beth." I shrugged. "This clean-up, on top of everything else ..."

"I'll ring Ethan now." Her expression made it a suggestion, though her tone said otherwise. "At least that way, he'll be coming before we've left and get here sooner. I'll feel better about that."

I nodded. "Okay, do it. I'll finish loading the boys."

While she ducked into the cab to make the call, I set to work. Having to drag one body up, climb in to slide him across, before repeating the process sapped my strength.

By the time I'd finished, sweat trailed paths across my body.

I rubbed a forearm across my head, as Beth climbed from the truck and held out her phone.

I took it from her. "Hello?"

"What the hell are you playing at? Do you have—"

"Did your mum tell you where to find me, Ethan?"

"Yes, but—"

I cut him off, passed the phone back to Beth. "Sorry. He'll have all night to rant once this is over. Wait for Jess, then head home."

"Sure, Jem."

I strode away from her unsure smile and headed back to the house. Through the kitchen, I yanked on the cellar door, jogged down the stairs.

Okay, baby, I'm all yours.

At the whoosh of rapid movement through air, I ducked—narrowly missing the steel bat as it skimmed across the hairs of my head.

"It's me," I hissed.

"Thank God." Jess's breath heaved with her words. "I thought you were one of them."

"Well, I didn't think you wanted to cave *my* head in." I searched for Sean as I spoke.

"Did you bring the keys?" Jess asked. "I can't get him out."

I studied the cage. "But you got the plants out."

"I sealed them in bags, chucked them outside."

I crossed to the door, my attention on Sean, where he'd wedged into the corner, as I tried to locate the correct key.

Jess came closer. The keyring left my fingers.

Unable to take my eyes off him, I vaguely heard as she tried different keys in the lock.

He looked bad. Weak, filthy, barely conscious—at least he'd stopped changing. His scent, for the first time ever, smelled pungently strong—musky, with a powerful staleness that could have only been created by someone who'd perspired for days.

"Got it," Jess whispered.

The key connected, the lock clicked, and the door swung open.

I marched in. Dropped to my knees.

Palms down, I pushed my head forward, eyes peeled for signs of recognition. My nostrils searched for a stronger dose of him as my ears listened for sound.

When he didn't move or speak, I edged nearer—cautious.

Reaching him, I lowered my head farther, raised only my gaze to study his downturned face, and so close to him, my suppressed sob erupted.

No longer caring if he attacked, I pushed my face into his, into his throat, around his neck. Beneath his ears, I sniffed at him, drowning in his aroma, trembling at the contact.

"Jem?" The word arrived so low, I couldn't be certain I'd heard it at all.

I found his chin with my fingers, tilted his face to mine.

At the gentle fluttering of his lashes, I sighed. When his eyes opened, despite them only achieving narrow slits, my first tear of relief spilled over.

"Baby, it's going to be okay." The promise came out a hushed whisper. He'd hear me, though—he always did.

He attempted to shift his body, his fingers brushing my arm, yet his eyes held confusion. Logic would warn of a trick while every one of his senses would scream that his mate knelt before him. Mingled with the deep uncertainty was the high glisten of desperate hope. "Jem?" he murmured again.

"Sean, it's me." I brushed my lips across his cracked, dry ones.

Another attempt to shift came with a low groan from deep within his chest.

I took the hand he willed higher, linked his fingers with mine and leaned my cheek into his contact. "How long until he's strong enough to move, Jess?" At that moment, he looked as if he'd be going nowhere.

"I honestly don't know."

"Isn't there something you can do for him?"

"I wish there was."

"Haven't you got something—anything? You've always got something, Jess."

"I bloody left them behind." She groaned. "Unless ..." Her footsteps scuffed the concrete behind me.

I tore my attention away from Sean and looked to her.

"I *might* have something. Not sure how well it'll work on him. But ..."

"What?"

She sighed and dug into her pocket, seeming to cringe as she handed over a foiled strip that resembled most over-the-counter treatments.

I stared down at it. *Pro Plus. Caffeine pills?* She had to be kidding me? My eyebrow made a slow upward journey as I peered back at her.

"They *could* work ... if you give him enough ... maybe."

My eyes narrowed. "How many's enough?"

"The lot?"

I counted the undamaged spots on the strip—nine. Anything had to be worth a try, if it would provide enough energy to get him out of there.

Right?

"Okay." I nodded before waving her off. "I've got this. I need you to head back with the others."

She shook her head. "I'm not leaving you here."

"There's only two of them left, and Ethan's on his way. I've already spoken to him. I want you to get the boys home for me and wake them up."

She stared down at us for a moment. Clearly, she didn't want to leave me with an invalid wolf to watch my back.

"*Go!*" I said to her.

With one final glance in Sean's direction, she took a step back and obeyed.

I listened to the sound of her passage, until certain she'd left the house and hadn't gone after the remaining witches. Only once her footsteps faded to a muted run did I give my full attention back to Sean.

"Baby, I need you to open your mouth."

His pupils dilated, unsurprising after days of raging in and out of violent changes, when I gripped his chin and tilted his face.

After fumbling single-handedly, to release one of the pills, pushing it past his lips took little effort. The hard part came with getting him to swallow. I cringed as I clamped his jaws together and pinched his nose until the bob of his Adam's apple assured me the tactic had worked.

When I prodded at his lips with a second tablet, a low growl brewed in his chest, and my head tilted toward the cellar stairs for sound, though even the threat of the last two witches flying down them didn't alter my position. Sean had to find strength. Given the choice between taking down Stephanie and Marianne, or remaining by his side, I'd have chosen the latter every time. I poked some more until I'd deposited another inside his mouth and blanked how long it seemed to be taking.

His teeth ground beneath the force of my hand pinning his lips closed. He gave a feeble attempt to tug himself from my grasp. I held him tighter, pressing my forehead to his as I once more smothered his airways until he swallowed.

"I'm sorry," I whispered against his temple.

Desperation bled in, jerking my movements, as I ripped the packaging in search of more and rammed two tablets into his mouth.

At his groan, I slapped my hand across his mouth and nostrils.

He coughed, the pop of his lips hitting my palm, and I grabbed the back of his head to force him steady.

"Come on." A tear leaked over my lid. My temple rolled across his hairline as I drew him closer. "Swallow it for me."

His jaw shifted. A quiet crunch followed.

I released him only long enough to snatch up the silvery packet. Four down. Five left. With trembling fingers, I poked the remaining pills from their pockets, and grabbing his cheeks until his lips parted, I shoved them all into his mouth in one go.

That time, his chin flicked upward, another attempt to shake me off, as the thunder within his chest vibrated against my forearm where I pinned him.

"Damn you, Sean." The whisper hissed through my teeth as I forced his face down and ducked forward until he would see only me. "You *will* take these tablets, and you *will* swallow them. That is an order. Do you understand me?"

His eyes stared into mine, though I had no idea what he saw, if anything. The tightness of the skin surrounding them told me his discomfort remained. What had I expected? That the stupid tablets would wipe out every ailment he had in a flash? Jessica had done too much over the past few days for me not to put my faith in her once more. I just hadn't expected the hope to be unfounded.

His shoulders bounced up before a cough erupted. His eyes shone bright—from the water suddenly invading them rather than the return of any life to his expression— as he heaved one breath after another, his mouth working as though to process what I'd force-fed him. If possible, he slumped even more against the wall, his head leaning back. Quiet rasps arrived with each rise of his chest.

My forehead slid down until it bumped his shoulder. Frustration at the situation encouraged another tear to escape. I wanted nothing more than to be able to scoop him up in my arms and carry his arse out of there. I'd never wished myself stronger than I did in that moment, but my body had limitations. Ones I'd almost reached the end of.

Hoping the tablets worked, if only eventually, I twisted to sit with my focus on the only entrance and settled in to wait.

With Sean's closeness heating my back, the virtual clock in my head chimed out every second we sat there. Floorboards creaked somewhere overhead, and more than once I braced myself for discovery, my head whipping up as my muscles tensed to act—only to sag again at each false alarm.

An hour could have passed in that cellar—it certainly seemed as if it did—but after what must have been closer to mere minutes, Sean's nose poked against my hair. The suck and blow of his sniffing tickled the flesh there, and I tilted my head, my lids threatening to droop. When his chest met my shoulders, and a hand slid across my hip to my stomach, I could fight them no more, and my eyes closed as I leaned into the one I should have been supporting.

Awash with peace after days of heartache, my restful position lured me in. Each nudge of his nose swayed my body. In my contentment, I scarcely noticed when his inhalations deepened, or as a slight tug drew me backward.

Perhaps Sean hadn't been the only one who required healing.

His free hand smoothed along my shoulder and weaved into my hair, tilting my head farther, and his lips traced the outline of my jaw.

A long, low moan of pleasure vibrated from me. My legs drew up, my fingers found his thighs.

"What the heck's going on?"

My eyes shot open at Marianne's screech, yet the cellar held nobody other than the two of us.

The first footstep hit the top stair, the rest in rapid succession. Her feet appeared, followed by her body, her head. She slammed to a halt.

Marianne's eyes scanned rightward, her gaze falling on us, as the swing of the single hanging bulb she'd caught with her head intermittently illuminated us.

Her mouth opened. She appeared unsure of which way to move, but turned back toward the open cage door with the keys dangling from the lock.

As she darted forward, I lunged from Sean's arms.

We hit the door together. A metallic clang rang out. The bars imprinted into my chest and shoulder as the power of my dive claimed control.

The door whooshed outward, and Marianne flew back and hit the wall—just not hard enough. She scrambled to her feet, leapt for the stone steps, and raced from the cellar.

The metal-framed door resonated against stone as I barged from the cell. On hitting the bottom stair, I halted, spun back to Sean.

His body no longer slouched in the corner. He'd attempted to get to his feet—almost succeeded—and his eyes showed sufficient alertness that he seemed to understand the reason for my hesitation. "Go!" His voice held the hoarseness of days with little speech. "*Go!*"

I took a step toward him. "But—"

"How many?"

"Two. And just you and me. Ethan on the way. But he won't be here for a while."

He pushed upright, swayed once and steadied himself with a hand to the wall. "Then, go."

I danced out my uncertainty before I got my head screwed on straight. "I'll be back for you." On my promise, I whirled and took the steps two at a time.

32

Marianne's short legs didn't seem able to carry her at high speeds. Maybe she should have worked out instead of sticking her beak into spell books. She stood no chance of getting away, not from someone who'd spent months trying to keep up with a pack of werewolves.

A few metres from the rear gate, I caught up and body slammed her with my shoulder.

Marianne collided with the wall. On an expelled grunt, she slid to the ground, but pushed to her feet with a headshake and turned to me. Venom filled her cold eyes as a murmured chant flew from her lips. Fists curled, she began to circle me.

I tilted my head, as I twisted to follow her path, trying to make out her words. When it clicked, I burst out a laugh. "Oh, this is just classic." My hands came to rest on my hips. "You're *cursing* me?"

She didn't answer, but her lip curled, and her tone continued to spit out words that sounded more malicious by the second.

I rolled my eyes, while hoping like crazy the deflection held up. "Oh, stop already."

Her lips didn't cease, the incantation continuing to roll out of her, the circling and fist clenching showing her increasing wrath.

A gasp broke her flow. She clutched at her stomach. Shock registered on her face.

Smiling, as it dawned she'd gotten what she intended for me, and hiding my relief that Jess had protected me, I strode forward.

Grabbing the front of her cable knit sweater, I yanked her up and threw her.

She landed about ten metres away with a thud and a cry.

My lips twitched as I moved closer. "We'll make it fair. You give me your worst shot, then I take a turn." I tapped my chin, pretending to ponder. "That makes it your turn. Come on, hit me with it."

She chanted another curse, her lips speeding through the words as she staggered to her feet.

"Oh, for goodness sake. You must have figured it out. It isn't going to work on me." I curled my fingers in invitation. "Get your arse over here and fight me properly."

The fact she didn't came as no shock. If I'd been her, up against me, I would have been on my toes already—running in the opposite direction. Her remaining presence, her continued efforts to win, only confirmed her loathing of me.

I folded my arms, feigning boredom. "Tell me when you've finished, won't you?"

Another cry of pain told me she had. She grasped at her arms, rubbing the length of them. Her frantic eyes suggested it had begun to sink in that she experienced the results of what she aimed my way.

"I already told you, Marianne." I squatted to bring her to eye level. "You can't beat me this way." The look she sent me surpassed even a glower, but I didn't care. "I bind you, Marianne, from doing harm." I smiled at her. "Is this a spell you're familiar with?"

"No!" She screamed the word.

I straightened my legs. "Rule number one, know thy enemy. You should have checked me out a bit better before you decided to take me on." I strode forward to tower over her, dropped back down to her level. "I come from a long line of witches. Powerful witches. You must be familiar with the eternal binding spell. All witches who know their stuff have heard of it—the only successful one ever achieved."

Her eyes narrowed as her glare deepened, the icy chill of their blueness glinting beneath the earth's natural lantern.

"I know you've read about it. Your choosing werewolves to merge with witches was no coincidence, was it? I bet you thought it would work. I mean, why not? The two worked well together before, right?" I grabbed her sweater front, brought her close. "The difference, Marianne, is that the original merging was no fake. The couple it was performed on were in love. A concept I'm sure you're unfamiliar with."

"How can you know anything about it?" she hissed. "You're nothing but a thug. You're no pureblood. You're—"

"That's where you're wrong." I smiled. "The witch who performed that binding ceremony was my mother."

I watched her as I waited for it to sink in, knew when it had by the widening of her eyes. She parted her curled lips, but I didn't wait to hear what she had to say. A yank drew her to me, and a harsh shove tossed her tumbling away across the lawn.

I marched forward, catching up a split second after she landed. My hand reached, my mind more than happy to play with the bitch.

"Come, now, Jem."

I halted at the sound of my mate's voice and looked up to see him making forced strides toward me.

"What have I told you about playing with your food? If you're hungry, just eat her already."

I couldn't help the smile or the flutter of my heart, or the moisture that invaded my eyes.

Compared to my last sighting of him, he looked hot to trot. Not perfect, not back to full strength—but that didn't matter when the only issue he had to contend with came in the form of an unfit witch. The only indication of Stephanie's struggles, he held her securely about her throat, were her darting eyes, the squawks she gave, and the occasional flap of her hanging feet.

She could have tried a bit harder. I certainly would have if swung around one-handed by a naked man.

Not surprisingly, Marianne jumped to her feet during my distraction and took off at a sprint.

I twisted to check which way she went before turning back to Sean. "Shit! Now I'll have to chase her."

"The bloody hardship." He grinned, my stomach tightening at the sight. "I found this one upstairs, hiding." He waved Stephanie about like a ventriloquist's dummy. "You want her, Jem?"

"No, baby. You can take her."

When I tore my gaze away, looked back toward the gate, Marianne had pulled it open, and the soft squelch of her running feet hit the damp grass beyond. I took a step, peered up at the moon, smiled at him over my shoulder. "Looks like the hunt is on tonight, after all."

His chuckle followed my pursuit of the witch, but I stopped as it dawned on me my mate hadn't reached my side—I'd never hunted without Sean. I spun to him, almost asked if he was coming, but one look at him told me I'd be asking too much.

Regret filled his eyes for an instant. "Go on, Jem."

I dragged my vest over my head and tossed it aside, did the same with my jeans.

Sean's eyes never once left me. "You sure you don't want me to save this one for you, Jem? I was looking forward to some entertainment."

"No. She's all yours." I trotted back over to him, pushed up onto my toes to kiss his lips. "The wolfsbane was her idea."

Rage darkened his stare as I turned and flew toward the gate.

Sean roared as Stephanie's scream of, "*No!*" reverberated throughout the garden.

I'd had enough of the toying—of Marianne still breathing, of being unnecessarily parted from Sean—and saw no point in messing around. On limbs weary from

337

fatigue and my change, I raced across the field until I could almost drink in her sweat-saturated scent.

Picking up speed, I circled round to block her path.

Her feet skidded in her halt. A high-pitched scream pierced my ear,s before she raced to the left.

As I leapt across, dashing into her path again, she fell forward onto her hands, yelping out her terror.

Another spin, another dash for freedom, a squeal at her route blocked once more by a huge wolf, and she still seemed to believe she held chance of escape.

Four or five times, I allowed a glimmer of hope to enter her eyes. Each time, I cut her off with a growl.

A rough ram of my shoulder into the back of her legs sent her sprawling to her face. As she rolled, I stepped over her, her black waves fluttering beneath my snorted breaths. Dread seeped into her eyes. A strong waft of urinary secretion told me understanding had finally dawned, and excitement shivered through me. My lips vibrated beneath the pressure of my slow-released snarl.

Clamping my teeth around her throat, I gave a sharp yank and tore it free.

As the spark of life died in her eyes, I chuffed the scent of her blood from my nostrils, gave a vigorous body shake to flick off her touch, and stepped away to change back.

Silhouetted by the moon, Sean's frame filled the gateway, as I made my return. With my fingers hooked over the waistband of the dead witch's jeans, I took one awkward step after another, hauling her beside me as I willed myself to get to him sooner. Metres from the gate, my fingers uncurled, and she slid down my leg to thump on the ground.

Sean's crooked finger beckoned me over, and being a dutiful mate, I stepped straight into his arms and pressed my face to his chest.

"How long until Ethan gets here?" he asked after a while.

"An hour ... maybe."

"Where are we?"

"Place called Little Hampton." I pulled away to look up at him, sent him a small smile of regret. "Time to start cleaning up."

He nodded, reluctantly it seemed, and trailed me into the garden.

I headed straight for an outside tap beneath the kitchen window. To delete all traces of Marianne, I turned it on and splashed the icy cold water onto my face, shivering with each droplet that hit my naked skin.

As I straightened, I considered where to begin. Though none of the bodies lay near, I knew they all awaited disposal. The damp grass chilled my soles as I stepped toward where Amber had dropped on the far side of the property. The orange glow radiating from the wood burner tempted me to bask in its shared heat as I passed. Softness met my feet when the arranged picnic blanket took place of the lawn.

A sharp jab caught the back of my legs.

My knees folded, hands flew out. I hit the blanket on all fours. Rolled with an erupted snarl, cut short by Sean plummeting toward me.

His palms hit the ground either side of my shoulders, and his mouth crushed to mine.

My body responded, curving to mould into him, clinging to hold him lest he stop. Soft moaning sighs and gentle gasps breathed out past my engaged lips.

God, how I'd missed him.

His mouth released me. "Seems a shame to waste all this, Jem." His whisper held huskiness. "The blankets beneath the stars, the warmth of the heaters ..."

I lifted my head to peer round the garden. "But ... cleaning up—"

"Let Ethan do it." Before I could argue, his mouth smashed back down.

The ravenous tastes he took, the tease of his tongue, and the nibble of his teeth told me he'd gotten enough of his strength back—*everywhere*.

My body arched to take me closer. I slid my fingers to the back of his head, deepened the kiss and raised my legs in invitation, gasping out a cry as he entered me.

His steady rhythm kicked straight in, and I matched him, thrust for thrust. He moved to my shoulder, gave warm laps of his tongue, soft skims of his teeth, tender caresses of his lips. Finding his flesh with my own mouth, I treated him to the same pleasures.

One hand swept beneath my back, the other pushed up and tangled in my hair. My fingers dug into his rear to encourage him further, my other hand grasping his shoulder, afraid to let go. As though desperate for the sight, touch, taste of one another, our heads lifted, our gazes connected, and our efforts grew frantic.

Holds tightened, breaths infused, heartbeats hitting the same tune, we rocked against each other. The almost silent air filled with our urgent gasps and growls of passion. Our scents of arousal and desire took over the atmosphere. As the warmth of climax reached boiling point, the cries of our release symphonised the night.

He collapsed upon me. His hot, panting breaths teased my neck.

Legs still around him, my arms still clung, unwilling to free him.

"I missed you, Jem." The muffle of his voice couldn't disguise the emotion behind his words.

"Baby, I missed you, too."

He pulled back, eyes glistening bright. The prisms affecting my vision told me mine held the same shine. As he rolled to his side, he took me with him, snuggled me into his arms, and lay watching me as though committing every feature to memory. The damp grass held freshness.

The wood smoke swirled to tickle our nostrils. If not for the venue, it would have been a romantic moment.

A tilt of my face brought the moon into focus. Its fullness seemed imposing as it hovered directly above, the white face huge as it beamed down on us unmarred. Just the sight of it hastened my breaths.

"It's beautiful, isn't it?" he murmured.

I nodded, hypnotised by it. I knew he stared also, would be doing so with almost the same effect.

The distant clang of church bells broke the spell. I smiled at their echoed music. Only when I picked up the even more distant booms and fizzes of fireworks did it register. It hadn't been bells but clock chimes announcing the arrival of midnight.

I twisted back to Sean, brushed my lips across his. "Happy New Year."

Confusion filled his eyes. "What? How long have I been gone?"

"Too long—far too long."

"But ... Christmas—"

I placed a finger to his lips. "It's not important. We'll reschedule."

He gazed into me for seconds before he smiled. "Happy New Year, Jem."

Strengthening his hold once more, he rolled me, whispering a sensuous tune my body was more than capable of singing along to, and started the New Year as we intended to go on.

The forced shove to my head and its collision with Sean's woke me from my deep slumber.

Sean gave a grunt and low spoken, "Ouch."

I opened my eyes to Ethan, squatted above us, shaking his head.

"What the hell is wrong with you two? You stop for sex and a nap, when there's all this cleaning up to do?" The

341

undisguised humour in his eyes belied the quiet harshness of his words.

A smirk played on my lips as I settled my gaze back on Sean. "You do it, Ethan. I'm dog-tired. You can wake me when you're done."

He responded with a barked laugh.

"Is that a no, then?" I asked.

"Come on—move." He got to his feet and scooped beneath my arms, hauling me up. He looked down at his brother with a grin. "Need help?"

Sean shook his head and slowly pushed up. If he'd needed help, he'd never have admitted it, anyway.

Ethan stepped forward, as he straightened, gave Sean a manly slap on the shoulder, then, as though realising nobody but the three of us would see, pulled him into an awkward embrace that lasted about twenty seconds. "Let's get to work," he said gruffly as he marched off.

After Ethan had explained the entire home situation to Sean, and the house and grounds had been cleansed, we headed off to dispose of the bodies. It took a while to find deserted woodlands in the unfamiliar territory, dig for and burn the bodies, and cover them back over. A few hours later, with the truck a few bodies lighter, we hit the road to home.

Sean hogged the back seat to get some much needed rest, but I couldn't help my constant visual checks.

Ethan paused in his mumbled rant, when I looked back again. "He's not going anywhere, Jem."

I turned back to the windscreen.

He ducked his head a little closer. "According to Jess, he was half dead when she left you," he said, his voice low. "How—"

"Pro Plus."

"Pro Plus?" he asked after a few beats, like he hadn't heard me right.

I sighed, though my lips twitched. "Yup."

After a deep chuckle that sent his shoulders into a jig, he returned to his moaning.

He went on about my 'escapades' and 'underhanded search and rescue'. His wounded pride showed its face when he rambled on about being left behind. Didn't I know he had plenty he wanted to do to the witches himself? That seemed to be the crux of his disgruntlement.

I didn't argue with him, just let him get it out of his system, thinking it better to preserve my argument for the ass slinging that would be awaiting me from Nathan when we got home.

33

Beth stood on the doorstep, when Ethan pulled onto the drive at five thirty. Sean's position had altered to sitting, thanks to the constant disturbance of Ethan's drivel, and he scrambled from the truck before Ethan or I could even reach for our handles. Beth had already folded him into her arms by the time our feet touched the ground.

I paused by the pickup, allowing them some space. He needed it—Beth, too, no doubt—so I waited, as they reunited after over ten years apart, and maybe shed a tear or two.

When Beth pulled back, she waved me forward. Her arms flew around me, crushing me to her chest. "You brought him home," she murmured against my hair.

Sean smiled down at the two of us, until Beth tugged him into the embrace, too. His chuckle tickled the top of my head.

"I'll warn you," Beth said as she took my hand. "Nathan's waiting on you."

I blew out a sigh.

"I've got you covered," she whispered as she led me inside.

Nathan 'waited' for me in the kitchen. The second I stepped into the room, he shot from his seat, fists clenched at his sides.

"How dare you drug me, Jem!"

I came to a halt as my mouth opened and closed.

"I cannot believe your irresponsibility over this ..."

I wanted to disagree, thinking I'd done a good job, but stayed mute.

A snarl ripped from him, before he snapped out, "... plotting and scheming behind my back ..."

I had to give him that one, almost nodded before I caught myself.

"... and your dishonesty. You knew all day where they were, didn't you?"

Another fish impersonation answered him.

"How could you keep that information from me?" He stabbed a finger at mid-air. "How could you show such disloyalty ..."

Huh? My eyebrows shot up.

"... and disregard for others?"

"Not fair," I mumbled. "I was trying to protect you all."

His finger did some more air pokes. "And how could you go off without even leaving a note?"

Yea, I hadn't thought of that one. *Too busy scheming disloyal and dishonest manoeuvres, that's why, Jem.*

He gave another low growl as he rubbed at his hair. "Do you have any idea how terrified we were?"

I could have hazarded a guess.

His index curled back in, as his fist reformed to punch at nothing. "And what bloody right did you have to take Beth along with you?"

"Now, just you wait right there!" Beth snapped.

Nathan's head whipped to her, but she gave him no chance to retaliate.

"I have a mind of my own, Nathan Holloway, and for you to suggest otherwise is nothing short of a damn insult."

"She had no right to take you," he said.

"I gave her no choice," she threw back.

"Then, you had no right to go."

"I forgot." She took a step forward, planting herself in front of me. "You lot like your women compliant and feeble. Well, you're out of luck, honey, because you damned well went and looked in the wrong place, if you didn't want a woman with a mind of her own." She spun to glance at Connor. "So did you." She whirled on Sean. "And you most definitely did."

345

Sean's chuckle broke the tension. Ethan's, too. As Nathan's focus fixed onto Sean, the fire cooled in his eyes.

Connor stood from his seat. "Thanks, Jem, for bringing my sons home." As Nathan's cold stare turned on him, Connor added, "But you could have been more responsible about it."

Once certain they'd finished their attacks, I asked, "Where's Jess?"

"Tending to the boys," Connor said.

"I'll go give her a hand."

I made my escape. On the landing, I poked my head into the lilac room, found Josh still sleeping like a baby. Turning to the left, I opened our bedroom door.

Kyle tugged his T-shirt the rest of the way over his auburn head and smiled.

I crossed to him. "You're awake."

He nodded, rubbing his face. "Thanks to your sister. She seems to know stuff about ... well, stuff."

"Confirmed by your condition." I smiled. "What did she do? Not more Pro Plus?" His eyebrow lifted, but I waved him off. "Never mind. Tell me."

"Well, I woke to find a decent looking female pouring smelly water over me and bathing me with a sponge. Then it registered that I was actually in the bath. So then I thought it was a dream. But then she started explaining who she was and what had happened." His lips twitched. "The dream concluded when I spotted Dad and Nate observing like a couple of pervy old men. That drove off the last hints of sleepiness."

I snorted out a laugh at his details before I grew serious. "But you're okay?"

"Thanks to you, I hear."

"Don't say that within earshot of Nate, for goodness sake."

"You're in trouble for it?"

"Like never before." At his chuckle, I smiled. "Josh is still asleep."

Kyle frowned.

"Which room is Dan in?"

"I believe he's in the midst of his visit to the spa right now."

I stepped forward, planted a big wet one on his cheek. "I'll go see how he's doing."

At the end of the landing, I pushed through the bathroom door, and discovered Daniel still in the tub, with water splashing about him and a pink-cheeked Jess unnecessarily sponging his shoulders while explaining what had happened.

"Room in there for one more?"

Daniel thrust up and out, almost drowning Jess in a tidal wave of water. His arms lifted me, his nose nuzzled into my hair. "Jem."

I sniffed at the strong citrus odours clinging to his wet body. "You okay?"

"Sure, I'm good." He tickled my neck with a few forceful kisses before setting me back on my feet.

I grabbed a towel, used it to dab at my soaked front and passed a second to Daniel, which he rubbed at his hair with. "Kyle's awake," I said. "I just left him in our room. There's some stuff of yours in the bottom drawer if you're getting dressed."

He reached for the door handle. "Where's Josh?"

"The spare room," I said, adding, "Not done yet, though," in case he barged into there.

He grinned. "I'll go see Kyle, then."

"And your dad. Your dad's been going out of his mind with worry."

As he left with his smile still in place, I turned to Jess. "Need a hand with Josh?"

Averting her eyes, she bent and pulled out the plug.

"Jess?"

"I've already done Josh." She twisted back to me as she straightened. "It didn't work on him."

My pulse picked up a notch at her incomprehensible words. "What d'you ..."

"I can't wake him up," she said. "I tried him, the same as his brothers, but it didn't work. I don't know why." She lifted her palms. "I don't know if he's in deeper because of the longer length of time Marianne worked on him for, or because she used binding before she did everything else ... I just ... don't know."

My fingers flexed. "Can't you try something else? You can't leave him like ... *that*." I almost spat the word as I stabbed a finger toward where he lay.

"I don't know what else to suggest."

"But ..." I took a step toward her, just as quickly moved back. "You must have some idea. How did you figure out how to try waking them in the first place?"

"I took a stab at what may have been in the sleep potion and made one to counteract it."

"Then, we can do that again. Try a different one." My feet fidgeted. "Let's give it another shot."

"It's not going to work."

"'Course it will. We just need to double the dose."

Sadness filled her eyes as she shook her head. "It won't—"

"Make it work!" I growled, fists clenching against the urge to grab her shoulders and shake until she agreed. "You come along here. Convince me you're a witch." I *pfft*'d out my frustration. "You can't even do this one little thing."

Jess didn't speak. Her gaze never left mine, though.

I stabbed a finger toward her. "When do I ever ask you for anything, Jess?"

No response.

I flung out my arms. "It's not as if I come knocking at your door every five minutes, begging favours. For the first time in my life, I'm asking you to act like a big sister here. So, quit messing around and get on with it."

Her eyes darkened—the first sign that she even listened to me.

"Or maybe you're not the witch you've led us all to believe. Maybe you don't really know anything. You just like to think you do. Well, guess what, Jess? This isn't playacting. This is real life. Josh's li—"

"You know what? I'm sick of listening to you rant on about what is, or isn't, real based on what you've seen for yourself."

I glared at her.

"I wasn't joking when I explained just how deep a sleep the witches put the pack under. A magical sleep." Her expression remained serious, her gaze never left mine. "And yes, you have no choice but to fight magic with magic—whatever you think of it all. Though, how you can come from the lineage you do and say you don't believe in all this shit is beyond me. You can't hold your history and not believe, surely? Or, are you going to discount everything that worked over the last few days and make sense of it with some sceptical bullshit?" Irritation sparked in her eyes as she poked a finger my way. "If Marianne was looking for something of yours at Connor's, like you claim she was, then she would only have been doing so with the intent to hurt you. Yet, nothing came of it. Because you were *protected*. By *magic*. You know Ethan had a bigger hit of that confusion spell, but he was not affected. Because he was magically protected by *your* hand, Jem. You must believe. You believed enough to call me in. What did you do before that? Nothing! Because you already knew, deep down, that you could only fight magic with magic. Because you—"

"I'm sorry," I cut in.

"How can you be so in denial?"

"I said I'm sorry, Jess. It's just ... damn, all this witchcraft bull has been a lot to take in, you know?"

"Because a human changing into the form of a wolf is so much easier to swallow?"

My tongue played around inside my cheek as I failed to conjure a response.

"You didn't believe it before you met Sean. How many arguments did we have about the possibility of werewolf existence?"

I couldn't dispute that. We'd debated the subject on numerous occasions. She'd wholeheartedly believed. I hadn't, and then I became one.

I took a deep breath to steady myself. "So ... it only took the bathing to wake Dan and Kyle?"

She stared at me for a second before nodding.

"What did you bathe them in?"

"Just some herbs, citrus oils—ingredients to invigorate, mostly. The opposite of what I'd put in a sleep potion if I made one."

"Makes sense, but ... Josh? You sure we can't try something different?"

"I'll keep looking. But I can't stay here indefinitely. I've already called Ray twice to ask him to have the kids longer."

My brow creased. "I didn't know that."

"You needed me here," she said. "But I have to go back. My kids need me at home now."

"But ... *Josh*," I whispered. He had to wake up. She had to try.

"I tried, Jem."

"Try *harder*." I snarled but checked my temper and balled my hands against my eyes. "Sorry."

She stayed quiet for seconds before she spoke again. "I'll keep searching. Once I get home, I promise you I'll keep looking for a way to wake him up. As soon as I have something, I'll call. You won't need me here to do the magic. You're more than capable of that yourself—if you haven't figured that out after the past week ..." She sighed. "I've got to go home."

The hairs on my arms fluttered as she walked past. I lowered my hands, kept my eyes closed as I listened to her trot down the landing and enter our room. Within minutes, the zip of her case sounded out, then her heightened breaths as she struggled with it toward the stairs. Her luggage bashed the top step, and she gave a low grunt.

Mentally scolding myself for taking my frustrations out on her, I turned from the room and strode along the landing. She'd only gone a few steps when I reached out and grabbed her bags.

"I'll take these for you."

Jess smiled up at me. "Thanks, Jem."

After receiving profuse thanks from everyone, Jess bid her goodbyes and climbed into her car. I stood on the doorstep, watching the white Punto rumble down the drive. The scent of cooking bacon and potato cakes wafted through from the kitchen, courtesy of Beth. The initial hint of morning broke into the sky above, but as Jess's tail lights disappeared from sight, the great weight of my emotions descended.

Jess's departure made it definite. She knew no other way to wake him. None other than those she'd suggested and tried.

Yet, I couldn't bring myself to go in the house. To go inside and close the door would be like shutting the door on so much more than the damp frosty air, the lightening sky, the outside world. It would be like closing out Josh, and I couldn't do that, even if it would reduce my shivers inflicted by the cold.

As the heat of Sean's hand came to rest on my shoulder, I leaned into his touch. His chin tucked over my collarbone, his arms slid around my waist. I tilted my head as his sigh drifted over me, listened to his body talk and reassure me he'd really come home, alive, well—or as well as could be expected after what he'd been through.

"Mum said I have to convince you to eat," Sean whispered at last.

My gaze upturned to the kaleidoscope of colours as the sky altered its shades even more. "I'm not hungry."

"She told me you'd say that."

I breathed out a quiet laugh.

"You coming in?"

I shook my head.

"I'll stay with you, then."

I gave another headshake. "You need to eat. You've lost so much weight."

"So have you, Jem. You should have looked after yourself better."

"I had other things to keep me going."

"And I'm back now, so you can eat."

"But—"

"Josh will still be there." As usual, he understood. "Take the food upstairs and sit with him, if it will make you feel better. Just ... please eat." When I didn't answer, he struck with his lowest blow. "If you eat, I'll eat. I promise to match you, mouthful for mouthful."

I withheld my protest as I went to tell him I didn't want anything. I'd learnt my stubbornness from the best and knew he wouldn't move unless I did. With a reluctant nod, I closed the front door and allowed him to lead me into the kitchen.

34

I talked Sean into resting before ignoring my own advice and going to sit with Josh. The others called in throughout the morning. Each time, they sat awhile and spoke quietly about the past week. I stayed without a break, chatting to Josh when alone with him—inane stuff we'd normally talk about, as well as stuff we wouldn't.

I talked about playing ball, about food, about Christmas, about food, about Poppy, and asked him a few questions I knew he couldn't answer even if awake. Didn't matter that some of the subjects I brought up were personal. Josh and I often found time for private chats—nothing untoward or conspiratorial—just us, just friends, just chatting.

After a few hours, I promoted myself from slouching in the chair to lying on the bed. My fast-evaporating energy'd had enough of holding up my weary head. It took effort to nudge the lump aside to make room for me. Once there, I tucked my hands behind my head, stared up at the ceiling, and resumed my mumbled commentary, until frustration got the better of me.

I rolled onto my side, poked at his ribs. "Hey, I'm talking to you."

He just lay there—eyes closed, body still, breaths shallow.

I gave a rough shove to his shoulder. "I'm getting a little sick of you not answering me, buster."

No response. I hadn't really expected one. Hoped, yes. Expected, no.

I tapped my fingers against his cheeks. "How much of a one-sided conversation do you think a girl can have before it gets boring, Josh?"

Nada—nothing.

What had I really expected? That if I hounded him enough, he'd give up the game and open his eyes just to shut me up?

Yeah, right! How could he answer when he was in some sort of bloody coma, for goodness sake.

Jess told me there was nothing to be done, unless she could find the right ingredients to work against the spell. I either believed what she said, or I didn't. I couldn't keep agreeing whenever it suited, or decide her ideas were ridiculous each time they didn't.

I groaned. Mental arguments didn't bode well for my sanity. "Come on, Josh."

I climbed on to sit across his hips, leaned over his chest to lift one of his eyelids. The eye beneath didn't move, or flinch—didn't even dilate when introduced to the light.

My forehead lowered to rest against his. I stared at his blurred features beneath me, brought my hands to his cheeks. "Don't do this to me, Josh."

Footsteps hit the landing then paused across the threshold.

I inhaled, though why I expected it to be anyone other than Sean, I didn't know. "He won't wake up," I whispered.

"Then, you may as well sleep, too."

"How can I?"

"Josh isn't going anywhere, Jem." As though aware of the reminder he'd just made, he added, "And you'll be of no use, if you don't rest soon."

"Do you have any idea how much you sound like your mother?"

He chuckled, drawing my attention to the doorway. His head jerked toward our room. "Come to bed with me, Jem. Feels cold in there without you."

Though my lips formed the smile, I could still sense sadness in my expression as I climbed off the limp body beneath me. Sean's embrace offered nothing but warmth after Josh's lack of response, and I allowed him to fold me

into his arms as I peered back at the bed. "He will wake up
..."

"He will. Everything's going to be just fine, Jem."

I let Sean's words wash over me, the deep assurance in his voice somehow adding credence to the declaration, and nodded to convince myself further that he spoke the truth.

Besides, Josh *would* wake up. The pack *would* go right back to the life we were accustomed to. Everything *would* be fine.

I'd make sure of it.

Two Weeks Later ...

35

Whiteness reflected back at me from the ceiling above—a blank canvas of nothingness. For two weeks, I'd spent a few hours each day in the lilac bedroom. For two weeks, I'd prayed for a miracle. For some kind of enlightenment. Or, at the very least, for Jess to find a way to wake up Josh.

Some days, the emptiness dulled my senses to a warble of incoherency. Thankfully, on those days, Sean came to my rescue, reminding me life still existed beyond the four, pale purple walls. Somehow managing to convince me that everything would work out.

If Sean believed Josh would awaken, what right did I have to dispute him?

If the rest of the pack believed, who was I to douse their flames of hope?

Yet, no matter how many hours, how many days, how many *weeks* I spent at Josh's side in a show of optimism, the ache in my heart belied any positivity I feigned.

Rolling onto my side caused the mattress to dip, but even that didn't stir Josh. I flicked at an errant, dark blond curl, poked at his cheek. Still, he didn't move, didn't flinch, didn't acknowledge my prodding.

Again.

Poor kid had probably been poked more in the past fortnight than he had his entire life.

As my heavy sigh eased out, footsteps ascended the stairs outside the room. I knew from sound alone who they belonged to, didn't even need to inhale to confirm. That didn't stop me, though, and my lids lowered as my mate's bouquet found home within my olfactory.

Seconds later, Sean's body filled the doorway and cast a shadow across the carpet. "Hey."

"Hey," I whispered without looking up.

"Anything?"

I tapped my fingertip along Josh's jawline, willing him to react, yet knowing he wouldn't.

Josh hadn't moved the entire two weeks he'd been under. Heck, *we'd* barely moved him. No toileting. No sweating. He didn't seem to feel, hear, taste, see or smell.

All thanks to being in a death sleep, Jess had said.

I'd slaughtered the witches responsible for putting Josh under—for bewitching him in the worst possible way. At the time, their deaths had seemed fitting. That had been before I realised Josh's predicament.

With a small headshake, I rubbed my hand along Josh's arm, as if the friction would help a body lacking in heat. "I've been thinking."

"Thought I heard the turning of rusty cogs."

My gaze skittered to the left and landed on Sean's lopsided smile. Dark hair stood on end above the dark eyes staring back at me. All male, all muscle, all *mine*, Sean Holloway got me like no other.

"You going to make me pry it out of you, Jem?"

Rolling my eyes at the suggestiveness of his tone, I brushed a kiss across Josh's cheek and wriggled off the bed. At the door, I grabbed Sean's hips and steered him backward across the landing and into our room.

His left eyebrow arched up. "You *do* want me to pry it out of you."

I breathed out a laugh as I trotted over to the bed and sat cross-legged, tugging him along with me until he mirrored my pose.

Nudging his hand up, I placed my palm flat against his, studying the size difference as male dwarfed female in a way I rarely noticed. "I've been thinking about what you said."

"About?"

"The grimoire."

"Ah."

My sister had stumbled across 'the grimoire' when hunting for proof of our binding, proof of our history. Sean had been the one to put two and two together, that the details in the grimoire could only have been written by a member of my family—one who'd been present when the ritual that bound us for eternity had transpired.

"Did you tell Jess what I believed?" he asked. "Did she agree with you?"

"No, I didn't tell her yet. But ... what if you *are* right?" I pressed our fingertips together and threaded my fingers through his. "The more I think about it,"—and I'd had plenty of time for *that*—"the more I think it's in the wrong hands."

He tucked a finger beneath my chin, lifting until I met his gaze. "You want to go and get it." A statement, an understanding, rather than a question.

"I think I *have* to get it."

"Okay." The word came out measured and slow, but even beneath the narrowing of his eyes, he didn't appear to dismiss the idea. "You know the pack can't just barge in there and demand it back, don't you? We'll scare the woman, who has it, to death."

"That's why we're not going to take the entire pack."

"He won't go for it." He meant his dad, Nate, our Alpha. "He's barely let me out the house since ..." Sean shrugged, though I knew he meant since I'd rescued him from the same witches who'd cursed Josh. "He'll never agree."

"Of course he will. I've been wanting to head out and poke Jess about Josh." I smiled. "When I tell him we're going to her house, I just won't mention the detour we'll take on the way."

***

For the short few weeks since I'd met Sean's mother, I'd come to adore her—but she terrified me with her astuteness when it came to any attempts I made at secretive missions. It took until early evening for Nathan to head upstairs alone, and after checking Beth's preoccupation with prepping dinner in the kitchen, I padded the length of the landing to their bedroom.

Still soaked from his post-work shower, Nathan towelled off his dark hair, as I nudged the door open a little. Thankfully, he had a second towel fixed about his waist— I never had quite gotten comfortable with seeing my mate's dad naked. He paused, his body stilling, telling me he'd sensed me before he even turned.

I smiled. "Hey."

His eyes narrowed.

Pretending I hadn't noticed, I pushed farther into the room, hoping he didn't spot the subtle positioning of my body that would allow me to keep an ear out for an approaching Beth. "I have a ... proposition." I shoved my hands into my pockets to keep them from twiddling. "For you."

His shrewd gaze sharpened, until I inwardly cringed at the hint of distrust in his pale blues. I couldn't blame him, though. Last time I'd had a grand idea, he'd ended up drugged unconscious, while I raced off to save the pack. He still hadn't forgiven me the misdemeanour and probably never would. He turned away, slid open his top drawer, and fetched out a pair of boxers. "I suppose I should be grateful you're actually bothering to speak to me about this one."

Nope, definitely hadn't forgiven me.

He stepped into his shorts and drew them over his hips, tossing his towel aside. "So, what do you need now?"

I averted my gaze. At six-foot-five with a body of solid muscle a man half his age would have been proud of, Nathan in boxers was only marginally less embarrassing than Nathan in his birthday suit. "Well, I figured, with Beth being home now, the two of you would maybe like to spend a little time together."

Fabric swished across his flesh as he tugged on his shirt. "We have been."

I refrained from rolling my eyes. The males of the pack *got* romantic notions about as well as a worm would. "I meant *alone.*"

He halted in his reach of his jeans, his shoulders stiffening for a second. Without even glancing my way, he asked, "And you'd get what out of this?"

"Why would I have to get anything?"

He chuckled as he scooped the jeans up. "So, you thought you'd offer to disappear for a few hours simply because it would be good for Beth and me?"

"Yes."

"And you needed to corner me for that?"

"I didn't corner you." I swung my arms into the gap between me and his exit. "You have plenty of room to make a break for it."

Another pause, as he slid the denim over his thighs, accompanied a twitch of his lips.

I feigned exasperation in an exaggerated shrug. "Okay, okay, so maybe I'm going a little stir crazy, too."

His humour vanished in an instant. "Where did you want to go?"

Gotcha. After my solid stint of flitting in and out of the lilac bedroom to natter to an unresponsive Josh, Nathan was probably relieved I'd shown interest in something else. "I thought I'd visit Jess." Not a lie. "Maybe go through her spell books again." Still sticking with the truth—just not all of it. "We might get lucky and find something we missed to wake Josh up." I didn't even have to fake the wistful desperation in my tone.

"Okay." He buttoned his jeans and smoothed his shirt. "I presume from your badly-performed ruse you expect Sean to go with you?"

"He's going to need to leave the house at some point, too."

"It's only been two weeks since he came home, Jem."

"And he's already strong." He truly was, despite having been tortured for days—something else the witches had

361

paid for. "We'll take Ethan. He'll watch our backs. You know he will."

It took fifteen long seconds for the indecision to clear from Nate's eyes. "I'll let Ethan know."

"Thanks." On my way out, I peered back over my shoulder, hand on the doorframe. "And don't forget to start planning."

His eyebrow quirked up.

"You know ... house to yourselves ...?"

His rumble of a chuckle chased me the length of the landing, as I ducked from the room, and I smiled to myself—until I reached the top of the stairs and spotted Beth blocking my way with her arms folded across her chest. My eyes did a shifty dance. I ordered them still and tried for a casual smile. "Hey."

Her lips curved a little.

I waited for the tirade to begin.

She merely walked away—sending me a final glance over her shoulder, before vanishing into the hallway.

I should have been relieved. I knew better, though.

Despite the earlier lack of bombardment, I should have been better prepared when I ended up cornered that evening by a very inquisitive Beth. Shoulder-deep in bath water, I couldn't even make a break for it.

She sat on the lowered toilet seat after closing the door behind her. "So ... an offer of a day alone for Nathan and me?"

"Yep." The sponge floated over my legs, and I swept it up, reached for the soap.

"Generous of you." Her dark eyes, ones she'd passed on to both her sons, settled on me like an anchor refusing passage.

"Not really." I shrugged, sweeping the sponge the length of my arm.

"You sure you're not planning anything ... underhanded?"

I ducked my face with the ruse of washing my ankle. "Just a need for some fresh air, and to feel like I'm doing something more constructive than spilling my beans to Josh. I don't know if he can hear me when I waffle on, but ..." Hot water poured from my other leg as I lifted it and began scrubbing upward. "... poor kid must be feeling like my personal agony aunt."

"Maybe I should go and ask Josh what you're up to, then?"

I breathed out a laugh at the absurdity of the idea, before sobering as it dawned that a very sedate Josh was what made it so ridiculous. "Yeah, good luck with that," I muttered.

"I guess you have a point," she said. "Because only another woman truly recognises when a fellow woman is up to something." Beth stood from her perch, stepping forward until she loomed over my spot. "Don't lead my boys astray, Jem."

Peering up at her, my mouth opened with a tonne of protests ready to spill—mostly ones about how I hadn't even known *how* to misbehave before I'd met Sean—but Beth spun away before I could voice them.

When she reached the door, she glanced back at me. "I've only just got them back. Don't jeopardize that."

"I promise we won't be doing anything dangerous."

Beth nodded before exiting and leaving me alone. Blowing out a breath, I only hoped beyond hope I'd be able to keep my promise.

36

Leaving the house, walking away *from Josh*, had been hard, even if it would only be for a few hours. For moments, I'd stood staring at him, until Sean reminded me that if prompting Jess garnered some answers, the trip would be worth it and would quell my guilt. I still spent the entire journey with my head pressed to the truck's rear passenger window, the vibrations of the engine humming through me as I tried to focus on what I headed toward, instead of what I left behind.

After following printed-out directions through busy Shrewsbury to a quiet side street, we finally came to a stop. All three of us climbed from Ethan's pickup into the early January temperatures and stared at the shop whose façade looked nothing at all as I'd imagined.

With the sign that headed the front: FACT OR FICTION, I expected some crummy store with alien posters in the window, maybe a crusty-smelling man, afraid of life, peering out with tinfoil on his head. Instead, broad windows, simply dressed in venetian blinds, and an 'open' notice hanging on a clean door greeted us.

"Is this it?" Sean asked.

I shrugged. "This is the address Jess gave me."

"Why don't we just go in and check it out," Ethan said, "instead of standing out here freezing to death and trying to decide from the exterior if it looks like the right place?"

"Nag, nag, nag. Ethan, you sound more and more like your dad every day, you know that?"

His eyebrow lifted as he faced me. "I don't see why I had to come, at all."

"I told you—I might need your help."

"But you told Dad, *and me*, for that matter, we were going to visit Jess. Why would I want to come to a bookstore?"

"Because I'm asking you to. Besides, we *are* visiting Jess. Afterwards. Now quit moaning."

Before he could gripe further, I stepped forward and pushed into the shop.

A bell over the door announced our entrance. The delicate tinkle seemed to match the dainty woman sitting behind the counter, her almond-shaped eyes tracing across an open book in her hands. With a fiery red, elfish haircut, she only needed to add in translucent wings and a patchwork dress, maybe knock off ten years, and she could have passed for a fairy.

Beyond the wide counter, a curtained doorway kept the store from whatever hid behind there, while books filled the customer side of the desk, stacked in tidy rows along shelves, library-ish but on a much smaller scale.

After an inhalation revealed no unfamiliar scents other than hers, and with it confirmed that no other customers hid behind shelves, I moved farther inside.

Ethan remained by the door, and Sean tailed me for a few steps before halting in place—one guarding the door, the other watching my back.

I glanced over the nearest bookshelves that held titles beginning with *A*. It appeared to be the biggest section. I blamed that on the aliens, although it covered topics such as astronomy and astrology, also.

My eyebrow twitched at a section on astral projecting. I considered picking it up, maybe buying it—for the half second it took me to realise I didn't particularly want to try *that* activity again.

Rounding the shelves brought me to *C*. I skimmed over a couple of titles on Chupacabra and changelings—and a misplaced dragon book. My fingers ran across the spines, as I took in a handful of themes and titles and danced through the alphabetical order of the store: folklore, ghosts and haunting, legends, Loch Ness. *M* sported literature on mysteries, magic, minotaur's, the Mothman, mythology—world mythology, A-Z of mythology, Greek, Egyptian, as many types as one could imagine. *S* offered spells, the supernatural and shape-shifting.

I paused at the latter, entertained its proximity to the changes we experienced ourselves, as wolves, but continued through without further investigating.

In the final stretch of shelves, amidst books on witchcraft and Wicca, I discovered the world believed it hosted creatures such as vampires and werewolves.

Well, who'd have thought it?

At the two-legged, half-man-half-beast creatures illustrated on the covers of most of the werewolf yarns, a laugh snorted out—met with an almost silent chuckle from Sean.

"Baby, you should see these," I whispered, low enough only he would hear. "They make us look hideous."

"Don't take it to heart," he murmured, his tone equally as silent to any other than the two of us.

I emerged from between the bookshelves to Sean's amused eyes and sent him a smile as I crossed to interrupt the woman at the desk.

Placing her book down beside her, she stood as though she'd heard my approach. Her green gaze trailed over me, from my face to my empty hands and back up. "I take it you're looking for something in particular."

My head tilted a little as I tried to read her. "I hear you have a reference library." According to Jess, the shop owner had a private collection of spell books her regular customers probably had no clue about.

The woman's eyes narrowed. She leaned to the side, that intense gaze of hers flicking toward my escorts. "I'm afraid only certain families have the privilege of gaining access to those."

"I'm a Stonehouse." In reality, I had no idea if my surname would hold kudos with her. Still, I said it as if I considered myself important.

Straightening, she stared up at me for seconds before she nodded. "Which of the grimoires did you hope to read?"

I had to order my eyebrows not to wing up and my voice to remain steady. "The one that holds details of an eternal binding spell."

"You're not the first unfamiliar face to show an interest in that one." She inclined her head toward the doorway behind her. "Did you want to come through?"

I glanced over my shoulder, caught Sean's tiny headshake, and turned back to the woman with a smile. "I'd prefer if you'd just bring it out."

I expected her to disagree, but after a deep sigh, she left me at the counter and pushed past the curtain.

As soon as she'd gone, the door catch clicked, and a swish followed—that of an 'open' sign turning to 'closed' as Ethan secured us inside. My attention remained glued on the curtain, awaiting the woman's return, and my first glimpse at the book that held my past.

Three, maybe four minutes had gone by, when she pushed back through. She came straight to me, placed a heavy book bound in dark brown leather on the counter and turned away to sit on her stool again. Although she picked up her paperback, the twitch of her eyebrows made me suspect she continued to observe.

Staring down at the grimoire, running my fingers over its rough surface, a deep reluctance to open it crept in.

What are you scared of, Jem?

Before I could change my mind, I lifted the cover to find beautiful, elegant script decorating a yellowed and brittle page.

Step one achieved.

Sucking in a deep breath, I leaned closer to decipher the words, notes on an infusion of herbs, what the caster had expected to achieve and the end result—followed by ways it could be improved. Seemed innocent enough.

On the next page, my fingers slid carefully over the crispness of age. Similar notes and comments lay across that one, too. The next few pages also bore the same type of content, mostly antidotes for common ailments.

A few pages farther in, I discovered a love potion with its end result. According to the experimenter, she'd used too many red lobelia petals and not enough sweet orange. The second set of results concluded with a more positive outcome.

More flicking followed until, on the twenty-fourth page, I found it: The planned procedure for an eternal binding dated the fourteenth of July eighteen-oh-nine.

I released a deep sigh and began to read.

The blue moon was predicted, and they'd set the date for then. There had been a circle of candles—twelve to be precise—each of them scented with bergamot and vetiver. The exact incantation of the ceremony lay in print; some of the lines I recognised, having spoken them once without fully understanding their source. Below those, it stated the importance of directing the request to Hecate, using the power of the blue moon, drawing on the earth's natural power—specifically insisting the *intent* with which the words were spoken held more import than the *content*. The exchange of hair braids had been described, too, encouraging forth a distant memory I'd already resurfaced.

Beneath those, it mentioned the significance of the triad of witches who'd performed the ritual.

I paused.

Triad? Of witches? Three?

With a head tilt and frown, I read on.

The ritual had been carried out by three related witches, a mother and her two daughters, which made the third person in the clearing my ... *sister?* The three witches positioned themselves to form the three points of a triangle, the symbol of the vulva, with the object of desire opposite the one who wished to snare him.

Snare him?

My frown deepened. That didn't sound right.

I glanced back at Sean. He lifted his eyebrow again, but I spun back to the book.

The more I read, the more it sounded as though the entire ritual had been *my* idea, *my* doing, *my* intent. I couldn't help but wonder just how much say Sean had had in our binding. I'd only ever thought we held such a strong connection because of the bite—an act of panic on Sean's behalf when he believed it the only way we could be together—because of what *he'd* done to *me*.

What if I'd got it wrong? What if the binding had been just as responsible for the bond between us? What kind of manipulated relationship did that make ours?

I shrugged it off, growled at myself to get a grip, told myself, *what we have is real, dammit*, and quickly read on.

At the bottom of the page, the author had added she only ever considered performing the magic because of the extreme devotion of the two subjects. If not for the intensity of their love for one another, she'd have had no doubt of the failure.

Lids lowering, my tense shoulders unknotted, and I blew out a breath as my worries diminished. With my eyes reopened, I turned back to the woman. "How do they know this even worked?"

She lowered her book.

"It only states here they did the ritual, and how."

"That's because they wouldn't know if it would work," she said. "There'd be no proof, unless the ones bound actually returned to the earth."

Failing to mention that living proof of its success stood right in front of her, I asked, "If they did, how would anybody know?"

With a sigh, she placed her novel on the counter and reached out for the tome before me. She flicked through until she neared the back, where she stopped and tapped her finger upon the page. "Nineteen-oh-six." She smiled. "Somebody recorded the return of the two werewolves upon whom the original binding had been performed."

Frowning, I peered down at where she pointed.

The handwriting didn't match the earlier pages, and whoever had written it didn't say much. No pages of theories or thoughts existed, but a simple note: Eternal binding spell of 1809 successful. Both subjects returned. Reunited. History repeated. Destiny acquired.

I straightened again. "How can they know this is genuine? Anybody could have written this in. What proof is there of it?" I probably sounded terse, but I needed to *know*.

Rather than appear bothered by my tone, her mouth curved into a genuine smile. "You're the first person to ever ask me that question."

My lips parted. No sound came out. I'd no idea *how* to respond.

"I inherited this particular grimoire from my mum who used to collect them," she continued after a few seconds.

I stared hard at her, the sudden, unasked for explanation throwing me even further.

"Most, she found in house-clearances ..." As she pointed a child-like finger, I tracked its route, my attention lingering on the grimoire. "... just like this one. I don't know where she discovered, or bought, it, but I do know it wasn't the only book there. Mum found a second one, secured with this one. Although I own the two of them, I've never put the second book on my shelves, not even within my reference collection ..."

The longer I listened to her cryptic ramble, the faster my pulse thrummed.

"Nobody has ever asked for it, or asked to see it. But if I tell you that's where I believe the writer of that particular page got confirmation, I have a hunch you'll be different."

My gaze flicked back to her face, to the earnest expression in her eyes.

"Would you like to view it?" she asked.

Resisting the urge to look to Sean for guidance, I gave a small nod.

With a smile I had trouble interpreting, she wandered off into the back again. She took longer the second time before the beads tinkled an announcement of her return.

Expecting another heavy volume, I frowned at the small, ribbon-bound notebook in her hands. A gentle tug with her fingers released the fastening, and she handed it to me with pages splayed.

As I took it and peered down at the handwriting of the opening entry, my breaths hastened. A tremble visited my fingers.

"Jem?" Sean whispered as though he'd sensed my unease.

I spun with the book in my hands, my frown almost overhanging my eyes.

With an expression to match, he stepped closer. "Jem, what's wrong?"

"It's my journal," I whispered as I passed it over.

Written in my own hand, the title page almost matched one I'd composed months earlier. Unlike that one, though, the record held no message for Jem Stonehouse.

The message had been left for Jem *Holloway*.

I'd known Sean and I had wed during our initial existence, but had no idea about our second time together. I guessed it made sense. Even in the early twentieth century, living in sin would have been frowned upon.

Sean leafed through the pages, one after another, his attention practically glued to the content.

"You know, I wondered if its original owner would ever show up here and ask for it back," the shopkeeper said.

My head snapped back to her. Beside me, Sean lowered the book.

"I know what you are." Only her fiddling fingers on the counter betrayed her nerves. "I knew the second you all walked through my door."

What the—

"I must admit, I did wonder what three—"

Please don't say it.

"—werewolves would want with a bookstore like this."

My panic rose. I opened my mouth, but nothing came out.

Sean turned fully toward her, as Ethan shifted from the door.

"Please"—the shopkeeper held up her hands—"don't be alarmed." Her focus fluttered left and right, until it stuck on Ethan. She probably considered him the biggest threat—rightly so. "I understand the importance of anonymity, just as I understand the risk I took in speaking up."

"You're mistaken," I said at last.

She turned back to me and shook her head. "It takes the mother of a werewolf to recognise when there are three standing in front of her."

My heart raced faster. "Your son is a werewolf?"

She gave a slow nod.

"Sean," I whispered, "more will come. What if—"

"What pack does he follow?" Sean asked her.

"He doesn't."

Ethan stepped close enough to shadow the tiny woman, ensuring her attention returned to him. "What do you mean?"

"He isn't part of any pack," she said.

"A loner?" Surprise deepened Ethan's tone.

She nodded again. "My son was a result of too much wine and too little self-restraint. I never saw the man again to tell him I was pregnant. Don't even remember his name." Her delicate shoulders lifted in a small shrug, a casual gesture that clashed with the slight tightness in her tone. "But ... I found out what my son is, what his father must have been ..." She took a deep breath. "When he hit his teens ... his body changed."

"Fucking irresponsible bastard," Ethan muttered too low for the woman to hear. He rubbed at his face. "And your son's never sought help? Looked for others like him?"

A flash of anger reached her eyes. "He's come across a few. And they were nothing but bullies. Not one of those he's met offered anything but intimidation. Why would he go looking for help from people like that?" She gave each of us her attention, fists clenching at her waist. "My son runs alone. When he was younger, I used to take him, then wait in the car and bring him home in the morning. If you think I don't understand how vital it is to contain a life-altering secret, then you're wrong."

I studied her, tried to judge her character, to decide if she could be trusted. She'd appeared too emotional in the way she spoke of her son to be acting. "If you think you know who and what we are, you must understand both these books belong in my family," I said.

Her chin dipped in what could've been considered agreement.

"Are you going to cause problems, if I take them? I need to put them back where they belong."

A few seconds passed, then she sighed. "No, I won't stop you."

I blew out a small breath. "Thank—"

"On one condition."

My eyes narrowed.

"I'd like some advice regarding my son. If I could convince you to stay a little while ... I'll make coffee." She sent a glance toward Ethan before turning back to me. "In return, I'm asking for help."

37

In a back sitting room-come-kitchenette, we sipped on coffee, while Shelley Lewis—the shopkeeper—ran through a condensed version of her life as an unsuspecting mother to a werewolf. Even after an hour of listening to how she'd discovered his unusual genes only after he'd experienced his first change right in front her, I doubted I grasped the full extent of how difficult it must have been.

"Of course, I can smile about it all a little now," she said, sipping on her second mug of coffee. "But then, it's always easier to—"

Banging echoed through the building from the direction of the shop.

All four of us shot to our feet, growls probably too low for Shelley to catch rumbling from Sean and Ethan. More banging, followed by, "Mum!"

Every hackle rose along my nape.

"It's okay." Shelley rounded us. "It's just my Gabe." She paused and turned back at the beaded curtain, worry lining her brow as she gestured toward our chairs. "Please ... sit down. It'll be fine." The beads clinked together once she'd passed through.

I stared after her exit, my heart thrumming at the idea of meeting another werewolf, no matter that his mother had spent the previous sixty minutes convincing us of her son's vulnerability.

'It'll be fine' she'd said. *Sure it will.*

At the end of the day, female werewolves were rare, and *he* was male. In my minuscule experience, any contact with male werewolves other than those in the pack hadn't been to my advantage.

"What do we do?" I hissed as tension coiled my muscles.

"Nothing," Ethan muttered, as Sean whispered, "Relax, Jem," like he hadn't been poised ready to spring himself.

The twist of the catch carried through to us. A deep voice trailed behind a second later. "Thought you'd gone home for lunch, or something."

"Nope," Shelley said. "Just entert—"

"What's that smell?" Audible sniffs followed, before footsteps thudded toward us. "Who you got here, Mum?"

The beaded strips smashed apart, clattering against the frame, as a young pup the size of an adult werewolf barrelled through. He slammed to a halt, and from beneath a crazy mop of pale blond curls, aqua eyes seemed to assess the situation in an arced scan of the room.

As his gaze landed on Ethan, his fists clenched. "What the fuck is going on?"

"Gabe!" Shelley pushed in behind him. "Language!"

As though she hadn't spoken, the bulky teen strode forward, his body leaning like he had every intention of knocking Ethan flat on his arse. Ethan didn't even flinch when the pup pulled short a couple of inches from butting noses with him. "What d'you—" His nostrils flared. His head whipped my way, a hint of surprise lightening his eyes. "A female," he muttered and bulleted toward me.

Sean's growl rippled past my ear, as my instinctive step backward bumped me into him. His hand shot around my shoulder, smacking against Gabe's chest.

The pup's gaze snapped up to Sean, the snarl he tossed at him as aggressive as the one Sean gave—which left me wedged between two huge wolves facing-off.

Just great.

"Sean, we're in his territory," Ethan said.

"And he's about to breach mine," Sean said, his palm still in place.

"Only because he doesn't understand." Ethan clamped his hand over Sean's arm and nudged it down, giving his attention to Gabe. "Care to back up a step? Because trust me, you don't want to be messing with a wolf when it comes to his mate. And you definitely don't want to be messing with me when it comes to my brother."

A long pause followed, during which the teenager's head made a slow twist toward Ethan.

"Gabe?" Shelley tugged on her son's arm. "Come on, sit down. Give them a chance."

"I can't believe you'd do this, Mum." Despite his tight tone, she pulled him away until the backs of his legs hit a chair, and he sank into it.

The moment he did, Sean's body relaxed against mine, the rumble in his chest dying down to a hum.

"Why the hell would you let these people"—Gabe's chin jerked our way—"in here?"

Ethan crossed to the chair farthest from the pup and lowered onto it.

Less height equalled less of a perceived threat, and I knew we should do the same, but Sean's arm wrapped about my chest like a steel barrier told me he'd no intention of that—confirmed by his whispered, "Let him handle it," when I went to step forward.

"We're here at your mother's invitation," Ethan said.

Gabe's scowl lifted, making way for a frown, as though he struggled to process Ethan's words. He twisted to his mother, and Shelley's nod only seemed to increase the creases knotting his brows.

"My name is Ethan." He drew the teen back to him. "We didn't come here to seek you out. We came to visit your mother's shop. The only reason we're still here is because your mother thought we might have some advice to share."

Gabe's lip curled. "What? Like stay out of your way? Or, if you see me again, you'll turn me into a pup kabob? I've had about all the advice I can stomach, thanks."

"Gabriel!" Shelley snapped.

His head swung her way. "Sorry, Mum. But what, exactly, have you been inhaling today, to think this is a good idea?"

"Don't be so bloody cheeky." She moved to the sofa Sean and I had evacuated and sank into it a few feet to Ethan's right.

Gabe dived forward and grabbed at her arm, drawing Shelley to the end of the sofa beside his own chair.

"Really, Gabe." Shelley heaved out a sigh. "They've been here over an hour and haven't eaten me yet."

"That's not even funny, Mum. Didn't I tell you the chemicals on all them book pages would fuzz your head? Now you ..." A dark glower entered his eyes as they flittered toward Ethan. "Spill your great advice and then get the hell out."

Ethan gave a slow nod and shuffled forward in his seat a little. "As I said ... I'm Ethan." He thumbed over his shoulder. "This is my brother Sean, and his mate. We're a part of a pack, bu—"

"And you've come to tell me to leave town like some kind of shit western." Gabe's fists clenched and unclenched where they hung over his knees.

"No." Ethan shook his head.

"They're not even local." Shelley reached out and uncurled Gabe's hand closest to her, folding her own tiny fingers around his. "They're just passing through."

"How come you get to be here without recrimination, then?" Gabe's intense focus bored into Ethan.

"Because we're not sticking around. If we'd expected to be here more than a few hours, then I'd have contacted the local Alpha, to let him know my business here and request permission."

Gabe scoffed out a laugh, but no humour entered his eyes. "Hate to drop it to you, but the locals don't take too kindly to stray mongrels hanging around, no matter the timeframe."

Ethan's head twisted toward Sean, his gaze narrowed, before he turned back to the pup. "I'm not altogether convinced it's the local pack you've been bumping into, Gabe ... can I call you Gabe?"

"Whatever." He gave a sharp half shrug. "What makes you think that?"

"Because if a pack got wind of an outsider in their territory—one with permanent residency—they'd have spoken to you about a place with them."

Gabe rolled his eyes, his lips twisting into a smile filled with bitterness. "Yeah, right."

"Who's Alpha here?" Sean muttered.

"Jack Brosen. Not his kind of stunt to bully, when he could be acquiring." Ethan faced Gabe again. "How long have you been in Shropshire?"

"Little over eighteen years," Shelley said. "Gabe was born here."

Ethan frowned. "And you've never met Jack Brosen?"

"I don't even know who the hell he is," Gabe said. "Look, this is real interesting, and all, but can we cut to the chase of you saying something interesting?"

When Ethan breathed out a laugh, my eyebrows shot up. Generally, Ethan only found himself amusing. "Okay." He stood, reaching into his back pocket and sliding out his wallet. "I've told your mother all there is to tell for now. I'm sure she can relay it so I don't have to bore you any longer. But ..." He removed a piece of paper from his wallet and placed it on the small coffee table in the centre of the seating. "... here's my card. My number's on there. You have any questions ... call. Anyone else gives you any problems, call. I might be able to help."

My jaw nearly dropped, but Shelley sent Ethan a smile full of gratitude, and Gabe didn't flick the offer back in Ethan's face.

"We'll get out of your hair now," Ethan said, waving us toward the curtain.

I sent Shelley a smile as I passed and met Gabe's gaze as it darted toward me for a split second, before ducking through the beads with Sean close enough on my tail for body heat transferral.

Back in the dim bookstore, we strode straight for the door, and a quick flip of the catch released us of the shop's confines, allowing winter daylight to bleed into the room.

"Well ... thanks for staying a while," Shelley said behind us. "And for the number ... I appreciate it."

"No worries," Ethan said. "It was nice meeting you both."

Despite the chill outside, relief swept through me at being away from the scent of unfamiliar male. I hugged the books to my chest that I'd refused to let go of since Shelley had conceded them, allowing the merged scent of old leather and city air into my senses.

"Hey."

I halted at Gabe's call, twisting back at the same time as Sean and Ethan.

"What's it like?" Gabe leaned against the doorjamb, hands in pockets as though going for nonchalance but not quite pulling it off. "You know ... running with a pack?"

Ethan smiled. "A million times better than running alone."

38

Back in the pickup, Ethan drummed his fingertips against the wheel. "You almost lost your cool in there." Although I couldn't see his face from my spot on the backseat, I knew he spoke to Sean.

"You saw how the kid came at Jem," Sean said. "What did you expect me to do?"

I ran my fingers over the two books in my lap, something trying to click in my mind but not quite catching. "The kid has issues," I mumbled absently.

"Yeah," Ethan said. "But no amount of surface attitude can diminish the stench of fear. The kid's scared. And confused. And as frustrated as he has every damn right to be."

"And that made him a risk," Sean said before twisting in his seat. "You okay?"

I placed the diary on the seat beside me and flipped up the top cover of the grimoire, like that'd help me figure out the niggle to my brain.

"Exactly why I gave him my card," Ethan mumbled on. "Better to keep an eye on a stray like that .... Besides, he's just a pup ..."

"Hey." Sean's finger slipped under my chin, and he tipped my face up until I looked at him. "You with us, Jem?"

I nodded but tapped the two books. "Something's bugging me about these."

"What is it?" Sean asked.

"Somewhere along the line, these couldn't have been in my possession. No way would I have left them where they could be picked up by someone else by mistake."

His eyes darkened. "You don't think they're yours?"

"I know the diary's mine, because the penmanship's mine." I met his gaze, as he tucked a stray hair behind my ear. "But whoever owned this grimoire couldn't have been me. And whoever they were, I must have entrusted my journal to them, also. So, it must have been another family mem—"

"Jessica!" Sean tossed his hand up, holding it suspended for seconds. "I can't believe I didn't make the connection before."

I stared at him, brow arched.

"Jessica was your sister's name before, Jem. And now you have a sister called Jess."

"Are you kidding me?"

He shook his head. "I doubt it's coincidence. Nothing ever is, when it comes to you."

I frowned, not quite sure I followed.

"I mean, we meet because the binding curse has already predestined it. Your mother went to great lengths to keep me at your side even after our initial lifetime together. Who's to say she didn't go the extra mile and create a backup plan?"

"Do you really think—"

"That Jess was your sister before?" He nodded. "The more I think about it, yes. It makes the most sense. I just never put it all together, because you never call her by her full name—it didn't click. And even when I met her ... I *felt* as though I recognised her, but with everything else"—he meant with getting the taken pack members back from the witches' evil clutches—"I just couldn't place her."

"So, Jessica—"

"Must have been the fourth person at our binding ceremony. It had to be her."

I nodded. "So, as the firstborn—"

"That grimoire belongs to her."

Jess lived in a three-bedroomed semi on the bendiest road Witchurch had to offer—the quietest, too. My rap of her letterbox sounded on par with an explosion as it boomed through the air.

The cold that crept into the neighbourhood alongside the afternoon seeped through the fabric of my sweater, as I waited with Sean and Ethan at each shoulder. Luckily, only a handful of seconds passed before footsteps thudded inside, and the distorted outline of Jess's bony frame appeared through the frosted glass pane. In the next breath, the keys jangled, and the door swung inward.

Brown to my blonde, hazel to my blue, and a couple inches shorter than my five-seven height, Jess whipped her attention to a spot above my right shoulder. "Ethan." Her lips curved up as a thousand thoughts I didn't even want to contemplate flittered across her face. "Good to see you again."

"Good to see you, too, Jess."

Although nothing had happened between my sister and Sean's brother, Jess had made it clear she would happily get close and personal if ever given the chance. As for Ethan? He was never easy to read, though he did always smile at Jess, and Ethan had a tendency to place all his warmth in reserve for only those he deemed worthy.

When Jess continued to stare, I cleared my throat, and her gaze dipped back to me. "You're here to nag me about Josh?"

I gave a non-committal sideways nod.

"Wondered how long you'd last. You didn't have to bring the goon-squad as backup."

I frowned. "That's not why they're—"

"I know. I'm just kidding. Come on." She spun from the door, heading for the kitchen, as I stepped into the hallway. "I'll put the kettle on."

The three of us followed her into the pale cream room at the back of the house, lack of sound from upstairs telling me her two children must have been at their father's for the weekend. I sank into one of the four seats at the kitchen table and indicated to Sean and Ethan to join me.

Jess snatched up her kettle en route to the sink, peering over her shoulder as she filled it with water. Though, as her gaze followed my lowering of the grimoire to the table, she gave a slow shake of her head. "Oh, no ... tell me you didn't ..."

"We didn't," I said.

"Then, explain to me why you have a grimoire that I know belongs to the woman at *Fact or Fiction*."

"Maybe it didn't belong to her," I said

Her eyes narrowed. "What do you mean?"

"I mean, it was never hers to begin."

Her brows twitched, but she didn't speak again as she moved back to flick on the kettle and grab cups. Within minutes, Jess had placed four mugs of coffee on the table.

Rather than take the only empty seat, she leaned over its back and tapped the book I'd placed down beside me. "Did you steal this, Jem?" She glared at Ethan and Sean. "Tell me you two didn't terrorise the poor woman into handing it over."

Ethan merely rolled his eyes with a smile on his lips.

"Give me a chance, and I'll explain," I said, before Sean could voice the annoyance showing in his dark expression. When she didn't argue further, I gestured to the chair in front of her and waited until she'd sat, meeting her questioning and expectant gaze. "It was Sean who figured it all out ..." I held up my finger as she opened her mouth. "So, you can thank him after I've finished explaining."

Jess glanced toward Sean and back to me. "Okay."

"Good. After you first told me about finding the binding spell in the grimoire, Sean thought of something I hadn't and that you should have."

Her gaze flicked to Sean again, and she lifted her palms. Code for: *Well ...?*

"That the book had to belong to a member of your family," Sean said. "Because it was Jem's mother in eighteen-oh-nine who performed the spell, which means she was most likely the one who recorded it in there."

A few seconds of stunned silence passed while Jess seemed to be processing his words.

"Holy crap, you're right." Jess's attention slapped onto the book with more hunger than a starved animal. "So, what'd you do? Just march in there, declare that the woman had something belonging to you, and she handed it over?"

"Not exactly," Sean said.

"Jess, there's more," I said.

She dragged her gaze back up to me. "What does he mean, *not exactly*? And what do you mean, *there's more*?"

"Never mind about the not exactly. We didn't scare the shop owner into giving us the book. She handed it over without argument. But as for the more?" I smiled. "Sean remembers the name of my sister during the time the binding spell took place."

With her neck craned forward until she resembled a long-necked turtle, Jess jigged the palms of her hands in a *Come on!* gesture.

"Her name was Jessica," Sean said.

Confusion clouded her eyes for a brief second. "Are you saying what I think you're saying?"

Sean and I had gone over and over and over it on the drive, and could find no reason to refute the idea—the *connection*.

"Yep," I said, to Sean's deep, "Yes."

"Oh, my God!" Her gaze flittered from Sean, to me, to Sean and back to me, finally settling on Ethan. "Can you believe this?"

Ethan gave a skewed shrug and chuckled.

"There's more," I said.

Jess snapped to face me, her brows lifted.

"This all means ..." I smiled. "... you've as much right to this grimoire as I do."

Jess's gaze dropped back to the book, and I couldn't help but laugh at the ping-ponging of her eyes. She even licked her lips as though I had the tastiest morsel at the table, and, dammit, she wanted a bite. "You know you don't really have a use for it, right?"

I laughed. "Yes, I know." After placing my diary aside, I slid it across the table beneath her nose. "Which is why I think you should have it."

An inane grin spread across her face. "This is really mine?"

"Yes," I said.

"And you swear you didn't kill the shop owner to get it?"

"Of course not." I guessed it would have been easier to explain about the tit-for-tat, but I could hardly expect Shelley to keep my secret and then spew hers at the first opportunity, so I merely added, "Actually, she was pretty cool about it."

"I can't believe it." Jess scooped it up from the table and trotted from the room like she had every intention of hiding it from us just in case we changed our minds.

I tracked her footsteps up the stairs and across the landing, catching Sean's smirk of amusement and Ethan's narrowed eyes that told me he didn't quite get the excitement.

After the scrape of drawers on runners grumbled a couple of times above us, Jess retraced her route and slunk back to her seat empty-handed, already pointing at the second book. "Okay, so, what's that?"

"Would you believe me, if I said it's even more unbelievable than the grimoire belonging to you?" I asked.

She jerked her chin up. "Show me."

I laid it on her outstretched palm, but didn't speak, instead waiting for her to figure it out on her own.

Her fingers loosened the satiny binding. She peeled back the cover, and it took around thirty seconds for her eyes to pop wide. "Dayam!" Her gaze flicked up to me, full of disbelief. "Where the hell did you get this?"

"Apparently, it was with the grimoire when the shop acquired it. I must have said some secret keyword, or asked the right questions, or something ..." I shrugged. "But I didn't even have to ask to see that one. The shop owner just went and grabbed it and handed it over."

"Flipping heck!" she said. "I take it you're keeping this one yourself?"

"I am."

"This's almost as awesome as the spell book." She handed it back. "So ... are you guys staying long?" She smiled. "Because I now have a date with a tome."

"Charming," Ethan muttered.

I laughed. "We'll get out of your hair. We've already extended our time away, anyway. But before we go ..." I sobered as I recalled my initial reason for visiting Jess. "... back to Josh. Found anything?"

She shook her head, her defeatist expression telling me just how much her lack of progress irked her. "Not yet."

Any lightness I'd temporarily been washed with vanished and made way for the hollowness to return.

"I keep thinking I'm looking in the wrong spots, because maybe I'm viewing his problem from the wrong angle," Jess said. "I'm pretty sure there has to be one I haven't investigated yet. As soon as I figure out what that is, I should have more to go on." She reached across the table, folding her fingers around my arm, as the corners of my lips headed further south. "I promise I'll figure it out. However long it takes."

I nodded, hoping she'd figure it out soon—for the rest of the pack as much as my own sanity.

Stony-faced, Nathan thumbed through my diary without looking up from his spot at the kitchen table. Sitting beside him, Beth stared my way, the slight lift to her eyebrows telling me she'd known all along I'd been up to something and I'd just proven exactly that.

Several seconds of quiet surrounded the sound of flipped pages, before Nathan folded the cover into place and leaned back in his seat. "Why didn't you tell me your real reason for wanting to go out?" Although perfectly calm, his voice held an undercurrent of disappointment.

"I did." I scratched at my head, averting my eyes—because even I knew my answer only bordered on the truth.

"Just not the entire story of where?" Nathan asked.

I glanced up to see Ethan's arched brow, his louder-than-screaming silent way of saying 'I told you so'.

"You, too," Nathan said Sean's way before I could respond.

"Je—" Sean sent me a quick glance then scratched his head—exactly as I had—and I knew he'd been about to spill the beans, to tell his dad that I'd said I would handle it, and he hadn't exactly played any part in the deceit. He'd never leave me to take all the slack, though. Instead, he muttered, "No, I didn't tell you because I knew you'd never permit it."

Strict silence fell over the room as we waited to see what Nathan would say. With my chin tucked close to my chest, my fingers wrapped around my seat as though to brace myself, I met Nathan's steely stare, forcing myself not to recoil from the discontent in his expression.

"Is this going to be an ongoing motto of yours, Jem?" His attention remained wholly on me.

My lips went to squish as I wondered what he meant.

"Act first, repent later?" he went on. "You must realise you're potentially endangering others, as well as yourself?"

"It wasn't dangerous," Ethan piped up. "Not even close."

"Maybe not this time," Nathan said. "But what about next time? It's exactly this kind of gung-ho behaviour that gets the pack into trouble."

"Yeah, but look at what was achieved today," Ethan said, and my eyebrows lifted a little as he came to my defence. "Jem retrieved valuable items out of the wrong hands," he continued. "Not to mention the contact made with the pup. Surely, you have to agree some outcomes are worth the risks?"

Nathan gave a slow nod. "But whether or not to take the risk in the first place should be my decision, not yours. I need full disclosure, if I'm to keep you all properly protected. Is this too much to ask?"

Somehow, the quietness of his tone made the reprimand all the more cringe-worthy.

Unsurprisingly, a trio of 'No's mumbled from the three of us, and Nathan's definitive nod announced us dismissed.

39

"Hmmm." I peered up at the page I held hovering over my face. "July ninth, nineteen-oh-seven. The day I woke up." Elbowing Josh's supine form in the ribs, I tipped my head back to bring him into view. "You listening, Josh? You could catch a few pointers. This is interesting stuff."

Sean chuckled from the wicker chair in the corner of the room. "You should be careful. He's probably listened to every damn word you've said." His eyes squinted. "Wonder how many secrets he's heard that I don't know about."

"Ha! None." I turned a couple pages over. Two days had passed since leaving Jess's house. I'd already whizzed through my old diary once, but couldn't resist a more thorough perusal—not when it took my mind off waiting. Again. "If he can hear me, he's probably praying for me to shut the heck up because I'm driving him nuts."

"There's no safe way for me to respond to that," Sean said.

I snorted and flipped back a page, scanning the contents. "*'Everything smelled strange when I woke up'*," I read. "*'Strong, too strong, burning my nostrils with pungency.'* ... Yeah, I can relate to that," I muttered. "*'Sean assures me my body will adapt to my heightened senses. I would take note if I were actually listening to him. Right now, I have only thoughts of murderous intent toward the—'*" Another snort erupted, though it diminished when I lifted my head to find no humour in Sean's expression, but a deep hurt cutting lines across his brow. "If it makes you feel any better, I crossed out the bad name. Guess that means I forgave you, at some point."

"Yeah." Forearms resting against his knees, he ducked his head down a little, before his dark eyes, filled with emotion, met mine. "For some reason, you always do."

I rolled up to sit, closing my diary and placing it on the bedside table. "What's up?"

"Nothing." He brushed a hand over his hair, blew out a breath. "I just don't deserve you."

"What's brought this on?" I clambered from the bed and crossed the room to him. "Why would you even think that?"

"See?" His brows knotted tight. "You don't even see how selfless you are."

"Selfless?" I breathed out a laugh, hooking a knee alongside his thigh as I sank astride his lap, leaving him no choice but to lean back. "Every day I'm with you, I feel like the most selfish person on the face of the planet, lost in a permanent self-indulgence of exactly what I want, everything else be damned. How on earth does that make me selfless?"

"Because you're so bloody accepting, I sometimes feel as though I have no right to ask any more of you. Yet, somehow, I still do."

"Wh—"

"You find out who I am—you accept me. Hell, you find out *what* I am and still accept me. You end up bitten—*by me*!" He tapped against his chest. "And even *that's* not my fault, according to you."

"Because it w—"

"You get snatched by another pack—even when that happened, you refused to allow anyone to take the blame but yourself."

"For good re—"

"You had a life before I stepped back into it. What happened to that? Oh, yeah, you gave it all up." His fingers gripped my shoulders. "For me!"

"Not all of—"

"And I repaid you by tossing you into pack life, expecting you to adapt with barely time for consideration."

"You hardly toss—"

"And now this? All this!" He released a low growl. "More crap you seem to think you're to blame for but probably would have happened, anyway, even if you hadn't been around. Then where would we all have been?" His chin jerked to the right. "Still stuck with those fucking witches, probably." He paused, the fire in his eyes moving aside for a deep hopelessness to take its place. "These past two weeks have been the most down I've ever seen you, Jem. *Ever.* The one time I should be able to give you something back ..." He heaved out a sigh and released me, raking his fingers through his hair. "... and I have no idea how to make everything all right again for you."

"Don't you get it?" Taking his cheeks in my hands, I peered through the glossiness that painted his eyes a dark, melted chocolate. "Every time you walk up those stairs, every time I hear your voice ... every bloody time I inhale your scent, and it brings me a calm I find nowhere else—*nowhere*—and every time you hold me until I fall asleep at night .... Sean, you're already doing everything I need."

"I love you, Jem."

"I know," I whispered, brushing my lips across his. "That's why I'm here."

My usual response failed to bring the desired reaction. Any other time, he'd have smiled or chuckled and burrowed into my throat, full of lustful intent. Too much had happened, though—or maybe too little.

When I'd first found Sean in the witches' lair, our reunion had been fast and furious and as hungered as one could expect after almost two desperate weeks apart. That had been before we'd returned home to find Josh hadn't woken. Since then, the entire pack seemed to have been in a depression, obsessing over the missing limb that prevented us from being whole. Even the trip to Jess's and the elation of retrieving the diary and grimoire were no more than they'd appeared—a temporary reprieve from the problems that still faced us on returning home.

Nothing but a heavy sadness hung over Sean, as I stared deep into his eyes. I knew if I didn't tug the both of us out of mourning for Josh there and then, and snatch at least a few hours for ourselves, it would take a whole lot more than words to lift him.

Ducking closer, I kissed him. Long and deep. Lips parted. Fingers weaving into his hair.

His response seemed automatic—for a few beats. A low groan bubbled from the back of his throat, his arms slid around me. And he dove into the embrace like the man starved of attention he'd become.

As he stood, my legs hooked around him, and in a dozen strides he'd taken us to our room.

The mattress met my back. His fingers grabbed my sweater hem, and he yanked upward. I raised my arms, wiggling and grappling to get it off fast before fisting a handful of his T and sending it the same way.

I sighed at the flesh on flesh contact, when he lowered back down. Gasped at the scrape of his teeth along my throat. Moaned, as his lips melded to mine.

He reached for the fastening of my jeans. Jerked the denim against my waist. A second time. Third. "Dammit," he muttered against my lips. "Bloody button."

I breathed out a laugh, stretching down to help him out. As I unhooked and wormed out of my jeans, he pushed back from the bed and stripped himself of his own. When he returned, not a scrap of fabric separating us, his arousal beat out his impatience against my abdomen.

For seconds, we simply stared at one another. The rumble within his chest vibrated through mine until it spilled from his lips as a long, low growl.

I trembled beneath him, my thighs parting in anticipation, my chest rising higher with each breath.

Still, he didn't move as he peered down at me, though his arms bulged in their rigidity, his jaw working as if he struggled with some internal debate, and the first beads of sweat glistened on his temples.

I lifted my head, captured his lower lip between my teeth.

His entire body seemed to buzz as the rumble evolved into a thrum that affected every inch of him—though who he meant to punish by holding back, I couldn't be sure.

"I need you," I whispered, darting my tongue out to tend the nip from my teeth. "Please, Sean, I—"

I gasped, as he thrust into me. My lids threatened to fall, when he drew back, but I ordered them open.

His eyes glistened above me as he stilled once more. For a moment, I wondered if he'd stop, if I'd failed in bringing calm to his turmoil.

His face dipped. His gaze dropped to my mouth.

I waited, breaths stalled, body tense.

As his lips smothered mine and his hips drove forward again, I let out a half-sob of relief and allowed myself to hold him at last.

As if his resolve had snapped, his mouth, his hands—*he* seemed to suddenly be everywhere. Lips across my jaw. Whispers of my name at my ear. A suckle of my throat.

All while he filled me over and over, while his scent saturated my senses all the way through to my soul, and while his hands caressed—each and every touch sending a searing heat to my middle until I could do little more than cling to him.

Sweat soaked his hairline as my fingers tangled within the strands. His muscles bunched and released beneath my calves. My back arched higher and higher into each embrace, and his arm slid beneath me, pressing me closer. Not even a sliver of air separated us as his lips returned to mine, and his thrusts grew to a frantic pace.

"*Jem.*"

The ragged whisper seeped into my mouth, chased by a low snarl that warned of his end, and I gasped as a shiver rolled the length of my body.

Beneath the high shine of his glossy stare and the waves of pleasure visibly rippling across Sean's flesh, the euphoric spasms began to uncoil low in the pit of my stomach. Each and every muscle I possessed clenched tight.

My breath stalled as though awaiting permission to erupt, as the buzz of muteness filled my hearing to capacity, allowing no other sounds passage besides the beating of our hearts, and my vision tunnelled until I saw only him.

For one beat. Two. Three.

On the fourth, darts of pure bliss splintered outward, bulleting to every precipice of my soul. My cries merged with Sean's, until we were both left panting, our chests meeting beneath each heave, our pulses thrumming out an unsteady tune.

For seconds, neither of us moved other than the tremor in our limbs.

With his temple pressed to mine, his breaths warmed the side of my face, and he dipped lower and kissed my eyelid, my cheek.

"Please rest, Jem." He brushed across my lips. "You need to rest."

As he pulled back, I took a moment to absorb the dark circles surrounding his eyes, the tightness to his jaw, and mentally screamed at myself for not realising how my restlessness had been affecting him. "Just ... hold me a little while," I whispered.

"I'd hold you forever if I thought it'd keep your demons at bay."

Within minutes, I'd settled half on my stomach, Sean snuggled against my rear with his leg hooked over mine, his arm wrapped as far around me as it could possibly go, and I fell into the deepest sleep I'd had in a fortnight.

40

Quiet tapping broke into my dream of running through the forest as wolf on the tail of a fox cub. My lids fluttered open, and a few blinks through descended gloom brought Ethan into focus, leaning against the doorjamb with his hands in his jeans pockets.

He smiled. No jibing, no snarky comments about sleeping in and slacking off—just smiled. "You've got a visitor."

Sean roused beside me, rubbing at his face as he released a yawn. "Who?"

Ethan's smile warmed even further. "Jess."

I stared at him. Jess didn't make off-handed, spontaneous, unannounced visits. The only time Jess had ever called round had been when the pack needed her help.

In fact, the only reason I could imagine for her coming was ... "She figured out a cure?"

Ethan shrugged, as I swung my legs over the mattress edge, already reaching for Sean's discarded shirt from the floor.

"She didn't say?" I tugged the jersey over my head, as jostling at my rear told me Sean made a move, too.

"She said, as it'll involve you, she only thought it fair you be there when she explains." He shrugged again. "Seems pretty itchy over it."

"Tell her I'll be right down." As Ethan turned away, I marched across for a pair of shorts from the drawer, barely missing Sean as he headed in the same direction. "Oh, someone should call Con—"

"Already on his way," Ethan said. "See you downstairs."

Of course they'd called Connor. Whatever Jess had to say regarding Josh, his dad had a right to know. His brothers, would most likely show up to hear the scoop, too.

In under two minutes, Sean and I padded into the kitchen—me in Sean's dirty T-shirt and a pair of his boxers, and Sean in pretty much the same except his shirt smelled fresh.

Jess peered up at me from my spot at the table, where she sat triangled-in by Nathan, Beth and Ethan. She sent me a smile. "Hey."

"You have some news?" Of course she did. The fact she'd come on a school night and hadn't brought the kids with her confirmed she'd dropped everything. I scraped back the end seat opposite Nathan and sank into it, as Sean took the spot across from Jess. "You figured it out?" I asked

"I've had an idea that I think might work." She should have looked smug—usually, would have—but only a deep seriousness affected her features.

"That's great. Tell me."

"It's not quite as—" Her gaze flicked up at the conservatory door flying inward.

In the next breath, Connor, Kyle and Daniel spilled into the kitchen, all three of them tugging shirts on, which told me they'd changed and run through the forest.

It didn't surprise me they'd taken the fastest route. The only reason Josh still occupied the lilac room, instead of his bed at his own home, was because none of us had expected him to be under so long—though leaving him behind at the end of the day seemed to be growing more and more difficult for his family.

Connor leaned against the doorframe as his sons settled into the two remaining chairs.

A couple of chest heaves and composure breaths later, Jess had the floor. "As you've probably suspected, I've had a breakthrough in my research," she said.

Stillness encompassed the room. All attention settled on Jess like a brain-frying laser beam.

"Turns out, I'd been going about it all from the wrong angle. I already suspected I had, but couldn't figure out the angle I should have been looking from. Now ..." She sent a small smile my way. "Thanks to Jem's retrieval of the grimoire—"

My eyes widened at the thought I could have been holding the solution in my hands just days before.

"—and certain ... recordings in there giving a big enough hint, I think I know the kind of spell we'll need to wake Josh."

Silence. Of the stunned variety. Of the 'dare we hope for this to be true' kind. As if we all stood on a pinnacle awaiting the tiny nudge that would topple us into soaring blissfulness.

"Okay, we're listening." Nathan broke the spell first.

"Well ... the thing is, I've spent the last couple of weeks so intent on trying to figure out *how* the witches put Josh under the way they did that I lost sight of the bigger picture. What I *should* have been paying more attention to was much simpler. The actual tools, ritual, ingredients used were merely a means to an end, so it's not those we need to overcome. It's not even the spell we need to overcome." She glanced toward me before giving her attention back to Nathan. "It's the aftereffects—the *result* of the spell—we should have been concentrating on."

More silence filled her pause, though I believed more confusion than anticipation housed that one.

Jess blew out a breath. "Josh has been—*is*—in a death sleep. Or, to be pedantic, the sleep of the dead." That much, we already knew. "It's about time we started treating him as such."

Connor straightened in the doorway—the only one of us to move. "Care to elaborate, Jess?"

She dipped her chin a little. "We should treat him like a dead person."

"Excuse me?" Connor stepped Jess's way, but stopped when she held her hand up.

"I mean figuratively. Not literally. As a means of approach. And I can't believe I didn't figure it out sooner." She shook her head, rolling her eyes. "But this revelation is a good thing. Trust me." Her gaze darted around the room, landing on each of us in turn, until settling on Nathan. "Because the dead can be contacted."

"Like a séance, you mean?" Nathan asked.

Jess gave a slow nod. "Now you're starting to think along the right lines. Except, it won't be a group séance. Because I doubt that would work. Chatting to Josh won't do shit, if he doesn't come with a visual of his physical form surrounding his soul. So, I delved deeper in my research. Found a spell—one that would enable the caster to reach a departed one via sleep." Jess's attention swung to me. "And we already know someone capable of that."

The whisper of heads turning spun through the room—no doubt toward me—but I couldn't take my eyes off Jess, or the fact she'd yet to show triumph over her revelation. No high shine to her eyes. No self-gratuitous smile. A flutter of concern flashed through her expression before she controlled it, but not before I'd caught it.

My eyes narrowed. *What aren't you saying?*

"So, what would it involve?" Sean asked, his hand slipping over my knee beneath the table. "What would Jem need to do?"

"Pretty much the same as she did before, when you guys were with the witches, and she mentally searched for you. It works almost the same way, except the soul she'll be seeking won't be in its body."

"Sounds simple," I muttered, my gaze still linked with my sister's.

"It does, doesn't it?" she said—a non-response, in my opinion.

"So, how does contacting him bring him back?" Connor asked.

Nobody else seemed to have noticed the eyeing session between Jess and me. She turned Connor's way.

"Normally, a ritual would be performed to call him back to his bod—"

"Necromancy?" Nathan shot to his feet, his chair tipping as he leaned over the table. "Tell me that isn't where you're headed in your ideas, Jess."

Jess met him head on. "If we didn't have Jem, that would be your only option, Nathan." Her hand waved toward me. "But you do have Jem. Hence the dream search."

Nathan's brow arched up. "So, this is in no way a form of necromancy?"

Jess stayed silent—for a few beats too long—before she said, "It would be. If we didn't have Jem."

"Explain," Nathan said.

"Sit down." Beth's quiet command, said as she squeezed Nathan's arm, seemed to work, because Nathan lowered back into his seat. "Jess came to help. Don't terrorise her before you've heard her out."

Nathan sent a glance toward his wife before giving Jess his attention again. "Go on."

"Jem will go under, thinking of Josh, just as she did in her dream searches before, with Sean. Hopefully, she'll land where she needs to be to find him. Then all she has to do is grab hold of him and bring him back with her when she returns."

Tension had begun a slow build throughout the room during Jess's explanation, with Sean's most palpable as his hand tightened over my knee. "She'll leave her body to do this?" he asked.

Jess cocked her head a little. "Like astral projecting."

Shit. I hated astral projection. Once had been more than enough—even if it had been the situation I'd loathed rather than the experience itself. No matter the strength of my inner groan, though, I kept my opinion to myself. A hint of apprehension from me would likely result in the entire plan being called off before it had even been fully formed.

"And," Jess added, "if she doesn't find Josh within an agreed timeframe, we'll wake her up and bring her back."

"And Josh gets left behind?" Connor asked.

"You were there, Connor, when Jem tried reaching out to the guys through sleep before. You already know it didn't happen on the first attempt. Though, whether or not Jem tries again will be up to her."

All heads turned to me, but no one spoke. Not one of them would ask me to do it or try to sway my mind. Yet their stares still held an oppression of responsibility. A twist of my head to the left connected me with Sean. His eyes held little expression, though they absorbed me into their depths. He probably hoped I'd say, *oh, hell, no—find another way*, but no way would he verbalise that kind of opinion. Not when he'd understand that, no matter the dangers, I'd throw myself into the task if it meant we'd get Josh back.

I broke from Sean's gaze and turned to Jess. "What do we do?"

41

Whether or not Jem tries again will be up to her.

Since I'd left the kitchen to give Jess space to prepare, her words had bugged me—along with the fact I'd yet to see her smile.

I rolled onto my side, white ceiling switching to lilac walls, before the object of my upcoming search and rescue filled my vision. I needed the reminder of the purpose, I guessed, the importance of it, because something niggled the hell out of me about it all.

It had since Jess had explained her enlightenment.

Why, though?

What, even?

Did I think she'd been dishonest in what she said?

She'd have had no reason to.

"You're fretting," Sean said from his regular perch in the corner.

My gaze flitted across to him. "What makes you say that?"

"Because you get this cute little groove"—he pressed a finger between his eyebrows—"right here when you're stressing, or worrying, or thinking too hard."

"Humph."

"You don't have to do this, Jem." His quiet voice told me he realised pretty much that I *did* have to do it. "You can change your mind."

Another sentence said without conviction because he knew as well as I did that I couldn't—that I *wouldn't*. I'd wondered if he'd be able to stay silent forever. Wondered if we'd get through the ritual without him stating his case. Should have known he'd try and make it sound as though *I* questioned my decision, instead of him outright expressing *his* opposition.

"Nobody will think any worse of you, if you do. *Nobody.*" That time, passion deepened his tone as he spoke the one statement we both couldn't question.

Neither of us looked away as minutes passed.

"Talk to me, Jem," he murmured. "What's putting that frown on your face? Let me in, for God's sake, because it's already driving me crazy, the thought of you doing what you're going to do."

"You think I don't know that? You think I don't understand the strength of will it must be taking for you not to argue with me, to try and forbid me to go ahead with it?"

"If I asked you not to do it, would you listen?"

"Yes," I said.

"But you wouldn't comply."

"No. But you'd never ask me to begin." More silence. More heavy staring. "Would you?"

He shook his head, deep resignation clouding his eyes.

"Because you want Josh back just as much as anyone else. And if it was anyone but me facing the ritual, you'd barely even be questioning the risks."

"I know." His head ducked a little, showing me his crown as he brushed a hand across his hair, mussing it up. "Doesn't make it any easier, though." As he dropped his forearms to rest across his knees, he lifted his face until we'd reconnected once more. "Which is why you can't shut me out, Jem. Because this is already hard enough as it is."

"It shouldn't be hard for you at all. Last time, I wasn't in any danger. Why should this time be any different?" Easy words that in no way matched the unease humming through me.

"So, if you truly believe that ... again, why the frown? Because the worry I feel in me"—he placed a hand to his chest—"I see reflected in your eyes, Jem."

Evidently, I hadn't done a decent job of convincing him. There went my plan to duck off and find the source of my

402

niggles alone. Silly of me to have believed I could—on either account.

I drew in a deep breath and let it out on a slow release. "I think we need to go and talk to Jess."

The kitchen erupted around me. Every pack member had climbed to their feet. Every pack member growled out their discontent in Jess's direction.

From beyond the bubble of momentary panic surrounding me, Beth tugged at Nathan's arm, Connor stalked left to right, a three step back-and-forth. Kyle thumped a fist on the table, while Daniel's arm swung in my direction as whatever objections he had spewed from his lips.

Cornering Jess and demanding to know what bugged her arse hadn't exactly gone how I'd imagined.

From the instant she'd admitted she believed Josh to be in some kind of 'in-between', and told everyone that for me to return from there, I'd have to open a 'doorway' to pass through, the pack had gone ape-shit. Though, I guessed her closing comment of 'Anything can potentially follow her back' had been the catalyst for that.

The only one of them around the table not screwing was Ethan, though the bunch of his muscles, the slight tic to his jaw, and the way he stared at his brother showed me where his thoughts had landed.

To the right of the fray, Sean stood, his hands linked across his nape, his eyes closed tight. It didn't matter that he didn't speak, didn't yell like the others. His thoughts on the matter screamed from his tightened features loud enough to mute all other argument in the room. Yet, when his lids lifted, and his gaze immediately sought mine, his stare held only a deep acceptance—solidified by the jerky nod he gave.

"Everyone, stop!" His voice arrived loud enough to slice through the racket, and every head turned toward him. "Quit hounding on Jess, when this is Jem's decision."

As if he'd powered them to do so, they all followed his gaze to where I stood by the cooker, expectation and fury all rolled into a bundle of contrasting stares.

After no more than a fleeting glance for each, I ignored them all and looked directly at Jess. "How much danger will I be in?"

She didn't waver as she answered, "I don't know."

"Can you protect me?"

"Yes." No hesitation—for which I was seriously grateful.

I released a breath. "Is there any other way?"

"I don't even know if *this* is the way." She shrugged. "But it's the only one I've found so far that has potential."

"Okay." I nodded before taking in each of the pack. "You want Josh back? You're going to have to let me do this."

Not one person argued as I stalked from the room.

The spare bedroom smelled like a cross between a florist, a perfumery, and a gardener's bonfire bash. Lilac bunches of flowers hung above my spot beside Josh and had been tucked beneath my pillow, along with a photograph of him—the necessary components of the Wisteria dream spell.

The tiny burps working their way up my throat tasted of the ginger Jess had made me eat, to prevent my body from being used as a vessel.

I didn't want to delve too deep into what she'd meant by that.

On the bedside tables, hacked up mugwort lay shrivelling in clay pots, consumed by flames that burned shades of red and brilliant blue—for protection, Jess had said as she'd secured bracelets she'd made from mistletoe about both my wrists. The latter scratched my skin, but I didn't complain—not when that would be the key to opening the door through which I'd be able to drag Josh back with me.

The homemade bangle on my left wrist jiggled slightly beneath Sean's thumb brushing across the skin there. He'd drawn the wicker chair to the bedside, where he alternated between intense gazing at me and watching Jess with curiosity, his two hands crowded around one of mine.

"You okay?" he whispered, low enough no one else would hear.

I nodded, because I was. A couple of moments alone with Jess had reassured me. I'd asked why, if the process was an in-and-out and she had confidence in her ability to watch my back, she'd looked as if she was on a fretting marathon since she'd shown up at the house. In response, she'd smiled and told me, 'You're my sister. It's my job to worry about you.' She'd also admitted the whole reason she hadn't wanted to say anything was because she'd known as well as anyone that the extra information wouldn't have changed my mind in a million years—so, what would have been the point of adding stuff for me to stress over that she could deal with on my behalf. After all, thinking about all the what-ifs would only hinder my attempts to focus solely on Josh.

Nathan and Connor stood vigil in the doorway, their too-broad-for-the-gap shoulders making them an impenetrable barrier. Though they both stood perfectly still, the tight lines pulling at their eyes and mouths showed a nervous energy anyone unfamiliar with them might have missed. While simple dislike for the situation shone from Nathan's pale blue stare, Connor's green eyes, each time they locked with mine, held a quiet desperation.

It had to have been a tough call for him to make as a father—yearning for his son's return over allowing me, the pack's only female werewolf, to perform the one task his superior strength and abilities couldn't help him with: saving his son.

After setting light to one more bowl—full of sage—Jess crossed to the dresser where she'd left a couple of Tupperware tubs. The instant she peeled the lid off the bigger of the two, my nose scrunched halfway up my head. Even Connor, Nathan and Sean shrunk back.

"What the heck's that?" I asked.

"This ..." She lifted her hand, and a ground mixture of earthy colours sifted through her parted fingers into the tub below. "This will keep everything contained to this room ... just in case. And for the 'just in case' ..." She opened the second tub, filling the room with a spiciness that might have been pleasant, had the contents of the first box not been so overpowering. "... we have asafetida."

"Smells like a dodgy curry house in there," Kyle called from the landing.

Although Jess had banned everyone bar us from the room, none of the others had obeyed her request to stay downstairs, and I suspected Sean's and my bedroom— being the closest—would smell of a combination of the pack by the time we finished.

"Well," Ethan's voice carried in, "I guess if nothing else works, at least the prospect of food should get Josh to come back."

"It'll be fine," Jess said, glancing to me. "I have every faith in Jem." She half-shrugged a shoulder. "And in myself."

"She better," Sean mumbled beneath his breath.

"Okay, from this point forward, I want nobody in this room who doesn't need to be here ..." Jess scooped out a handful of the stinky powder and began sprinkling it in a fine line around the bed. "And once this circle is formed ..." She worked her way behind the headboard, shuffling backward as she went. "Nobody must cross it ..." She reappeared behind Sean's shoulder in her reverse manoeuvring. When she'd only a couple feet left to complete the circle, she halted, her gaze lifting to Sean. "Time to leave."

I spotted the stubborn set to his jaw, even before he said, "I don't think so, Jess."

She sighed. "Things could get ..." She trailed off, rubbing her forearm across her brow as she straightened. "I can't protect you, as well as Jem."

He shrugged.

"You'll be vulnerable."

"I don't give a shit. I stay, or Jem doesn't go in."

My own sigh eked out. "Sean—"

"It's not negotiable." He cupped the back of my neck and drew me to him until his lips brushed my ear. "I *need* this, Jem," he whispered. "Do not make me leave."

Pulling back a little brought the darkness of his eyes into view, and I stared into them before admitting a small part of me was relieved at the thought of having him there at my side. I nodded to Jess. "He stays."

"Should have known." She waved an arm in our direction. "Fine. You'll need to give him one of your mistletoe bands. Once you've got that on, Sean, you can*not* break contact with Jem. Do you understand?"

"Not even an issue," he said.

"Good. As soon as you've done that, Jem, start sniffing on the handkerchief I gave you, and let's get this show on the road."

42

Heat radiated against my left palm from Sean's hand, coolness against my right from Josh's. Uncomfortable with having my face covered, I'd tucked the oil-saturated handkerchief into my bra strap, and the powerful bouquet of lavender and clary sage wafted up and in to dull my brain.

Breaths slow and deep, I stared from beneath my heavy lids at the minuscule cracks in the ceiling, my mind musing over what I might do with my days if we managed to bring Josh back. Would I miss the constriction of the four lilac walls that had become my prison almost as much as his?

"Jem, if you don't settle down, it'll never work," Jess said.

My gaze slid to her. "I am settled."

"Your flicking toes are telling a different story."

Flicking toes? I hadn't even noticed—not with the fingertips of Sean's free hand sweeping tiny circles the length of my inner arm and lulling me into a state of calm.

"Deep breaths. In and out. Close your mind. Fill it with just enough of what relaxes you. I already told you, Josh can be shoved in there at the last second."

I tightened my hand around Sean's and tugged him closer. "Hold me," I whispered.

He stared into me as though he wanted to say something, but only gave a small nod. The moment his arm came around my ribcage, and he ducked close enough to nuzzle my neck, I drew as much of him as possible into my senses, and my lids drooped the rest of the way without protest.

"I love you so much, Jem," Sean whispered against my ear as Jess resumed her chanting. "I'll call to you once you're there ..."

My breath eased in, out.

"... I'll keep calling your name ..."

My pulse slowed.

"... All you have to do is listen ..."

Jess's mumbles became nothing but background static.

"... You hear me, Jem? ..."

Darkness crept inward from the outsides of my brain.

"... Listen for me, and you'll know the way back."

Total blackness.

I blinked.

Still, blackness greeted me.

As though I'd been dropped into a well of infinite nothingness.

More blinks. Same result.

The blackness shifted. Just a little.

Shadows?

I tracked the slow dance of the one I'd seen move. Twirling. Swirling. Macabre fingers reaching out, beckoning, pointing, all of them gnarled and deformed.

Not shadows, I realised the more I studied the subtle alterations. *Fog.*

Thick, black fog.

Everywhere.

Disorientation in its most terrifying form.

I took a deep, shuddering breath. My entire self stiffened upon realising nothing entered my body.

You have no body, I reminded myself. *No body. No breaths.*

Yet, somehow, I sensed the solidity beneath my feet, the clench of my spiritual hands, the grit of my non-existent teeth. The thuds against the inside of my ribcage, though, surprised me the most.

For some reason, I'd expected to feel ... nothing.

I chanced a step forward. After all, I'd never find Josh if I spent the entire time in one spot. When nothing bad happened, I moved my feet again until I'd taken a half-dozen steps.

As though disturbed by my movements, the soup-thick fog parted a little, and I received my first glimpse of tree after tree after tree.

The view should have calmed me. At least a little.

Instead, it only filled me with dread.

None of the limbs I could see held the promise of life—not like the forest at home. Trunks as thick as my body length and far higher than the fog allowed me to see rose from the ground. Around those trunks grew grassy weeds that entwined into traps and clung to the blackened bark.

First glance insisted the webs would make the trees climbable.

Rationality argued the mesh couldn't possibly be safe.

I attempted an inhalation. No go. Zilch. Not only had I lost my ability to breathe, but my smell sensors had gone poof right along with it.

I'd almost drowned once. One wrong inhalation and the water had suffocated my body with an oppression of almost no return.

The atmosphere of the forest reminded me of exactly that.

My heart beat a little wilder.

"Hold it together, Jem," I whispered through my teeth.

Rolling out my shoulders, I dropped into a squat. Once more, my movement sent the blackness into motion like greying spirals of smoke.

A pitter-patter hit the ground to my left.

Head tilted, I tracked the sound as it scurried, coming my way. A wave of my arm urged the fog to lessen, as the tapping grew closer, until what looked like corporeal feet appeared beneath the lower level mist.

They halted and shuffled around until toes faced toward me, no more than three metres away.

I didn't straighten from my crouch, didn't announce my presence—didn't dare blink.

Time passed. Neither seemed willing to move.

I stared harder through the wisps at the toes, trying to match them up with what I'd seen of Josh's feet and wishing I'd spent more effort getting to know them better.

Unable to take it any longer, I nudged my face forward and whispered, "Josh?"

The feet came at me so fast, it took all my effort not to back up as I shoved to a stand. The fog spun, coiling tight before dispersing. In its place, two enormous eyes stared back at me from a head tipped to the left with long, dark straggles of hair hanging low over one shoulder. A quick up and down with my eyes revealed an emaciated body, hands curled claw-like, and a body pretty much poised to strike.

"You're fresh." Its voice came out a hiss, as the scary-as-hell features twisted into a smile that chilled me right down to the pit of my stomach.

I rammed my elbow up as fast as it'd go until it slammed into a jaw. As its head snapped back, I shoulder barged the manky female-looking-creature out of my path and bulleted off to the left.

Though no breaths left or entered my lungs, I still went through the motions of panting, my cheeks contracting and expanding.

Though each impact of my feet against ground made little to no contact, my limbs still seemed to register every single jolt.

I didn't glance back as I raced. Couldn't have risked it even if I'd wanted. Not when every trunk I swerved past loomed up out of the fog with less than a second to react.

I had no idea how long I ran. Lack of breath, lack of fatigue made it impossible to judge. So did the constant scenery that never seemed to alter whichever way I turned. I could have been trapped in some kind of loop and wouldn't have known the difference.

At least I seemed to have created a cleared pathway. Though, that might not have necessarily been good, as it led directly to me.

When I eventually slowed to a stop, my body automatically doubled over, palms pressed to my knees for support. I swayed there, eyes closed tight, wondering what the *fuck* I had gotten myself into.

For Josh, came my mental reminder, and I opened my eyes.

"Please be here, Josh," I whispered.

My head whipped to the right, at a crashing sound, like trampling and the snapping of brushes.

Heading toward me.

I dropped to all fours. Why the heck I kept doing that, I didn't know. Maybe I thought making myself smaller would help me stay hidden.

A blur streaked past my face, missing me by inches, close enough to stir the hairs trailing across my brow.

Instinct had me jerking back.

The body tried to halt, bundling over itself a couple of times before finding its footing. When it whirled back to me, it held little more height than me in my crouch, and it took me a single blink to realise I stared at some kind of Mastiff.

Its head cocked to the side. Its ears twitched up, too.

I stayed as still as possible. The canine may well have looked like something off a *Chum* commercial, but my last encounter had my defences up high. Shoulders raised, face lowered, I peered at a spot just below lips that resembled black rubber bands.

One paw nudged closer. A tiny whimper escaped.

Another pad pushed forward. Its head still angled, ears high on its head, the whimper rose into a quiet growl.

Drawing my own lips back, I released a warning growl of my own.

The dog halted. Whimpered. Stepped forward. Growled.

I allowed the rumble to brew a little longer before emitting another warning.

The dog sprang.

Its shoulder collided with mine. I flew backward, arms flung wide. A quiet *oomph* erupted from me as I hit the ground. Allowing no chance for composure, the dog draped over me. Big, beefy paws pressed either side of my head as it sniffed along my jawline.

Maybe I wasn't the only one unable to help themselves going through the motions.

Hopefully.

The dog sniffed lower, its nostrils tickling across my clavicle. It paused over my left breast and gave another of its whimpers before sliding lower still.

On the verge of me barking out, *Oh, hell, no!* the dog stalled at a spot just below my navel, and its nose went into overdrive. Sniffs in. Snorts out. Again. And again.

As it pulled its head back a little, its face lifted upward, and the whimper built into a pitiful half-howl full of pain. Ducking its face again, it pawed at my stomach, tapping against my vest covering it, prodding with its nose, rising only to let out another mournful cry.

Throughout the entire episode, I dared not move. My hands lay fisted at my side. My chin tucked tight to my chest. Not once did the dog hurt me or mark me with its inquisitiveness.

A howl arriving from who knew what direction snapped me round. What if the dog had called for backup? What if more were on their way? What if the dog just intended to save me so it could present me to others and share me as a snack?

Yeah, Jem, and what if you've lost your mind?

Ignoring my ridiculous mental rambles, I thrust up to sit and pushed at the dog.

It didn't protest, just backed away, giving me one more tiny whimper, before dashing off through a cluster of brush to the left.

Head tilted, I tracked its path, checking it didn't double back, needing to be certain poochie reinforcements wouldn't suddenly appear.

When its steps faded off into the distance, I rubbed at my face. My hands, when I lowered them, somehow ended up on my stomach, stroking at the spot the dog had been so antsy over.

Catching myself, I stopped. "This place is bloody nuts."

After clambering to my feet and standing still for long enough to ascertain no other intruders had appeared, I moved on, taking cautious steps straight ahead, hoping for it to be a new direction and not the way from which I'd just come.

Uncountable minutes passed. Minutes that could have been hours, for all I knew. Still, I could scarcely tell one tree from another. Discounting the bushes that resembled slate-coloured afros and giant, gnarled roots breaking free of the granite-hued earth, the ground I trod seemed to lay completely flat. No hills, no bumps, no rises.

I did spot more 'people', though—a lot more.

Each time, I watched from behind trunks I was too leery of to touch, or by peering over bushes prickly enough to slice.

Some of them had as much creep factor going for them as the first woman had.

Others? I had no idea what to think of the others.

The first 'other' had been a female with hair the colour of corn, stunning in a gown of gold and rich reds even the dimness couldn't disguise. Reassured by her 'normalness', I'd almost called out to her—until she'd flickered like a badly-connected hologram. With the tiniest frazzle of sound, only a faint female outline remained—like a body-shaped heat signal. That and a pulsating glow. Right about where her heart would have been.

After I'd stared for too long, blinking like crazy just in case something had gone awry with my vision, she still

414

fizzled in and out as she crossed the gap from one trunk to the next.

I'd lost count of how many presences I'd encountered, when the crunch of footsteps had me stalling again and hiding out like a kid trying to escape curfew. The trunk I'd ducked behind had branches growing outward, as low as a foot from the ground. Accompanying moss, thick and springy, hung from limb to limb like a spider's web and lent the entire plant a mildew-green tinge. With my legs and torso hidden by the trunk, I peered through a gap between branches, as a masculine head and shoulders emerged from a flurry of fog.

A swing of his leg seemed to boot the mist from his path, exposing the male's entire form—broad shoulders, tall. Blond hair, darkened by the gloom, surrounded eyes that the shadows and his semi-profile wouldn't let me distinguish.

He flickered, the throb in his chest exposed.

My heart beat in response, a stuttered thumping against my inner sternum, and I stared harder.

He came a few steps closer, each movement slow and measured—almost as though he knew of another nearby. As he halted, his head swung back around.

The instant his face came into full view, the face of a stranger, my chest ached a little, my eyes stinging against the threat of tears, and I realised just how much I'd hoped for him to be Josh.

He waved his arm, separating the fog before him.

I froze in place, praying he couldn't hear the rhythm inside my chest.

A few long, excruciating moments followed, with his head slanted, twisting side to side, and he moved off toward the other side of the tree.

As soon as he'd vanished, I crab-walked to the left, weaving my body through the low-based branches, gaze darting left to right, just in case he doubled back around in an attempt to sneak up from behind. After going full circle and spotting his retreating back, I quit with my acrobatics, my shoulders sagging in relief.

Yet, I still continued to watch even once the mist reconvened in his wake, and would have stood even longer, had the hackles not risen along the nape of my neck.

43

A *whoosh* of motion stirred the hairs at my crown. A heavy thud hit the ground right behind me.

Fingers grabbed my shoulders, and my body spun.

Scenery blurred.

My back hit something solid, head cracking back with enough force to spark lights into my vision.

Before my body could even begin its downward slide, a crawling sensation raced over my wrists, scurrying along my forearms, like an army of ants homing in for the win.

Legs kicking at air, I whipped my head to the side in search of the bugs.

Not bugs.

Oh, God!

Definitely not bugs.

Meshy vines protecting the trunk had begun a rapid creep over my upper limbs, and the tickling across my abdomen told me they invaded there, too.

A long, low growl rumbled from the surrounding denseness through smog that performed like the mud of a disrupted riverbed.

I snapped back around in time to see bared teeth and rippling lips emerge.

"Shit!" I booted my right leg straight out.

The mouth shot backward as my foot connected. A grunt took the place of the snarls.

Chest heaving, I searched the haze while hanging there, legs braced, ready to defend.

The face thrust from the swirls so fast, I barely had time to scream, before it pushed into mine and a hand clamped around my throat.

I yanked my head away, more willing to take my chances with the bloody tree than some dodgy psychopath. When I spun back, my own snarl spilling from my lips, my gaze locked with eyes of green so familiar my pulse stumbled in its flow.

"Josh!" The word erupted on a gravelly sob.

Fury battled with shock in his expression, revealing the exact moment my voice registered. He stilled. Blinked. Lines creased his brow. "Jem?" His hands cupped my face without actually touching, and his eyes closed as he pressed his forehead to mine—though only for a beat before he twisted away.

Tugging started up around my left wrist, as Josh sawed at twine with what looked like a jagged stone. My arm slipped free, and I folded it against my chest.

Josh shifted to my right wrist, gritting his teeth as he scored the vine. The wolf in me had my nose urging forward, nostrils flaring in search of reassurance over Josh's health.

"Won't smell anything," he muttered, still sawing away. "Haven't smelled anything for months ..."

I frowned. *Months?*

"... Not since I got here. It's been driving me fucking insane. You might want to hold onto me unless you want to drop."

I gripped his shoulders. My fingers probably dug in harder than necessary, but I had to be sure he actually did stand there—had to be sure he was *real*. "They're all over my stomach, too," I said. "I feel them beneath my top."

"Shit! Okay. It's okay."

"What are they, Josh?"

"No idea. It's like I've spent the last few months on another planet, or something."

Or another plane.

The binding about my middle yanked taut when my right wrist broke free, and I slammed that hand onto Josh's shoulder, too.

He fiddled with my vest until he'd worked it loose enough to shove up. "You know, you could always wrap

418

your legs 'round my hips for added security." His face lifted, and he flashed me a grin.

A wash of relief filled me at the first hint I'd seen of Josh as his easy-going self. I breathed out a laugh. "Nice try."

His shoulders shrugged beneath my palms. "Can't blame a guy."

"I never do."

I blanked the tightening and loosening happening about my waist, as well as the bunching of Josh's muscles that told me just how much effort the cutting took.

Minutes seemed to pass before he looked up again. "Nearly done. Might want to brace yourself—you're a foot above the ground."

I clung tighter and pointed my toes down like I could somehow reach base. A moment later, my body jerked downward, the tree scraping at my lumbar.

As Josh's hands grasped my hips, he fizzled in and out—just as I'd seen others do. His skin went translucent before fleshing back in, yet the heat from his hands still pressed at my hips, the hairs flopping over his forehead still tickled at my breastbone.

"Josh?"

"Well, this is different." His head ducked lower, curls fluttering across my stomach instead. "Why d'you have two?"

"Two? Two what?"

"When you fade ..." He pushed up, his face coming back to mine, concern softening his green irises. "... you have two glowy spots, Jem."

"What? What do you mean?"

"Everyone else I've seen with them has only had one—"

"And what do you mean, fade?"

"Some of the people here have been doing this hooky vanishing shit. Now you're doing it."

"Me?" With the weirdness happening to *me*, my voice arrived high, my so-far-contained panic showing the first signs of spiralling out of control. "I saw it. I saw it on others I've passed. I saw it on you just now ..."

"On me?"

"... Did mine just do that? Is it doing that now? What the hell does it mean, Josh?"

He pressed a finger over my lips. "Shhh, not here. Let's get somewhere safer. Then we'll see if we can figure this lot out."

Around twenty feet above ground, I sat astride a limb twice my width. The minute he'd broken me free, Josh had hoisted me up, insisting the trees grew less dangerous the higher he climbed, as well as being safer from whatever trolled the forest. I'd argued, of course, trying to make him understand that we needed to get going, yet somehow we'd still ended up on the branch.

"How did you find me?" He scraped away at a dip in the bark where branch met trunk. "How'd you know where to look?" He glanced back over his shoulder. "Bloody got no clue where the hell I am, myself, so shit knows how you found me. Why *are* you alone again?"

How the hell could I respond without freaking him out? I watched his digging instead. "The rest of them couldn't come," I eventually said.

He reached back with one hand, depositing a sharp, flat stone similar to the one he'd used to cut me free between us. "Why not?"

"Because ..." I blew out a steadying breath. "Because you're not currently on earth, Josh."

His entire body stiffened. His face tilted toward a sky hidden by the mist. Some time passed before he burst out a laugh that held no humour and shook his head. "Figures."

"Josh ..." My whisper trailing off, I reached for his arm.

"You know how many times I thought I'd died, or something, but rammed the idea into a corner of my mind because I didn't want it to be true? I mean, that had to be what happened. I knew it really. Because no way would the pack have left me lost for this long. They'd have found me, right? Or I'd have figured out a way home."

"Josh ..." I tugged at him until he twisted.

His face held such sadness when it came into view. "The worst of it is? I have no fucking idea how it happened. I don't remember a thing. And then you showed up after all this time and—" His words slammed to a halt. His frown deepened across his brow, somehow spreading lower over his face until torment took over every one of his features. Before I could stop him, he'd spun from my grasp, his arms tense and wrapped about his head, his hands fisted at his nape.

"Josh, wait—"

His cry shook the leaves and echoed from an invisible landscape until it escalated into a howl so full of rue every hair erected across my body.

Shit! I thrust forward, wrapping my arms around his chest.

"Josh, it's not what you think."

The slight rocking of his body took me along with him.

"Josh ..." I slipped a hand up to his cheek, tried to turn him toward me. "Please, listen to me."

His torso twisted, his arms flinging around me hard enough to crush. "Not you. Oh, God. Why'd it have to be you, Jem, why you, not you ..."

His words tumbled into a mess of incoherency, and I dug my fingers into his hair, burrowed my lips against his ear, whispering over and over, "Josh, I'm not dead, it's okay, I'm not dead ..." as tremors ran through him and vibrated through me until there seemed to be only us in a void where nothing else existed—no fog, no trees, no damned in-between or oddities I didn't understand, no pack troubles, no witch spells to conquer, no infinite non-space separating us from getting home, separating me from Sean.

Eyes closed tight against my thoughts, my hand soothed across Josh's back as his shudders lessened, as his sobs quietened.

"Not dead?" he whispered, pulling back until I could see his face.

I shook my head, a tiny, singular gesture.

"Then ..." Though his eyes shone bright through the dull light as they seemed to search my face, no tears patterned Josh's cheeks or dampened his lashes. "Where the hell are we, Jem? What the hell is going on?"

"You're stuck, Josh. In some kind of—"

His hand slammed over my mouth as his body dove on top of mine, crushing my chest, crushing my words, bloody well crushing *me*, and my legs swung in the air before flopping back down to overhang the branch.

My heart boinged like something possessed inside my chest as I stared at him. His focus seemed to be on something below. When he tipped his face down until an inch from mine, placed a finger to his lips and pointed toward the ground, I understood.

"What is it?" I whispered the instant he'd released my mouth, trying to twist my head far enough to see what he did.

His lips tickled my ear. "No idea. I've seen them before, though." He eased up enough for me to roll over and leaned to the right, his lips back at my ear, chin resting against my shoulder as I peered over the branch at the five 'people' below. "This lot are always together ..."

Each of them resembled the condition of the one I'd initially encountered. The group moved forward as though run by the same remote control, stopping every couple of steps.

"... I think they're hunting ..."

In unison, their heads tilted. The one with the slight lead had a grubby mop of rusty hair, and with his head lift, his eyes narrowed to slits.

"What's there to hunt here?" I whispered, somehow unnerved simply by watching them.

Those below took a few more steps and halted, their heads twitching to the side.

Josh's heartbeat thudded hard against my shoulder blade with his muttered, "Us."

Four more paces, and the fog swallowed those we observed.

"What do you me—" My body tugged to the side, slicing my words with a low grunt.

"Jem?"

Like an invisible lasso had snaked around my middle, my body jerked again. I scrabbled at the bark with my fingertips when more air than trunk showed beneath me.

Josh's arm wove about my torso. "Jem, what's happening?"

Another yank. Another jolt. My grunt forced out as I rebelled against the draw, followed by a gasp as its source sank in. *Sean!* If not him, Jess. Had to be. The sensation held too much similarity to the summons back to my body during astral projection to be anything but.

"We have to leave," I whispered. "Now."

"And go where, Jem? Those things have barely even left."

"They're the least of our problems right now." How on earth could I tell him that if he didn't get a move on, he'd end up alone again in that Godforsaken place? I twisted until I could see him. "If you don't leave with me now, Josh, you'll get left behind."

"You've figured out a way back?" Confusion and frustration bled into his face. "Because I don't even know where we are."

"I know. But you need to trust me."

"I always do."

"Good. Then, we need to walk and talk. Just don't let go of my hand, and everything should be fine."

Getting out of the tree without losing contact with Josh took skill—I only hoped Jess was right when she said dragging him back with me would work—but the instant we landed on solid ground, my body shot backward a couple of feet, breaking my hold on him.

"Jem!" He dove after me.

I kicked a heel against the ground, springing myself back toward him, grabbing hold of his hand already reaching for mine.

"What is this shit?" he asked.

"It's Jess and Sean." I fisted my free hand into his shirt. "They're calling me back."

"Calling you back from where?" He stared off over my shoulder as if he could see them. "To where?"

Another backward slide, my soles scraping at dirt, Josh lurching along with me. "From the in-between, Josh ..."

Jem!

With Sean's deep whisper echoing through my head came another slide, another haul on Josh's arm. "... It's where your soul's been all this time ..."

Jem!

The next thrust to my body almost doubled me over, smacking my temple against Josh's chest. "... I came here to bring you home."

Jem!

I gasped as my rear jerked outward like it had an agenda of its own. "Whatever you do, don't let g—"

Josh flew sideways so fast, his hold ripping free from my hand, that I barely registered the dark blur that'd ploughed into him.

With scarcely any time to react, to even *think*, my own body shot backward. "Josh!"

My arms flailed as the fog embraced me.

Only snarls and the scuffle of feet carried through the suffocating denseness.

"Josh, *no*!"

424

I dug my heels against every gnarled root that tripped me.

Still, I continued to whip backward as if a grappling hook had wormed through me and latched onto my middle, zip-wiring my hide into awaiting maws.

I flung an arm out to the side, but it's collision with a branch smacked it back against my face, searing pain through my shoulder.

Jem!

"Jem!"

The cry of my name blasted from both sides.

Footsteps thudded upon the ground toward me.

Mist swirled and parted before crowding once more, and I thrust out my other arm, fingers flexed, scrabbling for something—*anything*—to latch onto.

I grunted out my relief when I snagged in some kind of nook.

My body arched against the sudden stop, my arm twisting with the pressure, while the summoning force continued to snatch at my body.

"Jem!" The trampling hit the ground somewhere in front of me.

My fingertips slipped a little with each passing beat. "Josh, hurry!"

The fog billowed, plumes gathering in thick formation before darting aside as if repelled. Through the thinning clouds, Josh's face appeared, determination lining his features, each pump of his arms cording the muscles. "Jem, get out of here!"

"Take my hand!" Without thinking, I swung it in his direction, my fingers outstretched. It took only that release for my body to be flung backward. "*No!*"

Like I'd been sucked into a too-tight pipeline, my body folded in on itself, my brain seemed to crush, and a rush of wind blasted against my ears.

Not before Josh leapt toward me.

Not before I registered the scramble of his hands and the enfolding of his arms about my torso.

Not before the darkness chasing him so closely revealed pure malevolence, marring its features into ugly voids of nothingness. Clawed fingers reached. Hungered jaws widened. And the snarl of a hunter's victory spilled from thinned lips.

44

I didn't even realise I screamed, though the sound shrilled through my ears until my inner drums thrummed. I didn't acknowledge the all-consuming pitch of the surrounding blackness, either, until light flashed through my shuttered lids bright enough to burn.

My body seemed to spasm—a singular jolt as though I'd been paddled.

"Jem." Sean's voice. Right beside me. Fingers dug into my shoulders, and my body shook. "Jem."

My eyes flew open. The light bulb above appeared suspended in air and blinded me for a second, before I caught the shine of alarm in Sean's dark-eyed stare.

Gasping, I shot up to sit, spinning to Josh on the bed beside me. He lay supine, his eyes still closed, unmoving, unflinching.

"Josh." My yank on the hand still threaded with mine jerked him a little. "Josh."

"What happened?" Connor demanded from behind. "Did you see him?"

"Connor, do *not* cross the line!" Jess snapped.

I released Sean's hand long enough to bang a fist against Josh's shoulder.

A gasp burst from him. His eyes snapped open. "Jem, run!" His torso bolted up, but he went less than a foot before his body flopped back down, his arms limp, his face slackened.

"No! Josh!" I flipped back around and threw myself down beside him, my grip on his hand tighter than ever as I renewed my connection with Sean. "Send me back!"

"Over my dead body!" Sean threw an arm across me as though to deny Jess access.

I lifted my head, sent a glare toward my sister. "You *have* to send me back."

Sean's head whipped Jess's way, too. "Don't you dare!"

Jess strode across to the cupboard, where she snatched up the small tub. "Tell me what happened, Jem."

"Something tried following us. I think it has Josh. But if you send me back, I can help him ..."

Sean growled. "Like hell—"

"I can help him fight. He can't find his way home on his own."

"Calm down." Jess scooped out a handful of the coffee-coloured spice and crossed to the bed. "You've just shown him the way—which means he should be *right there* on the other side. You can guide him from here." Her posture altered, arm tense like she planned on tossing the stuff all over me, legs braced as if to fight, and she jerked her chin toward where Josh lay. "Now, call to him. In fact,"—she sent a glance to the doorway—"*all* of you call to him."

By the time I'd scrambled back to my knees, the rest of the pack had flooded the landing, their shouts of Josh's name squeezing through the doorway. Sean clambered to Josh's other side, took his other hand, creating a three-way protection as he joined in the chant.

Within seconds, Josh's legs twitched.

The calls to him escalated, though none of them quite so heartfelt as Connor's pleas to his son.

Josh's body arched up, his head tilted back, his arms splayed to the sides with enough strength to force me and Sean along with them, almost breaking our connection.

The roar began low, thrumming through Josh's chest, lending vibrations into every one of his limbs. On a vicious snarl, he lunged forth from the bed, his deep yell of, "*Go!*" rumbling out as he flung himself at Sean. The action, along with Sean's backward jerk, dragged me along with them.

Sean hit carpet first. His legs tangled over the bed, arm already curled to capture my fall.

Josh slammed into Sean's right shoulder, as I smacked against his left.

The wrap of Josh's arm along with the knitting of our three sets of legs created a cushioning cocoon that prevented me from jumping back up to see what the hell Jess shouted a load of mumbo-jumbo at—to see what made the unholy screeches filling the room, the thunderous crashes like waves against rock, what sounded like fuel-fed winds as pulses of heat and light throbbed against the walls.

To figure out what the heck had shut the pack up like they'd had their vocal chords axed.

Sudden quiet deafened me, leaving my ears filled with static, like the buzzing of a thousand bees.

With a groan, I lifted my face from its crushed position against Sean's chest. The instant I did, his eyes absorbed me—relief, terror and panic all warring within to darken them even further than usual.

"You scared me," he whispered. "Don't ever do that again."

"Seriously not planning on it," I said.

We both turned toward Josh, as he groaned and shifted up onto his elbows.

Beneath blond curls long enough to overhang his brow, he blinked until his green eyes held only lucidity, a smile tugging at one corner of his mouth. "So ... about that threesome we discussed ..."

Sean rolled his eyes but breathed out a chuckle. "Welcome back, Josh."

45

Within no time, the lilac room stood as though nothing had ever happened in there. No powder on the floor. No plants hanging from the ceiling. If not for the overbearing stench of sulphur, I could almost have convinced myself the entire occurrence had been nought but a bad dream.

I knew different.

As though he'd sensed my thoughts, Sean's arm tightened around my middle and his chin resting on my shoulder snuggled in closer to my neck. "Guess you'll be looking for somewhere new to hang out now, then?"

"I guess so."

"You know, there's a room across the landing. You'd be more than welcome to hang there more often." His shrug brushed my shoulder blades. "I'm pretty certain the owner wouldn't mind."

My lips twitched. "Sounds like a decent offer."

He took a step back, his arm taking me with him. "No time like the present."

Living in the present suddenly seemed like a great idea—especially if it would help me forget what had gone down in the murky forest on the 'other side'.

I turned and followed him into our room. "Maybe everything will go back to normal now." Or as normal as it could get for the life we led.

"It'll go back to normal. Because never in any of my lifetimes will I agree to you vanishing on me like that again."

"I was right there. On the bed."

"In body, maybe. But you were not there in soul, Jem. I know. Because I could not *feel* you." He shifted closer, his palm pressing to my heart. "And I *always* feel you.

Always *need* to feel you. I'll never let that be taken away from me again."

"But I heard you," I told him. "And you brought me home."

"It's where you belong. Not ... alone, not ..."

There went unsaid, as did *away from me, our hearts separated, our souls flailing in the dark.* I could predict how he'd have ended because the thoughts echoed through myself.

When we'd discussed what had happened, what Josh had experienced, what I'd seen in even the short time I'd been there— twenty torturous minutes, according to Sean—his expression had grown darker and more troubled, and his body tighter and tenser, with each additional word.

His hand slid up my chest, around my neck, until his fingers weaved into the hair at my nape. A gentle tug took me nearer. "Don't ever leave me again," he murmured before pressing his lips to mine.

A synergy of emotion spilled forth with his kiss. Relief. Desperation. Fear. Love. All of them seeped into me until a low moan bubbled up, and I clung to his arms, as he held me snug to him, my body moulding against muscles I knew as well as my own, my eyes peering into warmth and devotion that could have intimidated anyone unaccepting of something so powerful.

Wrapped in his embrace, I tried to force all remnants of the dark forest from my mind.

All except one thought fled, one that had gnawed away at my subconscious since Jess had spoken the words.

We'd told the pack about the body fizzling, explained about the inner glow.

'Yeah, I'd heard something about this', Jess had said. 'Some believe the differentiation is for those who've passed and have yet to move on, and those whose bodies are still alive because they're not technically dead.' She'd shrugged. 'Like patients stuck in comas, for example.'

431

What had the glow symbolised, though, if it separated life from death? Josh said he hadn't seen another there with a duet of pulses. Why me? What made me so special? Why the hell would I have two of what Jess described as the soul's life force—like a heartbeat keeping the carrier alive until in unison with the body?

I stilled, though my grip on Sean's arm strengthened.

He pulled back a little, his glossed gaze searching mine, lips slightly swollen from the heat he'd created.

Like a heartbeat for the aura ... "I had two." My breath hitched before I swallowed it down, as my thoughts roamed even farther.

Sean frowned, worry in his eyes. "Jem?"

Weeks before, I'd drunk from the witch's fertility potion meant for the male pack members. Did that mean I'd been ovulating when I'd also made love with Sean beneath the power of the Blue Moon—exactly as the witches had planned for themselves?

"Oh, my God," I whispered. "I'm pregnant."

ACKNOWLEDGEMENTS

Okay, let's hope I remember everybody.

With HUGE thanks to:

My family: Mr B, The Boy and Boop. They always come first for the thanks because they're simply that worthy.

My sister, Jenny: for reading the first draft of Lured (then titled Blue Moon) chapter by chapter and telling me when I'd strayed, and for knowing exactly where I was heading with my ideas when I emailed her for research help and understanding me enough to help me get steered in the right direction for where to take Resonance (now the ending in this book). Thanks to her, I stepped entirely from my comfort zone, and I wouldn't have been able to do it so readily without her support and knowledge.

To my beta readers: Carla Huxley, Aimee Laine, Jennifer Turner, Wendy Seagondollar, Elaine Hart and Dawn Whipps, whose feedback (and encouragement) always mean so much.

Aimee Laine: for helping to mould Lured from first draft long-windedness to who-knows-what draft with less waffle so we could save on the syrup.

Julie Reece and Jocelyn Adams: for helping me tear Lured apart ... just ... one ... more ... time.

I mustn't forget Zoë: for not being mad when something happened to a character for whom I had stolen her name.

And to you guys: For reading something I've written, for every single word of encouragement that has brought a smile to my day, and for helping me to believe I have something special in the Holloway Pack.

Cheers!

ABOUT J.A. BELFIELD

Best known for her Holloway Pack stories and The Therapist, J.A. Belfield lives in Solihull, England, with her husband, two children, a spoiled dog and a cat who likes to vomit in unfortunate places. She writes paranormal romance, with a second love for urban fantasy. And now she writes erotic romance, too. Because she can. ;)

In 2016, Instinct [now part of Beginnings] earned J.A. Belfield International Bestseller status when it featured in the Paranormal Attractions anthology. J.A. Belfield now hopes to claim that same status solo.

To stay updated on everything J.A. Belfield, join her on Facebook in the Belfield's MotherBookers group.

TITLES BY J.A. BELFIELD

HOLLOWAY PACK

BEGINNINGS
CALLED
LURED
CAGED
UNNATURAL
CORNERED
HEREDITARY
ENTICED

EROTIC ROMANCE

THE THERAPIST

PARANORMAL ROMANCE

HER MANE ESCORT